LIFE GOES SLEEPING

By Reed Farrel Coleman

THE PERMANENT PRESS
SAG HARBOR, NEW YORK, 11963

Copyright © 1991 by Reed Farrel Coleman

Library of Congress Cataloging-in-Publication Data

Coleman, Reed Farrel, 1956–
    Life goes sleeping / by Reed Farrel Coleman.
       p.   cm.
    ISBN 1-877946-05-2 : $19.95
    I. Title.
    PS3553.O47445L5   1991
    813'.54—dc20   90-42709
                                               CIP

All rights reserved, including the right to reproduce this book, or parts thereof, in any form, except for the inclusion of brief quotations in a review.

Originally published by

THE PERMANENT PRESS
Noyac Road
Sag Harbor, NY 11963

Manufactured in the United States of America

This work is dedicated to Rosanne, Betty and Brian, as they've managed to dedicate some part of themselves to me.

I'd also like to thank Tom McDonald and Linda Allen for their technical expertise and inspiration.

". . . Mendy's not as bad as you think. He has a heart."
"So has a snake."

—Raymond Chandler from *The Long Goodbye*

Sunday Breezes

On this Sunday the sun's light was too brilliant for life to go sleeping. Moist, ocean gusts blew the smoky perfume of Nathan's Famous hot dogs beyond the boardwalk and down Coney Island Avenue towards the traffic circle at the entrance to Prospect Park. A struggling, brown three year old, attached to the world by his tippy toes and momma's unrelenting grip, fights vainly to reverse the earth's momentum and pull his world to the origin of Brooklyn's delicious breeze. At a bus stop impatient mariners, mostly ancient, dressed in once blue Mets caps and black banlon socks turn their hearts and noses into the wind. And just for a breath they let go of their beach chairs and their impatience and too many years to count. They smile a three year old's smile and twitch their fingers with the remembrance of grips that once held them to the earth on a Sunday in Brooklyn, or in Budapest, or Berlin. But buses pull in only to bury those grips again in a trail of deisel fumes and rattles. No, life would not go sleeping; for everyone in Brooklyn, this day, would always be one breath younger.

Washing My Hands

No one wailed or fainted and only the limo drivers wore black. My dad and my Uncle Saul reminisced, not about my mother—that was for later at the house over hard-boiled eggs and bagels. Now, they pointed at close-by blocks of New England granite, recounting stories about the putz buried by "that" one or the schmuck laid out under "this" one.

Apparently, the putz had misappropriated, pocketed, purloined some temple funds in 1952 and exited with some leggy, Vegas showgirl dubbed Vera. When the *gelt* ran out so did Vera. He made his way home in '53, tail planted firmly between his legs, begging forgiveness. So the rabbi, fancying himself a Hollywood priest, forgave the putz his sins and worked out a payment schedule that would cross a loan sharks eyes. Within a year every penny was paid back triple. In fact, the putz turns his whole life around. He too, like the rabbi, fancies himself a good Catholic. He's so imbued with the spirit of life, forgiveness, rebirth and hardwork that he becomes a pillar of the community. His newly founded appliance business booms. He meets the Yiddish girl of his family's dreams and gets engaged.

On the wedding day, in the middle of the cantor's aria, Vera appears like Elijah on the first night of Passover. Only Vera is a little heavier than Elijah. In fact, she's forty pounds heavier than the '52 model of herself and she's dragging behind her a screaming, rat-faced, two year old boy. She smacks the kid a few times for effect, takes a deep breath, points to the putz and announces to the congregation that he's rat-face's father. It was just the putz's luck, too, that his was the only Jewish wedding staged in the last half of the twentieth century without a single doctor in attendance. So they buried the putz, my mother's oldest brother, my Uncle Larry—whom my brothers' and I always referred to as our "dead Uncle Larry"—that Monday morning.

Dad and Uncle Saul both loved telling that story. They liked to hear themselves tell it. I especially loved hearing it today. I couldn't be mad at them. They'd have enough time to mourn, we all would. In February there'd be a bounty of sleeting, gray nights for mourning. All the old stories and Valiums and Kinescope reruns in the world can't stop the emptiness from filling you up, eventually. At least that's what I'm told.

February was half a year away and the dancing, brilliant sun made it a tough day for grieving. For now I was satisfied that no one, not even the hearse driver, was wearing a Walkman and listening to the Mets' game. Though I must admit to being rather curious about the score myself.

Back at Rosensweig's Memorial Chapel, I'd turned down an invitation to view Mother's open casket. My brothers took this as a sign of cowardess, selfishness and poor etiquette. They were a little bit right on each count, but mostly they hadn't a clue. Now, standing across the trench that would be my mother's grave, I spied my brothers avoiding my eyes. I wondered angrily why they should be any more right about me today than last Thursday or a year ago last Thursday. There was no reason, naturally.

They looked paler than I imagined myself looking; Jeffrey and Joshie, my brothers. They looked lost, is what I mean to say. Well, not Jeffrey, not exactly. He's the oldest, the grayist, the achiever. And being those things, he had lost his biggest fan the moment my Mother's heart stopped pumping. A philosopher, Berkely I think it was, once wrote, "To be is to be perceived." Across the narrow trench I could almost detect Jeff's wondering interrupting my own, "Where would the applause come from now?" My dad, you see, wasn't much of a fan.

As the outdoor ceremonies drew to a close I could see Joshie screwing his face up into that pseudo-gargoyle pout of his. I guess he was just trying to frighten away some tears. Lord knows, it still frightened me. You couldn't argue with his success. Like I said, there was no wailing, maybe just a sniffle here and there. Shouting! Shouting! Now that's what I bet Joshie really wanted to do. Shouting he was best at, comfortable with, not tears. None of us were anymore. No, Mother was, but she had done all her crying.

I was thinking that she'd be pretty pissed off at the lack of easy tears. Then I was thinking that we were all pretty pissed off at her.

The presiding rabbi, not inclined toward Catholicism like some who had come before him, shooed us away from the grave as if he'd caught us flipping baseball cards in front of *shul* on Saturday morning. And like guilty little boys we picked up our invisible cards and stepped back from the hole.

The $1300 worth of satin and oak that contained Mom's body took its time touching bottom. She always felt more comfortable on the local and why shouldn't she feel comfortable today? But I could swear the sun was setting faster than that coffin was moving. It was probably the heat; yet I thought I could detect all the men at the graveside rubbing their faces as if to feel their beards growing. I rubbed mine, too. In spite of it all, this moment struck with a silent grace. For me, the world had never been so quiet. Finally, after a week full of seconds, the oak kissed earth, gently.

The pace picked up some from here on out. The lowering ropes were removed rather unceremoniously after a few "Repeat-After-Me's," three Amens and the first measurable sobs of the day, though I couldn't quite trace them back to points of origin. Maybe they were canned sobs provided by the undertaker. You know, as a way to break the ice at a tight-assed funeral. I'd have to check his bill carefully. Well, it didn't work anyhow.

All the mourners formed a single line in back of Dad. It looked like a busy concession stand in Coney Island.

"Step up, step up! Throw a shovel full 'a dirt on the casket and win a stuffed 'dollee' for your sweetheart."

Dad tried his hand first and when his little mound of loam made a hollow smacking sound against the bare oak he went white. I mean *white;* blood-drained, vampire-victim white. His legs liquified from shoe top to belt buckle, but reflexively he planted the shovel in a pile of waiting soil and propped himself up against its weathered handle. Color returned to his face, substance to his legs and, having made the initial investment, he chose to leave the 'stuffed dollee' for someone further down the line. He made his way over to my dead Uncle Larry's grave to visit a little longer.

My brothers and I added our dirt in birth order. Jeffrey bit off a huge chunk of real estate and slammed it down directly on top of the smaller spadefull my father had contributed, overwhelming it. Christ! I'm thinking, are you trying to wake her up? Then I woke up and realized all the racket wasn't meant for my mother at all. Jeff woke up, too, about the same time as me and noticed neither one of his parents had witnessed his prodigious feat. He dropped his heart with the shovel and melted back into line kissing his wife's forehead.

Joshie carved out a meticulous pie-slice of topsoil and held it steady above the coffin. With eyes closed he waited. We waited. In one smooth, rapid stroke he pulled the shovel back to his side. The surprised soil seemed to hang suspended in the air for a heartbeat only to fall dutifully through the vacuum Joshie had created. Whispers and thuds took the place of hollow smacks as dirt hit dirt, now, as opposed to coffin wood. Joshie, like Jeffrey before him, fell back in the ranks with his wife. I should say I assume he did so, as I was too busy sweating out my try for the 'dollee.'

I took a small unshapely spade full and made sure to drop it as far away from the family pile as possible. I didn't hang around to listen for the echo.

On the ride back to my parents', I mean, I guess I mean, my dad's apartment, the limo was alive with chatter like a classroom on the first day of school. You know, no one says anything worth quoting, but everyone says anything. In the far back seat Dad discussed bagel logistics with Aunt Lindy, Saul's wife, my mother's sister. Uncle Saul was still in a story-telling mood and was busy trying my brother Joshie's patience with a fish story he dusts off at every family get-together. And, by Saul's standards, this was a family get-together. Who could argue with that? Jeffrey pressed his right temple against the middle window and fumed in silence over the perceived disrespect. Maybe he was fuming because we weren't. Maybe he was just fuming. Tess, Jeffrey's wife, and Anne, Joshie's wife, exchanged questions about each other's kids, questions they knew the answers to before the asking. Up front with the driver we debated the Mets' chances of playing in October. Chances were pretty good, we agreed. We were also more than curious about today's score.

By the time the black Lincoln glided to a stop at the rear entrance of Dad's beige-bricked, shoe-box-shaped apartment building, all the chatter had exhausted itself into an ugly quiet. The driver shook my hand saying he was sorry about our loss, as if talking in his sleep. I thanked him with equal enthusiasm and told him not to lose anymore sleep over it. My uncalled-for sarcasm missed its mark, in any case, and the driver excused himself, reaching over my lap and popping the trunk release. The rest of my family had already abandoned ship.

Outside now, I leaned against the Lincoln, closing my eyes to the sun, which, it seemed, had moved back up into the sky since the burial. The air carried the smells of brown salt water and sewage and the smoky hints of hot dogs. With the wind I remembered just how close to Coney Island we were.

"Come on," Joshie nudged me.

"Huh?"

"Your stool, go get your stool?"

The only thing I moved were my eyes and noticed that Joshie was holding what looked like a cantaloupe box with woodgrain racing stripes. We all had to sit on these cardboard monstrosities for like a week. Oh great, just great!

"Where's T-woman and Annie?" I asked Joshie about my sisters-in-law for no apparent reason.

"They're upstairs, with the kids, checking if the mirrors are covered and—"

"O.K."

I dutifully picked up my cantaloupe crate, closing the trunk behind me, and got on the back of yet another single file line forming at the apartment house back door. This was "Jewish Death Ritual #8"; washing the cemetary soil off your hands. So we stood at the back door pouring water from a glass pickle jar over our hands to the mumbled rhythm of unpracticed men chanting Hebrew.

All the ritualized goodbyes were acting on me now like Ritalin on hyperactive kids. I could feel the strength run out of my body through my hands into the pickle jar water and onto the cement. This is not how I needed to say goodbye to anyone.

I wiped dripping hands on my pants legs to stem the flow of energy onto the pavement. I found my cardboard companion waiting faithfully at my side where I'd left it and proceeded to drop kick it across the parking lot. That stopped the chanting, I can tell you. They were so stunned that I was halfway to my car before anyone spoke up.

"What the fu—" Jeffrey stopped himself. "Where are ya going?"

"To my car," I spoke straight ahead without stopping or turning to face him, hoping the wind would carry back my answer. "I'll be up."

I lied a little. I was going to my car. Then I was going to find the source of the breeze and perform a goodbye ritual of my own.

Swatch and Medal

I wore the mustard like a yellow medal on my right lapel. No act of Congress needed, no battlefield commander necessary; I bestowed it upon myself for desertion of family under duress. On my left lapel I wore the mourner's black swatch, awarded earlier by one or other of the Rosensweig brothers for death of a close relative during a slow week at the chapel. I plunged my left hand into my trouser pocket for a paper napkin to wipe away a touch of of the glorious yellow, but came up only with another black satin reminder. So I stood by the grill wiping mustard off my suit jacket with a yarmulke and, as at the graveside, the earth again was quiet. Then I ordered another two hot dogs, "to go," in a voice that sounded something like mine.

I retired to the front seat of my VW. Once shut in and planted firmly, I washed down those hot dogs with french fries. I washed the fries down with orangeade and baseball. The score of the game almost brought the meal back up. The Mets were losing by two runs to the Cardinals in the top half of the seventh. The bases were full of *birds* with nobody out. Even so, I figured we'd get to the seventh inning stretch by the next flyover of Halley's Comet.

I grinded my way into first gear and began to ease the car into the sparse traffic on Surf Avenue when I remembered some baggage that needed unloading. I yanked up the once functional parking brake lever more out of hope and habit than anything else. Once in neutral the old bug dashed my hopes and rolled lazily back to the curb. I opened my door a crack, dropping the yellow-stained yarmulke into the vacuum backwash of a passing Camaro. I found first again and headed into Brighton Beach with all the urgency of a broken bat pop-fly to short.

Luck Changes

Brighton Beach had changed, but only in subtle, poisonous ways, since I'd called it home. The elevated subway still clacked and shrieked and rained sparks over the forever dark avenues below. Unsuspecting cars parked in the shadows of the tracks fell prey to the hot metal by-products of grinding wheels on rails. At night the sparks were shooting stars that burnt your coat when they hit your back or stray bullets when they brushed your skin. In the end, cars suffered the most.

Each block along Brighton Beach Avenue mimicked the next. Rows of sooty red brick "taxpayers" went on for a long mile. Each block had its Kosher butcher shop with ten dead chickens hanging by their crimson feet in the window. Each block had two, maybe three, produce stands featuring soup greens, wilted scallions, and bruised cooking apples on sale. Each block had its "Mom and Pop" superette where Momma always worries and Poppa just shakes his head. Each block had an "Appetizing" store filling the atmosphere with the seductive scent of sour pickles and the sweet sulphuric perfume of creamed onions from the pickled herring. These stores were here when my mother was a kid and they're still here, but you have to look carefully to notice the evolution.

Oh sure, Momma and Poppa still shake their heads with worry, but they do their worrying in Russian now. The makeshift signs that once proudly and self-consciously proclaimed, "Yiddish And English Spoken Here," were here no more. The too familiar, always mysterious right to left squiggles of Hebrew lettering have been displaced by the harsh shapes of the Cyrillic alphabet. "Appetizing" stores smelled now of salted fishes that hold no romance for me. The Democratic Party Club—two doors over from Hirsh's Knishes on the boardwalk—once the center of left-wing politics in all of New York—was now a garishly decorated night club mockingly called The Onion Dome. During the thirties Brighton Beach was a hotbed for Unionism and naive American Communism. Even in the fifties, I hear, the flame still flickered. One of my aunts marched in protest against the execution of the Rosenbergs. A lot of aunts and uncles from Brighton Beach marched. In the seventies and eighties, however, the neighborhood had become a landfill sight for unwelcome Communist outcasts and wanderers.

I played a game of shadow and light, steering my ancient little car out of the artificial darkness of the elevated tracks and into the sidestreets, quietly passing daylight and back, again, into the darkness, I serpentined through these old streets fishing for an anchor, someone or something to hook onto or to hook onto me. Somewhere in Brighton Beach a hint of the neighborhood I'd grown up in, like my mother before me, would reveal itself and give me some relief.

I crawled past the schoolyard of P.S. 252 looking to catch some late afternoon stickball action. The schoolyard had never been emptier. Not even one ghost of a chalkbox strikezone looked back at me from the beige school walls through the chainlink fence. I guess stickball isn't too popular in Soviet Georgia or the Ukraine.

I parked in front of every kid's house whose address I remembered, even the kids I'd fought with or hated or who hated me. But none of them lived here any longer and I knew that. They probably didn't hate me anymore either; I'm sure they didn't care. Their houses meant nothing to me now and I meant less to them.

Whatever it was I'd come here looking for was gone, buried long before my mother. And what exactly I was hoping to find, I couldn't say. So I resigned myself to facing all the crap and questions awaiting me at Dad's apartment. At least I'd catch the prayer for the dead.

"Shit!" I slammed my steering wheel. "Shit! Shit! Shit!" I slammed my steering wheel again and again and again until the knuckles on my left hand chapped, swelled, and, finally, bled.

Things were too quiet again. The ballgame was still on, but the chain-saw-like drone of the engine had quit. I guess I let the clutch slip during my amateur hand surgery. A horn blew behind me, then another, then another. Half a block away a "D" train squealed and rumbled by, burying the choir of horns at my back. I took my time finding neutral and turning the key. Nothing. Again . . . nothing, but this time the game on the radio blipped out. It had to be a loose battery cable. With my one good hand I turned the steering wheel hard right, hopped out of the car, and pushed it into an empty space behind a black, overwaxed Lincoln Town Car. The ass end of my VW hung out into the blacktop, making passage somewhat challenging for the hornblowers who had so politely suggested that I, "move the fucking piece of shit excuse for a car!" I gave my best mocking bow to each driver as he or she squeezed through the slim gap. I didn't look up to register their reactions.

Feeling better, with the exception of my throbbing left hand, I plopped the whole of me down on the right front fender of the Lincoln. The finish was so smooth that I almost slid off like scrambled eggs out of a Teflon skillet. And just as the last ounce of my two hundred pounds plus clothing settled on the slippery finish, sirens, not quite loud enough to be heard in the Bronx, imposed themselves on this late Sunday afternoon. Sirens so deafening they swallowed the whines and chatter of two passing trains. None of me felt very tip-top now, especially my ears. I sailed easily off the fender and stood there in the street, naked and guilty and diminished.

I waited and watched for accusing heads and wagging fingers to pop out of second story windows. This was Brooklyn; they had to come. Some did. A few eyes, necks and shoulders appeared briefly to take the mandatory number of disdainful glances, only to shrug and vanish. Then again, in this neighborhood there was nothing novel about the screams of alarms. No doors opened that I could see. Apparently, I wasn't worth investigating. I sampled the air for police sirens above the Lincoln's wailing, but didn't hear any nor did I hear the footsteps advancing behind me.

I jumped. I swear to God, I jumped across the street when his hand cupped the contour of my right shoulder. By the time I put my guts back in place and turned around he was inside the black sedan fiddling with the dashboard. Silence, relative silence broke out everywhere. The car had quit its crying, but my ears kept reminding me of its howl. My almost forgotten left hand did some reminding of its own.

"I am sorry sir, but my car already has a hood ornament," the little man mouthed with a hint of a smile.

"No need to be sorry," I said looking over his head at the semi-attached, two-story house behind him. "I apologize; I should've known a car service limo like yours would be alarmed to the balls around here."

He stopped hinting and screwed his thickish lips into a broad smile, "That's funny you know, very funny." He followed my gaze over his left shoulder to the building he'd come out of. When he turned back my way I was almost past him heading toward the house. He followed and stood parallel to me at the bottom of the stoop.

"Your hand is bleeding rather badly, I am sure you are aware."

"Yes," I agreed quickly looking down at it. "My family witch doctor used to live in this house. His office was up there on the second floor."

"He no longer—"

"—lives there. Yeah, I know. He no longer lives, period. The old bastard dropped dead about fifteen years ago. "—All of his female patients freaked out. That white-haired old quack's funeral was better attended than Valentino's.

"I'm really sorry about the alarm and everything. I don't mean to be lecturing you on local history, but my luck's run bad lately, very bad." I nodded over my shoulder at the dead VW.

"Luck changes," he said slipping his right palm into mine and giving it a shake. "I am Alexander Korin."

"Dylan Klein," I shook back.

"My pleasure, Dylan Klein. Well . . . you know, for all the blood and bruises, your hand will heal. And your car will run again with some prodding, I am sure. Even that yellow stain on your lapel will . . . ," he drifted to a halt. "Who?"

"Who, what?"

"The patch," he pointed at my other lapel.

"My mother. This morning," I continued, two words to the sentence.

"I am so sorry. What a fool I can be."

"Welcome to the club."

"Here I was lecturing you, filling the air with my crackerbarrel— I think that is the expression," he looked at me for approval, speaking in an accent that tried to hide its Russian origin.

I gave him an affirming nod.

"I was spewing out my crackerbarrel philosophy, about to tell you that things can only improve and that luck changes."

"Stop beating yourself up over it. Here, look," I pulled the black patch and pin out of my lapel and put it in my pocket. "No apologies required Mr. Korin."

"Alexander, please."

"Alright, Alexander. Please, let yourself off the hook. Believe it or not," I turned back to the building, "in some ways I've been looking for this place for hours. You know, most kids don't like going to the doctor, but I sort of enjoyed it, coming here. It was like a trip to the neighborhood zoo."

"Would you like to come in and sniff around the old zoo then," he offered, urging me up the front steps with a gentle push. "I cannot say how much has changed, as one, maybe two owners have made this place their home since the passing of your doctor. Maybe three, I do not really know."

"Maybe," I repeated, "maybe. Certain things I think are better left to memory." I acted out my ambivalence by leaning back against his guiding hand.

"Maybe," he parroted back, "maybe. You will never have your answer standing here. Come in and share a drink with me; after all you did rouse me from a nap to come down and shut my alarm. Also, it is the least I can do to make amends for my insensitivity. In any case, your hand is bleeding and needs some attending to. You can use my phone to call road service and—"

"Stop! Stop! Stop! I relent. You win. Christ, Mr. Korin—"

"Alexan—"

"Christ, Alexander, you should have been a lawyer."

"Do you think?" He loved the idea or was amused by it and smiled broadly. "Come, come. Tell me all about this doctor of yours. What was his name?"

"Potamkin."

"Potemkin. Yes, like the battleship."

"Potamkin. Yes, like the car dealer," I chimed.

We laughed without sound through the passing of a train. I found myself up the front steps just behind the still laughing little man. I could hear him now. Keys jingled. Locks clicked. We were in. No, I was. Alexander Korin stood back and waved me in. He waited anxiously by the doorjamb, no longer laughing. My ears told me that much and though I couldn't see his eyes, I felt him excitedly twitching in anticipation. Would I pull a faint or hang my head and sob? Would I break into a joyful smile, having been reunited with old memories? I headed up the stairs towards Potamkin's old office.

Neighborhoods change. Luck changes (so I am told), but hallways remain the same, mostly. This one had. I knew this place with its tan, threadbare carpeting. I knew its darkened, discolored mahogany woodwork and handrails. I touched a finger to the banister searching for some traces I might have left some twenty years before. The wood had the waxy feel of melted crayons that your grandmother's coffee table had. Oh, I remembered this place alright, but in a warped way. If you've ever gone back to your elementary school ten years older and two feet taller, then you know how it feels.

I turned to the door that was once the entrance to my doctor's office. Alexander Korin, using the subway noise to cloak his approach, made short work of the stairs between us.

"Please," he spoke to my shoulder blades.

I understood and awkwardly reached across my body with my right hand to twist the crystal doorknob. This time the little Russian blew past me babbling and disappeared through yet another door. I didn't catch a word of it, but I assumed he wanted me to sit, relax, whatever. I rejected his offer for the moment.

This used to be Potamkin's waiting room. I didn't know this place at all. No old carpet here, chum. The once peeling, tobacco stained, white walls were now buried by brushless coats of steel gray satin latex. The anemic green patchwork linoleum was replaced by a deep-pile mauve twill that could swallow a man's shoe up to the ankle. A bank of angular, low backed, flat-black finished wooden chairs lined up against the south wall trying to decide whether to be "Art Deco" or just "New Wave." The chairs these had long since replaced used to have difficulty deciding whether they were really chairs at all or just firewood.

The only other piece of floor-bound furniture in the room was a squat, bow-legged, Chinese-flavored coffee table finished nothing like your grandmother's Maple monster. Neatly rowed magazines—ranging from "Spy" to "American Heritage" to *"Stern"*—and a woman-shaped, mauve vase tastefully devoured the coffee table's ample surface area. A singular green-stemmed, long-tongued flower with one pink petal and a cotton-white, bullet-like mass stared back at me out of the curvey pottery.

A Hopper lighthouse poster, an unfamiliar Miro print and a signed O'Keefe took their places well on three of the gray walls.

Reflected glimpses of dying, orange light barely fell through striped cracks of vertical blinds hanging in an east-facing window cut into the fourth wall. I put myself uneasily onto one of the black chairs, listening for the passing trains.

"How old was she?" Korin emerged from the door he'd disappeared through juggling two towels, a brown bottle of peroxide, gauze pads and adhesive tape.

"Who?"

"Your mother—how old?" He said it matter-of-factly.

"Sixty, I guess. I'll go through the permutations, if you require a more exact figure."

"No. That is fine." There was some air of embarrassment in his answer. I thought he might even be blushing, but it was hard to see in the dying orange light.

"Why do you ask?"

"I am a curious man."

I let that pass, thinking that he certainly was a curious little man.

"It has often been my undoing, my curiosity. At my age, however, even the most passive among us get curious about death. It is difficult to be so close to something you know so little about. Now let me see your hand."

He began to wash the wound with peroxide, holding the towel beneath to catch the runoff.

"I haven't thought about death that way," I got back to the subject of the day.

"Not yet, but I assure you you will."

"Degenerative kidney disease. She died of kidney failure and complications, if you're curious. I figure I'd save you the trouble of asking."

"Thank you. I would have asked, eventually." He let it drop and my hand with it. "While in my office I took the liberty of calling a mechanic friend who owes me a small favor. He will be over shortly to look after your car."

"Thanks, but I could've handled it myself," I said half-heartedly.

"Yes, and you would have ruined my excellent first aid work," he joked, tilting his high forehead at my newly mummified fingers. "Let me have your keys and I will see to the mechanic and the drink that I promised."

Korin scooped up his supplies and my keys and limped to the door mumbling, "needles and pins, needles and pins."

"Foot asleep?" I asked already knowing the answer.

"Very astute, Dylan Klein. It is the whole leg, not simply the foot."

"Old war wound—no doubt."

"No doubt, as you say."

"World War II, fighting your way into Berlin with the Red Army."

"Right war, Right army, Wrong battle. I see I have yet to corner the market on curiosity."

"*Touché*. I deserved that. Sorry."

"Please," he waved a hand at my apology. "There is no need for that."

He turned to the door flexing his left knee, all the while trying to get back some circulation.

"Watch yourself going down those steps," I said just as my Mother would have.

"Yes, I hear the carpet is worn." He hobbled out the door, leaving it ajar.

"You're no car service driver," I yelled.

"Once, yes, I was, but no longer. Not for some time," his drifting voice came back to me. "Such a curious fellow you are, Mr. Klein . . ."

I was curious. I had questions, a pocket full. I had questions about him. I had questions about me. And other questions, too. Now I had some time to list them, ponder them; What was I doing here on the day Mother was buried? What was my family thinking about me? Who was this little man I was waiting for? Why was I waiting? Who won the Mets' game, anyway?

An unseen subway rumbled by, shaking the blinds and rattling my cage. Suddenly I felt nothing but tired, even the pain in my hand seemed like last week's bad memory. Standing in the now near darkness, I twirled the lucite wand, opening the window blinds to reveal the coming of night. I noted a pair of overalled legs sticking out of the passenger door of my crudely parked car. "Pretty prompt," I thought.

I sat back down as Alexander Korin returned, flipped on a light and, sans limp, danced over to the Chinese table, giving the tropical flower an impatient shove. He plunked down a cheap fifth of Scotch and two chiseled glass tumblers, displacing a row of the tidy magazines.

"I hate Scotch, but if I was ever going to reevaluate the stuff, today's the day."

"Good. Ice?"

"Please," I said, "anything to help kill the taste."

"I anticipated as much," the Russian winked, pointing at one of the tumblers filled with ice. "I enjoy my Scotch cheap and neat."

"So I see. I had you figured for a vodka drinker."

"Yes, another bad assumption. You also thought I was a car service driver because I drive a black Lincoln."

He handed me my poison.

"Thanks, I guess," I accepted the tumbler without enthusiasm.

"To the life of your mother and the world into which she passes!" he spoke loudly, raising his glass.

I liked that. I liked that a lot. We clinked glasses and drank. He sat next to me. I still hated scotch; razor blades would've gone down more easily. I coughed and cleared my throat not quite eleven times before I managed a few choice words.

"Got any battery acid to wash that down with?"

"Sorry, but I gave my last few drops to the mechanic working on your automobile," he laughed.

"You surprise me, Alexander."

"Why, because I did not toss my glass at the wall after finishing my drink? That is, after all, what Russians do."

"Well maybe just a little. Actually, I was hoping you'd break out your balalaika or do a sabre dance or two."

"Excuse my sarcasm," Alexander replied.

"Excuse it? I like it too much to excuse it; I'm comfortable with it. You really do surprise me, though. You're a hard man to read."

"Thank you. An easy man to read is a boring man to be. What confuses you or surprises you about me?" he asked with obvious delight.

"Your car, your office, your Scotch, your manner, your . . . What is it that you do for a living anyway? I mean besides offering liquor to wayward mourners you meet on the street."

"Law. I *am* a lawyer. Your mother would approve?" He asked in an explosive whisper."

"No, my mother always wanted a doctor for me," I laughed too loudly. "So I was right about you before. I told you you should've been a lawyer."

"You were right," he paused, "in your way."

"What—"

"Ah!" he put his palm up like a traffic cop to stop me. "This is all I will say about myself for now. It is your Dr. Potamkin I want to hear of. My curiosity is scratching at me again and only your words will soothe it."

"And when I'm done?"

"I will peel off this great shroud of mystery which surrounds me," he said self mockingly.

"Fair enough."

"Another?" he held up the bottle of Scotch.

"No thanks. One's my limit."

"Would it be rude of me to have a second?"

He began pouring himself a few fingers before I could give him my say so, I guess he read minds, too. Either that, or he didn't give a damn about my approval.

"No. No. Go ahead and have another. Anyhow, it'd be a major pain in the ass for you to pour that juice back in the bottle now."

The little Russian drank the Scotch in a thirsty gulp, slammed the glass down, and said,

"Now, Dr. Potamkin."

"Dr. Hyman Potamkin was a piece of work. They didn't break the mold after they made him. There wasn't any mold at all. He was strictly spare parts. I mean he was a round-shouldered runt of a man, but women couldn't get enough of him. The guy needed a road map to find your pulse, but the old bastard had a practice to shame a TV doctor. Patients sat in here," I waved at the four walls, "bunched together in the summer with no fan, no air conditioner and lined up into the hallway and onto the stoop. They were mostly women; grandmothers, bored housewives, housewives with bored children, bored housewives with sick children.

"He was pretty ugly. He stood about 5'4" but would've been about 5'8" if he could've gotten the curve out of his spine and the hunch out of his shoulders and had a shock of white hair like Einstein."

"Yes, but the women . . ."

"His eyes. It was his eyes, Alexander. They were the most sincere shade of faded blue."

Alexander poured himself another drink stating, almost disappointedly, "so he looked like Quasi Modo with nice eyes."

"That's part of it, yes." I held my glass out for a refill I knew I'd regret.

Another part of the magic was vitamin B-12. He'd herd ten women into his office at once and they'd pop out of there like bread out of a toaster. Ten neurotic, overweight housewives like my mother and my aunt went in there," I pointed again, "feeling like unloved, sexless pieces of shit and came out feeling less unloved and less like shit.

"The most vital ingredient was the easiest to see, but the hardest to recognize. He paid attention to them. They believed it was the B-12 shot that cured all without realizing it was the two minutes he gave each of them that made them well.

"When he died my aunt and my mother cried to each other on the phone for a week. They went to the funeral and the cemetery. I'm telling you I couldn't figure out if they were crying more for him or themselves."

"You will learn, as I have learned, that few tears are shed for the deceased."

With that and the scotch, tears uncried for twenty years welled up behind my eyes, fighting unsuccessfully to declare themselves free. Sensing the explosion, Korin fumbled for his empty glass.

"Thank you," he picked up the tumbler, "for sharing some of your history with me, and thank you for your company."

"Not so fast. I'm not going anywhere until you solve the great mystery," I said seriously. "It's time to hear about Alexander Korin."

"The solution will have to wait. I believe I hear your car engine running downstairs."

"I believe you believe correctly. Either that or someone's chopping down trees in the dark with a chainsaw. And in this neighborhood I think that's not likely."

My own words kicked me into reality. The sun had been fast asleep for some time now and, great mysteries not withstanding, I had to get to my dad's apartment for prayers and more goodbyes.

"How much does your friend charge for Sunday house calls?" I asked, reaching for my wallet.

"Now I told you before, this was done as a favor to me. He will not charge me and I will accept no money from you," he said, without overacting the part.

"Well, then, thank you for everything."

"Everything?"

"Not the Scotch, but everything else."

"You are welcome anytime in the old house of Dr. Potamkin."

"Anytime?" I tested him. "Tomorrow, let's say."

"Tomorrow?" he pondered. "No, not tomorrow, but Tuesday, for instance, would be fine. I am certain you will need a rest from the stresses of the week."

"Not as certain as I am, but I can't pin myself down to a day no matter how curious about you I might be. You understand."

"I do, completely. Why then did you ask about tomorrow?"

"Just interested in your answer, I guess."

"Well it has been my pleasure to meet you and share this time with you, away from your grief."

"Thanks again for the company, and for this," I waved my bandaged hand at him.

"Yes, take good care of my work, please. I only hire the healthy."

"Hire?"

"Yes, as in employ."

"You don't even know what I do except bleed well and tell a good story."

"Oh, on the contrary, I do."

"Enough with the 'I do's'! Somebody's going to start throwing rice in a second. I suppose you read minds."

"Not at all, but I can read a business card as well as the next man. A smart lawyer can always use a good insurance investigator."

"First off, I'm not that good. Second, I'm even worse than that, really. Third, where'd you get one of my cards?"

"On the dashboard of your car, when I left your keys for the mechanic. The card looked as though you had been picking at your teeth with it."

"I had been doing just that. Isn't that what everyone uses business cards for anyway?"

"Sometimes, yes, I do it myself."

"Here," I said reaching for my wallet again, "take a fresh one."

"No," he smiled, "I will hang onto this one." He held out the card he'd taken off my dashboard."

"For sentimental reasons, no doubt."

"For whatever reasons, it is mine."

"Another mystery! In any case, I told you I'm not very good at what I am."

"Do. What I do," he corrected me.

"Again with the 'I do's.' Am, do, it's not the point." I was getting too worked up over nothing.

"In this it is possible that you are correct. However, a smart lawyer should depend more on mediocre help that he can trust than on primadonnas whom he questions. Trust is a more valuable commodity than is skill."

"Thank you for your blind faith," I tipped an invisible cap to him, "but how did I earn your trust?"

"Many little things today; and then again nothing. Maybe I simply read your mind and saw that it was so."

With that, any building tension blew away like crisp, brown leaves in a wind tunnel. Chances were, I would never see the funny little Russian again.

We shook hands for a second time and I trotted down the ancient steps, feeling for my mother's buried footprints in the worn carpeting, thinking that mine were there too, but only much much smaller. Going out the front door I reached for my wallet again. I wouldn't insult the Scotch drinker's pride, but maybe the mechanic had lower standards and would accept a tip. I put the wallet back. The overalls and the legs within were gone, leaving the driver's door open and the engine running more smoothly than it had in a decade. Its ass still stuck out rudely into the street. Stepping into the driver's seat a newly familiar voice called down to me not quite from heaven.

"Dylan Klein . . . Dylan Klein," he got my attention, "try not—"

But even cupped hands around his mouth could not raise his voice above the grinding cries coming from the dark avenue. So I turned away from him and to the sparks showering the moonless night. With the subway now crying in the distance on its way to Sheepshead Bay, I gave my ears back to Korin.

"Say again," I called up.

"Mr. Klein," he obliged, "try not to set off my alarm as you leave."

"You can bet I'll try my best not to. You don't have to watch me, remember. You can trust me."

And he made no answer, abandoning his perch above my world.

On my dashboard I found a clean, crisp business card in place of the one my benefactor had taken. The card was one of his, with printing on both sides. The English print side gave me all the correct information: occupation, address, telephone numbers (there were two of them), hours, the usual stuff. The Cyrillic print side probably gave the same facts, but except for the phone numbers I was just guessing that was so. I reached for my wallet a third time, finally unfolding it, and hid the future toothpick behind a thin collection of dollar bills.

I turned right on Alexander's corner, listening for his alarm in my wake. Apparently, I'd managed to do as promised. The dark avenue, Brighton Beach Avenue, seemed less poisonous than it had in the light of the day and memory. I took my time circling back to my father's apartment and the anger that was waiting.

Meanwhile, the radio told me lots of things, some with great urgency. It told me the Mets' score, eventually. It told me something unexpected. It told me that the Mets had rallied to win in the bottom of this inning or that. The radio told me that the Cardinals had had a rally of their own, but that with bases loaded again and one man out, the Mets turned the freakiest double play the radio had ever seen. It told me a Cardinal player hit a screaming liner to the mound, but it deflected off the edge of the pitching rubber on the fly and popped into the first baseman's glove that was attached to the first baseman whose left foot was touching the bag. Double play! After that inning, the radio told me, the Cardinals went down quietly for the remainder of the game. With that I yielded to my desire for some quiet and stopped the radio from telling me anything more.

I thought about what the Russian had said about how luck changes. Maybe. At least I was willing to entertain the thought for the night.

Neither Brunt nor Teller

The incorporated village of Sound Hill fell neatly into one of the rough shoreline grooves that populate the north-facing coast of Long Island. It had fallen there about two hundred years before I had. Neither fall caused much of a stir in the world. Well, George Washington liked Sound Hill enough to commission a lighthouse to be built there. It still stands, blind to the water now, with no beacon to shine through the early morning fog at the southern Connecticut shore. These days the town kids use its white clapboard shell as a place to lose a few beers, or their virginity, or both.

Sound Hill is due north of the fork-split jaws at the eastern end of Long Island. The village, as the name plainly tells you, is located on a hill overlooking Long Island Sound. Townspeople are still constantly amazed at the number of "westerners" (outsiders, New York City residents, mostly) who can't figure out how the village got its name. On bleak winter days Sound Hillians brighten their spirits with stories of how old Mr. So-and-So convinced this "idiot westerner"—two words frequently used in tandem—that the village was named after a Revolutionary War general felled at Valley Forge or a hidden echo cave once used by pirates to conceal their booty or whatever. Not born a true Sound Hillian, and no longer a westerner, strictly speaking, I would never be the brunt of such a story nor could I ever be the teller.

For most of this century Sound Hill was surrounded by sod and potato farms. Lately, the farms have been sold off and converted into wineries by ex-hippies, college professors, and other assorted westerners with dreams and money to kill. Some of them turn a fair profit with fair product. Most don't. You can still find the harpoon vestiges of the village's whaling legacy in the lobby of the town hall, at "Ahab's Antique and Gift Shop," and down at the marina.

Until the last decade, Sound Hill had escaped the invasion of well-healed summer skippers that dominate the Hamptons on the south shore. Overflow was inevitable though; with each year a few more investment bankers, ad execs, surgeons, and theatrical agents would park their vessels in the harbor and their families in the area for the season. Even so, the harbor is a working one. Fishermen in white cableknit sweaters will still dominate the marina for a few years to come.

Summers here, even post invasion, are relatively uneventful. Then again, that's uniformly so for three out of the other three remaining seasons as well. Until recently, local tragedy was defined as cancellation of the annual Little League parade due to threats of hail. High drama would take place in the hours coming up to parade time—to cancel or not to cancel, that is the question. And to call it off only to have the skies clear would just about constitute a capital crime. All of it—the location, the longevity, the whaling, the small town values—gave Sound Hill an aura of quintessential rustic charm. But, as with all splendid things, the aura made for both blessings and a curse.

Curse? Yeah, curse. Or curses; that's how the locals thought of it, anyway. I was part of it or, more exactly, an example of it. The summer invaders were part of it too, but they disappeared as the clock struck twelve on Labor Day. Even if they did reappear in greater numbers every year, they could be thought of or dealt with like locusts or allergies. Their seasons came and went. You braced for their arrival, tolerated their presence, and celebrated their departure.

I was different; a few of us were. We had come and stayed. There was Johnny MacClough, Detective (second grade) New York City Police Department, retired. He'd been decorated more times than the interior of the White House, but at forty-three decided that his head couldn't take anymore pounding against the wall. Two years ago, while doing routine surveillance on a low level wiseguy, who was enroute to Orient Point at the very tip of the island, Johnny and his mark made pit stops in Sound Hill. While the wiseguy got twelve dollars of high-test, a pack of unfiltered Camels, a cup of black coffee with four sugars and some relief,

John Francis MacClough was downing a double Bushmills at the Rusty Scupper Lounge across from the gas station.

To hear MacClough tell it, halfway through the Bushmills he had a religious experience, something akin to Brigham Young's. Sound Hill, he decided, was the place he'd retire to. That was it. The next day he set out filing the proper papers. He bought the Rusty Scupper and moved into the apartment upstairs. At first Johnny flirted with changing the name of his bar to MacClough's Irish Pub. But when he found out what it would cost him to hang a new sign, Johnny decided he could get used to the original moniker. Besides, the locals liked it and, he reasoned, the name fit with the bar's close proximity to the docks. These days you could find Johnny McClough sipping his Bushmill's in back of the bar, staring happily at the gas station across the street.

There were others, as I was saying. One or two were stumblers like John MacClough, people who'd happened into town because they'd made a wrong turn, got the calling, and came back to stay. A few were ex-winery workers who stayed on as waiters or nurses or handymen even after their jobs had dried up. Some toughed it out in the vineyards or by the vats and grew into positions of local wealth and power. I was a stumbler myself.

No matter how we'd settled there, to the locals we were the increasingly expensive price of rustic beauty. Sound Hillians were never belligerent toward any of us. We just represented their position in the midst of an ugly world they'd miraculously avoided until now. In a way I guess they look at us like I looked at the immigrant Russians in Brighton Beach ten years ago: with suspicion and wonder. Eventually, Sound Hillians might move beyond suspicion and wonder to think of us as a curse. But for now, we were just convenient scapegoats, treated with respect, at least, if not with love exactly. It was a price most of us were willing to pay in exchange for relative peace and a night's sleep with the front door wide open.

To Make Up a World

I sat facing out, my back to the door. The marina was busy on summer mornings, even cloudy ones. Fishermen and charter operators didn't have much choice in the matter, if eating was a priority. The well-to-do tempted fate and electrocution at sea in an effort to make their leisure time cost-effective. The New York daily rags were spread out over my desk, masking a generation of dust or two. "The Lighthouse," Sound Hill's weekly contribution to the Third Estate, lay open but ignored upon my lap.

I noticed I was flicking Alexander Korin's bilingual business card between the fingers on my recovered left hand. All the starch and white in the card were memories now. It seemed as though I'd gone through this ritual almost every working day for a month. I'd get just to the point of calling him, then back down at the last second like a nervous teenager asking for a date. My mother'd been dead four weeks now and I hadn't been home to Brooklyn since the Friday after the funeral. I knew that calling Korin would be my first step back and I was not anxious to take it. That's a lie. I was anxious as hell, but frightened more by the possibility of letting go.

The phone rang behind me on the desk and I spun around to pick it up before the answering machine kicked in.

"Klein."

"How is the hand?"

"The hand," I looked at it, "is still attached. How's the scotch?"

"Cheap! Just as I like it."

"Alexander, I was just about to pick my teeth with your card. You must be psychic after all," I tried, unsuccessfully, not to sound unnerved.

"Am I interrupting?" he asked diplomatically.

"Yes, I suppose you are and thanks for doing it."

"I thought I should call you and check up on my handiwork."

"Nice pun," I complimented.

"Pun?" He sounded confused.

"Hand. Handiwork. Come on, you're making me feel like a jerk for pointing it out."

"And your car?" he asked, dropping my hand as the topic of discussion.

"Never better. That mechanic must've owed you a big favor. Could he have torn down my engine and rebuilt it in a half hour?"

"Nothing so dramatic, I assure you. I shall have to ask Boris the next time we speak."

"Boris?" I asked with a laugh.

"And why not Boris?" There was no laugh in his question.

"Look, I'm sorry. Maybe I should call you back when I'm feeling more human."

"No," the Russian demanded, "the job I have for you will not wait that long."

"Thanks for the vote of confidence, Alexander."

"Oh . . . ," he paused, "Yes, that was stupid of me to say. I am sure you are quite human enough now," tension in his voice fading away.

"You mentioned a job."

"I did indeed."

"There are a few people I can refer you to—"

"Thank you, but I do not need references. I need you."

"Need's a pretty strong word, considering."

"Maybe so, but—"

"But nothing," I interrupted. "I've never done a job for you before. You don't know anything about me other than how old my mother was when she died, what she died of, where my family doctor used to live, and that I don't like scotch. Christ, you don't even know if I can follow my own shadow without help or get proper directions from a map-maker, let alone follow some old lady with one leg to make sure she's not faking the amputation."

"Even if all of this were true, which it is not, that would be beside the point. I believe in using the proper people for the proper job and in this instance—"

I finished, "I am the proper person. But how can you know that?"

"I know. In any case, that should not concern you. At least come to my office tonight and hear my offer."

"I'll think about it," I answered with a negative ring.

"Do you always give your prospective clients such an argument? I am surprised you are not in need of public assistance."

He was waiting for my witty reply, but I was fresh out of them. Then he got impatient and called in his marker.

"I know it is wrong of me to ask, but as a favor to me, please come. If you choose not to discuss the work I have for you, then I will follow your wishes. At least we can share a drink, exchange stories, whatever you desire, I can clear up all the questions you had about me, if you are still interested."

I was going to tell him he had no right to ask and I didn't owe him a thing. But the fact was that I didn't and I did. There was nothing wrong with his asking; I owed him more than one favor. He knew as much.

"Oh, I'm interested enough, but not in drinking."

"Excellent. Then you will come?"

"I will come."

"Nine o'clock?"

"Eight thirty-nine, somewhere in there."

"If not Scotch, what would you like to drink?"

"Surprise me."

"That is funny," he said with no hint of humor in his voice.

"What is?"

"You do not strike me as a person who enjoys surprises."

"I'm not, but surprise me anyway."

"A challenge! Very well, until this evening then . . . ," he trailed off.

"Later."

I put down the phone and turned my gaze and attention back to the marina. I hadn't missed much. There wasn't much to miss. The clouds had gone from gray to black and the promise of rain was now a moist reality. Life in Sound Hill stood quietly before me in my crow's-nest. The working boats had long since gone. In a rare display of clear thinking, the vacation captains opted to do their sailing secured to the moorings, fueling their vessels with aged single-malt Scotch and varying amounts of gin, vermouth kisses, and mutant, midget onions. I was jealous of their journeys.

I tried to go back to killing my time quietly, without success. These were the moments when alcoholism seemed like a noble vice. My fantasy would have me reach into the third draw of my file cabinet, pulling out a bottle of amber liquid love. I could lose the empty hours in its warming fog while chain-smoking a pack of cornpaper Gitanes. It was a sweet fantasy, but I only smoked for fashion and Korin's liquor had served to remind me that there was no romance in a bottle of Scotch. I settled on listening to the rain and the awkward, fast beating of my heart.

By 6:00 pm the skies had cleared sufficiently for the sun to blind me all my merry way to Brooklyn. I didn't happen to own a pair of sunglasses, but to keep my equilibrium I didn't own an umbrella, either. I had no love for either. Almost all the blue pigment had been burnt off the skin of my Beetle by subway showers years ago. What little paint remained had been bleached to gray by the sun.

I made it to the Long Island Expressway in a turtle's twenty minutes, passing sod farms and farm stands like they were standing still. They were. Raspberries sent tart, crimson telegrams to me in an effort to flag me down. Eventually, I got their message. The stand girl, wearing a checkerboard gingham apron, flushed red to match the fruit with my wink and smile. She was at the age when presumptions of innocence were at least a year away from losing their validity. Eyes with the fresh crystalline texture of greenish ice looked up from the floor every now and then to peek and shyly smile. Her lashes—too long—and freckles—too irregular and numerous—were offset by a wiry mop of auburn hair. I bought two dry pints of the blood-clustered berries; one for the road and one for the Russian. The price was too high, as stand prices went, but her face was worth her father's profit. I wondered if she understood that. We simply nodded our goodbyes. Then, a few paces away from my car, I turned back, studying her for a moment, blinking my eyes like a shutter. I wanted to carry her picture with me back to Brooklyn.

All the poop about the L.I.E. being the world's longest parking lot was true. I suppose. This far east however, it was just another smooth six-lane highway peaceful enough to let a man ignore his four-speed and focus his attention on swallowing handfuls of unwashed raspberries. Forty minutes down the broken white lines there'd be a year's worth of traffic and no time for anything but clutching and shifting and clutching and shifting. For now the sun pulled down on the sky, pushing up scores of dirty brown hares from their holes dug into the earth along the roadside. Every day was Easter Sunday out here. They'd just sit there in frozen bunches facing the fading sun. The sight of them always caused me discomfort. I don't know, maybe I was just worried one of them would unglue itself from the dying light and dart out in front of my car. Maybe, who knows? What I did know was that I just didn't like it one bit. Closer to the city, the parade dispersed. My forty minutes were up.

The anticipated year's worth of traffic turned out to be a little less than eight months worth. I had time to kill and nowhere I wanted to do it. Dad was down in Florida trying to recover, so stopping by his apartment was out. Even if he were there, home I mean, I'd've managed to avoid that place. I'd been doing a perfect job of that now for weeks. Sadly, with my Dad out of town, there wasn't a soul left in Brooklyn I'd cancel a trip to the dentist for. The real sadness was that the converse was true as well. I made a lazy gas run.

The Merit station was one of those plastic, pristine monstrosities; a self service affair. You know the type, no garage bays, no bow-tied attendants. Your only human contact is barely human and the contact is, at best, indirect.

The man in the glass booth was resting his salt and pepper head on a bed of twiggy arms and jaundiced skin. I set about emancipating some paper money from my wallet and placed a freed note in the empty metal tray.

"Five bucks on number eight," I commanded in a distant voice while inspecting the lack of shine on my shoes.

No answer was forthcoming from the sleepy, yellow man.

"Five on eight," I repeated from less distance this time.

"We're closed. I'm dead. Go away." The voice was older than the still motionless body appeared to be.

"Well come, Lazarus, rise from the dead and give me five bucks on pump eight. After you have done your duty, you may return to the Bible."

"There's a Gulf station about ten blocks from here. That way," a finger moved pointing north.

"Sorry, Lazarus, I can't do that. The conversation's too stimulating here," I retorted.

The mechanical contribution tray swallowed up my five dollar bill with one relaxed gulp.

"Get your gas and go. Let me rest in peace," the detached voice came from the unmoving head.

I hesitated. Something in that remote voice hit a chord in me. I stood there searching my brain for the chord it struck. I couldn't find it.

"I know your voice from somewhere."

"Yeah, another life. I don't know anybody in this one. Besides, this isn't my voice; I just borrowed it for the evening. Your gas is waiting for you." His frail, blind fingers tapped out a code on a keyboard to the right of his head. "There's two bucks extra in it, so just go for it."

The chord was struck again, but I couldn't name the tune. I pumped my seven dollars worth while watching for any stirrings from the man in the booth. There was no movement from him, but I jumped when the last ten cents of the seven hundred poured onto my shineless shoes. In my head I could hear Lazarus the cashier's imaginary laughter. I laughed with it.

I made for Korin's house having decided that early was good for me. The scent of gasoline easily overwhelmed the delicate breath of raspberries. I sort of enjoyed the smell of gas. I remember liking it more as a kid, but that was true for lots of things.

I sat in my car out in front of the Russian's flat, half listening to the Mets game in between the subway thunder. His black Lincoln was shoe-horned into the too narrow driveway at the stoop side of the house. I guess he thought it was safer there with me coming and all. I could see light barely squeezing through the stingy slats of the upstair's blinds. I shut off the game, grabbed the gift pint of berries, and walked to the front door.

The door buzzed itself open before my left index finger could beg entrance. Apparently, Korin had been watching me watching his house. Without stopping to reminisce, I made my way up the familiar staircase two steps at a time. The waiting room door was ajar. I knocked anyway.

"Come in, Mr. Klein." His voice was friendly enough.

He stood, smiling broadly, a pace or two ahead of me. The room looked pretty much the same as it had weeks before. The bow-legged coffee table was still covered by neat rows of magazines, only the issues had changed. The exotic, long-tongued flower was gone from the curvy vase. In its stead stood a solitary red rose.

"You are disappointed?" he asked, chasing his smile away.

"About what?" I questioned back.

"I am not sure. You just seem so. Your face is blank."

"Not disappointed. I was just seeing if things were as I remembered. I was on fairly shaky footing the last time around."

"Yes, I should say you were. Well, are things?"

"Are things what?"

"The same as you recall," he continued.

"Basically. Your periodicals are current and you've invested in a new flower, but otherwise it's the same."

"Forgive me," the little man held out his right hand, "how have you held up?"

"These are for you," I put the pint crate of raspberries in his outstretched hand. "As well as can be expected, I guess."

He raised his brow at the berries and transfered the package to his left hand, extending his right back out to me. I took hold of it and shook it firmly.

"It *is* good to see you, Dylan Klein." The broad smile reappeared.

"I hate to admit it, but it's nice to be here."

"Now, let me see my handiwork."

I held out my left paw for inspection.

"So," he said, with self satisfaction, "you will live."

"It seems that way, but don't rush to hasty conclusions." What's this about work for me?" I tried cutting through some fat.

"Not in here. Come into my office." Korin waved me past the door that once led to Hyman Potamkin's treatment room.

On my way past him, I hesitated and took note that my host had gone formal for the evening. Well, he wasn't donning a tux, but his loose-weave, light gray, Italian silk suit with white cotton shirt and red paisley tie were head and shoulders above the sweat-yellow T-shirt and worn chinos from three Sundays past.

"Gone shopping I see," I let out casually.

"What?" His face went blank.

"The suit. The tie . . ."

"Yes." His smile came up. "No! That is, I purchased this ensemble some time ago, before we met. It is not fair that you should judge my wardrobe by what I lounge in on a late Sunday. These snap judgements of yours will do you in someday. Really!"

"I don't doubt it. Sorry." I looked at the room. "Nothing left in here that I remember except that window." I pointed vaguely in the direction of his desk.

His office sort of mirrored the waiting room. The wall coloring, the carpeting, all the same. No art on the walls to speak of, though, just a grouping of framed diplomas scribbled in dyslexic lettering. There was one from Brooklyn Law School I could make out well enough. The rest of them, who knows? They might as well have been car muffler warranties from the old country for all I knew.

Korin rushed by me and eased into a black leather swivel chair behind a desk that was first cousins with the coffee table in the other room. I put myself down on the middle of three chairs that faced the desk. These chairs were clones of the ones in the waiting room, not just relatives.

"A rare treat," he said, placing the well-traveled berries before him. "Thank you. Would you care for some?"

"Not so rare. You're welcome and no, I wouldn't; not now anyway. Nice office, Alexander. You've got good taste for—"

"For a little Russian immigrant. We all do not wear ill-fitting, ugly brown suits with thin lapels and floodwater length trousers. Our offices also are not required by law to resemble a produce market or a delicatessen."

"Is that so?" I couldn't help laughing.

"Yes," he barely managed before joining me.

It was an awkward moment when the laughter had stopped and we'd finished wiping the tears from our eyes. Neither one of us knew the words to say to get back to the circuitous road we were on. Korin solved the problem by producing that fabled bottle of cheap Scotch from one of the drawers of his desk.

"A drink?"

"Why not," I answered, regretting the words as the came out.

"Indeed," he said, pulling two glasses from the same drawer that gave birth to the Scotch. "Pardon my asking, but did you spill some gasoline on yourself this evening or is that some awful cologne?"

"The former. By the way, my car's never run better since your friend returned your favor."

"I shall pass on your compliments. Ice?"

"No. Let's get it over with.

He poured. We drank. I hated it. He loved it. He offered another. I passed. He didn't. He loved it again.

"Cigar?" He flipped open a walnut humidor.

"Not for me, but I'll take one for my Dad." I half asked and half stated.

He didn't bother to ask if I minded and went through the rituals of cigar smoking which are its real appeal.

"Work for me. You were asking where we were, Alexander. You have some work for me."

"I asked no such question," he replied clearly off balance.

"Well, you should have and I figured one of us should get around to it."

"Eventually, but first I feel obliged to clear up any questions you have about me. I cannot expect a man to work hard for an employer he is unsure of."

"Sounds fair, but I have a suspicion that you're a hard man to know."

"Ask your questions and reach your conclusions then."

"Okay. What's your *schtick?* You drive around in a gaudy limo that smacks of immigrant inferiority from here to tomorrow, but you don't act the part. Well, actually sometimes you do—act I mean. Your English is almost perfect, but every few sentences you'll mix up your syntax or flip-flop phrases as if by formula. Then there's this place. The damned staircase is basically unchanged since I came here as a kid. Even the carpet's the same, worse in fact. I walk through the door at the top of the stairs and boom, it's designer showcase; clean, fine, tasteful. The cheap Scotch, the good cigars, I don't get it."

"You are not supposed to," he said, almost without an accent."It is not really for you at all. You are correct, it is sometimes an act; the car, the mixed-up phrases, the decor."

"Who for?"

"I am not really certain any longer. At first, and still, to some extent, it is for my clientele. For them, I must walk a curious tightrope between the evils of the past and the promise of the future. I must have all the symbols of success, or rather what success means in their eyes, and yet maintain some rough edges."

"Tough way to assimilate. It's an awful lot to go through to gain some trust and customers."

"I suppose to you it is, but people raised in the Soviet Union are not a trusting lot. They may live here now and some may have attained all their dreams, but they still do not trust the system." He pointed at me for emphasis.

"Good for them. I don't trust it either."

"Yes you do. If you search deeply enough, you will say there are parts that need changing, but, given the human condition it's not that bad. On the other hand, we have been taught forever the evils of capitalism. We have been shown the decadence of the west; crime, poverty, wars fought over religion. Therefore, though we may flourish here, only our grandchildren will find comfort in America.

"As for the Soviet Union, what would you have me say? We were not taught the failings of the system; we lived them. Stalin was lesson enough for any man, but that is not to say that the system had no merit. I should tell you that if Jews were allowed their religious freedom, Brighton Beach might be a ghost town. These people feel trapped, and for them to trust me I must be symbolic of their plight."

"How religious of you," I commented, with more than a pinch of sarcasm.

"Guilty as charged, also a little over-dramatic, but the basis of what I say is quite true. Intellectually, I am certain you understand, but emotionally, viscerally you could not possibly." His response was relaxed and easy.

"Let's say I buy all this and I have no reason not to, really. I mean, it's not like you don't share anything with these people. Isn't trust a by-product of common experience? You come from the same place, speak the same language, practice the same religion, whatever. Doesn't that buy you a little acceptance? And if not, why hang here. From what I hear, see, and surmise you could move in bigger circles than this, much bigger."

"I rather enjoy this small circle. I wax poetic at the sound," he hesitated, waiting for the earth to stop shaking, "of elevated subway cars rambling through the night. I find it amazing how we humans can tune such sweet noise out until we want to hear it."

"Yeah, almost as amazing as that answer. Sorry, Alexander, I don't buy it, not two words of it. I get the impression you'd rather be a thousand miles in any direction from your fellow emigres. Hell, if you like subway noise so much, you could record it and pipe it all through your house in Malibu or Kenosha."

"You are unconvinced? I will leave it there for now," Korin pronounced, pouring himself another scotch before delicately attacking the raspberries. "Here!" He slid a check over to me with his free hand.

"One thousand bucks! Very impressive, but who's this guy 'Cash'? What would a soul have to do to earn this money besides changing his name?"

"Not a thing." His three syllable answer was too long for me.

"See ya in church," I stood up to leave. "Thanks for the company."

"Sit Down! Dylan Klein, you are the most impatient person. Stop the drama and sit, please," he said, backing away from his imperative tone. "This amount is simply a retainer—a signing bonus, if you wish. Listen to what I have to say; then make your decision. If you choose to feel that I have injured your pride, you may do a dance of indignation on my desk, but at least show me the courtesy of hearing me out."

"I should've worn my tap shoes."

"Yes, and maybe those shoes would have smelled less like regular unleaded," the little man shot back effectively.

"Regular leaded. I'm listening."

He wasn't talking, but rather reaching into his top drawer to pull out a 5″ × 7″ manila envelope. He undid the metal clip, pulled up the unglued flap, and blew into the exposed seam expanding the girth of the envelope. Using his right index and middle fingers as tongs, Korin pulled out an old black and white photo and laid it gently down in front of me. He still wasn't talking.

Forty faces looked up from the grainy, browning print. I guess there were around forty, men and women both. Some were old and worn and withered. Some were newer to the world. A few had flat Slavic cheekbones and wore rumpled hats over their unkept hair. Some women wore babushkas; most really, but not all. None smiled. None! These were people from a different age, people uncomfortable around cameras. These were people who knocked on wood; to whom superstition was the unifying force of nature. One could not judge any of them stunning or handsome, hideous or deformed. Their dress and discomfort and the quality of the print made those sort of determinations troublesome, if not impossible. I didn't know whether they were irrelevant, yet.

"Yeah, and so what happened? I've got one just like it. My

mother's side of the family is from the Ukraine. Did my family steal a horse from your family?" I asked, tongue in cheek.

"That may be, but those people are not my family. Flip the photo over."

I did as he suggested. In the upper left hand corner was a faded black stamp consisting of an official looking seal and foreign lettering. In amongst the print were underlined blank spaces filled in with ink by human hand. The writing itself was script and had almost dissolved into oblivion.

"*Deutchland, Deutchland uber alles.*" I half sang.

"You recognize the markings, then, I see."

"It's not too tough. Half the people in this country may not be able to name the seven continents or name our national symbol, but most of us recognize the swastika as the mark of Nazi Germany—the twisted cross and all that jazz."

"You take it lightly," Korin asked and stated in one breath.

"No, not really. Look at my hands."

"They shake!"

"So do my guts. When I was a kid I had a long romance with WWII. I watched every movie about it I could, especially about the European war. Then when I got older and was exposed to truths about the Holocaust and the twelve million who died in the camps, romance turned to morbid curiosity. I was sure that if I were to ever go to Germany, I would visit a concentration camp."

"To what end?"

"To find answers, I guess. Being born Jewish, I felt like it was sort of a duty I had. Of course now I think that's nonsense."

"Your hands are liars then," he said.

"I said I think it's nonsense, not that it really is. You know, I made it to Germany one summer during a trip to Europe. No matter how I rationalized or intellectualized about how that was forty years ago and that these Germans were not responsible and blah, blah, blah, I couldn't feel comfortable. Everytime I'd see a sixty year old German I'd think—What did he do during the war? Did he drive the cattle trains? Did she light up a synagogue? Did he pull gold teeth from the gassed bodies?"

"Did you go to a camp?"

"No," I swallowed my response. "I was afraid to ask about how to go about it. You know it's not like taking a tour bus to Stonehenge or Notre Dame. They didn't have those little tourist flyers in my hotel lobby. This picture," I held it up, "is my first real contact with that ugly past."

"The persons in the picture you hold never saw the inside of a camp. Most were hanged within ten minutes after the photo was taken. The younger women lived slightly longer, long enough to be stripped nude, raped, and chased like herd animals around the corpses of their strung up brothers, parents, lovers, husbands, and friends. Finally, they were made to kneel over a ditch one at a time to be shot in the back of the head and tumble onto the bodies of those who had gone before.

"In the Soviet Union the Germans were less discriminating about who to kill. Being Jewish only enhanced your chances. Actually, most of those people were not Jews at all. They were rounded up at random when the Nazis overran the village. The killings were meant to show us what would happen if we were to resist. They made their point clearly. The Germans are a very thorough people."

"Yes, thorough enough to photograph their victims and arrogant enough to film the goings on. How'd you get hold of this?" I waved the sepia print at him.

"Germans," he corrected, ignoring my question, "are not arrogant. The Nazis, the believers, were arrogant."

"The photo?" I repeated.

"Jews are not the only hunters of Nazis on the planet. Some say twenty million Russians perished in the war. Maybe that figure is exaggerated. It may be too small, but whatever the number it does not interest me. I am an old selfish man. Only those people in the snapshot concern me, because I watched them die.

"In the Soviet Union you can buy anything on the black market, even files and pictures from high places. Truthfully, it was not that difficult to procure once I found the correct source. That was the difficulty. After all, this print is not a state secret and with so much documentation and so many dead to choose from—who will miss it? And now, if it is missed, nothing can be done about it."

"These people were family?"

"No."

"Friends?"

"I knew some of them, but none of them were close to me," he answered nonchalantly.

"Well, if they weren't your friends or family and they're all dead—"

"Ah, Dylan Klein," Korin cut me off with delight, "they are not all dead. That is why I need you. Do you see the clean-shaven man, third from the left in the second row from the bottom?"

"The one without the hat with curly hair," I answered, putting my right index finger over his face.

"Him. Yes, him. The Nazis wanted to show us that they could be generous and humane, as well as tough and unflinching. So they gathered this group of townspeople and set them off to one side in the town center, lining them up neatly, taking that picture, etc. The rest of us were herded to the other side of the square and looked on curiously like any good audience.

"After so many minutes a dark haired Nazi colonel introduced himself to us, spouting on about what we could do, what we could not do, and where we were permitted and not permitted. Funny," the little Russian laughed almost to himself, "I cannot remember the bastard's name. If this were the movies, I would never have forgotten his name, but . . .

"Yes, he finally came to the climax by pointing to those people across the square. One of them, he tells us, will be made an example of to indicate the serious consequences of disobeying their rules and orders—a seriousness none of us doubted to begin with. This colonel walks directly up to me followed by his interpreter and pulls me out in between both groups. I thought I was dead. I am not proud to tell you that I urinated down the leg of my trousers. 'Do not be afraid,' the interpreter tells me, with the colonel whispering German at me through a smile. 'You will choose the example, not be him,' I am told, as the colonel points to the neatly rowed group across the square.

"This colonel snaps his fingers and a private comes running to his side, gesturing with the proper show of respect. The private produces a babushka which he proceeds to blindfold me with. Again, I feel I am a dead man and the blood is pushing through my veins so quickly that I feel light-headed and nauseous. A man tugs on my arms and leads me some steps to my left. I can taste the vomit in my throat. I am spinning. Suddenly, I am spinning. Arms are twirling me in a tight circle, faster, faster. The same arms that spin me, hold me up from falling. The vomit is exploding up through my mouth. Now, I am free of the twirling arms and fall. I collapse into a crowd of bodies, spewing my insides out as I tumble.

"I am up again, unblindfolded, covered in my own vomit and urine, next to that man," Korin pointed at the picture, "also full of vomit."

"This guy with the curls?" I asked for asking's sake.

"Mikhail Brodsky. We are both standing there in absolute silence, too frightened to pray or to beg. Whom would we pray to, after all, and what for? The dark haired colonel comes to inspect the two stars of his little Passion Play. His cackling is so loud and infectious that some of his troops join in, along with one or two of the villagers. He stopped laughing just long enough to bark out some orders to his men. One of the orders was to dump some buckets of water on Brodsky and myself. At least, we thought, we will die clean, wet, but clean. The other order was to start marching all of us to the eastern edge of town."

"To a makeshift gallows and the ditch."

"Just so. Just so."

"So you picked the survivor, not the example," I concluded.

"Yes and no. Brodsky was both an example and the survivor. We were all the examples. The Nazis, not unlike Stalin, were showing us that there are games for sure, but never any rules for sure.

"So, this colonel slaps Brodsky on the shoulders and shook my limp hand. Rifle butts guided us back into the audience, their faces fixed on the hanging ropes."

He sounded as drained as I felt uneasy. Great story. And for my money, that's exactly what it was. I just didn't like it; bits of it, parts of it, the all of it. Throughout his retelling I kept being reminded of a documentary I'd seen, a book I'd read, something I'd once heard. The fact was that despite his protestations to the contrary, it sounded rather 'movie-ish.' I tried not to let on so Korin could finish playing out the hand.

"Brodsky's here and you want me to find him for you. For that I get the thousand dollars and my daily bread," I threw out for discussion.

"I have found him for you. I simply want you to follow him. He drives for the Kiev Car Service on the avenue near Ocean Parkway."

"Thanks. I think I can find it, but what's the pomp and circumstance for, anyway? You know he's here, where he is. Go have a *knish* together and save yourself some money."

"That is solid advice, Dylan Klein, but I have my reasons for acting in this manner, believe me." He sounded sincere enough.

"Care to discuss them?"

"Not at the moment, but they will become clearer to you."

"I haven't taken the job yet. I don't even know what it is I'm supposed to do exactly." I wasn't lying.

"You are a loud thinker, Mr. Klein."

"Yeah, I guess I am. You know how some people wear their hearts on their sleeves? Well, I wear a cerebral cortex on mine. I think it's congenital. I'll try to keep it down."

"If I read those noisy thoughts of yours correctly, I would say that you are having a difficult time accepting my story."

"That's a fair assessment. Difficult? Yes. Impossible? No, not really," I lied a little bit. "Besides, even if I believed the whole nine yards, I still wouldn't understand the surveillance routine."

"I anticipated as much. In your place, I would feel as you do."

"In my place, would you take the job?"

"Probably not . . . ," he paused, "not unless the money was good enough to persuade me not to care. Are you persuaded?"

"No, but I'll take the job anyway. I figure I owe you one." I regretted my words even before he could hear them. "And just for the hell of it, do you think you could give me a few more specifics about just what it is I'm supposed to do with this guy? I can't cha-cha with him twenty-four hours a day, seven days a week."

"In a moment. First, what is your per diem fee?" he asked, holding a Mont Blanc pen over a scratch pad. "Expenses, of course."

"What would life be without expenses? As far as the fee goes, I haven't decided. Since I don't know what I'm supposed to do, it's tough to come up with a number. I'll start with the grand and when that's exhausted, I'll bill you according to my mood."

"Yes," he dropped the pen and smiled, "please bill me. I am certain you are a reasonable man."

That was my cue to leave. I didn't take it. I learned a long time ago not to trust clients who are happy to be billed at a later date with no set fee. Their pleasure with that arrangement usually indicates they have no intention of paying.

Korin stood up from behind his desk, opening his mouth to speak. I stood, in kind, to stretch my legs. The little Russian's copper eyes looked past me. Suddenly, something hissed over my left shoulder, warming my cheek on the way. A dime-sized red dot appeared just above the bridge of Korin's proud nose. His eyes went blank as a puppet's as he stiffened for a long moment, only to collapse quietly into a puddle of himself. The only noise came from the weight of the body crushing the raspberries and the balsa container they came in.

Frozen, I didn't get a chance to see the gun or who was attached to it. I squeezed my eyes shut so tight they burned. I waited for my bullet in the frantic calm, but it wasn't coming, at least not yet. I got a gun butt—I think it was a gun butt—instead. I was happy for it. My face and the floor were destined to meet, but I fought gravity long enough to puke all over myself and the carpeting. On the way down I wondered if I'd live to consider the irony. It's funny what you think about.

I woke up where I'd fallen. I hadn't dreamed. The crushing pain told me I had used the rest badly. My eyes popped open mechanically. The room, nearly black, let in enough light for a foot's visibility. My left cheek was buried in a pool of vomit and spit. Instinctively, I jerked my head up off the floor. Christ! My whole body shuddered. I got sick again pressing my palms against both temples in an attempt to keep my brain from exploding through my battered skull. Each convulsion sent shock waves down my spine, ripping me in two. I was certain death was the preferred option.

I stood up, piece by piece, on the rolling deck of a ship, slipping on my lunch and nearly flopping backwards. I'd've thrown up for an encore, but my guts had given their all. A few dry retches were the best I could manage. A screeching train naively assaulted me, cutting at my brain through the ears. I searched for a lump at the back of my head and found it still leaking some blood. I took ten deep breaths in the dark, waiting for the seas to calm.

When the waves had steadied to a windy chop, I took baby steps towards Korin's desk and body or, rather, towards where I thought they might be. My ship hit land. My fingers read the obstacle's contours and told me that I'd sailed in the right direction. I found the dead man's back with my right hand. With touch as their radar, my eyes followed and the sparse light allowed for a hazy picture of

Life Goes Sleeping

the still body. But even in the haze, I could make out that there was something drastically wrong with the torso's outline. My left hand fumbled to find the switch for the black metal, giraffe's neck lamp hiding on the desktop.

My eyes struggled to focus in the virgin light and I struggled against accepting what they saw. Korin's body lay almost where it had dropped, widthwise across his desk, but his head was gone. I should have run or fainted or screamed. I did none of them. I stood there strangely numb, feeling not much like a human. All the humanity I possessed had been bludgeoned out of me some time before. Now it trickled down my shirtback and putrified in puddles on the rug.

A maroonish bathtowel, heavy with blood, was fixed about the stump of the dead Russian's neck with a once white, nylon cord. A spreading red blotch grew on the carpet just below the towel. In my fog I'm sure to have missed no more than a hundred details, but I couldn't help noticing there was less blood than I would've expected and that splatter marks were conspicuous by their absence. How rare! A neat butcher in Brooklyn.

Numbness makes calling the cops easy to forget. Numbness gives you license to do things, without hesitation, that normally you would never do. Things like disturbing evidence or frisking the headless body of a man you'd just recently shared a Scotch with. I patted down the back of the stiffening corpse all the way to its shoes. I didn't find what I was looking for, whatever *it* was. Numbness was going to let me flip the cadaver over until pain intervened.

Another attacking subway screamed into Brighton Beach station, sending my hands up to my head and me to my knees. When the suffering let up, I opened my lids onto the flesh and lumber landscape of Korin's desktop. Rapsberry juice had stained a semi-circular blast pattern out from the body's right side. Following the crimson stain from its spotty, outer tentacles into its source, my eyes latched onto an incongruity in the corona. A rectangular piece of puzzle was gone from where the juice would have sprayed across the little Russian's writing pad. The pad itself was still there alright, but at least the top sheet had been torn away. And continuing to trace the stain back to the torso, I found the missing top sheet soon enough.

From the curly twist of his white-blue fingers one might have concluded that Alexander Korin had died with a sand wedge in his right hand. I knew better. Even if he had expired with a short iron in his hand, the club was gone now. In its stead was a folded piece of red-spotted stationary. I'd completely missed it in my numb frisk just a minute before. With some effort I freed the paper from its hardening prison, unfurled it and laid it over the stark white rectangle on the desktop. Perfect fit! Strike up the band! The stain was complete. I was nowhere. Confused. Hurting. Nowhere.

I raised myself up to circle the desk and sit down before calling the law. A dead man's chair never felt so much like a womb. I almost passed out, but the demolition in my brain put the skids to that notion. Reaching for the phone, I stopped to wonder how the paper had gotten into the corpse's fingers and why. The "how" part didn't take too much wondering. The murderer had put it there. After all, Korin was dead before he hit the red berries. He was in no shape for breathing, never mind tearing and folding. I'd watched him fall. And even if he had lived a minute with a bullet in his brain, his busy fingers would have smeared the fresh juice on the paper. Neither the stained sheet nor the cool, rigid hands showed any signs of deathbed finger-painting.

I flipped the spotty sheet over a few times looking for hints that might have been there, but I couldn't find. There were no obvious visible signs on the paper to suggest why it had been folded and placed in the stiff's fingers; no coded writing, no secret creases, no mysterious pin pricks, no Braille, no dots, no dashes. Well, the cops could worry about the "whys" of the matter from now on.

The numbness must've been lessening. I checked my watch so I could give a time frame to the reporting officer. It was near 2:00, real near. That meant the Mets' game would be long over by now. I was still numb enough not to care about the score. My moist left palm found the phone, but it sang to me before I could dial 911. I picked up the receiver and somewhere Pavlov was proud.

"Good morning Mr. Klein," a calm voice offered.

"Maybe for you."

"Sorry about the bruise. I have faith you shall survive it." The accent was remotely English.

"Do I have a choice?" I asked.

"Why yes, you most assuredly do." He sounded like a Czech or a Pole who'd learned the language from a native speaker or in Britain itself. "We always have choices. Do exactly as I instruct and I can insure your survival, within limits of course. Deviate, even slightly, and I shall see you lifeless as the fellow on the desk."

"Place the—"

"Fuck you!" I cut him off, slamming down the phone and holding my breath.

He couldn't hit me in the back of the head, after all. I eased my eyes open and watched the red second hand count to ten on the black plastic band that passes for a watch these days. I was waiting. A slow subway, moving under yellow, made its knife grinding turn where the elevated tracks crossed Coney Island Avenue, ending my wait.

The dead man jumped. Only an inch, but that was enough. I reacquainted myself with the floor. The train came to rest and with it silence ruled the avenue. The desk light showed me where the bullet had come clean through the blind slats slicing two or three on the way. Bits of shattered glass perched on the sill. My phone pal had used the subway to cover the shot and as long as that cover remained in the station, I was safe. I thought I was.

The train stayed put, but the body jumped again. This time I heard the glass crack and the dull smack of metal on meat. I also heard the electric insect singing. I pulled the receiver to the floor so hard that the whole phone followed, crashing down beside my head.

"Mr. Klein, do I have your attention now?" The question was rhetorical, but I figured I better answer it.

"Sorry, can you repeat the question?"

"Please Mr. Klein. I enjoy a bit of repartee as much as any man, but can't we save it for later? Time is short and you've so much to do. You may climb back into the chair now."

"I'll pass on that."

"But Mr. Klein," he sounded genuinely disappointed, "surely you realize I could have just as easily put those two shots into your thorax as into that carcass. Why should I lure you into the chair after such a demonstration?"

"Because you like games, mister. Games like using train noise as shot cover even though you've got a silencer. Me and the rug are great buddies anyhow. So, if it's all the same to you, I'll stay planted."

"As you wish." He closed that chapter and went on to the next. "As I said, you have much to do, so be quiet and listen to my instructions. If you so much as breathe too loudly from this point forward without my permission, a third bullet will end your life. Is that clear?"

"Abundantly, old chap."

"Take the piece of paper you found bundled in the corpse's fingers and place it somewhere on your person. The place is of your choosing. Open the bottom left hand drawer of the desk. There you will find a plastic drop cloth, a blanket, and some nylon cord. Lay the plastic—"

"You're out of your fucking mind. I'm not cleaning up your mess." I was beginning to feel very sick again.

From the marksman came only silence. Above the avenue an engineer blew pressure from his brakes and began to pull his cargo toward Ocean Parkway. The dead man's leg twitched. Bits of fabric and flesh with a blood chaser rained down on me.

"Alright. Alright," I shouted into the phone, "I'm listening."

"Lay the plastic out on the floor as near the desk as possible. Lay the body on the mat trying to keep it centered. Bind its feet and hands. This will take some effort, but if you must break a bone or two, do so. I doubt if there will be any protest from your friend. Once this is accomplished, fold the plastic around the body and secure it tightly with the cord."

"Don't shoot! I've got a stupid question. What do I cut the rope with, my teeth?"

"A fair question. No, use the scissors in the top drawer. The rest of your work is simple enough. Roll the wrapped and bound body into the blanket. Carry it down the stairs, out the door and place it in the trunk of that tasteless Lincoln. You will find the keys and registration on the coffee table in the outer office. Along with that, I have provided a towel, a comb, and some mouth rinse so you might freshen up. In any case, we can't have you drawing attention to yourself.

"With all that accomplished, you simply have to drive the car back to Sound Hill, park it near your office, and get some well-deserved sleep. Whenever you wake up, you'll find that awful car gone and your Volkswagen in its place. Yes, we've taken the liberty of borrowing your car for the evening so as to transport it out east. You can't very well drive two cars, can you? No, of course not."

"How kind," I coughed up. "Then what'll you do, shoot me

through the ear or just call the cops and pin your chopping party on me? I mean, I don't mind getting fucked, but come on . . ."

"Oh nothing so dramatic, Mr. Klein, I assure you. In fact, we'd like you to complete the investigation that you were hired for this evening."

"Brodsky?"

"Quite so, Brodsky. Only I should inform you that your Mr. Korin was neither who nor what he claimed and that locating Mr. Brodsky will involve more than phoning the local taxi service."

"Any helpful hints?"

"None, I'm afraid." He thought he was funny. "By the way, if you're entertaining thoughts of escape or avoidance, please drop them immediately. The house is surrounded."

"That line's kinda worn."

"True, nevertheless."

"So let's say I go along with this. How do I contact you?" I couldn't believe I asked.

"You needn't concern yourself with that," he assured me, "we'll contact you whenever."

"No, that's right, I needn't be concerned. You blew a man's brains out in front of me, bludgeoned the back of my head bloody, decapitated a corpse, fired shots a foot from my scalp, and have set me up for a murder rap. What's to worry about?" I was screaming in an odd whisper.

"Just do as we say, Mr. Klein. The evidence will disappear. Find Mr. Brodsky." He hesitated. "It is now 2:07. I want you out of the house and in the Lincoln by 2:20." The body moved for a fourth time. "Just a reminder, Mr. Klein, to do as I say." The phone went dead; no dial tone, no nothing. Just dead.

I didn't pontificate overly long about whether to comply. Doing what the man said would buy me time; time to think, time to breathe. He, or they, wanted me alive, at least for the immediate future. How immediate was out of my hands. I slipped my wallet open and slid the stained top sheet in beside the big check made out to 'Cash.' What's another piece of evidence here or there linking me to the murder scene gonna hurt? I thought about leaving my name, address, phone number, and palm print to make the law's job less complicated. The pain in my head sent me back to work.

I found the touch pad on the wall and raised the light just enough to get a fair look at the mess. Funny thing, as the lights came up so did the smell of my former guts. I located the drop cloth and blanket as instructed and set about my grim job. The dead man made it easier on me than I'd anticipated. Nice bundle, except for the spot of vomit I got on the blanket near his feet. It bothered me that even in better light I couldn't find any splatter marks worth mentioning. Too bad for me.

Playing TV detective I knelt down along the wall adjacent to the door which led back out to the waiting room. Turning the handle and pulling, I moved the door back a few inches revealing nothing. A few more inches showed me the room as it was hours before, with the addition of some items on the bow-legged table. I freshened up to the tune of a D train, maybe an M. I spit the mouthwash back into the towel and went to get my package.

Carrying it wasn't a breeze. My left shoulder ached more than the rest of me under his weight. Spinning slowly, I took one last look around. Korin's feet slammed into the desk lamp. It staggered like a punch drunk pug in search of his legs. The lamp steadied, refusing to go down. Navigation was a task with the added weight, but I managed to reach the bottom of the stairs without scuffing halls. I laid the blanket down by the vestibule door before checking the air outside.

Again, no bullet. The salt air burnt my nostrils, but rescued my lungs. The street was bright with those stupid, buzzing, amber lights. An ignorant old Plymouth passed by me, stopping at the corner to wait for green. I waited for it. When it turned right, I went for the Lincoln's driver side door. The correct key made getting in struggle free. Nice interior; I liked gray leather. I popped the key into the ignition and leaned toward the trunk release when a sweaty chill froze me. It froze me on two counts.

First, I was staring at the numbered keypad of a combination alarm. If the thing was active, I'd have anywhere from five to thirty seconds to punch in the proper code. These things never stopped the pros, but they did tend to hamper amateurs waiting to deposit dead Russians in the trunk. How could I have forgotten that fucking alarm; it's how I met the bastard. In less than thirty seconds the neighborhood would be treated to a symphony. In the thirty seconds after that a prowl car from the 61st precinct would arrive. And after I was cuffed, it would take the boys about thirty more seconds to find the car's rightful owner ripening quietly by the vestibule door.

Second, I hadn't followed my instructions exactly. Instead of bringing the corpse with me and placing it directly into the trunk, I'd come out of Korin's house empty-handed. To my friend with the British manners and whispering rifle, it might appear as though I was making a run for it. And if that's how he chose to interpret my actions, I'd be dead before the alarm could sing.

I remained frozen on the outside. Inside, my heart pushed and sucked blood so hard my ears hurt from the pressure. Those few pieces of clothing that had managed to remain free of sweat or blood or vomit until now, were relieved of that honor by my pores. My cheap Swiss watch spoke in loud ticks, no need for translation.

No lights. No sirens. No broken glass. No bullets. I wanted to melt into the ashen colored cowhide, but twisted the ignition key instead. The trunk popped open on command and I made my way out of the car leaving a moist outline on the driver's seat. Taking measured steps back up the stoop, I peeked over my left shoulder at the empty space where my VW wasn't. I hadn't thought of checking before. Truth was, the time I'd bought was running out and I hadn't come up with any ideas; brilliant or otherwise.

With the rolled blanket on my shoulder I stepped through the front door. Turning to the right, I shut the door behind me saying some 'farewells' and 'thank you's' for the benefit of any audience I might have other than the one I was aware of. A Manhattan bound train buried my steps during the short hike down the brick stairs to the rear of the Lincoln. I raised the trunk lid to its limit and placed the headless cadaver across the cargo space as if it were a fragile glass heirloom or delicate paper sculpture. I figured throwing it in like a side of beef might get the attention of any potential spectator.

I backed the boxy, black auto onto the street and headed toward the light at the corner of Brighton 5th Street and Brighton Beach Avenue. I looked for company in my rearview mirror and found it a half a block behind. His headlights grew bigger and brighter in my mirror as my foot on the brake pedal waited for red to turn to green. Nerves, more than anything, put my head on a right to left-left to right scan like a spectator at a tennis match. I hated watching tennis, but the nervous scanning paid dividends. A blue and white patrol car made its lazy way down the avenue, coming at me from my left. Bang! Two things clicked inside me at once, and in combination they might just help me stay alive. The first part required a little help from the local constabulary.

I gambled, flooring the big Lincoln through the red light, tooting its horn as I went to insure the cops would notice. They noticed. Their sythesized siren, roof-mounted bullhorn, and Christmas tree display told me so. I drove straight across the avenue towards the boardwalk and into a maze of tight, one way streets and dead ends. I'd wanted the cops to put themselves between me and my tail. They obliged. In return for the favor, I heeded their warnings and pulled over a quarter block from the boardwalk. The bigger gamble would come now. Electricity pulled down my window and I waited.

In my sideview mirror I studied the approach of the blue shirt. He was a light-skinned black man, no more than twenty, maybe twenty-one. His nervous, cocky walk told me he was new to the job. His partner hung in the shadows to the rear passenger side of the Town Car. The partner was white, older and carried a full-sized spare around the middle. But his gut didn't prevent his right hand from dangling about his holster. Another younger, darker hand put down on the car door.

"Thanks, officer," I said, throwing him a curve and stealing his initiative. "Here!" I handed him my driver's license, Korin's registration and one of my business cards. I also made certain he got a good long look at the blue enamel and gold detective's courtesy shield, which bore Johnny MacClough's old badge number, that I kept pinned in my wallet.

"Do you realize that you went through a red light back there and exceeded the speed limit by at least twenty miles per hour for three or more blocks?" He recited his question rather than asking. My appreciation and the badge had rattled him.

"Yes, officer, I do. I did it on purpose and I blew my horn so you'd see me do it. Thanks, again. You saved my ass."

"Don't give me any shit, Mr. . . . ," he paused to read my license, "Klein. And don't think that baby shield's gonna do ya any good. Have you consumed any alcoholic beverages this evening?" He went back to the script.

"One, I think, much earlier."

"Hey, Newkirk," another voice broke in, "are you proposing marriage to this clown or trying to give him a ticket?"

"Hey, Rizzo," the black cop carelessly turned away from me, "stop bustin' on me. The gentleman here's busy thankin' us for somethin'."

"You green idiot, don't ever turn away like that," the fat cop scolded. "Now finish your business."

"But the man's got a baby detective shield and it's numbered."

"Praise the lord, Newkirk, so does my Aunt Carmen. Switch spots with me."

"But, Rizzo—"

"Now, Newkirk. Now." The two blue shirts played ring around the Lincoln, exchanging my papers as they went.

Rizzo put his fleshy face in mine, "Let's see that pretty badge again Mr. Klein."

I paraded it for him and, while he studied it, he instructed Newkirk to check the Lincoln's tags. That couldn't hurt me unless the car had been reported stolen.

"Looks real enough, but these things are easy to come by," the fat cop lectured me.

"Not numbered ones and you know it," I begged to differ.

"If you say so. Who owns the big brother badge to yours?"

"MacClough- O.C.C.B."

"Johnny MacClough? That slobby, Irish son of a bitch." Rizzo molded his face into a smile.

"Sounds like a good description of him." My gamble was paying off.

"Lives out in Greenport, don't he?" Rizzo was testing me.

"Close. Sound Hill, actually. Owns a bar a block from my office. Check the address on my card and license."

"Already have, Klein, a long time ago. Living in the same town don't earn you one of those," he took away his smile, referring to my courtesy shield. "They're meant for family."

"Let's say he promised it to me over a bottle of Irish Mist and you know MacClough's a man of his word."

"Sounds like Johnny. How's he doin'?"

"He's his own best customer, but he pulls in enough to keep going."

Newkirk got out of the patrol car and started toward Rizzo. Rizzo stopped his advance, "What's the good word, Newkirk?"

"Car's clean."

"Fine. Get back in there and listen to the box," Rizzo ordered his partner before returning to me. "So you know a cop I know, a cop I like, but that don't explain the red light routine. Let's have it."

"Fair question. I'm sure you heard me blow my horn at you going through the red." He nodded yes. "Fact is I had somebody on my ass and you got 'em off, for the moment anyway. I'm sure they're still there about a block back, lights off, motor running."

"A little less than a block, the way I see it, parked on the west side of the street. What'd'ya do to make yourself so popular?"

"I'm working an insurance job, the usual thing. I'm watchin' a house to make sure who's wearing the crutches. You know."

"Yeah," he said incredulously, "I know. A little late for this sort of business, ain't it? Most cripples I've met don't wear their crutches to bed."

"You'd be surprised," I shot back. "This is when people've got their guard down. Besides, the lawyer I'm working for lays out the schedule, I just follow it. He even provided my transport so I'd fit in with the rest of the limo drivers."

"Korin?"

"That's the man."

"Kinda' close to his house, ain't you? Were you spyin' on his next door neighbor?" Rizzo wasn't liking my story.

"Hey, I was just tryin' to brush my tail off. I ended up near Korin's office, it's not where I started."

"Even so, none of this adds up to you gettin' chased around Brighton Beach at 2:30 in the morning by a couple of thumb-breakers."

"Maybe not, but a lot of people could stand to make major bucks from the case I'm workin' on. That means those people could also stand to lose money they've yet to be awarded, but already spent. These Russians have gotten the hang of capitalism pretty quick. Besides, this wouldn't be the first time I've been roughed up for doing what I do."

Rizzo thought it over. "Your story stinks like week old *baccala*. I just want you to know I know that. Now get the fuck outta here. I'll hold your company back for a few minutes."

"Thanks, Rizzo, but how you gonna hold 'em?" I asked a stupid question.

"Maybe I'll let Newkirk try to give 'em a ticket," he laughed. "Go!"

"Thanks again."

Rizzo started for the blue and white but stopped halfway for some parting words, "Tell MacClough he owes Tony Rizzo another one."

My thumb sent a window up to seal the Lincoln shut. In the rearview, I watched Rizzo and Newkirk backing up the street. One down. One to go. I had one more stop in Brooklyn, an appointment at a gas station, an appointment that had little to do with the filling of tanks.

Joey Piccolo was small time. His family was small-time connected, mostly numbers and making book. They were fringe players. In high school Joey dealt a little weed, boosted a few cars to support the only thing big about him; his habit. Joey was a born user. We'd played JV football together and he sold me my hash, but there was no love between us. Our doings were measured by the yard or by the ounce. Our bond was so weak that it was easy to forget I'd ever known Joey Piccolo. Now I needed him as much as I'd ever needed anyone.

The man in the glass booth was still resting his head on a bed of twiggy arms.

"Wake up, Lazarus." I whispered into the little, silver speaker.

"We're closed. I'm dead. Go—"

"Sorry, Lazarus, I've heard that speech once tonight. There's business to do."

"How much? On what pump?"

"Not that kind of business, Joey." I said the name tentatively even though I knew it was him.

Joey Piccolo raised his yellow-skinned head, his black eyes popping out of their sockets. Everything about his face was smaller than I remembered. Everything, that is, except those eyes. I saw recognition in them, but his mouth said otherwise. "We're closed." His head drifted down.

"Come on, Joey, please. It's Dylan Klein. I know you remember me." I could hear myself sounding desperate.

"What if I do?"

"I need a favor and there's money in it for you."

"What kinda favor?"

"I sorta need a car boosted."

"You don't need me, Klein." His voice was calm. "You need the AAA."

"Will you pick your fucking head up and listen," I screamed.

He complied, but now there was fire in his cheeks, "I don't see you for six years, maybe seven, and you come in here pushin' me like I owe you. I don't owe you. I didn't used to like you and I still don't. I got no hash to sell you or your dickweed friends, so go back to actin' like I was a bad memory."

"I can't do that." I pressed the thousand dollar check up against the plexiglass booth. "See it? It's yours. Yeah it's a check, but it's made out to 'Cash.' It won't bounce. Look, we're not friends, but we've done business before. My money's never bitten back. How many weeks you gotta work here to earn a ten buck note? How many?" I was feeling sick again and fell against the booth.

He didn't blink. "Let me hear about what I'm gonna turn down."

"I want you to boost this Lincoln," I said, pointing at it with a thumb over my shoulder. "I'm gonna drive it to one of the long term lots at JFK. I'll call you from there and give you the lot number and aisle number. In the glove box you'll find the check and the registration. Problem is, I can't leave you the keys, so you'll have to help it get going."

"Then what?"

"I want you to lose it somewhere; a garage only you know or a boatyard, anyplace away from people. It's got to be a place where nobody asks questions or, even better, where there's nobody to ask questions. Write down where it is and mail me the location."

"Easy," was his reaction.

"You'll do it?"

"Are you fuckin' nuts? What's with the Lincoln?"

"That's my business. I can tell you it's not hot, not even warm," I said, neglecting to tell him about the headless torso in the trunk.

"I want the bread up front." He pushed out the electric cash collector.

"Are you—"

"Now," he cut me off. "Now, or you can use plan 'B,' if you got a plan 'B.'"

I didn't. I put the check down on the tray and followed that up with one of my cards that I'd written my dad's address on, "Send it to me at this address Express Mail or Federal Express." He sent out a gas receipt with his number.

"Why don't you save me the trip and leave the car?"

"I paid you to do what I asked, not what's convenient for you. When do you get off?"

"My relief shows up around five." He twirled a hand full of fingers at me so I could count to five in case I hadn't heard.

"I want you at the airport by six and gone fifteen minutes later."

"I'll be there by six, but it's been a while since I done any midnight auto work. I'll get it, get it started. You know, I got the perfect place to sleep that baby. Why don't I tell ya now and save some postage?"

"Because," I screamed, "I don't wanna know now. Mail it to me. Mail it to me."

"Christ, Klein, I heard you the tenth time."

A red Camaro with a cargo of cigarette smoking girls pulled up to the high octane pump at the far end of the station. The high-heeled driver was coming my way. It's the only thing I noticed about her, the high heels.

"Look, Joey, we haven't done business in a long time, but you always kept your word in the past."

"I'll keep it now." With that he put his head back down to show his new customer some salt and pepper hair.

The air-conditioned leather gave me a cold reception. I shut down the climate control and opened the windows, figuring the wind would help keep me awake. Passing the cashier's booth I didn't bother waving. What for? But I did catch a bit of conversation, "We're closed. I'm dead. Go away . . ."

The Belt Parkway was a pretty lonely place at 3:30 a.m., probably the only time of the day it is. The wind was doing me good until I hit the garbage dump at Pennsylvania Avenue. Rotten eggs would've been perfume in comparison. I made the Van Wyck airport entrance in an easy twenty minutes. In a like amount of time I found myself sitting in a spot in aisle C14 in Long Term Lot 2. I made certain the registration was in the glove compartment and I threw in a raspberry stained piece of stationary for good measure. I put the windows and the door latches in the up position. Before leaving I made sure the trunk was shut tight and took a last look at the tag number; 878 LLD.

After a few paces, I halted to take a piss between an old Porsche 914 and a Taurus wagon. The breeze blew some of the spray onto my shoes. I wondered if gas and piss fumes were toxic in combination. It might've made things less complicated, but all it did was make my shoes wet.

For ten minutes I walked a tight circle inside a bus shelter. For five more I followed the shuttle bus's meandering adventures while it made its way to me. Since there was no fare, I got on through the back door and found a seat across from the barren luggage racks. It was just the driver and me.

"Did you forget your baggage sir?" I could see his eyes working me over in his backlooking mirror.

"None to forget," was my response.

He just shrugged his shoulders and went into a rap about the course of our journey, "Eastern Airlines Terminal will be our first stop. On the upper level you can make connections for . . ."

I said my goodbye at Eastern. He shook his head, closed the doors behind me, and rolled away from the yellow curb. Inside I found a bank of phones and called Piccolo, but Piccolo didn't answer.

"So nice to hear your voice again, Mr. Klein." It was the man with the whispering rifle. "Bravo to your tango with the police, but I am a better dancer than you suppose. Enjoying the airport, are you? Mr. Piccolo was just explaining to me how you love to roam the long term lots."

"Is he alright?"

"More or less. Actually," he hesitated, "less."

"Let me speak to him." I demanded.

"If you wish, but I rather think his broken jaw will prevent him from answering. Oh yes, since Mr. Piccolo was unable to fulfill his commitments, he's consented to return your fee. You'll find it in the front seat of your car later this morning. Now do please finish what you started and stop these paperback heroics."

"Get him to a hospital." I said, ignoring the beautiful English.

"Will you cooperate?"

"Yes. Just get Piccolo to a hospital."

"Done."

"One more thing," I continued.

"Yes, Mr. Klein."

"Drop that fox-hunting accent. It doesn't suit you."

Click. I got a dial tone. I put the receiver back in its cradle and made for the exit. The parking lot shuttle bus came eventually. I took the front way in this time. The driver, my pal from the trip

Life Goes Sleeping

here, was still shaking his head when I sat down. Before he could comment, I said, "Forgot my luggage."

"Takes all kindsa' people to make up a world, all kinds," he spoke, eyes raised to the roof. "Next stop Northwest Airlines Terminal. Upstairs you can make connections . . ."

The only thing I could beat by rushing was the sunrise, so I strolled back to the Lincoln at a leisurely pace. I rattled the keys between my fingers and whistled some nonsense tune. The shrill music hurt my head, but I kept it up to drive away any lurking demons. You might say I was whistling through the graveyard. A few paces away from the black Town Car an iron hand grabbed my right bicep. I was beyond freezing or puking or fighting.

The man attached to the hand attached to my arm was about forty. He had gray-brown hair and a reddish mustache. His suit said he had his own tailor and his own business. "Will you look at this," he said, pointing at a pool of urine at the rear tire of an old Porsche 914. "What type of asshole does this sort of thing?"

"I don't know, but—" The ferocious whinings of a just-landed jet buried my sentence.

"What?" He let go of my arm.

"I said I don't know, but it takes all kindsa' people to make up a world."

He closed his mouth into a toothless smile and nodded his head in agreement. I stood there for a few seconds of silent commiseration. That's all he wanted to begin with. He hopped into the tiny middle-engined car without any sort of farewell. I knocked on his window.

"Why do you drive this bomb?" I asked.

"Because if I left my 911 here, people would piss on that, too. Goodnight."

Of course he was right.

Even with my encounter in the parking lot, I beat the sunrise back to Sound Hill. I got so punchy, I started talking to the stiff in the boot. He didn't talk back. I wasn't that bad off. I found out seven or eight times that the Mets had crapped out around midnight. Luckily for them, it only counted as one in the loss column no matter how many times it was announced.

The Lincoln looked completely out of place in Sound Hill, especially in front of my office. It wouldn't be there long, maybe just long enough to get a ticket. I left the keys in the ignition.

I found my way home like a wounded animal; by scent and by blind memory. I stripped down to my bones and took a restless shower. It seemed as if more had happened to me and I'd done more in the last eleven hours than in the last eleven years. I was beyond analyzing any of it. The only thought I had was of the gingham girl at the farm stand, but she was probably in a clean bed somewhere holding a white pillow and dreaming of boys named Billy. I had moved two giant steps away from her world tonight.

Morning Coffee

My last desire before drifting into unconsciousness was to sleep for a century or two. I never made it. I slept, and I use the term loosely, for about three hours. Then, to pass the time, I counted seconds with the clock. I showered again, not out of need but for distraction. My impulse for denial is a powerful one. I shaved around my beard, giving serious consideration to cutting my own throat before someone else slit it for me. In a way, I already had. The lump at the back of my head felt like half a golf ball, only harder. On the inside, most of the cobwebs were lost memories, but the residual pain refused to be forgotten. I swallowed a quartet of aspirins without water.

I dressed in my powder blue summer suit. It was as good a choice as any. The same went for my gray T-shirt. They were the cleanest things I owned. The refrigerator wasn't bare, but it lacked coffee. Plenty of milk, even some cream, but no coffee. I wanted coffee. I called Johnny MacClough instead.

"MacClough's Rusty Scupper," the familiar sleepy voice told me.

"When'd you change the name?" I prodded.

"It's a compromise in spirit. I can't change the sign, but I can answer the goddamn phone in my own establishment anyway I see fit. You'd make a poor Irishman, Klein, too concrete. No romance in ya, not a drop."

"You're a fine one to talk. The closest you been to Ireland is crowd control at the St. Patrick's Day Parade."

"You see, Klein, that's just it. You're a measurer. You want to put a label on everything, like a grocery store clerk. Well, you can't measure my Irishness. It's in my blood."

"That and a few quarts of stout," I added. "Listen, Johnny, all this stuff's a little beyond me now. I need to see ya."

"Suits me. When?"

I thought about it. "I've got to stop by my office, pick up the paper and a few cups of coffee. An hour?"

"Noon it is." He ended our discussion.

I found the marina abnormally hushed for a dry, hot Wednesday. Maybe it was the hour. More likely, it was me. After the past fifteen hours, I didn't see how anything could ever seem or feel the same again. Eyes closed, I turned to the mostly-risen sun, letting it bake my eager face. The slapping of salt water against boat hulls and pier supports rocked me into an upright stupor. I was lost and happy in a world alone, a world without black cars and headless cargoes, a quiet world punctured by the nasal proclamations of air horns on passing ferries. I was across the street from my office, across from where I'd parked the dark Lincoln. I turned.

It was gone, as promised, replaced by a once-blue Volkswagen. I got closer. The license plates told me the old bug was mine. I gazed through the driver's side window and spotted the retainer check Korin had written sitting on the passenger seat. Seeing it made me wonder about Joey Piccolo's health. I'd research that later, if my own health held up. I retrieved the check and found a folded, red stained piece of stationary hidden beneath it. Both objects felt at home in my wallet. My right hand located neutral, inserted the ignition key and twisted. It started! I had no intentions of going anywhere. I just wanted to see if it would do something wacky, like blow up.

I expected to find a note of one kind or another, a list of instructions, you know, I combed the interior; rugs, seats, sun visors. Nothing. A search of the glove compartment yielded two Nathan's Famous napkins, five expired insurance cards, an empty cassette box, but no notes. I even skipped through both sides of the cassette I'd left in the deck. Nothing there either, except over-played pop ditties from two decades gone by. I untwisted the key, put the car in gear and exited.

The phone was on its fourth ring by the time I persuaded my office door to open. I didn't rush to it, figuring the caller to be my

English accented inquisitioner. I've been more wrong about things in the past, but I can't recall when exactly.

"I found the car, the check, and I'll find Brodsky," I glared into the mouthpiece.

"I am most pleased for you. I hope the car is fast and red. The check, large and negotiable. And I hope Brodsky thinks about changing names." Her voice was my morning coffee. It was rich and resonant with a distinctively Russian flavor.

"Sorry."

"Is this Mr. Klein?" she asked.

"This is."

"My father suggested I call you. You will please excuse my lack of ease with such things."

"You're excused and we can get to 'such things' later, but let's back up a few steps. Who's your father?"

"A client of yours: Alexander Korin." She gave me the answer I'd expected.

I may have been a zero in math, but I could still put two and two together and be reasonably sure of coming up with four. I didn't like it. The hair standing up on the back of my neck told me not to. Korin might have had a daughter, maybe he had a dozen, maybe the woman on the wire was his daughter. I wouldn't bet on it. Her timing was bad. No. No, it was too fucking good.

"Are you still there?" she asked uncomfortably.

"Yes. How is your father?"

"I assume he is quite well. I haven't spoken to him in over a week."

"Forgive me. I haven't asked you your name?"

"Micki, with an 'I,' not like the mouse. It's not my real name, but I am used to Micki." She said it all naturally.

"Micki," I thought about the name, "I like it."

"Would you confess if you despised it?"

"I'd plead the 'Fifth'. The fifth amendment to the—"

"Mr. Klein, no condescension please. My father is not the only graduate of Brooklyn Law School in the family."

"Sorry, again. You know this is how my conversations with your father go." I remembered to use the present tense. "I'm always apologizing to him for doing or saying the wrong thing."

"He's too curious a man to be apologized to. My father's stepped on toes for a hobby his whole life. For my sake, don't ever excuse yourself to him again." There was a smile in her voice.

"I can guarantee you that I never will. Can I ask you what you called about?" I was running late for my meet with Johnny.

"Well, yes," she hemmed and hawed, "would you care to have dinner with me sometime? Don't feel obliged to accept because of my father. I—"

"Lady if I felt obliged, I'd turn you down. How could I turn down anyone with a voice like yours?"

"I wouldn't know, as my voice always sounds horrid when it's played back to me."

"Mine doesn't have to get played back to sound awful. I'm no bargain, you know. I don't know what Alexander told you . . . Where do you live anyway?"

"Joralemon Street. 21 Joralemon, top buzzer. While I have the courage, would tonight be good?" She sounded nervous enough.

"I'll be in Brooklyn later, but my plans are sketchy. Can I call you?"

She told me I could, gave me her number and bid me peace. How nice of her. By the end of the conversation I was pretty confused. She was quick when called for, uneasy when it fit, and just naive enough to be believable. She didn't overwhelm me with minor details about Korin in an attempt to prove her authenticity. His real daughter wouldn't have to, but it was going to take more than good style to convince me.

I rewound the tape in my answering machine. It played back a hang-up and two earlier messages from the alleged Micki Korin. Her recorded voice didn't sound too shabby to me. I pulled the thousand dollar check and soiled paper out of my wallet and wrapped them in a sheet of yellow foolscap. I put that sheet into a blank envelope and sealed it. I marked the envelope, "Insurance Policy," and slid it in my inside jacket pocket.

Life had picked up in my absence. Even in small towns people pop out of their cages for lunch. In winter, it was the only way to tell Sound Hill was inhabited. In summer we had the marina and Little League baseball. I stopped at the Star Spangled Deli for the papers and a large, sweet coffee for MacClough. He'd appreciate that. The stuff he served was sour as a pickle and thicker than pea soup. Too bad, Johnny would have to make due—the line at the deli was to the door. I scooped up the Times, the Post, Newsday, and the News, fished the exact change out of my pockets and left it on the counter.

The Rusty Scupper's innards were less than glorious. Taxidermied fish hung on the walls wherever one fit amongst the impotent harpoons and bogus brass portholes. Rusty anchors attached to rusty chains leaned against the green walls in every nook too small to accommodate a standing human being or a stuffed fish. Thick ropes, gray and brittle with age, wrapped themselves tightly around the carrying posts, so drunken patrons couldn't carve masterpieces into the wood. A quarter-a-game pool table with grooves in the slate and a distant recollection of felt made for one-third of the bar's appeal. The second attraction was a dartboard with mangled metal numbers and darts as sharp as bowling balls. And, of course, there was drinking to complete the triumvirate. The bar itself was once a pretty thing, sort of filigreed and Victorian. Neglect made certain you'd have to search for its beauty. In amongst all the paraphenalia, the only visible evidence of Johnny MacClough's ownership was a framed 3×5 inch color photo of him the day he graduated from the academy.

"You're late," Johnny announced to an empty bar.

"I knew that. Thanks for reminding me."

"Doing a ton of reading these days," Johnny pointed to the papers under my left arm.

"Not quite a ton, but close." I sat down at the bar. "I went to get you some real coffee, but the line at the deli was ridiculous."

"I would've liked a cup. Want some of this slop?"

"Not really. I've already had mine."

"I thought you said the line—"

"Figuratively speaking," I cut him off. "I'll be daring, pour me a cup of that ooze."

"Milk?"

"Light cream, no sugar." I threw the envelope on the pockmarked wood.

"What's so urgent we gotta talk?" MacClough asked with his back to me as he mixed my coffee.

"Here," I tapped the bar by the envelope, "I need you to keep this safe for me for a bit."

"Insurance policy," he laughed, "what's really in there?"

"It's a type of insurance," I sipped the coffee. "Oh, Christ, this stuff is horrible."

"Anything illegal?"

"Yeah, this coffee. You could get sent up for attempted murder."

"I don't like the sound of your voice, Klein and you look like shit. What about the envelope? Anything illegal?"

"Would it matter?"

"No," he said. "Besides, you just answered my question." He took the parcel and disappeared for a minute.

"Thanks," I offered, when he came back into view.

"Thanks nothing. What gives? This isn't your style and you're looking frightened to me." There was genuine concern in his voice.

"An old lady threatened to zap me with her walker if I didn't stop following her."

"You're not usually funny, Klein. Today your act is especially thin. Give me the poop and I'll see what I can do."

"I'll tell you, but not now," I assured him. "I don't even know what's going down myself. You've already helped me, anyway."

"How's that?"

"The little shield you gave me."

"What about it?"

"It," I said, "saved my behind last night. I got myself pulled over in the six-one precinct and an old buddy of yours helped me out of a painted corner."

"What old buddy is that?"

"Tony Rizzo."

"Tony Rizzo?" MacClough tilted his head to the floor, pulled down his eyebrows and squinted so hard it made my eyes hurt. "Tony Rizzo, Tony Rizzo, Tony Rizzo," he repeated three times aloud, lowering his volume with each rep. "What he look like?"

"About 5'10", 220, tire around the gut, brown eyes, thin lips, fat face."

"Don't know him."

"What are you talkin' about? He knew you, knew where you lived. Called you a slobby Irish something-or-other. Come on, for chrissakes," I choked and laughed with the same words, "there's gotta be a fucking bushel of Tony Rizzo's on the job."

"And I don't know one of them well enough to say hello to. Are you sure you got the name right?"

"Yes. It was clear as day on his name tag, too. His partner's name was Newkirk, a black kid. I mean, Johnny, these guys were riding around in a blue and white. It's not Halloween and they didn't say trick or treat. Maybe you just forgot him," I said, knowing better.

"Unlikely. Give me five minutes." MacClough went away again.

That sick feeling started expressing itself to me in the form of sweat. I finished the bad excuse for coffee and got on my horse, but pacing just made it worse. I tossed some dull darts into the wall that supported the dartboard. They just sort of bounced off. I considered telling Johnny the whole story, then quickly reconsidered.

"No Rizzo. No Newkirk, not even an old one." He reappeared.

"What?"

"Old-kirk, Newkirk . . . nevermind. It was funnier before I said it."

"Did you check with the precinct?" I was sounding panicky.

"Not in the six-one. Not in the six-zero. Not in Brooklyn. What's going on?"

"Later." I split before MacClough's next syllable could catch me.

I was nurtured in the age of conspiracies; the Kennedy assassination, the other Kennedy assassination, the King assassination, the Gulf of Tonkin, the Pueblo, the '69 World Series. Everything was a conspiracy and, if it wasn't, the reason it wasn't, was. But a few decades worth of exposure to conspiracy theories is like getting bopped on the back of the head. They both numb you out. Numb or not, I decided to start paying attention to the little boy inside my brain crying, "Wolf!" What I couldn't figure out was why anybody should conspire with, for, or against me. I wasn't nearly as important as the Kennedys. I'd have plenty of time to think about it on my trip into Brooklyn.

Brooklyn was forty-five minutes closer in the early afternoon than during the rush. The sciatic nerve in my clutch leg liked that, so did the clutch. I drove by the freckled girl's farm stand, but she wasn't in. A prune faced old woman with rimless spectacles and colorless hair sat behind the berries and dusty potato sacks today. She, too, wore a checkerboard gingham apron, but there wasn't enough blood left in her for blushing. I kept on going, listening to the tired tape in my deck for company. When traffic permitted, I'd toss a glance at the unread newspapers resting on the passenger's seat.

Brighton Beach looked too damned familiar. It should have. I'd been here recently. I was sort of hoping to avoid murder this trip, but the past twenty-four hours had taught me that my hopes didn't count for much. Maybe it had always been so, and I'd just started to take notice. The air had cooled and dryed since my last visit, but somehow that failed to console me.

I parked by a broken meter under the perpetual shadow of Brighton Beach Avenue. My spot gave me an unobstructed view of what was once Adelman's Discount Haven. It hadn't been Adelman's for years, but you could still read the store's motto—"Haven for the Shopping Maven"—written in the ghosts of glued on letters long since removed. From the looks of it, the current owners weren't much interested in discount stores or ghosts. They were busy running a car service: The Kiev Car Service. I wondered if Mr. Brodsky was in, but I decided to do a little reading before I asked.

The world had manufactured a considerable amount of news when I wasn't watching. The papers told me so. A Chinese DC 10, stuffed to the bulkheads with paying customers, had made a rather sudden and unscheduled stop on the side of a mountain. You didn't need an abacas or the fingers on one hand to count up the survivors. The IRA, PLO, Red Army, and the Hezzbollah had ambushed, truck bombed, and generally slaughtered some fifteen human beings in the name of God, or cause, or country. The home front was no less bloody. A double-crossed crack dealer in Jackson Heights evened the score by hacking to death five relatives of the guy who'd run the scam. Unfortunately for the victims, the hacker got his addresses confused. Accidents will happen. The last few spins of the clock had certainly produced a fair amount of news and none of it concerned mutilated Russians, make-believe policemen, or gas station attendants with wired jaws. It was all merely cold comfort to me. I wiped the black ink from my hands with a Nathan's napkin.

About three hours had gone by since the conspiracy bug infected me at MacClough's bar. I couldn't put anything together on that front, so I told the little boy to stop crying. There might well be wolves in Brighton Beach, but I sure as hell didn't see them. That wasn't the problem, anyway. The trouble was, they could see me and I still couldn't figure out why they wanted to.

Car service headquarters always looked and smelled the same. There were some exceptions, I guess, but the Kiev wasn't one of them. The available floor space was split in two between the waiting room and the dispatcher's area. The waiting room—where impatient fares paced, checked their watches and paced some more, or where idle drivers reread last week's papers and discussed past lives—was a compost heap of three-legged chairs, gritty linoleum, broken pay phones, almost-empty coffee cups, and cigarette smoke. In their area, dispatchers papered walls with street maps and air-brushed shots of Miss June, July and August. They answered phones, gave impatient directions to stray drivers and auctioned off big money runs to the highest briber.

My entrance caused about as much excitement as snow flurries in December in Minnesota. Over in one corner, a gangly man, dressed in conflicting shades of polyester and reading a Russian-language tabloid, sucked on an unfiltered Camel, exhausting the smoke through a pointed beak. He looked like he belonged here. I stood in front of him.

"You vant ride? Talk vid dispatcher," he instructed in an accent ten feet thicker than Korin's had been.

"No ride, just information."

"Information?" He looked up.

"Yeah, about one of your drivers."

"Tventy bucks," the polyester man demanded, working his pale lips and yellow teeth into a smile.

"Alright," I agreed too eagerly, slapping a portrait of Jackson into a waiting palm.

"Driver's name? Don't vorry, I know dem all." He assured me.

"Brodsky, Mikhail Brodsky."

"No Brodsky. Vat's he looking like?"

"Good question, but I don't have a good answer."

Like an idiot I'd left the group picture up in Korin's office. It wouldn't have done me much good, anyway. The man I was searching for would look forty years and thousands of miles older.

"Sorry, mister." The Camel smoker interrupted my self-pity.

"No, you're not. I wouldn't be."

I turned my back on the clothes horse and leaned on the counter. It nearly collapsed under the weight. A potbellied dispatcher, with fat brows, fatter lips and a dull demeanor, lethargically downed his coffee. He seemed hypnotized by the flashing lights and crackles coming out of his radio. An unintelligible voice came across the speaker and, without changing expressions, the fat man talked back to it in equally mysterious terms. Satisfied that the exchange was complete, the dispatcher terminated his coffee.

I cleared my throat loud enough to split crystal. That got me nowhere. I removed another twenty from my wallet and snapped it between my fingers, but the dispatcher's catalepsy continued. I put the money away and decided to try a little diplomacy.

"Hey, fat boy," I screamed loud enough to be heard above a squealing train.

The zombi rose from his seat and came to me with small, measured steps that didn't fit his girth. An old girlfriend of mine who worked in a psychiatric hospital used to call his kind of walk the "Thorazine Shuffle." With each petite footfall, his rubbery middle bounced with a life of its own.

"No Brodsky," he declared in a voice to match his manner.

"Nice deaf act. You should take it to Broadway. Are you sure about this Brodsky? Word has it he drives for you."

"Vord is wrong. No Brodsky here." He pronounced the 'h' in here as if he were about to cough up phlegm. The few Russian speakers I had met all had that habit with words beginning in 'h.' "Ve have two cars, four drivers, two dispatchers, no Brodsky. Juri," he pointed at my friend in the waiting area, "is driver here. If he says no Brodsky and I say no Brodsky, dere is no Brodsky."

"But are you certain?"

"Ve have two cars, four drivers—"

"Yeah, yeah. Two dispatchers and no Brodsky," I finished his speech. "Could be he used to work here."

"No, is original crew." The dispatcher paused and stared at the trunk of my body. "Your suit is very ugly, but not so ugly as you," he said with the same flat affect as everything that had come before it. This time though, the corner of his mouth twitched, which for him must've been a smile.

Before I could respond, the rotund man did a sluggish about face and began the long shuffle back to his chair. I followed his lead in the opposite direction. I shuffled to my car. Juri stopped thumbing through his rag just long enough to gloat and bid me a nice day. Since my money and stupidity had already perked his up, I didn't feel compelled to return the pleasantry.

A parking ticket on the VW's windshield served to remind me what an unforgiving place Brooklyn could be. Normally, I'd never check the issuing officer's name, but this wasn't normally. The carbonized signature on the summons looked to be the work of a south-pawed Chinese doctor suffering from acute Parkinson's disease. And although I couldn't say what name the scribbles translated to exactly, I was confident it wasn't Newkirk or Rizzo. Somehow, I guess, I was hoping MacClough's memory and sources had failed him. Life would be easier without hope.

I sat in the front seat mulling over my encounter with Laurel and Hardsky. It might well be true that Mr. Polyester and his roly-poly partner had never heard of Mikhail Brodsky, but they'd spent a lot of energy telling me so; a lot of energy, too much energy. Where a simple "fuck off" would have sufficed, I got opera. Where a shove out the door should have been appropriate, I got answers. Insurance work teaches you to listen for how something is denied, not the denial itself. This was tougher than two plus two, but it added up to something. I just didn't know what. Whatever it was encouraged me. I get hungry when I'm encouraged.

The car radio killed my appetite:

"and the Mayor called such reports ridiculous . . . Early this morning the badly beaten body of a gas station attendant was dropped off in the trauma unit of Brooklyn's Coney Island Hospital. The body has since been identified as that of Joseph Piccolo, age thirty-four, of the Gravesend section of the borough. Eyewitnesses report that the body was brought into the emergency area at approximately 5:30 am by another man. Several conflicting descriptions of the other man have been given to the police. A police spokesperson has revealed that a preliminary examination indicates that Mr. Piccolo had expired prior to his entering the hospital and that results from a complete autopsy are pending. Police refuse to speculate about the motive for the brutal attack, but have, for the meantime, ruled out robbery. Mr. Piccolo's wallet and belongings as well as the cash drawer and safe at the Merit gas station (owned by the deceased's uncle) were found to be intact. Other member's of the Piccolo family have been linked to the Gambino organized crime family and the deceased has a long record of drug-related arrests. When asked about any possible drug and/or organized crime connection to the murder, both police and Piccolo family representatives refused comment . . ."

I didn't like Joey Piccolo any too well when he dwelt among the breathing. I didn't suddenly like him now that he didn't, but a new bond existed between us that would last an eternity. I was the instrument of a man's death and any facade of guiltlessness I may have foolishly once worn was lost to me for good. The moral distinctions between myself and my phone pal with the silenced rifle had just melted away like cotton candy in the rain.

Kings of Brighton Beach

At points, the boardwalk was no more than a block away from the train trestle eclipse of Brighton Beach Avenue. Despite their proximity, they may as well have been planets apart.
    I put the parking ticket back on the windshield, locked the car door, and moved from one planet to the next, from the shadows into light.
    Behind me, bicycle tires rolled over weathered wooden planks like curious fingers down the keys of a piano. Bicycles are prohibited, by law, on the boardwalk, as is spitting on the subway. Brooklynites follow both edicts with equal fervor. Questioning authority is sort of a communal thing.
    On nearby benches, the last vestiges of my grandparents' generation sing silly Yiddish songs, out of tune, and argue Democratic politics. These are the souls too stubborn or poor to make room for the Russians by dying or moving to West Palm Beach. On other benches still, the new kings of Brighton lift, push, and drop chess pieces. They take their chess too seriously to call it playing.
    At the shoreline, ghetto kids ride the brown surf to sand before riding subways back to Bushwick and Brownsville.
    I look at a lifeguard's chair and recall some girls I gave first kisses to there. I wonder how they are, when I remember their names. I wonder if they remember. If not the kisses, then, at least, my name. You can wonder about such things in a world of light, but death gets in the way. My imagination's cast of Piccolo's crushed face pulled black clouds over the sun and my idle speculations.
    I found a phone and made a call in the first drops of rain.

Reading her number off a wet sheet didn't help my fingers punch up the unfamiliar sequence. Four aborted tries and three rings later, someone picked up.

"Is this Micki with an 'i'?" I asked before the person on the other end could speak.

"Yes. Who is this?"

"The car was slow and green. The check was small and rubbery. And Brodsky loves his name."

"Mr. Klein." She stated with a smile I couldn't see.

"Most people who ask for my company at dinner call me Dylan."

"Most! Then there are exceptions." She played lawyer.

"I can't remember any. But if there are, I'd prefer you not be among them."

"I didn't expect you'd call Mr.—"

"Dylan!" I corrected.

"Dylan. In some sense, I wish you hadn't. I'm feeling overly embarrassed about this morning's call to you."

"I can't tell you how to feel, but I was pretty flattered. That's why I'm sorry to tell you I can't make it tonight."

Her answer to that was silence, but I thought I could hear her thinking.

"Micki, are you there?"

"Yes, I'm sorry. Now I'm both embarrassed and disappointed." Her tone matched her feelings. "Is it something you're working on?" she asked, not hiding her accent.

"In a way. I've just decided to take myself off a job I've been on. In fact, this call is the beginning of an indefinite vacation."

"Was it a difficult job?"

"Too much of a puzzle. I don't like puzzles. I've hated puzzles even before I can recall hating them. That's what my mom used to tell me." I wasn't lying.

"Oh, I'm such an idiot. My father told me about your mother's passing, but I was so caught up in my own nerves this morning . . . I am sorry for your loss. Can you forgive my stupidity?"

"You can make it up to me over dinner sometime soon," I said. "I've got to go."

"I'll call you again, soon."

"I'd like that. Bye."

The rain had moved on, following the black clouds away from

the beach. Summer rains are funny like that. There were certain clouds, though, that would not be driven away with the reappearance of the sun. I walked up the boardwalk toward Coney Island and the cancerous skeleton of the parachute jump, trailing clouds behind me.

Makeup

Insurance and liability work lends itself to dead time, an eternity of it. You sit. You watch. You drink bad coffee. You read the paper. You take a picture. You sit some more, drink some more, re-read the paper, and take another snapshot. You even get to piss out the bad coffee into the cup it came in. All this excitement to ascertain whether or not some poor schmuck, who tripped on a cracked brick and broke his neck, is capable of sliding out of a car without the assistance of the local parish priest, two nurses aids, and a first cousin from Whitefish Bay, Wisconsin.

It gets so you get to be an expert at the waiting game. I thought a few days of playing the mountain to the lengthy list of Mohammeds from Brooklyn would be a breeze. I wouldn't even have to piss into a plastic cup. But this waiting game had its differences. I'd be setting myself up as a tethered goat to draw out the predators. Just a couple of problems with that arrangement. First off, I didn't know who and how many predators there were. Secondly, sometimes the goat gets slaughtered in the process. That wouldn't do, not at all. Oddly enough, using myself as bait was the only method I could figure to gain back any measure of control. I was important to them. The fact that I was still breathing convinced me of it. That meant they'd come for me or whatever they thought gave me value. That gave me power.

On day one of my vacation, I slept some and wasted a few hours on the problem of my importance. The whys continued to escape me. To block out the questions, I took a long, hot soak with T. S. Eliot and Ezra Pound; two of the literary world's great Jew-haters.

Life Goes Sleeping

Collge professors love to tell you those intimate little facts that add nothing to the work and make it more difficult to appreciate. You know: Oscar Wilde, wearing purple knickers and clutching a lily to his chest, lectured American gold miners about the intricacies of Victorian interior design. Lord Byron had a clubfoot, a pet bear and slept with anything that would. T. S. Eliot was a bank clerk, married a psychotic, loved Great Britain, and hated Jews. Ezra Pound edited Eliot's most important works, was loonier than Eliot's wife, did propaganda broadcasts for the Axis powers during WWII, and hated Jews. They'd tell you crap like that and then demand you ignore it. Only their works matter. Bullshit! Deeds have to count for something. They have to.

I threw the poets out of my tub and dried off. I pressed the lump at the back of my head; there was some residual soreness, but the golfball had been replaced by a marble. I looked in the mirror and considered shaving off my beard. Nothing unusual in that. Whenever I'm depressed or feeling particularly self destructive, I think about it. Beards are makeup for men and I hadn't seen myself without any for awhile; awhile, as in four years. Suddenly, I regretted not looking at Mom before they closed the coffin. Talk about moot issues. I shaved around my makeup.

The coffee and cholestoral special—two scrambled eggs, American cheese, crisp bacon on a buttered roll—that Tommy from the deli had delivered and left outside my door were both below room temperature. I conserved energy and put them down cold. I was more interested in the paper, anyway. Even in death, Joey Piccolo couldn't make the big time. Page eleven was as far as he'd ever get. An unflattering shot of him with a dirty-lip mustache, a pony tail, a biker's vest, and marijuana eyes looked up at me. The accompanying story added nothing to the radio account. He'd be forgotten soon enough. I cut the article out and magnetized it to the refrigerator.

I called The Rusty Scupper.

"MacClough's Rusty Scupper," an Old Bushmills' voice informed me.

"It's Klein. I'm takin' a few days off. Do—"

"Well, Hallefuckinlujah! Hey Stan," MacClough called to Stanley Long, who owned the gas station across from the bar and who divided his time equally between the two, "Klein's taking a vacation. Should we have a parade?"

I heard Stan in the background order another of whatever he had the first time. He refused comment on the parade, but told Johnny to tell me to enjoy my vacation.

"Tell Stan I say thanks." I waited for him to relay the message. "Do you wanna come over later and watch the Mets' game?"

"And what am I supposed to do with the bar, have a self-service night?" The whiskey went out of his voice. "Fess up boy. What was that hundred yard dash outta here for yesterday?"

"We'll discuss it during seventh-inning stretch."

"Like hell we will. You want something from me, Klein. The only time you get hospitable is when you need something from me. What is it?"

"The bar TV working?" I asked.

"If you use a broad definition of terms."

"See you at 7:30."

The fish weren't biting at the bait just yet, so I set the alarm for six fifty-something and went back to bed. I took the poets with me and hoped their songs would put me to sleep.

Most of me woke up to all news radio babble. My right arm was lost somewhere above my head looking for a little blood. The Norton anthology was pinned between my chin and chest, its back cover wet from siesta saliva. How attractive. My neck was stiff. My eyes were sore and I had a headache. All things considered, it had been a glorious nap.

My left arm found the right and began flexing it. With the blood came the pain. There were no whole aspirins left in the bottle, so I filled it with tap water, gave it a shake and had a drink. Since I was at the sink already, I whipped up some cold water soup, using my head for the meat and flavoring. The results were mixed. My eyes and head felt wetter and better, but my neck was still as stiff as a pressure-treated two-by-six.

I was dried and dressed and at The Rusty Scupper by the bottom of the first. The announcers said so. You couldn't tell by the action on the screen. The picture was about as clear as a sonogram in a snowstorm. Stanley Long was back, flinging darts and sipping his umpteenth Red Label. Two local fishing types were having a drunken game of eight ball. Ten empty tall necks adorned the pool table and the players were about to make it an even dozen. A GQ dressed westerner sat at the bar popping honey-roasted nuts into his million-dollar mouth. He was nursing his high-balled Campari and soda, sans twist, and trying to watch the ballgame. Johnny MacClough stood arms folded, legs crossed, back against the stainless beer cooler, overseeing his empire. The expression on his lined face was prouder than the Pharoh's gazing out at the pyramids.

"Black and Tan," I ordered.

"You know," Johnny spoke as he tapped the stout, "for a Jew from Brooklyn you got some strange taste in drinks."

"It's the company I keep. Some slobby Irishman I met once introduced me to the stuff. Now what was his name?" I squinted my eyes, looked up at the ceiling and rubbed my beard. "MacClough! That's it. That's the man that led me down the path to bad taste."

"Cute, very cute." He put my drink down in front of me on a silly green napkin. "You know, Klein, I had some visitors today just after you called."

"You're a popular fellow." I raised my glass to MacClough.

"Funny thing about it was, I got the impression they weren't very interested in me or my liquor. They seemed more concerned with my customers, in fact; where they were from, what they did to earn a buck, how'd I meet 'em. You know, stuff like that. They didn't exactly come straight to the point. No, they talked in circles, big circles. But the strange thing about circles is that no matter how big they are, their shape causes you to get around to the issue, eventually."

"Talk about talking in circles. What's the point?"

"You, my friend. You are, or were, the point."

I finished my stout and beer in a gulp. Johnny poured me another without asking. Mr. GQ gave up on the game, having exhausted the nuts, his drink, and his patience. His goodbye walk told me he wasn't coming back. MacClough served the pool sharks two more Bud bottles. He turned around from the register and bent over the bar, putting his elbows on the wood, his head on his balled fists and his face close to mine.

"What makes you think they were interested in me?" I asked in a falsely nonchalant voice.

"I used to be a professional circle talker," he answered. "Any cop worth his salt is. And these guys were pros."

"Cops?"

"I didn't say that, but they might be the type to dress like 'em."

"What?"

"I'll draw you a picture. Two guys; one's white, 5'9" maybe 10, about 220–230 pounds, gut like he's ten months pregnant with twins, brown eyes and skinny lips. His friend's a fair skinned black, maybe 6'2", 190–200 pounds, short hair, on the quiet—"

"Newkirk and Rizzo!"

"You're learning. Enough bullshit, Klein."

"I'll give you some of it now, all of it soon." I reached into my wallet and pulled out the article about Joey Piccolo which I'd pulled off the fridge before leaving the house. "Here. Read this."

While Johnny studied the print, Stanley Long stopped by to give his regards. MacClough nodded and gave a careless wave. I made small talk and in a town the size of Sound Hill, small talk is tiny. Stanley left.

"Murder," Johnny whispered with odd respect. "Murder's not your ballgame, Dylan." It was the first time he'd ever called me that. "You're a crutches and neckbrace man. What's your angle?"

"You know Piccolo?" I asked.

"I know the family."

"I grew up with him, not friends or anything. Well—"

"Cut to the chase, Klein. I've had enough circles for the day."

"I got in a squeeze, the same squeeze I thought your shield helped me out of. I offered Joey Piccolo some bread to help get me further out of it. Only he never got a chance to help or collect and he got dead because I involved him."

"So, I take it you're still in the deep shit."

"Up to my nipples and sinking fast."

"Murder," Johnny repeated. "Can you make it any clearer?"

"I was kinda hopin' you'd be able to help me there." I fought myself to say it.

"How's that?"

"Forget it MacClough. I have no right to involve you in this. Look what happened to the last guy I enlisted."

"The last guy you enlisted was a dime bag asshole with eyes for your cash," Johnny said angrily, pointing an index finger in my face. "I can't use your money and I'm as good as they get. Besides, if you won't involve me, I'll just rat you out and watch from the sidelines."

"You couldn't rat out Charlie Manson, if you liked him even a little." I smiled. "Cops are too loyal for their own good."

"Sometimes."

"If you wanna help, I can't stop you. Frankly," I put my right hand out for him to shake it, "I need you." He squeezed my hand and shook it.

"Details, Klein, details."

"One more day, Johnny, one more day and I'll give you the whole picture or, at least, the parts I've seen. For now I need you to check if your friends in blue know any more about the Piccolo case than they're letting on."

"One day. Twenty-four hours. That's it. You have your ass in here tomorrow night by game time or I'll be whispering in some friendly ears instead of letting them whisper into mine. Agreed?"

"Do I have a choice?"

"Don't let's get philosophical about it. Of course you have a choice, but it's not a very attractive one." He liked his words.

"Thanks, Aristotle, I appreciate you clarifying that for me." I gave a mocking bow. "If anybody else comes sniffing around tomorrow, I'll be in the office early."

I got up to go. We shook hands again. As I was about to release my grip, MacClough practically pulled me over to his side of the bar.

"Do you need something to carry on you?" he spoke close to my ear. "I've got a few extra pieces laying around collecting dust."

"But aren't you worried—"

"—that it'll get traced back to me?" he finished my thought. "They'll find Jimmy Hoffa before they trace anything to me."

"Thanks, I'll keep that option open. Goodnight."

"Game time." He let go of my fingers.

"Do you need this?" I picked the Piccolo article up off the bar and waved it at MacClough.

"Take it home and frame it."

I stopped by the Star Spangled Deli on my way home to pick up some coffee beans and to pay my bill for Tommy's morning delivery. Bob Street, the owner, was closing up. We made some more Sound Hill tiny talk and did some exchanging of money for product. I asked Bob if Newkirk and Rizzo had been in to see him. He said they hadn't. He asked me if I knew the Mets' score. I said I should, but I didn't.

I saw morning rain coming in the night sky. It's funny, but when

I lived in Brooklyn I never saw anything in the night sky. Christ, you could barely make out the stars for all the streetlights. Maybe weather just mattered more here. Maybe. I'd have to discuss it with Aristotle MacClough sometime, sometime when he wasn't trying to give me a gun or save my ass. I checked the clouds one more time, scratched my makeup, and headed home.

Importance for Necessity

Sound Hill was womblike with gray fog and rain on the second day of my vacation. The moist air pushed teasing hints of cool seasons through the open windows. This was stay in bed forever weather; lazy weather, "Mommy—I don't wanna go to school" weather. I got up anyway. I was in a rush, a rush to wait. Waiting was good. Waiting got results. Waiting was power. I stood at the edge of the bed wondering who might stumble into MacClough's empire today and strike up a circular conversation. I'd find that out later. Now, I had to wait.

I thought about showering and then stopped thinking. No matter how hot I made the water, I couldn't get the chill out of the air or my bones. Coffee! Coffee would do the trick. Coffee is magic. I ground up some of the newly-bought beans and suffered through the paper-cone filter and hourglass torture of hand dripped coffee making. What a pain in the ass. It seemed like too much work for such a lazy day. No, it was always too much work. But the snail's pace process gave me time to dress and the sweet results almost made it worth the trouble. Almost. The chill remained.

The muted atmosphere inside the deli reflected the weather. Business had been pretty slow so far today. I could read it in Bob Street's face. I scooped up the full compliment of newspapers and told Bob his beans made nice coffee. That brightened his life for nearly a second. He told me the Mets had won easy. I said I knew they would. Tommy thanked me for the tip I'd left him yesterday. I paid for the papers and left.

I didn't recall leaving the office door open, but it was. The knob turned quietly in my hand. Behind the door, someone was terribly busy shuffling papers, opening draws, closing them. Hell, it never sounded that busy with me in there. Maybe I'd have to make an appointment and come back later. Then again, no. I knew the proprietor personally.

The door fell open without noise and without resistance. She was on her hands and knees, ass facing my way, her face to the window. She was making neat piles of my files in the middle of the floor. The joint looked a mess, even worse than usual. Books and papers were everywhere except where I had left them. Someone had been searching for something or maybe he was cold and wanted to set a bonfire using my records for kindling. Dumb schmuck. Forgot the matches!

"Are you the new cleaning lady?" I asked.

"No, but by the appearance of this place I can see why you dismissed the old one." She answered in a voice I'd heard only twice, both times over the phone. She kept to her task without turning to me.

"Good morning, Micki."

There was no surprise in her reaction, only grace. She spun her head slowly over her left shoulder. As she did so, her thick, wedged, ebony hair traced the locus of her spin. She smiled, saying nothing. Why bother?

"This isn't exactly how I pictured us meeting," I said.

"And I wasn't certain that you ever pictured us meeting at all."

"Hence the visit."

"Do you find that so extraordinary?"

"Extraordinarily coincidental."

"How so?" She packed a lot of curiosity into two syllables.

"If you hadn't just shown up, I would've had no choice but to clean this," I said waving my hand around the room, "by myself." I lied a little.

"That's silly, Dylan. There would have been many options."

"Christ, Micki, you sound like MacClough."

"Mac—" she started.

"—Clough," I finished. "John MacClough, a friend of mine."

"There. You see. You might have called John for help."

"I don't think so, Micki. He's already too busy helping me."

She let that pass. Finished with her straightening for now, she stood up and faced me. I stepped out of the doorway, finally, and into the office.

The day's gray light did no justice to Micki Korin. I thought her Navaho brown skin too dark for a Russian woman, but it was summer and what did I know, anyway? The high cheekbones fit just right on either side of a slightly hooked nose, just long enough to mention. Her wide copperish eyes were bare of women's makeup and smiled at me from under skinny, black brows. I focused on her mouth. Her mouth was magic. Not like coffee magic, that's slight-of-hand. Oh, her mouth!

She kept it open a crack, revealing an inviting hint of her rough, pink tongue. The teeth were square and white and level. Her lips, however, did the real damage. They were thick and full and ripe with blood. Lipstick need not apply. Her moist upper lip arched high at midpoint and swept down to the corners, taking upward turns where it melted into her rolled back bottom lip. She seemed to look past my shoulders. I couldn't look past her mouth.

Eventually, I got the message and closed the office door. I held an awkward hand out for shaking. She ignored it and kissed me one cheek at a time. I skipped the continental mannerisms and kissed her mouth, tentatively, like a seventh grader. I mean like how seventh graders kissed when I was in seventh grade. She flushed red under the dark skin.

"It seems you've had a visitor," she said, stepping to the window and changing subjects.

"Besides yourself. Sure looks that way, doesn't it?"

"Do you suppose this relates to the case you mentioned on the phone?" she asked looking across at the marina so I couldn't see her expression.

"What case is that?"

"The puzzle."

"Yeah, the puzzle. I don't like puzzles too well."

"So you said. I thought you were taking a vacation."

"So did I, but I guess whomever broke in decided against taking his now." I counted a few Mississippi's in my head then continued: "Speak to your dad recently?"

"No, but that's not at all unusual," she responded calmly. If she was acting, she was good. "Have you?"

"Went for a ride in his Town Car the other night, but I haven't seen him or spoken to him since. Have a seat."

I plunked myself down behind the friendly confines of my desk. Micki moved around to the opposite side of the desk, pouring herself into a flimsy folding chair.

"Hey, thanks for helping me clean up. Was the door ajar when you got here or'd'ya just knock and come in?"

"The latter. Look, Dylan, I am very sorry about your office, but it's not why I'm here. Can we talk about it some other time?" She seemed down. Down like somebody whose got a fantasy of how things are going to go, but nothing's going according to plan.

"No problem for me. This doesn't concern you, anyway." I lied again, only this time the lie was bigger. "So tell me about how your dad got you to call me."

"There isn't much to the telling. I practice at a large firm in the city and am, by no means, starved for male companionship."

"That's honest enough, but I didn't figure you to be the hungry type."

"At the same time, though," she drove on, "the men I have contact with are homogenous, like so many quarts of milk. I am still uncomfortable with the insatiable American drive for money. The men I meet are uncomfortable without it. Well, my father heard this complaint one time too many and he decided to take matters into his own hands. Without my permission, of course."

"Of course," I parroted.

"There were names and numbers he'd supplied before yours, but I haven't bothered until now."

"You flatter me, but why? Wait! Don't answer that. You figured, doing what I do for a living, there's no way I could have a money obsession."

"That may be, but it is not why I called." Micki twisted up her lips and considered. "Your name. Yes, I liked your name more than the others. It's a bit paradoxical, isn't it?"

"Hey, don't take this honesty thing too far. My ego can't stand much more. But your answers are unique. No one's ever asked me out to dinner before just because they thought I had an odd name."

"Not odd, interesting."

"Have it your way," I tipped my head to her, "interesting."

"Can your fragile ego withstand another jolt?" she asked, flashing a coy smile.

"Give it your best shot."

"I called also because I had vacation time to use and—"

"Stop!" I threw my arms up in surrender. "I'm at my honesty tolerance threshold. Another word and I'll jump."

Now she raised an arm as a schoolgirl might to ask a teacher's permission.

"Be careful what you say," I mockingly warned her.

"Whatever the reasons for my calling, I couldn't be more pleased with the outcome. Let me take you to breakfast. And let me warn *you*. My delicate ego can only stand so much putting off."

"I accept."

The office phone rang. I wanted to let it ring until the machine screened the caller for me. On the fifth ring I returned to planet Earth and realized the answering machine was down on the floor, with the rest of my office, disconnected. I picked up.

"Klein speaking."

"Not for very much longer, I'm afraid," another familiar phone voice informed me.

"Hold on." I put my palm over the mouth piece and asked Micki to meet me downstairs. It was business, I told her, and I'd be about five minutes. When the door shut behind her, I stopped suffocating the phone.

"Good morning, Mohammed. Didn't your momma ever teach you that threatening people so early in the morning was impolite?" I asked, in as snotty a tone as I could muster.

"Your sense of humor escapes me, Mr. Klein. Really, it does. But it is refreshing to see a condemned man keeping his chin up."

"How British of me," I snarled. "And since we're on the subject, where ever did you get that accent, Mohammed, in Harrods?"

"Why do you insist upon calling me Mohammed?" he answered my question with a question.

"Because if I'm the mountain, then you must be Mohammed."

"That follows, I suppose. I don't think you comprehend the grave situation you're in, Mr. Klein. Do you know what Klein means in German?" He didn't wait for an answer. "It means small. Small is synonymous with the value of your life."

"Thanks for the grammar lesson, Mohammed, but I'd suggest you stop reading those second rate, tough guy novels. They're affecting your speech." I took a breath. "Now I have something to tell you. I'm tired of your threats, so if you're gonna pop me with that silenced rifle, shut up and shoot." I counted to three silently. "I'm not bleeding Mohammed. You're not gonna hurt me. I'm important to you. I don't know why, but I am."

"I will admit your continued health is, for the moment, consequential. And since we are exchanging lessons this morning, let me impart something to you that may better your perspective. The world's graveyards are crammed full of men who mistook their importance for necessity. No one is indispensable. The situation, as it stands, makes working through you more convenient than around you, but around you can be done. I assure you."

His words rocked me. I tried to cover with tough talk: "Nice of you to mention graveyards, Mohammed. I was getting to that, eventually. You gave me your word you'd get Piccolo to the hospital."

"And I kept my word," he interjected. "You, sir, did not specify what condition I was to deliver him in."

"Fuck you! You dickless bastard. You'll be joining him soon enough."

"Threats, Mr. Klein. Your momma would be ashamed. In any case, I'm taken aback by your violent overreaction. I have researched this Mr. Piccolo of yours. He was a supplier of drugs to children, a junky, a waste of our planet's limited resources. And it would not be inaccurate to judge that you and he were far from blood brothers."

"All true," I confessed, "but I don't feel inclined towards explaining my motives to you. What did you expect anyway? Did you expect me to thank you for bashing his skull in?" I took a long, loud breath. "Now stop bothering me. I'll find Brodsky for you. Then I'll repay the courtesy. I'm also a man of my word."

"Bravo, Mr. Klein. Bravo." He clapped into the phone. "Now that you've gotten that off your chest, I will continue. Yes, find Brodsky. Mohammed's voice got suddenly serious, "but he is a secondary issue. First, I need to know what you've done with Korin."

"Korin! I don't get it."

"Mr. Klein, Mr. Klein. My patience is at low ebb. You are good, though, I'll give you that."

"That's nice," I said, "but what exactly am I good at?"

"Where is Korin?" Mohammed ignored my question and asked one of his own.

"I had him stuffed and put on the wall. I thought it'd be a unique approach. Most people stuff the head as a trophy, but you've got that. I just made do with the parts I had left."

"Where is he?"

"Look, I don't know where the fucking body is, already. Why should I wanna know?"

"Why did you stop at the airport that night?" He moved onto the next question.

"To buy time." I gave an annoyed reply.

"Yes, but for whom?"

"Full of questions this morning, aren't we? I'd say you're asking the wrong ones to the wrong person. If someone snatched the body—"

"Body. What body?" Mohammed cut me off. "Oh, yes, that body."

"You losin' track of your victims—huh? Must be lots of 'em. Look, I don't know where the stiff is. Brodsky, I'll find him. The body's your problem."

"Our problem," he corrected. "One last time, Mr. Klein: where is Korin?" Whatever he paid you to help him can't possibly be worth your life, can it?

"I'm going to breakfast now. Say goodnight, Gracie."

"Remember my advice, Mr. Klein. Don't get too full of yourself. It's unbecoming of you and potentially dangerous for your friends."

"Say again."

He ignored my demand. "Take some of that money Mr. Korin filled you with and buy Mr. MacClough a new TV. It's so difficult to the see the matches on the one he owns now. Rather snowy, don't you think? Do tell him, though, that his honey-roasted nuts are impeccable. Take some time to absorb what I've said. I'll be back in touch. Goodnight, Gracie."

Puzzles. I hate puzzles. The further into them you go, the further away from the answer you get. The threats? They were just window dressing, but for what? Why would Mohammed care about the body, anyway? If someone borrowed it, I'd think he'd be relieved. Less garbage to dump. And why tip his identity's hand? He could have threatened me and MacClough easily without doing that.

She was standing in front of me when I picked my head up.

"Dylan, are you alright? You look pale."

"Fine," I heard somebody mumble in my voice. "What are you doing up here?"

"It's raining heavily downstairs and you've been a while. It's a good thing too, my coming up. I was standing here for a minute before you noticed. You needed someone to break the trance."

"Thanks. Let's get outta here."

She was tall, not taller than me, but about five-nine. I led her out of the unkempt office by the elbow, fast. We had places to go, breakfast to eat. Waiting was over. Waiting got me results, though the results were mixed.

The gray fog had gone, but the rain was thicker now. We stood just inside the downstairs doorway watching the water fall down.

"Do you find rain romantic, Dylan?"

"Rain is romantic when you're watching it from a leather sofa or a seat in a movie theater."

She laughed, a nervous laugh, like a skipping record.

"What are you laughing at?" I asked.

"You," she answered, only smiling now. "I think you find the rain very romantic, but are frightened to let it show."

Micki Korin leaned over and pressed her lips against mine. There was no embrace or exploration of each others mouths. A picture taken at that instant would seem rather tame, but there was nothing tame in that kiss. I would not soon forget it.

"Thank you," I said, for lack of a better phrase.

"My father was right about you."

"He said I was a good kisser?"

"I don't know you, Dylan Klein, but I want to."

"Breakfast?"

"Yes, please."

"Pancakes alright with you?"

"Perfect."

"Wait here," I instructed, "My car's about two blocks away. I'll pick you up in about—"

"Let's take mine," she said, pointing at a maroon BMW 2002, circa 1973 or 4, parked not quite ten feet to our left.

"Neat car."

"Do you think so? I'll have to tell Davy you like it."

"Davy?"

"A friend, an associate." Micki ran over some words in her head and then spoke them. "Living in Brooklyn Heights and working in the city are not conducive to owning an automobile."

I let the "Davy" issue fade into that mystical place where all potentially awkward subjects go. Micki's lips smiled at my lack of enthusiasm in pursuing Davy further. Just the smile made dropping things worth it.

On the way to Grandma's Revolutionary Pancake House, I did all the talking. Most of my remarks were confined to directional commentary. Things like: "Make a sharp left at the next flashing yellow light."

There was nothing revolutionary about Grandma's pancakes. And, after five bites, we found nothing exciting about them either. All pancakes are like that, though, your memory of them is always better than your bloated belly's reality. It took some time and a pot of mediocre coffee, but we pretty much cleaned our plates. With nothing left to eat, we took up conversing again.

"What type of law do you practice?" I asked out of genuine interest.

"International," she answered with a yawn.

"Back at the ranch you told me it was a big firm."

"Yes. Smythe, Kearne, Powers, and Whitney." That came with a bigger yawn.

"Sounds more like a group of Puritan church fathers. Do they practice law or burn witches at the stake?"

"Both, I think." Micki laughed at her answer. "The men attached to those names have been dead for quite some time. The more ethnic names begin appearing approximately twenty partners down the list."

"Any emigre Russian Jews on the list?"

"None that I am aware of."

"Then you'll be the first."

She began to cough and gag as if she were choking on a bone or had some hot coffee go down the wrong pipe. But she hadn't sipped her cold coffee for a good minute and pancakes didn't have bones.

"Can we go, Dylan? I'm not feeling at all well." She didn't look it, either, but I couldn't tell if it was the pancakes or the conversation that caused her ills.

"Just let me make a quick call," I said, rubbing my overburdened belly.

I asked our waitress for the check, some water for Micki, and the whereabouts of the payphone. The waitress asked me where I was from. I told her Sound Hill. She shook her head from side to side and asked where I was from, originally. I said Brooklyn. She said she thought as much; the way I pronounced water was a dead giveaway. I told her she had a fine ear and was wasting her talents serving people unremarkable pancakes, but that I really had to make a call. The phone was upstairs near the restrooms, above and to the right of the cigarette machine where payphones always are.

"MacClough?" I spoke before I was spoken to.

"Are you ready for our date tonight?" Johnny asked, recognizing my voice.

"I bought you a wrist corsage and put a fresh Trojan in my wallet. Do you have a pen around?"

"Wait . . . yeah, go ahead."

I gave him Micki Korin's particulars, as best I could over the wire. She could kiss and was real handy with a sloppy office, but I wasn't the trusting kind anymore. I had no way of knowing whether she had dumped my files or had been doing a good deed, really. I asked Johnny to get me the whole nine yards on her or as many as he could by tonight.

"Any other requests?" MacClough waited for an answer, tapping his pen against the phone.

"New York tag 304-AOG. That's 3—0—4 Alpha, Oscar, Golf. 1973 or 4 BMW 2002, maroon. Owner's first name, David."

"Yeah, what about it?"

"I need the owner's full name, home address, work address, phone numbers. You know."

"How about the size of his dick while I'm at it?"

"No, MacClough, I only have eyes for you."

"Christ! I was getting jealous there for a second."

"Anything about Piccolo?" I hedged.

"Relax baby, relax. We'll have plenty to talk about later. Don't you worry."

"Me, worry? See you later." I hung up.

Micki met me at the bottom of the stairs and informed me that the check and tip were taken care of. My right arm started for my wallet, but her gunfighter eyes told me not to dare. I didn't. There was a question I'd meant to ask her. It was gone now.

"I hate when that happens," I blurted out on the way to Davy's BMW.

"What do you hate?" she asked in a slightly startled voice.

"When I'm about to say something and," I snapped my fingers, "I forget. I wanted to ask you a question. It was almost out of my mouth. Now, I can't remember. Stuff drives me crazy."

"Was it about how I felt?"

"No," I gave an embarrassed laugh, "but since you brought it up . . ."

"Better that we're outside. Let's run down the alphabet. It helps me with my stubborn memory."

"Let's drop it. It'll come back eventually."

Except for the rain drumming its fingers on the roof, the ride back to Sound Hill was quieter than the trip to Grandma's. Not only did Micki Korin have a magic mouth, but her sense of direction was faultless. She turned the lefts, when coming, into the rights, when leaving, as if she'd driven these roads her entire life. Meanwhile, despite my words to the contrary, I searched the back of my brain for that elusive question.

After parking in front of my office, Micki brushed my left profile with the back of her hand.

"You'll remember the question when I'm gone," she assured me.

"It shows, huh?"

"Your beard is very soft. Beards usually intimidate me, but yours is soft."

"Thanks. I almost shaved it off the other day." I continued to look straight ahead.

"But why?"

"Something about wanting to remember my mother a certain way. It's real roundabout, don't bother trying to understand. I'm not sure I do."

"Will you be in Brooklyn again soon?"

"Tomorrow, probably. Why don't I call you during the day?" I turned to her.

"I was counting on that, but I thought you were on vacation."

"My visitor this morning put an early end to that." My wording was intentionally ambiguous. "I've got an office to clean, wanna stay and help?"

"Next time. *My* vacation's still on."

Both of our bodies met somewhere over the handbrake. My ribs told me so. I cupped her chin in my right hand and barely brushed her lips against mine. The gentility seemed to surprise her. I could tell by the stiffening of her jaw. When the surprise wore off, she relaxed her lips enough to let me taste her hot breath. It's flavor drove me to press harder against her mouth until it invited me in. My tongue barely scraped the enamel of her front teeth when the invitation came. I remembered! Micki, sensing the distraction, pulled away, but without violence.

"I remember the question now," I explained.

"Well then," she managed laughing, "you should ask it before you have a relapse."

"I don't know. I could force myself to enjoy this method of memory stimulation."

She nodded in agreement.

"It's pretty stupid."
"Ask it!" She screwed her face up in semi-serious anger.
"Did our waitress try to guess where you were from?"
"She did, actually."
"Right or wrong?"
"France. The waitress guessed France. Apparently, the way I said check was a dead giveaway."
"Was she disappointed?"
"At what? I told her she was correct and that I agreed with the gentleman's opinion. She was wasting her talents serving Grandma's Pancakes. She said that's what she told her husband before he bought the place."

I got out and walked around to the driver's side window. Micki Korin rolled it down. I told her that rain had more potential than I'd thought. She asked me if we could eat anything but pancakes the next time we dined together. I said I'd think about it and ran inside.

I thought about its driver as I watched the BMW push itself up the wet boulevard. The driver was sharp. The driver had style. The driver could kiss. But the driver was as much a Mohammed as any of my gentlemen callers. I pulled myself up the stairs, one step at a time.

Rainout Syllogism

There would be no game tonight. The return to fog and continuing rain made that a certainty. Bad weather is nature's insurance against balls and strikes. In New York, at least, that remains so. In Houston, Seattle, and Minneapolis however, nature can no longer buy into such a policy. Funky domes see to that. Domes and polymer rugs are baseball's insurance against nature and bunting for base hits.

Game or no game, I was destined for The Rusty Scupper this evening. I considered throwing a rainout syllogism—Meeting set for start of ballgame/No ballgame/therefore, no meeting. I could buy myself another day to clear things up solo. I put that notion to rest in a hurry. It would just be so much lawyer-ish bullshit to a man like Johnny. Cops grow to detest lawyers. They hate politicians, too. And, since most politicians are lawyers, its difficult to tell who cops loathe more. Besides, I had about as much chance of putting things together on my own as I did of being elected Pope. Truth is, I had a more realistic shot at Pope.

The sun was still up according to the clock, but the sky's opaque complexion made me doubt my Bulova. I didn't relish the prospect of even a short walk in this rain. Its appeal had diminished for me in the absence of certain lips. I threw on my faded Mets cap and hooded red sweatshirt and cursed my distaste for umbrellas. I stepped to the door when something knocked it from the other side. And I thought I was fresh out of Mohammeds.

"Go away, no one's home," I answered the knock and winced at the similarity of my words to those of Joey Piccolo.

"Nevermore. Nevermore." Quoted a voice that sounded more like a drowning ex-policeman's than a raven.

"Sorry, wrong house. I don't recall ever dating anybody named Lenore."

"Open up the fucking door, Klein, it's pouring out here."

I did as the man said. He was dressed in a similar fashion to myself, only he was considerably wetter. I waved him in. He shook himself off as a dog or a cat might, spraying water all about the doorway.

"So you were coming after all," MacClough announced, after giving me the once-over. "Started using your brain, finally."

"I thought about skipping our date, " I admitted, "but I know how much being stood-up hurts your pride. What are you doing here anyway? I thought self-service didn't suit you."

"It doesn't. My brother Billy's been after me to let him help out. I figured the work would do the lad good."

"But what are you really doing here?" I flashed a knowing wink his way.

"What we've gotta discuss isn't for public consumption," he said with a neutral mouth and unsmiling eyes.

"A beer for you?" I asked, already headed for the refrigerator.

"Nothing for me."

I stopped midstep. "Now you're making me nervous, Mac-Clough."

"And with good reason. But get us a beer, anyhow."

"Hang your stuff up behind you," I said, pointing to three porcelain and brass coathooks stuck on the wall just inside my front door. "Grab a towel in the bathroom and I'll meet you in the kitchen."

I was halfway finished with my first Anchor Steam when Johnny's bare feet stepped onto the worn linoleum. He wore a blue and white hotel towel tucked under his collar like an offensive lineman's neckbrace. I slapped a Budweiser into his right palm. He twisted off its cap as an afterthought and sipped at it more out of habit than desire. He looked disdainfully at the little brown bottle in my hand.

"What is that shit?"

"Anchor Steam, from San Francisco," I answered meekly.

"Queer beer."

"Hardly. It's sorta like English lager. Wanna taste?"

"No. I don't even want this," he said, holding up the bottle of Bud.

"Okay, MacClough, you're acting pissed off. What gives?"

"They got your prints off the glass booth and the money slot. They got a lot of people's prints, but you're the only one I know."

I almost asked him who had my prints. I didn't ask. I knew. That numbness flashed through me. I felt for the lump at the back of my head. It was gone now, but the ugly seeds that were planted the night I got bopped might have just started to grow.

"So?" was the best I could manage.

"So that puts you at the crime scene on the day of the crime."

"Me and every other customer that day. You even said the boys in blue had a bunch of prints." I tried, failing miserably, to sound unruffled. "If I get questioned, I'll say I was in Brooklyn checking on my dad's mail while he was away. It's not a crime to run below a quarter of a tank, is it?"

"Cute, but thin. Sure the cops have lots of prints, but how many of the people attached to those prints knew the deceased, grew up with the deceased, bought a few lids of Thai-stick from the deceased? I'll tell you how many: one. One is the answer. And you're the one.

"Nice, but circumstantial. I'll stick to the mail checking story."

"You're not gonna fool anybody with that line." Johnny's wise face looked its age for the first time since we'd met. "Good cops don't have to be geniuses. The best ones aren't."

"You said it, MacClough. I didn't."

"Good cops learn to trust the obvious, to hold onto it until something else drags them kicking and screaming away from it. Most of the time the most obvious suspect is the most guilty. Sherlock Holmes is for books."

"I didn't kill him, MacClough. You gotta trust me on that. I swear."

"Swearing is for four letter words." He sucked in a bunch of air and let it out slowly. "I know you didn't do it. It's not your style. And the cops won't think you did it either, eventually."

"Thanks, John."

"They won't think you did it," he continued, "but they also won't believe you're totally clean. The connection's too clear, too obvious. They're gonna wanna know what you were doing there. Christ, Klein! I wanna know."

I honored his request. I gave it to him once digested. I'd gotten it raw. I edited out as little as possible and threw in the few conclusions I had reached by my lonesome. John Francis MacClough took it in with a blank stare and a minimum of telltale body language. The lack of external expression was a cloak for the mental churning inside. He finished his Budweiser.

"Let me try some queer beer, Klein."

I got us both a bottle. "What do you make of it?"

"It's a lot to swallow in one sitting. Some of it's straight-forward enough. Some of it doesn't fit." He took a gulp of the amber beer and frowned as if it had been chlorine bleach. "God, this stuff tastes like shit. Get me another Bud."

"Let's start with the stuff that doesn't fit," I said, while exchanging bottles.

"The missing head routine. It doesn't go with the M.O." The ex-detective rubbed his red eyes. "That bothers me."

"Care to elaborate for the amateurs in the room?"

"Mutilation of the corpse or of the victim is always done for a specific reason. And this type of crime is usually committed by a specific profile perpetrator. Problem with your story is that the reasons and the profiles don't add up.

"A good portion of these types of murders are done by whackos, nut jobs. They're mostly male and their victims are usually female prostitutes. Your friend with the silencer is no psycho. He's a pro. The crazy act is for your benefit. I'll fill you in on that later. Nobody who can handle a weapon the way you tell me he can, bothers butchering his victims. Too sloppy, increases his chances of getting caught. Bad for business.

"The rock and powder boys from South America way sometimes do mutilation hits, but they like more publicity. They want photos of their victims on the front page of the Post. They use mutilation like you use Western Union; to get a message across. In your case, someone's sending a message, but the decapitation isn't the medium.

"Some killers dismember the body for practical reasons. In a few cases, chopping up the body helps to disperse evidence of a crime and it can make disposal easier. It's also done, sometimes, to hide the victims identity. Does the name Jimmy Hoffa ring a bell?" MacClough asked, rhetorically.

"Yeah, you mentioned him a few days ago." I answered just the same.

"Well, you're still alive to tell who the victim was, so the beheading wasn't done to disperse evidence or hide the victim's identity."

"Proof of the kill," I thought aloud. "Maybe he took the head to prove he'd done the job he was hired for."

"Come on, Klein, use that *yiddisha kup* God gave you. There's lots of body parts better suited for proof and ease of travel than some stiff's head. Even an instant Polaroid picture might do the trick. But that's all besides the point. He doesn't need physical evidence. He's got you."

"Me?"

"No, asshole, my Aunt Tilly," MacClough screamed. "Yes, you. You're his evidence. You're his witness to a job well done. Why do you think I'm here tonight instead of at your funeral?"

"Because the game got rained out." We both laughed.

"You're his messenger, Klein. You can't really hurt the assassin. You didn't see him do anything and you don't know who he is."

"But this morning he told me he was the guy munching peanuts at the bar last night." I sounded confused.

"Sorry to disappoint you, but that guy last night produces half the shows on Broadway. His name's Goodman and no, he doesn't speak with a second rate English accent. The rifleman had my place under surveillance; no big thing. He's playing you, manipulating you, pushing you. That's why Joey Piccolo was murdered."

"That's a little severe, don't you think?"

"Well, he can't kill you. Not yet, anyway. Killing Piccolo was his way of telling you to keep in line and do as you're told."

"And because I might be implicated in Joey's death, the pro thought that would increase my motivation to clean up shop and deliver the message before I had to explain myself to the cops."

"You're catching on." MacClough said proudly.

"So when I improvised by getting Piccolo involved, he improvised by using Piccolo as a punching bag. But why beat him to death? I thought you said marksmen don't get physical."

"He beat him for two reasons. First, he needed to get the lowdown on where you took Korin's body. Sometimes broken jaws are more inspiring than a pistol. Second, if he used a gun, you couldn't have been implicated."

"This guy doesn't like my improvising, does he?"

"No, but you're right, in that waiting gave you leverage."

"That's what the threat against you was all about this morning, a little motivation."

"As long as you don't deliver the message, he'll keep you around."

"But the longer I wait, the fewer living acquaintances I'll have. And eventually, he'll find and alternative messenger."

"That's it, on a silver platter."

"Like John the Baptist's head." I got another round of beers. "I take it that Brodsky's the man I'm meant to deliver the message to."

"That's the way I see it. Other than the dead end at the car service, do you have any clues about this guy Brodsky?"

"Only that Third Reich photo, and I left it in Korin's office like a schmuck."

"Okay, Klein, we're going to Brooklyn tomorrow," Johnny informed me.

"We are?"

"Separate cars, of course. You got an appointment to follow a driver from the Kiev Car Service around. Me? I got an appointment to go photo shopping at a dead lawyer's office. And while I'm in the area, maybe I'll flash my old blue and gold shield around. Maybe I'll talk to a neighbor or two. Then, if the spirit moves me, I'll look up some old friends from the six-one and the six-zero."

"Don't get that involved, MacClough."

"Piss on that idea, brother." He slammed his bottle down on the table. "Anytime my ass gets threatened, I'm involved, deep."

"So I guess we're going to Brooklyn tomorrow." I relented. "I was sorta planning on it anyway. But what'd'ya think trackin' the car service is gonna net me?"

"Us," Johnny correct, "net us. We won't know until you do it. Besides, when it's the only clue you got, you milk it dry."

"And when it's dry?"

"You milk it some more." He poured a bit of St. Louis' finest down his throat. "But don't lose sleep over it, Klein, that car service got some ripe tits. You just gotta find where to squeeze."

"You know, MacClough, it's true: the Irish can sure turn a phrase."

"My ancestors thank you, you sarcastic son of a bitch."

"Did you get the information I asked you for this afternoon?"

"It'll cost you another beer." My drinking buddy's already reddened face lit up like the Christmas tree in Rockefeller Center, as he produced a folded piece of yellow paper out of thin air.

"Is that envelope I gave you safe?" I asked with feigned indifference.

"The one with the thousand dollar check and the stained stationery?"

"How the fuck . . ." I stopped mid-question.

"Even before you filled me in, I didn't exactly think it was a list of your ten favorite Elvis recordings." He answered the unfinished question. "And now with all the details, it was easy to figure."

"Your beer, sir." I slid it across the table.

Upon receipt of the bottle, MacClough unfolded his yellow paper and began reciting: "David Ben Avraam, born Netanya, Israel 9/18/51. Relocated to United States of America 1975, March. Naturalized American citizen as of July 4, 1982. Currently resides at 24 Colonial Avenue, White Plains, N.Y. 10605. Phone- (914)287-9999. Employed by Blue Sabre Worldwide, Inc., 182-13 182 Road, Jamaica, N.Y. 11434. Phone- (718)995-8765. Position- Executive Vice President of Operations. Marriage status: single. Automobiles: two, both registered to employer."

"I bet one's a maroon BMW." I cut in.

"Christ, I wish I could be as smart as you for just one minute."

"Yeah, look how far it's gotten me." I finished my last Anchor Steam and moved backwards to Budweiser. "What about Korin's daughter?"

"Very little so far. She works where she says she works and lives where she says she lives, but other than that we've drawn a blank. I'll see if I can fill in the numbers tomorrow."

"Where do you think Newkirk and Rizzo fit in?"

"You tell me." MacClough shot back. "Let's not worry about them just yet. I—"

The phone rang, ending Johnny's sentence without a period. He seized the opportunity to let out a little liquid. I held mine in and answered.

"Hello."

"Is this Mr. Klein speaking?" A bored, flat voice questioned.

"Why, has he won Lotto?" I went tit for tat.

"If Mr. Klein is at home, please put him on the line. This is Detective Brian Fazzano of the New York City Police Department."

"Concerning?"

"I'll discuss that with Mr. Klein when he picks up the phone." Detective Fazzano was now sounding both bored and annoyed.

"Hold please." I covered the mouthpiece. "MacClough!" I screamed.

"What?" He screamed back.

"You know a Detective Fazzano?"

"Yeah. He's about as sharp as the darts in my bar."

"I got him on hold on the other end of the line."

"He probably wants you to come in for questioning. Talk to the man, but don't say anything. You're good at that. I'll be right there." The toilet flushed.

"This is Klein," I spoke into the newly uncovered phone. MacClough returned.

"Mr. Klein, would it be possible for you to come into Brooklyn tomorrow, for questioning concerning an ongoing investigation being conducted by our department?" He was back to just boredom.

I made the phone deaf again and consulted MacClough. "You were right. What should I do?"

"Ask him what it's about. Say you'll go, but don't sound overly cooperative. And, for Chrissakes, don't mention lawyers." The ex-detective advised.

"What sort of investigation, Detective Fazzano?"

"Murder investigation, Mr. Klein. The deceased's name was Joseph Piccolo. I believe you knew him." He was sounding perky now.

"Belief is your burden, detective. But I guess we can argue that tomorrow in Brooklyn, when we meet."

That pleased him. He was an easy fellow to please. He wanted me at the 61st Precinct at noon. I told him he'd just have to wait until 1:00. He didn't like that too well. He was an easy fellow to displease. MacClough gave me the "thumbs up" for the hour delay. I hung up and made it to the toilet before Fazzano heard the click.

I returned to the kitchen feeling a little less like an overstressed water balloon. Johnny's hands were full. The left one held a familiar brown bottle. The right one held tan leather and metal.

"Take this."

"Sorry," I said, waving him off, "no more beer for me."

"Here." He landed his Bud on the table, caught my right arm

with his left, and slapped the holstered gun into my palm. "It's a short barrel .38. The handle's taped against prints and it's loaded."

"Should I shoot myself now or wait until you go?"

He ignored that. "The holster ties around your ankle. Look." MacClough pulled a trouser leg up revealing more metal and leather. "Don't wear it into the precinct tomorrow, but keep it on otherwise."

"Okay." I wasn't up to a debate. "About tomorrow, what should I say?"

"For now, stick to the mail checking routine. Tell them you knew Piccolo, but you hadn't seen him for years until that night. They won't buy it, but it will ring with enough truth to make the cops back off for a few days. Let's hope nobody spotted you at the gas station twice the night Joey got sent to the angels. That'll take the truth right outta the ring."

"What if they have such a person?" I was feeling numb again.

"They don't." Johnny stated matter-of-factly. "If they did, they wouldn't be making polite phone calls. You'd be pacing inside a holding tank instead of your kitchen."

I *was* pacing. I stopped, put the covered pistol down and re-started.

"You're making me nervous, Klein." He picked up his beer.

"Good. We're of like mind now. Which car should I follow tomorrow?"

"Flip a coin. The one you don't follow tomorrow, you'll follow the next day."

"Are the Yankees playing tonight?" I asked out of left field.

"Yeah, they're on cable now," MacClough answered haltingly.

"Who they playin'?"

"Minnesota at the Homerdome."

"Fuck the Homerdome!"

"Fuck the Yankees!"

I went back on my vow and grabbed another Budweiser from the fridge. This was one night I needed to sleep well and beer was the closest thing I had to Valium. I was fresh out of Valiums. Valiums go fast the week of a funeral; I can vouch for that.

"Before you go," I began.

"Am I going?" My arms dealer asked with counterfeit surprise.

"I think so. When you came to the door earlier, what was that 'Nevermore' shtick?"

"I know you like poetry. The weather seemed right. And 'The Raven' is the only damned poem I remember, even a little bit."

"Come on, MacClough, the Irish are all born poets."

"What do I know about the Irish?" Johnny asked, scowling at his empty bottle. "I'm just another schmuck from Sheepshead Bay."

"Now I know you're drunk. Get outta here."

I walked him to the door. He didn't need the escort. Years of drinking on duty, on the beat, on surveillance, behind the bar had taught the man well how to mask alcohol's physical effects. The emotional ones were harder to cover. He slipped into his Mets cap and still damp sweatshirt as if they were a second skin.

"Don't wear the piece into the precinct," he warned me for a second time as he twisted the doorknob. "We'll speak the day after tomorrow." He walked out into the night.

I caught the door before it shut and watched MacClough disappear into the dark, the fog, and the rain, but his splashing strides reported back to me for another fifteen seconds. I vacated the doorway, returning the door to its rightful position. Behind it, I flopped onto the couch and turned on the Yankee game.

Budweiser Forest

The TV was still watching me when I reopened my eyes. I'd passed out, fully clothed, on the couch. Too many brews and American League baseball will do that. Knock me out, I mean. The top of my head felt like ground zero just after the neutrons got let out of their cages. I guess I'd have to fault the beer and my nerves for the hurting. You can't, after all, blame everything on the designated hitter.

The sun's climb back into the sky was about an hour old when I stumbled onto the street. The only tangible remnants of the Earth's previous turn were the pothole puddles out in the gutter and the ache above my brow. The captive water would evaporate by noon. I doubted that the pain in my head would vanish so quickly.

I stepped back inside, shut off Big Brother, and wandered into the kitchen. The white handled gun and holster were still on the table amongst the empty glass trees of the Budweiser forest. As I reached down to play lumberjack, the tainted breath of last night's beer stuck its finger down my throat. I tried to convince my digestive tract that puking twice in any seven day stretch was definitely against my religion. I wasn't persuasive enough, but I made it to the toilet just the same. My knees got off the tiles, eventually and I whipped up another batch of cold water soup. Someday, I thought, I'd have to use someone else's head as a filler. My hair was losing its flavor. It was an especially sick thought, considering my situation. I laughed anyway. I was allowed.

I headed back to the bedroom, promising my alarm clock that I'd try sampling the new day again at ten. A red dot told me the clock would keep its end of the bargain. I wasn't as confident about mine.

The Last Word

I pulled off the road for a minute to give the aspirins I bought and swallowed at the Star Spangled Deli a chance to take effect. Besides, you ever try to drive a stick and drink hot coffee through a straw at the same time? There's no profit in the venture. Unless, of course, you own a dry cleaners.

The farm stands along 25A were busy as beehives today with the sun's resurrection. Adventuresome westerners, hoping for the nickel tour and a sample of the fair for free, flock to the wineries on sun and blue days like vultures to a side of beef. The farm stands, in turn, feed off the vultures. "Nature, red in tooth and claw." Tennyson wrote that, and he'd never even been to Sound Hill in the summer.

Farm stands take on this sort of religious significance for cityites. It's a revelation to watch grown humans treat fresh fruit like the Holy Grail. In the five boroughs they pinch it, sniff it, bite it, and bag it. Out here, they revere it. I watched one schmo, a guy about my age, cradle a sack of onions like the Virgin Mary caressing the baby Jesus. That clinched it. My headache wasn't, but I was gone.

"What assholes," I thought, pulling back onto the blacktop. "What incredible assholes." I got people cutting head's off my clients and there's some putz over there worshiping lily bulbs.

By the time I got to the Nassau County line all the wonder went out of me. My headache was also on the canvas with the referee counting to ten. I forced down another set of white tablets to make sure the pain would never get off the mat. The coffee in the cup between my legs was cold by now, but it was just wet enough to help

Life Goes Sleeping

me swallow. With the hurt almost exorcised, maybe I could control my cynical panic for awhile. Who knows, maybe produce and religion had possibilities.

The old 61st Precinct was situated on Avenue U; half a block from the Avenue U Bar and Grill, half a block from the Avenue U subway stop, a full block away from the Avenue U Diner and two full blocks from the Avenue U Movie Theater. Everything on Avenue U, it seemed, was named for the thoroughfare itself. No, that's not entirely accurate. The Chinese restaurants managed to maintain some ethnic integrity.

The old 61st had integrity. At least it looked like a goddamned police station was supposed to look. It was a mass of beige bricks, green walls, white glass globes, and workable windows. It looked like precincts looked when New York State still fried its guilty and the city dressed its patrol cars in green, black, and white. Just driving by it used to get me nervous, but I wasn't driving by today.

The new 61st precinct was a textured concrete affair with acoustic tiles, dropped ceilings, and handicapped access. My junior high school was more intimidating. No desk sergeant, seated like a justice on the bench, was to greet me here. That job fell to a fidgity lieutenant named Boyce. He and some civilian employees sat in a white tiled area that resembled a nurses station.

"Can I help you, sir?" Boyce asked, flicking his thumbnail with the tip of his index finger.

"I'm here to see Detective Fazzano," I replied, putting my elbows on the tiled partition.

"Name?"

"Klein."

"I'll get him for you." He picked up a phone. "Please, take a seat," the lieutenant jutted out his chin, pointing at a row of molded plastic chairs that must've escaped from a city bus, "over there."

Fazzano didn't give me a chance to sit. A thick hand clapped me on the left shoulder not quite hard enough to register on the Richter Scale. After I'd recovered sufficiently from the shock, I turned to meet my inquisitor. There were two of them. MacClough joked that cops were like socks: they always come in pairs. These cops were like my socks: they didn't match.

The one closest to me, the amateur chiropractor, was dressed in a light blue, short-sleeved shirt with brown racing stripes under the armpits. His too wide, navy blue tie couldn't have reached his frayed brown belt with a ladder. His gray, doubleknit pants were okay, if your taste ran to gray doubleknit. I was afraid to look at his shoes.

It must be hard to find nice clothes on a cop's salary when you're that big. He stood six-six, if he stood an inch. His balding head was too small for its pedestal and the remaining rim of curly, brown hair made him look silly. His lids hadn't woken up yet today, but you could make out that there were brown eyes under there somewhere.

"I'm Detective Malone," announced the big man in a rather squeaky voice. We shook hands, sort of. "This is Detective Fazzano," he tilted his tiny head in the other man's direction.

Fazzano stepped forward to receive what was left of my hand after Malone had crushed all the bones in it. He was the same half inch short of six foot as myself, so we could look each other in the eye. His were almost black. Very appropriate, I thought, for a homicide detective. Black was his color alright. His hair was black. His tastefully baggy designer suit was black, as were his tassled Italian loafers. At least his shirt wasn't black, but it wanted to be. It settled on turquoise.

"Mr. Klein," He nodded. "We're glad you could make it."

Not me, but I wasn't about to say so. "I'm happy to help, if I can."

"We'll just see about that," Malone cut in. "Please come this way."

I played follow the leaders with Black Bart and his pinheaded sidekick. We went through some doors, down a corridor or two and into a stark white room. No one got the hot lamp treatment in here. The lighting was strictly florescent. A green metal card table, surrounded by four similarly hideous chairs, was the room's centerpiece. Two steno pads lay shut on the table. Fazzano and I sat down. Malone chose to prowl along the windowless walls.

The preliminaries took a few minutes. Fazzano would read a list of facts about me from his pad for me to confirm or deny; name, address, business number, etc. His info was fairly accurate. I corrected his spelling once and changed a digit here and there, but nothing major. Fazzano assured me that I wasn't suspected of anything and that I could stop the questioning at any point, if I felt the need to consult a lawyer. I told him I probably wouldn't feel the need. Malone paced without speaking.

"Do you know why you're here?" The man in black asked his first serious question, while admiring his manicure.

"I figure you found my prints at the crime scene, did some checking, and found out that I knew Joey once." I answered.

"You figured nothing," the quiet man stopped being so, but kept walking. "You're buddies with Johnny MacClough. He's the man that educated you. When ex-cops start nosing around about cases that don't concern them, that makes us curious," the big man squeaked. "We ain't as dumb as we look."

I wanted to tell him that wouldn't have been possible, but Fazzano interrupted me and told Malone to calm down.

"He's just edgy today," the dark eyed detective explained. "Malone's got ulcers. What about MacClough?"

"What about him? I know the guy. Sure we talked. If you were going to buy a diamond and you knew a jeweler, wouldn't you talk to him before you invested in a stone? So I was coming to talk to cops today and MacClough's the only one I have the pleasure of knowing."

"Nice answer, Mr. Klein," Malone's ulcer was feeling good enough to let him speak, "but that don't explain why your friend and our brother in blue was asking around even before we called you."

"Look," I turned around to address the orbiting policeman, "If you wanna know why Johnny MacClough does things, ask him. You," I pointed at Fazzano, "asked me to come down here to discuss the Piccolo case. Are we gonna discuss it, or not?"

"Sorry, Mr. Klein," Fazzano apologized, playing his part as the good cop, "we're naturally curious. What were you doing in Brooklyn the evening Piccolo was murdered?"

"I came in to check my dad's mail and to see if his apartment was secure. He's down in Florida. My mom died a few weeks back and he's there trying to get over it. Around Flatbush Avenue I noticed I was running low on gas. I got off at Knapp Street and pulled into the Merit station."

"Sorry to hear about your mom," the good cop said. "How long had it been since you last saw Piccolo?"

"Before that night," I made like I was calculating, "about seven, eight years maybe. I'm not sure. I didn't even recognize him when I was getting the gas, although his voice sounded familiar. Later that night I put the voice with the face."

The next group of questions dealt with timing; when I left my house, when I got to Brooklyn, when did I get to my dad's apartment, when did I leave, when did I get to the station, etc. We talked about how long it took to go from place to place and did I know if anyone noticed me at any of those places. Malone acted angry and paced. Fazzano played it neutral to friendly. Malone got disgusted and left. I didn't like it.

"Nevermind him."

"I know, ulcers."

"Piccolo was a dealer," the nattily dressed cop informed me.

"I know he used to be one, but if he still was it wouldn't shock me."

"A big user, too."

"Doesn't shock me either." I was feeling real uncomfortable. "I haven't done drugs in forever. I hadn't seen him for years before that night. What's the point, Fazzano?"

"Hey, you're a friend of MacClough's. MacClough is a good man. I like him. He likes you, so I'm trying to make this as easy as possible."

"Thanks," I said, beginning to sweat. "What is it exactly you're trying to make easier?"

"I wanted to tell you before Malone gets back in the room. This way maybe we could work something out, just you and me, without Malone." His black eyes took on the hungry glint of a predatory animal.

"You're a great dancer, Fazzano, but I'm getting tired of waltzing. Say what you gotta say or I'll be wishing you a good day." I got up.

"Hey, that rhymes. I like rhymes," he said, producing a pack of Marlboros out of his suit jacket. "It takes two words to rhyme. Two is a word that should interest you." He lit a nail and threw the spent match on the linoleum floor.

"How cute! You made a rhyme of your own. Good day, detective." I turned the doorknob.

"We got a witness that makes you at the station twice that night," Fazzano whispered to my back. "Why don't you take a seat and make yourself comfortable, Mr. Klein. I don't think you'll be going anywhere just yet."

I wasn't feeling too well again, but I couldn't show it. Fazzano had thrown a bomb in my lap. Now I had to determine whether it was genuine or bogus, whether it was fact or fabrication. Either contingency called for a little defusing. I calmly walked back to my seat, using the time to plan the counter-offensive.

"Do you wanna call your lawyer?" Fazzano asked with an icy smile.

"I told you before I didn't see the need for a lawyer. I still don't. You've been watching too much television, Fazzano. What, am I supposed to shit in my pantaloons because you throw a curveball at me? Am I supposed to break down now and spill my intestines? Come on, be real. You got no witness." I fired a few volleys, figuring some of them would hit.

"You make nice speeches, but you sweat too much. We got a witness, believe you me."

"Well, if you got a witness, he didn't see me."

"I think you're the one who watches too much tube, Klein. You gonna tell me you got an evil twin brother now?" The inquisitor laughed at his sense of humor, flicking ashes on the floor and blowing smoke into my space.

"Blowing that smoke at me's the perfect metaphor for what you're doing here. You know what a metaphor is?" I asked sarcastically. I didn't wait for an answer. "If you got a witness, slap the cuffs on and tell me about Carmen Miranda."

"Look, Klein, we don't think you offed Piccolo. We just want the real info about why you were there. Was it drugs or cars? Cooperate a little and make all our lives easier." Fazzano lit another cigarette. "We won't even use your name. Just point us in the right direction."

The bomb was a dud. They had no witness. The dark clad detective's admission concerning my guilt or innocence told me as much. I didn't want to let on yet that I knew there was no witness. I was probably going to be here for a few more hours rehashing things. Those hours would go a lot smoother if I let the cops play their cards at a pace that suited them.

"If you got a witness, let's hear what times I was there and what kinda car I was driving." I demanded, keeping up the charade.

Malone trudged in. He'd probably been listening at the door. He sat down for the first time since our little question and answer session had started.

"No statement, huh?" he looked at Fazzano with rehearsed disgust. "Go get yourself some coffee. Me and Mr. Klein got some things to jaw over."

"Mr. Klein tells me we ain't got no witness," Fazzano related to his eager partner.

"Is that so?" Malone asked no one in particular, rubbing his hairless forehead. "We'll just see about that."

"Either one of you want a coffee while I'm going?" The black detective querried, halfway out the door.

"Mr. Klein's not thirsty. Are you, Mr. Klein?" The bad cop stated, then questioned.

I nodded that I wasn't. Malone nodded he wasn't either. The door shut behind Fazzano. This time I could hear footsteps moving down the hall. I took a deep breath to prepare for the inevitable.

One deep breath wasn't nearly enough. Malone fed me the same threats and questions as Fazzano, only minus the sugar coating. The pinhead didn't like MacClough, didn't like me, and wasn't interested in making deals. He kept demanding that I stop wasting everybody's time and the taxpayers money.

When Fazzano returned, the smoke he blew at my face tasted like old coffee in my lungs. Malone stayed put and they double-teamed me for a week-long hour. I was more bored than steamed by now. Eventually, the dynamic duo went back to tag-teaming interrogation. Malone took a piss. Fazzano got more java. Malone got coffee. Fazzano took a piss. No matter what combination they used, my answers remained the same: "I was checking my father's mail. You have no witness." Class was dismissed at around six o'clock.

"Alright Klein," the turquoise shirted detective exhaled, "get outta here."

I moved to the door of our square white world without uttering a sound. My eyes snapped a farewell photo of them and I nodded my goodbyes. They appeared untouched by the last five hours. I felt a thousand years older, give or take a century.

"Don't plan on visiting your relatives in Fiji any time soon," Malone added the obligatory disclaimer before I was through the door. "We'll be in touch. You can take that to the bank," he assured me. "And don't for a minute think we bought a word of the bullshit you fed us, not a blessed fucking word."

I almost turned. I almost spoke back. I almost spit in his face. I just left. The last word is too damned important to some people. Getting out of there had it all over the last word.

I died and went to heaven in the front seat of my Volkswagen. It felt like heaven, anyway. I left the windows up and let the six o'clock sun bake through my skin to the bone. Five hours of air conditioning, questioning, and lying had chilled my soul thoroughly. I needed to defrost and to turn the calendar back about nine hundred years.

By 6:35 my eternal spirit was young enough and warm enough to let me get on with business. I found Johnny's leather clad .38 and strapped it to my right ankle, banging my forehead on the steering wheel for good measure. I wondered if the inventor of Velcro had holster clamps in mind when he or she hit upon the notion. Somehow, I doubted it. This morning's coffee cup still held a finger's worth of liquid. I used the remainder to float a few more aspirins down stream. I pissed five hours worth into the empty cup. It was the only thing I'd done today that felt natural and familiar.

On the way into Brighton, I dumped the cup's contents onto the rear wheel of a double parked police car. I know it really wasn't, but it sure felt like the last word. The last word is too damned important to some people, and I could be one of them.

Condors in California

Steiner's Kosher Delicatessen was busy dying a slow death when I pulled up for breakfast, lunch, and dinner. Steiner's was the last of its kind around here. In fact, a fair measure of just how little remained of the neighborhood I'd grown up in was the current scarcity of kosher delis. Hell, when I was a kid there used to be more kosher delicatessens in Brighton Beach than condors in California. It was no longer the case. Birds, unlike ethnic food stores, can be coaxed into captive breeding.

I stood for some minutes on the sidewalk gazing through the neon, glass, and pickle-jarred facade at the neatly ordered frankfurters grilling patiently on an ancient bed of aluminum foil. Behind the glass a life-bleached counterman, dressed in whites, impaled the sleeping dogs only to cover them with bread, boiled cabbage, and brown speckled mustard. Satisfied with the foreplay, I stepped through the door, made my purchases, and drove off for the task at hand.

The Kiev Car Service's entire fleet, all two cars worth, was parked directly out in front of its offices. I put my VW to rest a few spots behind the less than mighty armada and went to work on the food from Steiner's. Above me, a Manhattan bound local covered the noise of my chewing and the telltale sounds of my passenger door opening.

"Save some for me."

I choked and jumped out of my car, sending celery tonic, hot dogs, and waxed paper flying. When my guts got in synch with the rest of me, I checked out the source of my surprise.

Life Goes Sleeping

"Fuck you, MacClough," I slammed my hand on the old car's roof, "Fuck you!"

"Likewise, I'm sure. Now get in the car before you draw the rest of the neighborhood's attention."

"Whose side are you on?" I asked, repositioning myself behind the wheel. "Are you trying to kill me, too."

"Don't get hysterical," he grabbed the back of my neck. "Nobody's tried to kill you yet."

"That's a real comfort."

"I was just tryin' to make a point. Be more alert." Johnny let go of my neck, but smacked the side of my head for emphasis.

"Just tell me next time. I'm not from Missouri." I chided.

"How'd it go today?" His voice strained as he bent over to retrieve a frank.

"As smooth as a fall through broken glass. Some pinhead named Malone—"

"Brendan Malone?" he cut me off.

"I was too busy keeping my head above water to ask. Why?"

"He's a real prick, really enjoys playing the bad cop."

"That's the man," I confirmed. "He and Fazzano didn't buy my story for a second."

"I told you so."

"They didn't think I did the crime, either."

"I told you so."

"Well, here's something you didn't tell me," I got MacClough's attention. "They claim to have a witness that makes me at the scene twice."

I expected Johnny's jaw to drop to just above his ankles, but all he did was smile like a tomcat familiar with the flavor of canary meat. "They have no witness," he laughed. "It's an old ploy. They threw the one thing at you that might shake your tree. Then they stand around and wait to see what kinda fruit falls out. I woulda done the same."

"Why didn't you warn me that they'd pull that on me, whether or not there really was a witness?" I was yelling now.

"I told you last night they didn't have a witness," he replied in between bites on the scavenged hot dog.

"That's not what I asked."

"Okay, Klein," MacClough focused on my eyes, "here it is. That tale you told last night was pretty bizarre, just bizarre enough to make most people think you couldn't have made it up. But, I'm not most people. One thing you sacrifice as a cop is trust, and you don't suddenly get it back when you turn in your shield.

"I like you. God knows why, but I like you. I also happen to think you're an honest guy. Unfortunately, I've seen a lot of honest, likeable people slit their wives' throats or testify against their best friends. Circumstances can do funny things to honest, likeable people. So, no matter if I believed your story, there was still a chance you croaked Piccolo and fed me the other crap to cover your tracks. I had to let the cops shake your tree. I also had to do some checking on my own."

I turned away from his eyes and stared straight ahead. "Fair enough, John. Do you trust me now?"

"As much as I trust anybody." He went back to finishing my meal.

We didn't talk. I watched the shadows spreading, throwing themselves onto the perpendicular side streets, previewing the coming of night. A wiry old man wearing a tan cap and a pencil behind his right ear walked out of the Kiev Car Service. He sat himself behind the wheel of the red, white, and blue Kiev car parked furthest away from me. Within a minute's time the flagship of the fleet was headed into traffic, flickering underneath the shadows and boxes of light created by the spaces between the rails.

MacClough nudged me, prodding me to follow. I ignored the suggestion. I was too busy being hurt to tail the vanishing taxi. Johnny was perfectly justified in acting the way he had. Christ, his instincts as a cop are what made me go to him for help in the first place. He just couldn't turn them on and off at will. Rationalizing helped a little bit, but feelings are amazingly resistant to rationalization. Feelings are funny that way.

"There's been a fire in the neighborhood," Johnny interrupted my hurting.

"Just one?"

"Just one that matters to us. Your old doctor's house burned to the ground a few nights ago."

"What?" I rejoined the action. "Korin's house?"

"Potamkin, Korin; same house. Yeah, and the neighbors claim he was planning to go on a long vacation, but none of them could remember to where."

"Convenient fire," I mused.

"Convenient vacation," he added.

"Micki didn't bother to mention either one. I'll have to ask her about them."

"Don't!" MacClough admonished. "Play stupid for now. Let her keep underestimating you. The less she thinks of you, the more likely it is that she'll fuck up."

"You're right," I agreed. "Playing dumb comes pretty easily to me."

He grabbed my neck again. "Klein, your problem isn't stupidity; it's inexperience. And that's a good thing. Look what experience has made out of me. I'm an untrusting, suspicious old prick."

"Well . . . two outta three, maybe. Let go of my neck."

As he did so a more familiar figure appeared at the door of the Kiev Car Service. It was Juri in all his polyester glory, furiously smoking an unfiltered cigarette. He was taller and thinner than he had looked sitting down. Juri was carrying a clip board in one yellow hand and an overstuffed brown envelope in the other.

"Wish me goodnight, MacClough. That handsome fellow there is my assignment for this evening."

"Are you wearing the present I gave you?" He sounded like my mom when she'd ask me if I had my gloves on cold days.

"No, Mom," I giggled, "I returned it and bought an ugly-colored tie instead." I waited a few seconds and then lifted up my trouser leg to reveal the metal and leather. "Look!"

"Good man." Johnny clapped me on the right bicep. "Call me tomorrow."

As Johnny exited my car, Juri entered his. I let the Russian put some space between his '83 Chrysler LeBaron and my faded blue VW. With that patriotic paint job, the Kiev car would be hard to lose as long as daylight held out.

His initial stop was a coffee run. I was fairly desperate for a cup of my own. A sip of celery tonic quieted my desperation. Juri's first few fares were astoundingly routine, never taking us too far out of Brighton Beach.

I followed somebody's grandma to Las Vegas Night at the Shore Haven Jewish Center on 86th Street. After the old lady paid her tab, Juri ferried his empty car over to the Pathmark on Cropsey Avenue. There, he picked up a young black couple with six bags of groceries. Ten minutes later they were dumping their bags onto the pavement at Avenue X and Stillwell, right by the Marlboro Projects. Stillwell Avenue is also covered by a canopy of elevated subway tracks. It's the avenue Gene Hackman chased the train along in "The French Connection."

Over the next hour Juri and I continued to take on uneventful fares. The long hour was profitable for the Russian. For me, it was a waste of fuel. After yet another coffee run, the lanky driver and his stars and stripes Chrysler hit the Belt Parkway going east. Wherever he was headed, he was in no hurry. He stuck to the far right lane and kept a lazy pace at 45 mph. Within twenty minutes all of the Brooklyn exits had been eliminated as possible turn-offs and we moved into Queens. About a football field short of the Van Wyck Expressway-Kennedy Airport off ramp, Juri's right directional popped on. So there was a fifty percent chance I'd be making my second trip to the airport in a week. This time there'd be no headless cargo in my trunk.

Summer nights were busy ones at JFK. The airport's brown-black vapor dome almost glistened in the last gasps of sunset. Turbofans roared in whiny defiance of gravity. Acrid fumes of heated metal and burned kerosene infiltrated my eyes, my nose, and my recollections. When I was a kid, my dad used to drive me out here on Sundays. He'd park on one of the airport border roads at the edge of a runway. When we got out he'd boost me up onto his shoulders and we'd silently tempt fate as descending jets created noisy vacuums just above our hairlines. In following years my friends and I carried on the tradition with the help of beer and acid and teenage bravado. Now, the tradition was just a memory, like most of the delis in Brighton Beach.

When he hit the airport circle road, Juri picked up his pace slightly. I closed the gap between us. With the creeping darkness and the intense traffic I couldn't afford the luxury of a big cushion. As he passed the British Airways terminal, the Russian moved to the far left. I figured he was positioning himself for a pick up at the International Arrivals Building. And when he balked at the turnoff for TWA Domestic, I felt very comfortable with my figuring. I shouldn't have. Juri turned left at TWA International, adding speed as he went. He back-tracked past British Airways and headed for an alternate airport exit which was situated in the cargo area. I mirrored his moves. They were evasive moves, at that. Someone less familiar with the territory would have lost him for sure.

The cargo area was darker, but less congested, than the terminal circle road. I let the gap between our two cars widen again, tucking my bug in behind a lumbering yellow tanker and using it as moving camouflage. Every few seconds I'd inch the VW left, keeping tabs on Mr. Polyester and his tri-colored car. If he'd spotted me over by the passenger terminals, my current absence in his mirrors would help to convince him that I was just a bad memory or that I'd never been there to begin with. My gut feeling was that he hadn't seen me at all and that his evasive maneuvers were sort of preplanned. Tailing my marks without detection is one of the few things I'm pretty competent at.

At a traffic light by the base of an alternate exit ramp, the crafty chauffeur hung a rocket left turn, against red, nearly colliding with an oncoming flatbed truck. The flatbed driver jumped on his brakes with both feet and skidded through the intersection, losing his load in the process. The light went green for me, but a barricade of cardboard garment boxes suggested that I not hit the gas. I got out of my car and picked up Juri's taillights disappearing into the fully fledged night.

The flatbed driver, also out of his vehicle, waved me over to help him assess the damage. I obliged. He was a short, well-muscled white man in his late twenties wearing very faded jeans, a classic white tank top and a look of heart-felt disgust.

"Did ya see 'dat fuckin' hole?" The driver asked, not giving me space to answer. "I'll kill 'dat lanky-assed mothafucka."

"Seemed to be in a hurry," I said. "You gonna need a witness?"

"Nah, but thanks anyway. Union'll cover my butt. It's just sucha hassle, you know?"

"I do."

"You need some duds?" he questioned while checking out some broken boxes. "It's gonna be an insurance job," again not waiting for an answer, "so nobody's gonna lose sleep over a missing piece here and 'dere."

"No thanks, but you go ahead."

"Are you sure? The Port Authority cops are gonna be here soon. Christmas don't come early every year."

"No thanks," I repeated, "but help yourself. Merry Christmas!"

He didn't move. "Nothin' fa' me either, my friend. First thing I learned at Kennedy was to neva' trust an honest man. Too easy for honest men to stick a knife in your back when it suits 'em."

"Solid advice."

Distant wailing sirens were getting louder, closer. Apparently dissappointed by my refusal to partake in the spoils, the flatbed jockey's mood turned sour.

"I'll kill that asshole," he mumbled, referring to Juri.

"Gotta find him first," I put in my two cents.

"No problem," he smiled sardonically. "I see 'dat ugly fuckin' car here two, maybe 'tree times a week. Prick don't lose me so easy. I'm gonna ring 'dat geek's neck."

"You see that red, white, and blue car here three times a week?"

"I just said so, didn't I?"

"You did," I assured him while reaching for my wallet. "I was just making sure. Here's twenty bucks to tell me where it is you usually see the geek and his car."

The flatbed man snapped the Jackson out of my palm in a flash: "Over by El Al Cargo or United Airlines Cargo or outside the Guy R. Brewer Blvd. Exit, where all the freight forwarders are."

"Those three places only?"

"Can't ya count?"

"You made your point. Now what'll it cost me to have you forget about what happened here? What would it take for you to tell the cops you hit your brakes to avoid squashing a small fur bearing animal?"

"Mister," the muscled man shook his head from side to side, "you ain't got 'dat kinda money."

He was right. I didn't. I tried the only thing I could think of on such short notice. I reached down into the broken cartons and pulled out anything my fingers latched onto. Without so much as a peek at what I'd taken, I ambled over to my Volkswagen and threw the uninspected booty into the back seat.

"So much for honest men," I shouted at the trucker.

He surveyed the misplaced cargo with eager eyes. "Why is 'dat jerk so important to ya?"

"Let's just say that he's gonna lead me to the promised land, and he can't do any leading from a hospital bed."

"Go on," he waved at me with both arms, "Moses is forgotten."

I opened my mouth to thank him, but the words would've been wasted. The flatbed driver was too busy snatching up his bounty to pay me any further attention. He knew exactly which boxes to go for, as if they were marked cards in a doctored deck. From where I sat, I could see why he was so hot for the fallen goods. Men's silk shirts and women's silk dresses were being yanked out of the split boxes at superhuman speed. He'd be able to peddle those items around the airport for some high numbers. They wouldn't hurt his wardrobe, either. Just as he finished tucking his stash in the flatbed's cab, the cavalry arrived.

I hit the starter and backed up past an oncoming squad car replete with red lights whirling and sirens screaming. The cops ignored me and I returned the favor. As I pulled away I watched the tank-topped driver's performance. He went through a varied array of histrionics attempting to describe the animal he'd almost crushed. Arms were flailing, heads were shaking, and feet were stomping. I just continued my journey, in reverse.

I had a vague idea where to find United Airlines Cargo and El Al Cargo. Although miles apart, they fell within the confines of the airport. I was less familiar with the freight forwarders' domain. It ran along the far boundaries of the cargo area back to the Belt Parkway and beyond. That's a whole lot of space to cover in one hour. I turned my bug around, finally, and tried El Al first.

No luck waited for me there. I picked up my first strike amongst the squat, drab rows of warehouse buildings that counted El Al Cargo as a paying member. If Juri had been here, he was gone now. If he had yet to arrive, I couldn't afford to hang around. I had places to go, other cargo buildings to see.

Fifteen minutes and three wrong turns later, I was cruising up to the one man guardpost outside of Hangar 8; United Airlines Cargo. A tired old body with yellow-gray hair gave me the automatic wave through. Security at JFK was as tight as ever. I turned left and rolled slowly along the cyclone fence that ran perpendicular to the hangar. About twenty yards short of the corrugated steel structure, I cut the motor and opted for some leg stretching.

Both huge hangar doors were peeled back. The belly of the building was bathed in an eery pink glow. Its guts were stuffed with multi-tiered metal racks, shiny aluminum aircraft containers, oversized wooden vessels, and cardboard crates in every configuration imaginable. Frantic forklifts navigated the maze with the ease only familiarity brings. Mixed in with the freight and forklifts were a few cigarette-smoking, coffee-drinking, blue-uniformed cargo handlers. But no ill-clad Russians that I could see.

Outside the hangar, trucks fell into a serpentine formation waiting to drop and/or pick up a load. With its mission accomplished, one of the vehicles would leave the loading dock. Another would break formation and fill the void. As the night wore on, each lorry would get its chance to sit at the head of the snake. I retreated to my car and put it back into service. I drove a curvy parallel along the body of the beast. Maybe the car service Chrysler was hidden in the serpent's skin. No Juri here, either. Strike two!

I drove up to the guardpost, unhappy at the prospect of having to search uncharted ground. I could look all night and never find Juri. The old body was already waving me out. I ignored the free pass.

"Hey," I called into the little hut, "can I ask you a question?"

"You just did," the yellow-gray head shouted back.

"Another then. Have you seen a red, white and blue Chrysler LeBaron pull in or outta here tonight?" I asked without great expectations. "It's a Kiev Car Serice car. Driver's sorta ugly, smokes Camels, dresses like—"

"Why do you wanna know?" the voice from the hut cut me off.

"Because my wife left something valuable in that car tonight and I mean to collect it." I lied. I was getting good at it.

"Why not call its home base and have the guy bring it in?"

"Sure, warn the guy he's carrying a big ticket item and he'll drop it off somewhere, claim she didn't lose it in his car. Sorry, I can't afford to be that stupid or generous." I sounded properly impatient.

"I see your point," the security man offered, waving an eighteen wheeler past me. "That car you're looking for left here about twenty minutes ago."

"Shit!" I slammed my hand on the steering wheel. As I raised it for a return match, I recalled the last time I'd pulled this stunt. It was out in front of my old doctor's house the day they buried my mother, the day this nightmare began. I put my hand down.

"Relax, son," the yellow-gray head instructed. "I don't know if this'll do any good, but that car's here almost every night. Sometimes the driver's different, but it's a good bet it'll be back tomorrow night between 8:00 and 10:00."

"Thanks. That helps a lot."

I sailed out of the airport to look for a phone and some gasoline. As I prowled along the North Conduit, I smiled to myself, a sick kind of smile. The kind of smile you smile when you find out you've got cancer, but it's in a treatable state. The screaming little boy in back of my brain was telling me we'd made progress tonight. That the ride around JFK was going to be the key to the cure of my disease. The rest of me didn't see it quite that way. The rest of me was just relieved not to have to go searching for Juri in an uncharted area. There was no finding him tonight, but I'd be waiting at Hangar 8 tomorrow. We'd pick up the two strike count from there. I guess this was progress, after a fashion.

As usual, I spilled the last few cents of gas on the floor, but I missed my shoes. I pulled my bug up to the phonebooth and dialed a Brooklyn exchange.

"Micki. It's Dylan. Sorry to call so late."

"I am just glad you called. I've been waiting," she said with a hint of impatience.

"I didn't mean to hold you up, but I got tangled in a job tonight and I'm just untying the last knot now," I explained.

"That's alright, really. Does your work tonight have anything to do with the person who broke into your office?"

"Sort of, I guess. It might." I did my best Jimmy Stewart. "That's not what I called about, though. I'd like to see you again."

"I don't sit by the phone waiting for most men to call. Would you like to come here tonight?" she purred.

"I'd more than like it, but I'm out here at the airport and—"

"Kennedy Airport?" she questioned.

"Yes, as a matter of fact. Why do you ask?"

"Like my father, I can be uncontrollably curious."

"That's a reasonable answer." I coughed and continued: "Like I was saying, I'm way out here and I've got to head back home tonight. How about meeting me halfway?"

"Where?"

"The Little Athens Diner on Flatbush Avenue. Do you know it?"

"I'll find it," Micki assured me. "When will you be there?"

"About twenty minutes, half an hour maybe. It'll take you a little longer."

"Hold a table for us."

"No problem. See you soon."

"So long, Dylan."

When that conversation ended, another one began. It was between me and that pesky internal voice of mine. It wondered why Micki Korin was so interested in airports. I told it I was wondering the same thing. I smiled again. Maybe the airport was the key. Maybe I was desperate for it to be. Maybe I was smiling at the vision of certain lips.

Spaghetti Curls

Except for the freshly painted stripes in the parking lot, the Little Athens Diner hadn't changed much in the last twenty years. Its chromium-bordered pane glass, beige-pebbled and stucco exterior stood as a monument to tasteless architecture. Funny though, no one ever bothered much about its external aesthetics as long as the strawberry cheesecake was the best in Brooklyn.

The banana-nosed host pulled a solitary menu out of its box when I came through the door. I told him there'd be two of us eventually, but that I'd like to get started. He cloned the solitary menu and sat me at a blue vinyl and formica booth with a clear view of the entrance. Banana Nose asked me if I would like some coffee to begin with. I said I would. He barked out some angry Greek at an unseen waitress and turned back in my direction to express his desire that I enjoy my meal. I thanked him.

Even now the joint was crowded with fat cops eating fruit Danish, disco misfits molesting Deluxe Athens Burgers, and wide-eyed truckers redefining the "bottomless" coffee cup. I knew what I was going to order when Micki showed, but I read through the menu to pass the time. The damn thing weighed a few ounces more than the Sunday Times and was just a couple pages short of *War and Peace*. I think Tolstoy made for easier reading.

The smack and rattle of cheap Chinaware against formica interrupted my studies.

"Milk's on the table. What can I get for you?" a testy voice asked.

"Nothing. I'm waiting for someone to join me," I said, looking up.

She was gone before I could focus. I guess she wasn't in the mood for idle chatter. That made two of us. I sipped at the coffee like it was hundred year old port, sucking air through my pursed lips and cascading the brown liquid over my rolling tongue. Despite my ritualized drinking, the coffee tasted burnt and older than fine port. I emptied my cup.

An ebony-maned woman stood just inside the doorway. Her head swivelled back and forth across the diner's expanse. Banana Nose hooked her elbow and pointed her my way. He made eye contact with me and smiled his approval behind her. If he didn't approve, I guess he'd make her sit at a separate table.

Micki flowed toward me under a loose-fitting, tan suede dress tied in at the waist by a wide leather belt. The belt sported artistic highlights of turquoise and silver. Only delicate patches of her brown legs could be seen peeking out between a low, sweeping hemline and the tops of her dusty chestnut, cowboy boots. The backwards bounce of her black hair and the fluid waving of suede lent her the illusion of walking against a passionate wind. I knew I shouldn't be so entranced by her, but it's difficult to deny a woman that walks in her own breeze.

She passed her side of the table, put both knees on the blue vinyl bench, and put her mouth softly onto mine. For that second my life's focus was confined to the anxious taste of Micki Korin's mouth and the perfume of her breath. My focus changed quickly when she removed her lips from mine and pressed the side of my face against the hot, bare skin above her breasts. Her arms encircled my head from the outside and the floral scent of her cologne, mixing with the moist salt air of her skin, captured me from within. I was getting lost somewhere in between the beats of her heart when the gentle cage around my head was removed.

I opened my mouth to speak, but Micki put her right middle and index fingers across my lips and shook her head; "No!" We weren't to speak. Most of me was in no mood to argue. She brushed the back of her hands across my beard-covered cheeks and dismounted the blue plastic bench. In anticipation of her next move, I dug three bucks out of my wallet and tossed them on the table. Micki shook out her hair and made for the exit. I trailed in the wash of her wind. Banana Nose followed us out with jealous eyes and a frozen grin that looked as if it had been put there surgically.

Outside, a breeze, generated by more than the gait of a beautiful woman, blew back my hair. She waited for me at the bottom of the slate steps, her suede skirt snapping like a sail in a squall. When I reached her, I trapped her left hand behind her, bent back her neck and pressed every part of me against her that I could manage, but no part harder than my mouth. I rubbed my tongue along the ridges of her teeth and thrust it back and forth. Micki formed her lips around my tongue, paring the juices off of it into her mouth. I withdrew my tongue and closed my teeth across her lips drawing blood, a sigh, and a shudder. With that I could feel fluid easing from the tip of my penis. Nothing! Nothing is more exciting than a woman's sigh.

Her right hand found mine and placed a set of keys against my palm. She sculpted my fingers around the keys and started off into the lot. We stopped by a maroon BMW, David Ben Avraam's BMW. My hormones instructed me that chivalry might well be dead, but that resurrection had its place. I opened her door and closed it behind her. Once inside, I buried the keys in the ignition. Micki sat facing me, sort of, with her back against the door. I ran my palm along the interior of her right thigh until my fingers encountered wet cotton beneath the suede. At that point there seemed to be a direct link between the nerve endings at my finger tip and those that controlled my erection.

As I moved my finger underneath the elastic rim of her panties to touch the moist blossom of her hair, she shuddered again.

"Not here, Dylan," she whispered as I drew closer to the edge of her pleasure. "Yes, Dylan, but not here."

Although she'd broken the silence, I didn't take it as a cue to engage her as to where she might prefer to have me. I drove to Plum Beach, fast. Between shifts, I reached under Micki's dress to stroke her. For a moment she slid back and forth along the seat with the rhythm of my fingers. Then she locked onto my right wrist with both hands, bringing her face forward and down to brush against my imprisoned arm. She relaxed her grip and ran her tongue over my forearm toward my hand, hesitating occasionally to grab some skin and hair between her white teeth. Micki's fingers cupped mine closed, only to uncurl my forefinger with her tongue. She encircled the straightened finger with her lips and rode it up and down, swallowing the flavor of her own moisture. A drop of burning saliva slipped onto my knuckles. By then, I'd lost track of how many shifts I'd missed.

Life Goes Sleeping

I never heard the snap, but I could feel the pressure release around my waist. The zipper seemed to open of its own accord. She worked her right hand under the loosened trousers, pressing her palm tightly against my abdomen to defeat the border of my underwear. Her thumb spread the beads of fluid at my penis tip along the blood-gorged skin. She withdrew my finger from her mouth and her hand from my pelvis. I took my eyes off the white lines to watch the brown skinned woman lick my semen off her thumb. She shook. I shuddered. The passenger side tires brushed against the curb.

Her hand found me again, her fingers conforming to the hardened shape. With increasing speed and friction, Micki moved her hand from base to tip and back again. My back, forehead, and palms were awash with the sweet sweat of inevitable orgasm. My toes curled inside my shoes as my quads flexed into happy numbness. Above all, I could feel my heart trying to beat its way through the chest wall.

She stopped, suddenly. I mean, her hand stopped. She bit my tightened neck hard, painfully hard, joyously hard, then dropped her head into my lap. Micki's prominent lips folded around me with gentle authority, as her hand had previously. Her damp, abrasive tongue applied varying degrees of pressure—all of them agreeable—as she plunged toward the road surface and then back towards the sky. More friction-heated saliva poured onto my skin, running through a thatch of coarse brown hair and into the natural channels between my legs and torso.

Sensing my physical impatience, Micki made a tight circle at the trunk of my erection with her well-lubricated thumb and forefinger. Her sighs grew in frequency now, like a Geiger counter clicking as it measured a developing critical mass. She shook, breaking the circle. I obliged. The reflexive tensing of my muscles forced my thighs into the steering wheel, carrying Micki's head with them. The horn blared our arrival with my right foot kicking hopelessly at the gas pedal. For seconds after the flood, the barriers between Micki and me and my liquid surrender, vanished. The brief, unique oneness of the moment floored me.

Relaxing slightly, I could make out the exaggerated gulping sounds of a woman struggling with her own excitement and the residue of mine. I dug my hand into her wedged hair and made spaghetti curls with a fork of my fingers. Driving became instinctive again and the oneness was forgotten. It's the nature of the beast. I exited the parkway into the lot at Plum Beach.

"We're here," I announced, for the lack of anything else to say.

As Micki raised her head, I met it halfway with mine and ran my lips across her off-guard mouth. I kept my eyes opened and watched the wide surprise in hers. She fell back against the passenger door, turning her eyes to the baby-sized waves.

"Why did you do that, Dylan?" Micki asked, still looking off in the direction of the British Isles.

"Do what, exactly?"

"Kiss me then."

"Because I wanted to. I more than enjoy doing it and kissing has been known to lead to other interesting things."

"Yes," she changed her gaze back to me," but why after . . . ?"

"I gotcha," I assured her. "I kissed you then for the very reason you're surprised enough to ask. I kissed you to let you know how amazingly good you felt and that I'm not just gonna roll over and play dead because I've been satisfied."

"Is that how you operate?" she questioned in a tone that suggested sarcasm the way raised bridges suggest stopping.

"If you're asking, have I done it before? I have. I've tasted myself on other women's lips, but it's not done out of habit like brushing my teeth in the morning," I threw up my hands in disgust. "I did it because I wanted to, goddamit!"

By the last syllable of my disgust, Micki Korin was laughing with tears pouring down her brown cheeks. "Thank you, Dylan," she managed to chortle. "It was a lovely kiss." The confusion on my face added fuel to the fire.

I decided to scan the shoreline for enemy subs. None surfaced in the short time I watched. I also took the opportunity to readjust my clothing.

"Please forgive me," Micki implored, wiping the wet streaks from her face with the back of her hands. "I needed to laugh today very much."

"Always glad to help a damsel in distress," I bowed, "but why the need?"

"My father's insurance company contacted me today. Apparently, there's been a fire in his house and they cannot get in touch with him. Do you have any idea where he could be?"

I knew what he was: dead. Where he was was another story. In any case, I lied. "No. I haven't got a clue. Does he often disappear like this?"

"Not often," she answered calmly, "but sometimes. He is such a child."

"Wanna drive by there? We're pretty close?"

"No, Dylan," she leaned over and kissed my cheek, "not tonight. Let's go back to the diner. I'm starving."

The turn of the ignition key told her I was hungry, too. It didn't lie. I was also pleased she'd mentioned the fire in Brighton without any prompting from yours truly. Maybe she was who she claimed. Maybe. Christ, I could do with one less mess to solve. But if she were Korin's daughter, her father was extremely dead and she didn't have a hint. She'd find out eventually. She'd live. I did, after all.

"You're sad, Dylan."

"A little. Just thinking about my Mom. I'll be alright."

"I have no doubt."

At least one of us was sure.

I parked the borrowed BMW a spot away from my dormant Volkswagen. Back inside, Banana Nose gave us an all-knowing once-over, two menus and a shake of his perpetually smiling head.

"Your usual table, monsieur?" our host asked with an unexpected sense of humor.

"Naturally," I responded, sounding hurt that he'd have to ask.

"This way," he swept his arm toward our booth.

"Pardon me," Micki broke in, "which way to the lady's room?"

When the host finished his verbal road map, Micki excused herself and signaled that she'd meet me at the booth. Banana Nose escorted me to my seat.

"The girl is Greek?" he asked.

"Russian."

"Sounds Russian. Looks Greek." He walked back to the entrance shaking his head.

He had a point, but I brushed it off. She didn't look very Russian to me, either. Whatever that means.

I didn't bother with the menu again. I spent my waiting time eyeing the counter fridge where a piece of strawberry cheesecake had my name on it. A false-blond waitress delivered two cups of coffee without the asking. I gave a glance at the host and he nodded his head. The coffee was on him. I nodded my thanks.

"Milk's—" she started.

"—on the table," I finished. "Two pieces of strawberry cheesecake, please."

One woman replaced the other. The false blond moved on and Micki moved in. This time she sat across from me.

"The coffee's on your friend up front. I ordered you a piece of cheesecake. It's the best in Brooklyn."

"That's fine, Dylan," she held my hand across the table, "you're a lovely man. You excite me."

I could feel the blush rising onto what showed of my cheeks as I tried to respond. This time she put her fingers across her replenished lips, telling me not to bother. The jumbled words gladly jumped back down my throat. The rouge on my cheeks remained. Our cheesecake arrived on the arm of the wanna-be blond.

"Enjoy!" the waitress offered with all the sincerity of a politician making a concession speech.

"Thanks!" My appreciation was equally sincere.

The cake and coffee made fast exits from the table. The losing candidate returned to fill our cups.

"The cake was wonderful," Micki commented to the coffee pourer.

"Good. I'll go call the baker up and tell him you think so." The waitress went away.

"Is the help so friendly in the Soviet Union?"

"Don't be so rough on her," Micki scolded. "Have you ever waited on tables?"

"No."

"It is a job that can make you hate people. Probably tonight that woman got a table full of people that ordered food that came out too hot, too cold, too rare, too well done. There wasn't enough butter. There was too much. Their table was too close to the smoking section and their seats were too far away from the air-conditioning vents. Their Cokes tasted like root beer and the root beer wasn't full enough of syrup. After they finished driving the poor waitress ragged with complaints that were beyond her control, the customers probably left her two dollars on a thirty dollar bill and thought they were overtipping."

"I give up." I flew my white napkin as a flag of surrender. "I take it you've waited on tables."

"For two years, at a restaurant in Brighton."

"While your dad was driving a cab?"

"Yes," she sipped some coffee. "Coming to a new country, even one you want to come to, can be shattering. I imagine it's difficult enough for those who leave poverty, but in some ways I believe it can be more of a test for those who leave good jobs and status behind. Climbing a mountain the second time is less enjoyable and more dangerous."

"I see your point. I'm glad you made it back up." I found her hand again and squeezed it.

"What were you doing out at the airport, Dylan?" Micki asked as if she were asking the time.

"Work, following somebody." I gave her the time.

"Was it fruitful?"

"Yes and no," I told the truth, "mostly no," I lied. "I lost him. I'd tell you about it, but—"

"Professional ethics," she cut me off, "I totally understand."

"I appreciate the sentiment, but that's not it. Most of my work is pretty boring and the job I'm on fits that description nicely." Maybe sometime I could tell her the whole ugly truth. Maybe, but not now. "Do you know a friend of your father's named Brodsky?"

"You mentioned him the first time we spoke on the phone," Micki stated, but didn't answer the question. "Why do you ask?"

I should've anticipated her turning the question around, but didn't. Lately, there were a lot of things I should've done, but didn't do. What was one more added to the list? I took a long slug of coffee, buying time to formulate a reasonable answer.

"The last time I spoke to your dad, he mentioned a man named Brodsky who might be in need of my limited talents. Now that your father's gone on vacation without leaving word, I've got no way to contact this Brodsky."

"Sorry, Dylan, I can't recall my father ever mentioning such a man. However, my father and I are not so close that I would know all of his acquaintances. Maybe this man Brodsky is my father's client."

"I suppose that's likely," I said, scratching at my beard.

"In any case," she went on, "if this man needed your services, I'm certain my father would have given him your business card or number."

"You're right," I agreed, "but I'd hate to lose a potential client. My business is so up and down. Nevermind."

"As you wish."

"Can I see you tomorrow night, late?"

"I would've been hurt if you left without asking."

"And I'll leave hurt if the answer is no."

"Then you won't leave hurt," she smiled. "The cheesecake was marvelous, but would you come to my apartment?"

"Said the spider to the fly."

"Dylan!"

"All flies should be so fortunate."

"All spiders as well. What time is 'late'?"

"I don't know yet. Midnight, maybe. I'll try and call," was the best I could offer.

"If you can't reach me at home, leave a message on my machine."

I stood up and walked to her side of the table. Mimicking her earlier entrance, I put my two knees up on the blue vinyl and kissed her mouth. I moved my lips onto her closed eyelids, then to her ear.

"Goodnight, Micki," I whispered and walked away, throwing a five dollar bill onto the table.

Up front, Banana Nose and I worked out what the bill would be and I paid it. He assured me he'd let the waitress know the tab was covered. I stepped through the doors not looking back. I'd look tomorrow.

I almost didn't notice the hole in the driver's side window of my car, almost. It wasn't until my behind communicated its discomfort about having to sit on shards of glass, that I bothered to check for possible sources. The hole was small and neat and spread out into a crystal spider's web. I guessed that the damage was done by a bullet. I wasn't familiar enough with bullets to be sure. I didn't want to be. And for the first time since I strapped it to my ankle, I was conscious of MacClough's spare .38.

I looked for an exit wound on the passenger's side window, but no spider had visited there. The rest of the car glass was intact as well. Darkness prevented me from having a good view of where the bullet head might've buried itself, so I let my fingers do the hunting. They found something right off, but it wasn't a spent bullet. Wedged between the passenger bucket and door my fingers found a piece of paper. There was writing on it, but reading in the lack of light was an impossibility. I thought about using my dome light and recalled it hadn't worked in ten years. Besides, I had to split. Micki might come strolling into the lot any second and I didn't want to have to explain a bullet hole in my window. I drove down Flatbush towards Rockaway.

The overlit parking lot of a driving range seemed like a good place to do some reading. I got out of the VW and dusted the glass particles off its seat and mine. The paper in my hand was identical to the raspberry stained sheet I'd found by Alexander Korin's body. Only the red blotch was missing. In the light, what had appeared to be human writing in the darkened diner's lot turned out to be computer-generated laser lettering:

"Brodsky is close. You are close to Brodsky.
Where is Korin?
You will be behind the wheel next time.
Where is Korin?
I'll ring you up shortly.
     Cheers for now."

He even wrote in a corny English accent, but there was nothing corny about bullet holes where my head might've been. I folded the note into my wallet and started taping up the spider's web. I tried not to think about what the message meant, but sometimes trying just doesn't count for much. It would be a long ride back to Sound Hill.

Split-Brain Russet Potato

"At least if they send ya packing now, you'll die a happy camper," MacClough shouted back at me from inside the Volkswagen.

"It'll take more than a rolling blow job to make me a happy man," I spoke to his feet.

"You're too damned hard to please, Klein. Just hearing you tell the story gives me goose bumps."

"What?" I yelled in after him. "Stop talking to the door panel."

"I said," Johnny turned his head over a shoulder to look at me, "that hearing the story gives me chills. Nothing like that's happened to me since . . ." he drifted off, turning onto his back to lean against the door.

"Since when?"

"Since the wife of a mob hit victim decided to express her grief to me in a novel way. Her husband's Eldorado's parked in the driveway. He's in the trunk trussed up like a rump roast with a few vents in his skull that weren't part of God's original design. The homicide detectives have already grilled the wife about the technical aspects of the hit: When did you hear the car pull in? Stuff like that. I'm there to question her about his connections."

"Nice time to be questioning the widow," I said sarcastically.

"Not nice, but effective" the ex-detective shot back. "Grieving breaks barriers. A little crocodile sympathy at a weak moment'll net you more fish than fifty wiretaps or subpoenas."

"Yeah, so with the widow, what'd'ya find at the end of your hook?"

"Her lips," he flipped over and started to shout the rest of the details to me. "She told me she was feeling worn out by all the questions and all the cops flooding the house. She tells me she'll talk to me if we can go upstairs, alone, where it's quiet. I'm agreeable and . . . Wait! Here's the slug," Johnny popped out of the VW holding a tiny lump of gray metal between his right thumb and forefinger. "Looks like a .22; catch!"

I bobbled the misshapen metal a few times before making a shoestring grab: "What'm I supposed to do with this?" I asked about the bullet.

"Take it to the dentist and tell him one of your fillings fell out. I don't know," MacClough exclaimed, facing his palms to heaven. "Maybe you should give it back to me so we can compare it to the one they dig outta your carcass."

"That's a pleasant idea." I shoved the metal seed into a pants pocket. "What happened with the stiff's wife?"

"Another time. What's tonight's plan?" he asked, unsmilingly.

"Simple. I'll wait for Juri at Hangar 8 and follow his ass until he takes me somewhere that means something."

"How specific of you," Johnny spit out in a voice like a smack across the face. "Wake up, Klein. What if he takes you on thirty more trips to Pathmark? What if he never shows up at all?"

"He'll show," I slapped back, "he'll show."

"Why the sudden confidence?"

"The note that accompanied the bullet," I answered, already pulling the folded paper from my wallet. "Read away."

"Did you notice anybody following you?"

"I was a little too busy being a tail to see if I had one of my own. Besides, what would it matter if I noticed or not? The note proves I was followed. It also proves Korin pointed me in the right direction before his barber took too many inches off the top. The Kiev Car Service is gonna lead me to Brodsky. I can taste it."

"Well, if it tastes like shit, don't swallow," MacClough cautioned.

"Why all the sunshine, Johnny?" I asked sardonically.

"Something doesn't feel right. It's too easy."

"But you're the one who's tryin' to teach me to trust the obvious. I'm just putting the obvious pieces together. That's all."

"Yeah, and they fit too neatly." He shook his head, "Christ, Klein, the note tells you you're close to Brodsky. And if the author of that note can judge that you're close, then he must also know where Brodsky is. Why doesn't he just call you up and give you Brodsky's address and phone number. It would certainly speed up the process. You could go bear witness that you saw Korin killed and that you drove his headless body around for a few hours while it ripened. With that message delivered, you could live happily ever after.

"No. Something smells and it ain't Coney Island whitefish. I still can't figure out why the killer and the victim want or wanted you to find the same man. And where does the daughter fit in? What'd she just fall outta the sky onto your dick? Why's she so interested in the airport? Did you happen to ask her what insurance company carried her father's fire and theft policy? Of course not," he answered his own question. "No, you wouldn't. You were too busy, weren't you?"

"Hey, MacClough," I stopped him, "enough already. What gives?"

"There's too much goin' on for too little return."

"What?"

"We got a decapitation, a torture murder, bumps on the head, breaking and entering, fake cops, burnt down buildings, bullet holes, blow jobs, Nazi photos, threats, intimidation, and mysterious relatives. For what? All so you can tell some survivor from World War II that the guy who puked on him back in the Ukraine is now a headless corpse swimming up the Hudson, or buried in the Jersey meadowlands somewhere? Come on, get real here. There's nothing obvious about the whole routine, except that there's a bunch of shit we don't know about."

"You're right," I admitted, crestfallen. "When did you arrive at this conclusion?"

"Now, but I started thinkin' about it last night watchin' the Mets."

"Did they win?"

"Yeah, beat the Astros 5 to 1. And that was just it. Houston kept gettin' men on, stealin', hittin' and runnin', sacrificin'. You know, real carpet baseball. Well, it's exciting to watch, but they're not scorin' any runs. There's a ton of activity with nothin' to show for it. Started me thinkin' about you and this mess," he waved the note at me symbolically.

"So what am I gonna do now?"

"Be at Hangar 8 tonight and follow that ugly, yellow-toothed Russian geek. Who knows, maybe we can score a few more runs than we're supposed to. We just have to start stealin' the other team's signs."

"Great, coach, but who's on the other team?"

"Everybody, Klein. Everybody except me and you."

"Thanks, Johnny. That answer really clarifies things for me," I said with a smirk. "And since you're into clearing things up, why do you imagine the author of that note keeps asking where Korin is?"

"It's a reminder and a warning. He's telling you to be sure to deliver the message to Brodsky with all the gory details included. He's also lettin' you know: the same can happen to you."

"Talk about beating a dead horse. This clown must think I have the short-term memory of a split-brain russet potato. Why doesn't he just tie a ribbon around my finger to remind me?" I dangled my left middle finger out in front of my face.

"Maybe that's next," MacClough squeezed the back of my neck. "Let's go have a beer."

"On the house?"

"Fuck, no. My brother's been givin' away the store. Anyway, the Irish in me says I gotta start chargin' you for some of my services."

"Hey," I smacked his hand away from my neck, "the other night you poo-poohed your Irishness. You were just another schmuck from Sheepshead Bay."

"I am, and proud of it, but you're still payin' for the beer."

Caterpillars

My cheap timepiece spit out the seconds, launching them at my middle ear and on into infinity. Each tick was arrogant and precise and loud enough to be heard above the aircraft cries of hot spinning metal. It was a bad night for waiting. Caterpillars of sweat crawled over my brow and into my eyes, burning and tearing at them. I fought to flick them off with my fingers and the backs of my forearms, but the effort just helped them breed. Even the friendly perfume of spent jet fuel was no comfort. The brown airport atmosphere exploded in my lungs.

Maybe some night I wouldn't have to sit outside lonely buildings waiting for donkeys to pin tails on. Not tonight. It's never tonight. Tonight I'd wait for the donkey at the edges of Hangar 8. And tonight, just waiting would come at a price. The security guard recognized me.

"I thought I'd see you here this evening," the wilted little man remarked with an unpleasant 'I-told-you-so' smile. "You departed a touch too quickly for my liking last night. So long wishes and heartfelt thank yous don't cut the mustard with me, sonny. No sir. I could lose my job for passing out tidbits like I handed you yesterday. Information ain't like the air."

"Yeah, it's not brown."

"That's not what I had in mind, sonny," his yellow-gray head shook east to west and back again. "That's not what I meant at all."

"What color did you have in mind?" I asked with false interest.

"Green."

"Christ, no wonder you're spending your retirement working in that upright coffin. You sure take the long way around when it comes to extortion."

"Extortion!" he practically keeled over with righteous indignation. "Who said anything about extortion?"

"I did. Relax. What's a box seat behind home plate gonna cost me?"

"The seat's for free," the indignation, righteous or otherwise, vanished. "You're paying to keep my mouth shut. I could educate that friend you're waiting for. The one with the funny painted car. Maybe he'd be interested to know you're here."

"Maybe." I rolled two tens up into a ball and threw it at the small-time blackmailer. He went for the bundle of green paper like a trained dolphin jumping for fish. "That'll have to do. I've decided to sit in the cheap seats and sneak down."

He didn't seem to hear me. And I didn't seem to care. I found a particularly dark spot along the fence.

That was a half hour ago. The catepillars had calmed a bit and the ticking had spit its way into the background. The Russian had failed to show so far, but that was less than tragic. He still had almost two hours to make a liar of the little man in the security hut. I passed the time by running a few more micrometers off my one cassette tape. The Mets game wasn't on just yet. The pick up and delivery line outside the hangar was short and straight. There'd be no snake-like folds to hide in tonight.

The tri-colored car rolled up to the security coffin with two out in the bottom of the second and no score. I snapped the game off, adjusting my rearview mirror for a better look. I couldn't tell who was driving, but the shape behind the wheel seemed to be a familiar one. And when the Chrysler passed by my position, I recognized the polyester prince at the controls. Another peek in my rearview showed me the security guard's silhouette giving me the thumbs up. I returned the gesture by putting a finger up to the mirror. The finger wasn't my thumb.

Juri must've been a big man on campus. He pulled his hack right up to a side entrance, got out of the car, and marched his skinny self into the hangar. No waiting in lines for Juri. I wondered if he got into clubs in the city with similar ease. He went in empty handed, but exited in a different state of being. The Camel smoker came out with a canvas pouch tucked under his right arm and what looked to be an air waybill in his left hand. He tossed the pouch unceremoniously through the rolled-down window of the Chrysler and folded the waybill into his back pocket. He put match to tobacco, ass to seat, and car in drive. As one half of the Kiev Car Service fleet flew by the carelessly waving arm of security, I pinned a tail on the donkey.

Apparently, we were in no rush to get where we were going. We made a lot of slow, sweeping right turns to ease ourselves back into the heart of the cargo area. The red, white, and blue car's lethargic pace suggested Valium in the gas tank or in the driver. I wished they'd saved some for me. The lazy tempo forced me to operate my Volkswagen just above stall speed in order to keep a safe distance. A few more minutes at this rate and I'd forget where third gear was. Juri made sure I wouldn't forget.

The Russian hit his gas pedal so hard I was surprised his foot didn't come through the floorboard. I couldn't keep up as he weaved the boxy Chrysler in and out of the available traffic. The gap between his taillights and my front bumper grew with each turn of the tires. I stopped shadow weaving and let him turn left to disappear into the night. I recognized the squat, drab surrounding buildings and had a pretty good notion of where Juri was headed. I set a steady course for EL AL Cargo.

Fuck me and my notions. He wasn't there, not that I could see, anyway. The truck lines were short here, too, and the boulevard was wide and straight, giving me a clear view of all traffic in both directions. The caterpillars of sweat came out to play. They were angry now and crawled over me with a vengeance. I didn't try to fight them. I surrendered. Folding my arms across the steering wheel, I laid down my head.

I heard something; a too familiar sound, a sound I'd listened to recently. Someone was pounding on the steering wheel with a bruised fist, then two fists. Yes someone was really losing it, flipping out from all the dead ends and frustration. And since I was alone, it had to be me.

"Hey," a single syllable and a rough hand shook my shoulder, "I got 100% silk shirts and dresses at off-the-truck prices."

Recognizing the salesman's voice and product line, I wiped my eyes with my short sleeves and looked at the speaker: "Sorry, friend, I picked up some similar items just last night." I reached into the back seat and fished out a forgotten cut of silk.

"You're de guy from last night. *Ho-lee* shit!" the flatbed driver exclaimed. "You okay? You don't look good."

Life Goes Sleeping 139

"I don't feel good and thanks for noticing. How's the rag trade these days?" I asked, referring to his arm-full of silk.

"Rag trade?" the well muscled man repeated, momentarily perplexed. "Oh," the light of understanding lit up his face, "da clothes. Yeah, I'm doin' real good. My new bowlin' ball's already on order and my wife's gonna get dat anniversary band she's been buggin' me for."

"That should make her happy." I smiled an empty smile.

"For about a week." He wasn't smiling at all. "Did Moses lead ya to de Promised Land yet?" the tank-topped driver quickly changed subjects and asked about Juri.

"Forget finding the Promised Land," I shouted with rising anger. "I can't even find Moses.

"Yeah, den who's dat parked over dere, Ghandi?"

I followed the silk salesman's point past his fingertips, across the road and onto a Chrysler with a patriotic paint job. Clouds of cigarette smoke billowed out of the driver's side window. My notion had some merit after all.

The Kiev car was second in line behind a black and yellow Hertz truck carrying a twenty foot box. I guess Juri didn't have as much pull with the doorman at El Al. He was forced to wait his turn like every other airport stiff.

"Take it light," the flatbed driver slapped me on the shoulder. "I gotta split. Good luck crossin' the Red Sea."

"Thanks. Good luck with the new ball and the wife."

He fed himself into the cab of his truck leg by leg and rode off to deliver his load and push his Oriental wares. Calmer now, I pulled the bits of me I could gather back together and studied the scene. I didn't dare put the ballgame back on. If the Mets were losing, it might set off another steering wheel abuse jag. One every twenty years was about my limit. A good man knows his limits.

The bumblebee-colored truck backed into the dock at 9:00, dropped off its business, and was gone by the quarter hour. The yellow-toothed Russian let his car stay put while he carried his freight to the export dock. That freight seemed to be the same gray pouch he'd just taken delivery of over at United, though the thirty yards between us made positive identification an impossibility. Attached to the pouch was a white, numbered sticker and some fresh documentation.

Juri hopped up onto the dock with unexpected ease and grace. He was met by a bored-looking man in blue overalls. The Russian gazelle nonchalantly flipped the gray sack to the bored, blue man. That maneuver proved Juri wasn't shipping eggs or nitroglycerin. The cargo agent thumbed through the paperwork, caressed the pouch as if he were inspecting a cantaloupe, flashed a Mona Lisa smile at Juri, scribbled something on the attached documents, and ripped off a few copies. The agent handed the delivery boy one of the copies as a receipt. Juri buried the paper in his back pocket as he'd done at Hangar 8.

The Russian jumped from the dock, landing with the same surprising facility with which he had ascended. A filterless cigarette appeared just under his dirty mustache. I felt bad for the cigarette having to get so close to that geek's mouth.

He drove away and I let him. I wouldn't follow. I wasn't going to fall victim, again, to his pre-planned driving trickery. No. I would stay and gamble. I gave myself two minutes. Two minutes to show-time. I counted one hundred and twenty arrogant seconds with my cheap Swiss watch.

As the curtain rose on Act II, I revved up the VW and shot across the cargo road. A few feet short of the vacant export dock, I hammered my brakes and spun the old car to a stop. I flew out of the bug and stomped around like a professional wrestler with terminal jock itch: "Fuck! Shit!" A small crowd of blue uniforms gathered on the dock landing. Super, an audience. I'd keep this part of the show going until the agent who'd taken delivery of Juri's package joined the gallery. Hopefully, that would be soon. They take security seriously at El Al, so I couldn't drag out the madman routine much longer. Finally, he stepped up for a peek at the freakshow.

"Did some asshole car service driver drop off a gray document pouch yet?" I asked no one in particular. Before anyone could answer, I vaulted myself onto the dock with far less aplomb than the Russian.

"About five minutes ago," the bored agent offered. "What about it?"

"Goddamit! What a schmuck that Juri is." I used the Russian's name to see if the agent recognized it. If he knew Juri by name, it would lend credence to the rest of my story.

"Calm down, mister," he warned in a strong, even voice. Nothing on his face or in his manner told me whether or not he knew Juri. "What about the package?"

"I'm sorry," I toned down so the crowd would disperse. "I think it's the wrong package." And with that most of the onlookers drifted off. No more excitement, just another misdelivery.

"Who says? We never had problems with that guy before."

So he knew Juri. If not by name, then by face.

"Name's Klein, Dylan Klein," I reported, handing him one of my cards with an insurance company's logo on it. Sometimes in my line of work you need cards like that. "I work for Empire Interstate Mutual."

"Card tells me that." He was unimpressed.

"Anyway, we had some documents and computer software shipped to us via United domestic. Sometimes we use car services to do our pickups. It's a lot cheaper than using messengers or truckers. One of the services we use is Kiev, but not after tonight," I started raising my voice again.

"Please, mister, sometime this century. It may not look like it, but I got work to do."

"Sorry," again. "He picked up two packages at United, similar packages, both from the West coast. When we called to check if the pickup was done and if the goods were on their way to us, well . . ."

"I'm waiting for the gag line."

"We think he delivered the wrong package. That's it in a nutshell. So before you ship it to Tel Aviv, I'd like to take a look at the pouch." I crossed my fingers and prayed. Something else I hadn't done in years.

"No can do." He stated without hesitation.

"Wait a second. I think you misunderstood. I don't need to look inside the pouch. I just need to look at it. Our pouches are coded so we can recognize them as geniune. You know, sorta like the red fibers in American money."

"Tell me the code and I'll check for you."

"No can do," I gave his own words back to him. "That'd be tellin' and tellin' would mean losing my job. Come on, I'm only gonna look at it for ten seconds. You can stand here and watch me."

"Christ, if it'll get you outta my hair." For the first time all night, a hint of life showed on his stoic face. "Wait here." He walked toward the back of the warehouse, vanishing behind cardboard foothills of containerized freight.

The gamble was working, but it had been a blind bet. I didn't know what the payoff would be, if any. Maybe the air waybill, or the pouch markings would tell me something, anything. Maybe this blind bet was a dead end. I'd see soon enough.

"Catch!" the agent tossed the pouch at me. "You got you're ten seconds."

I gave the body of the pouch a cursory inspection. The white label told me the contents, whatever they were, were headed to London. I didn't bother with the shipper and consignee labels. I'd get that info off the air waybill.

"Time's up," he goaded.

"Are you always so literal? I'll be with you in a minute," I said in an appropriately annoyed voice.

"Sixty seconds and counting. One, two, three . . ."

The consignee was Edward Lugton, 4 Kimberly Close, Langley, Sl 37R4, England, U.K. That meant nothing to me. The shipper was Vivien Heiden, 410 Sheridan Ave, Palo Alto, CA 94306 U.S.A. That meant even less. The exporting agent was Blue Sabre Worldwide, Inc., 182-13, 182 Rd., Jamaica, N.Y. 11434, U.S.A. The issuing agent, the person who prepared the document was listed as David Ben Avraam. The owner of a certain maroon BMW. That meant something.

"Is it yours?"

I was numb. I couldn't answer.

"Klein, is the package yours?"

"Mine? No, it's not mine. I'll have to apologize to Juri. Here," I handed the gray pouch back to the bored blue man. "Thanks for the help."

"Are you alright? You're white as a sheet."

"Everybody keeps asking me that," I mumbled to myself.

"What?"

"Yeah, I'm fine."

"Well, if you're fine, get your fucking car outta the way and stop bothering me."

I did as he requested, taking a short leap off the dock and onto the pavement. My right ankle barked at me for making a distracted landing. That was nothing new. My right ankle hadn't ever forgiven me for a lifetime of schoolyard basketball in subfreezing weather. Fuck my right ankle and the phony Micki Korin.

Philosophy Tree

The sign was backlit plastic with red lettering against a rectangular field of glowing flourescent white. Each plastic letter was skewered on the curved blade of an equally plastic broad blue sword. Beneath the shish kebabed logo, the company's motto appeared in italicized blue lettering surrounded by plastic quotation marks: *"Worldwide and Worldly-wise."*

Parked on the silent, black street, just below the Blue Sabre sign, sat a driverless, passengerless Chrysler painted in like colors. The building's life-drained brown brick stood in stark contrast to both car and sign. From across the way I watched heads of shadows dancing behind softly smoked glass on the building's second floor. Occasionally, I looked away from the shadow heads to follow the glide to earth of landing lights in my sideview mirror. I'd lose track of the lights as they'd cross the fence along Rockaway Boulevard. The tarmac lay just beyond the fence.

I considered coincidence while sitting in my car watching the reflection of lights landing and the blur of shadows dancing. It wasn't impossible that the Micki Korin, David Ben Avraam, Kiev Car Service triangle was an innocent triad of chance. No, it wasn't impossible; it wasn't likely either. The man with the dimestore English accent and silenced rifle was perfectly correct. I was close to Brodsky, very close. I stopped being a spectator and drove off to find a phone.

I sank a quarter down the vertical slot and punched up the eleven digits that should've given me The Rusty Scupper. I got my quarter back instead. A computer generated woman, in a voice as flat as Nebraska and as even as the number two, politely panhandled for more change than I could manage. I hung up in the middle of her second courteous request. I thought about reversing the charges or charging the call to my home number. I stopped thinking and decided to call the second number I had in mind. It was a call I could afford to make with the cash on hand.

I fed the slot again and pushed the seven button code of Miss Make-Believe Micki. I got the computer woman and my quarter back once more, but this time I rewarded her civility. She thanked me. I cradled the receiver between my nervous left ear and shoulder. My mind raced with the first ring. What would I say? She picked up on the second ring and saved me from answering any tough questions.

"Dylan?" her voice was shaking. "Dylan?" she coughed.

"Yes."

"Please," she choked on too much air and saliva, "please hurry!"

The line clicked, then hushed, and then teased me with a dial tone. I didn't call back.

I put my car on auto-pilot, cruising around her block searching for anything which remotely resembled a legal parking space. No shot. In Brooklyn Heights parking spots only open up when there's a death in the neighborhood. And tonight, the community's population hadn't dropped. Not yet, anyway. After my second orbit I decided to stop circling the wagon train and to double-park my pony. I slid the VW in tight alongside a maroon BMW parked directly in front of 21 Joralemon. I figured the two cars could keep each other occupied with stories of the old country. It would also prevent any quick exits by my soon-to-be hostess.

Joralemon was a street of brownstones in a neighborhood of brownstones and churches. Number 21 was a classic, right down to its vestigial, wrought iron footscrapers, gas lanterns, and overgrown ivy. Most Brooklynites had trouble accepting this area as part of the borough. The locals had the same problem and called their neighborhood "The Heights." Considering the streets' tasteful Victorian charms, both sides of the argument had merit.

My feet swallowed up the front stoop steps two at a time. To the right of the front door a triple deck of doorbells gave me the news that there were three more flights for my feet to feed on, once inside. I took a step down, off the landing, to survey the street facing windows. A bump on the brain and two murders later, I was becoming a more cautious man. The ground and second floor windows were sealed and black with night. The third floor panes hung open over the face of the brownstone. Ivory curtains waved in and out at the neighborhood, as if energized from within the apartment by an oscilating fan. Behind the off-white fabric, her lights burned brightly in defiance of the night.

The front door looked as old as I felt, but carried its years with considerably more grace. It was a delicate balance of deep-stained hardwood, greenish metal, and etched glass. In a gesture of my newfound caution, I skipped ringing the bell and turned the doorknob instead, pressing gingerly against the glass. I fully expected the old door to resist my advances. It did no such thing, falling away easily with only a somber squeak of protest. The vestibule door responded to my charms with comparable ease. Some men have a way with women; I have a way with wood.

Three flights of stairs were quick work for my anxious legs. At the third-floor landing, I came to a full stop and spider-walked my right hand along the inside of my left leg. The tape-handled .38 felt awkward and, at the same time, intoxicating to the touch. It was like cupping a girl's breast in your palm for the first time. I approached the false daughter's apartment as quietly as I could. I must've looked like a total twit, tiptoeing to her door. I know I felt like one.

Conquests, like plane crashes and members of a conspiracy, must come in threes. I arrived at that conclusion after yet another door fell prey to the weight of my charm. But by the looks of the lock and jamb, I surmised that someone before me had already used charm in the shape of a crowbar to let him or herself in. I got down off my toes to rest my calves for a second. I thought about the nasty things a crowbar could do to a cranium and rubbed the painful memory on the back of my head. I was back on my toes. If someone attacked me with a recording of Swan Lake, I'd be ready.

A bare parquete floor greeted the tips of my shoes. An intense but indirect light played shrinking games with my pupils. When playtime ended, my eyes showed me a long hallway with soft aquagreen walls and a high, white ceiling. Glass fan wall sconces, placed just inside the door, accounted for the initial shock of light. About five yards ahead of me, the hallway spilled into a larger whitewalled room. More light filtered up the hall from there. I could make out the low hum of a fan and the faint whipping of curtains against the evening air. There was something else, another noise. It was more human, but too unfamiliar to decipher.

I did a clumsy ballet down the green corridor to the mouth of the white-walled room, my increasingly damp back leaving its signature along the walls as I went. The *other* noise grew louder now, but no more meaningful. I simply had to turn the corner. Turning the corner would answer some questions. However, turning the corner was something I could not do. I stood there, quiescent, letting the burning caterpillars spill into my eyes and trickle through the hair on my flat Jewish ass.

I got down off my toes and silently suffered through a foot cramp. I brought MacClough's pistol close to my face, letting its cool metal brush my cheek. Somehow, it wasn't like a woman's breast at all. I released the safety and let my thumb pull back the hammer. *One . . . Two . . . Three.* I turned the corner.

I located the source of that human noise perched on a Persian rug midroom. Dressed in a man's white Oxford shirt, it clutched hard to itself and rocked autistically on its haunches. The floorboards, muffled by the rug, creaked in time to its rhythmic rocking. It had a wedged mop of black hair. It was the pretend daughter of a headless Russian lawyer I'd left rotting in the trunk of a Lincoln in front of my office.

She huddled a few feet behind a swivel-headed fan, facing out at the flapping curtains. She wasn't going anywhere, so I took an unguided tour of her digs. The smartly done bedroom, porcelain and brass bath and closet-sized kitchen were empty enough to suit me. I went back to the room with the creaky wooden floor.

She welcomed me with disregard. I knelt down to meet her eyes, but they were previously engaged. They weren't quite closed nor were they looking through me. No, they were blind or rather more like mirrors with their backs to the world. She cut a lonely figure there on the rug. She was good.

I buried my left hand in her sable hair and stroked it to the beat of her sway. As I slowed the stroking, the swaying slowed in kind. The floor was silenced. I kissed her forehead, eyes, and cheeks while keeping hold of her thick hair. I peeked at her eyes again and this time there was somebody home.

"Are you alright?" I asked, in as concerned a whisper as was ever spoke.

"Yes," she whispered back, "now—"

As her ripe lips formed into an oval, I tugged heavily on her hair and placed the stubby barrel of the still cocked pistol into her stunned mouth.

"I'm not very experienced with these things," I screamed the truth at her suddenly wide eyes, "but you'll notice the hammer's pulled back. So even if you're a wiz at getting outta these spots, there's a pretty good chance I'll splatter your brains against the walls while you're tryin'. Nod if you catch my meanin'."

She nodded, very slowly.

"I don't know who you are, but I know who you're not. I'm gonna ask you some questions. When I get done askin', I'll pull this gun outta your mouth an inch past your lips. Then you're gonna answer. Understand?"

She nodded.

"Who are you?" I pulled the gun out an inch.

"Dylan, don't you recognize me?" she gasped frantically. "I am Mick—"

I shoved the gun back into her mouth, cutting her upper lip on the way in. "I figured you'd try that at least once. You had your chance and I'm not buyin'. This time I'm gonna ask you all the questions at one clip. Then you *are* gonna answer likewise, in one clip. If you didn't know, I'm already a suspect in one murder. When the cops find out about Korin, that'll make two. And if you pull the dumb act on me the next time I remove the gun, it'll be three. Ready?" I smiled at her.

She nodded.

"Who are you? Who do you work for? Why was Korin killed? Who is Brodsky? Am I going too fast for you? Nod once for yes. Twice for no."

She nodded twice.

"What's the connection between Blue Sabre, the Kiev Car Service, and you? Why was Joey Piccolo killed? And," I shrugged my shoulders, "why me?"

As I moved the .38 away from her bleeding lip, the gaze of her wide eyes moved from my eager countenance to somewhere above and beyond my head. I began to turn, but not fast enough. A circle of cold metal pressed itself onto the back of my neck.

"I vud like very much dat you drop your gun, Mr. Klein," a remotely familiar voice informed me.

"Hello, Juri." I dropped the tape-handled revolver onto the Persian rug.

Make-believe Micki picked it and herself up in one motion. She spoke to the man with the gun at my back in a foreign language, but it wasn't Russian.

"It's been a long time since I was bar mitzvahed, so could you repeat that a little more slowly please," I talked directly to the woman, trying to ignore the man attached to the gun attached to my neck.

"I wasn't speaking to you, Dylan," the pretender informed me in a voice completely devoid of a Russian accent. "I simply told Juri to watch you while I get dressed. Then we're going to make a visit."

"Great! Who are we going to see?"

"Someone you've wanted to meet for some time now," she smiled and walked to the bedroom. As she did so she barked a little more Hebrew at the geek.

"You like de airport?" Juri wondered of me.

"Love it."

"Good."

Night fell onto the back of my neck spreading fiery blackness and exploding stars across the white walls of 21 Joralemon. I dropped like a philosophy tree in the forest. I couldn't be certain if the floor creaked when I slammed onto the inlaid wood. I wasn't there to hear it.

Renaissance Woman

"Thank you for joining us, Mr. Klein," a man's overly cheery voice acknowledged the opening of my eyes. "We were afraid Juri had given you too big a dose of his gun butt. He's a very zealous young man."

Focusing seemed beyond my grasp. Life's colors had drained together into a searingly painful haze. I fought the hurt and blinked my lids until the haze cleared. Unfortunately, the pain lingered. I wasn't in Brooklyn Heights any longer. No, I was in a soft leather chair in a walnut-paneled office. The walnut panels were covered with plaques and certificates and various maps of the world. To my left, a large rectangle of lightly smoked glass looked out onto Rockaway Boulevard.

Three people shared the room with me; the false Ms. Korin, Juri the zealot, and the cheery-voiced man. He was in his late thirties and sported a thick red-gray mustache, a deep tan, and no hair on the top of his head. His eyes were blue and sparkled like the star in my father's old sapphire ring. The skin about his bright eyes and uneven lips crinkled as he smiled. He sat behind a mahogany desk, flanked on either side by Juri and the woman.

I mouthed some syllables, but nothing escaped my kiln-dried throat except a series of squeals and scratches.

"Hannah, get Mr. Klein some water, will you?" the smooth-headed man directed the woman I knew as Micki. "Be patient, Mr. Klein, relief is coming."

As she walked by me, Hannah hesitated and skimmed my cheek and beard with the back of her right hand. I slapped it away. Juri started to lunge at me, but was thwarted by the quick grasping hands of the smiling, seated man. The woman exited through a door behind me.

"Juri!" the man scolded after the door had closed. He laid some nasty Hebrew on the yellow-toothed boy and then turned his attention to me: "Please, Mr. Klein, there's no need for treating Hannah that way. It's my understanding she's treated you with considerably more affection."

I tried my vocal chords again. This time with more success: "*Worldwide and Worldly-wise.* That's your motto, isn't it, Mr. Avraam?"

"Excellent," he laughed from the bottom of his desk hidden belly. "Did you hear that, Juri? He's very good." Then to me: "I'd prefer you call me David."

"Fuck you!" I gave him a mocking bow that almost split me in two. "I'd prefer to call you a few other things," I rasped out the last word and coughed myself dizzy.

"I understand completely, but we'll work that all out in time," Avraam assured me. "Ah, here comes Hannah with your water."

She knelt down beside my chair and watched me drink. The concerned look in her eyes was enough to make me puke. I considered spitting a few drops into her face, but I was too thirsty to waste any. I was also struck by the notion that she was making herself a particularly easy target. They wanted me to lash out at her, though I couldn't say just why. Whatever the reasons, they'd have to work a little harder to get me to play along. I gave the empty cup back to Hannah and winked at the disappointment I thought I saw in her eyes.

"How do you feel now, Mr. Klein?" David inquired.

"About the same, only less thirsty."

"Yes," he shook his head up and down, "that was a stupid question. Well, onto the business at hand. Ben Avraam opened an unmarked folder and spread it out on the desk. "You are an acquaintance of a man who calls himself Alexander Korin, yes?"

"What day does Passover fall on next year?" I asked, ignoring his query.

"I have appreciated your sense of humor up to this point," he stopped smiling for the first time since I'd opened my eyes, "but the time for laughter has passed. Don't force me to use the crude methods you yourself tried on Hannah earlier. I can guarantee that we are rather more proficient at that sort of thing than you."

"No doubt, but you can still stick it up your ass. I'm not saying another word until we start exchanging some information."

"What do you propose, Mr. Klein?"

"We both have questions. You have the answers I need. At least, I think you do. And, apparently, the reverse is just as true. Why would I be here, otherwise? If you'll help me fill in the gaps, I'll tell you anything you wanna know. But if you figure on this being a one way question and answer session, you're headed down a dead end street."

"An unfortunate choice of words."

"Come on, Dave," I smiled at him and shook my head disapprovingly, "let's not slip into Hollywood gangster dialogue, okay?"

"No, Dylan Klein, you're right, of course," he put his happy face back on. "When mutual interests exist there's no need for threats. Will you excuse us for a moment, please. Hannah," he turned to the woman, "please keep Mr. Klein company while I make a call." Then to me: "Mr. Klein, may I count on you not to cause us any problems?"

"Start counting. Besides, the odds are three to one in your favor."

"Very well," Ben Avraam motioned me out the door. "Juri, stay put."

I stood up too fast. All the blood in my body flooded into my skull, attempting to pop my eyeballs out of their sockets like corks out of badly opened bottles of champagne. The earth tried to spin out from under my shaking legs. And my intestines were poised for an instant replay of breakfast, lunch, and dinner.

Hannah caught me under the elbow with her left arm and covered my mouth with her right hand.

"Can you make it outside?" she asked.

I nodded a pale-faced yes. She guided me out the door and into an adjoining office. Walnut trees had sacrificed themselves for the walls of this office as well, but the desk, which I sat myself behind, was less grand and the panels weren't as cluttered. No smoky windows on the world, either.

"Dylan, would you like some more water?" she sat facing me on the edge of the desk.

"No. It'll just add to how much I have to throw up later. Israeli intelligence, huh?" I changed the subject.

"Do you really expect me to confirm or deny anything?"

"I guess not, not until your boss gets off the phone with his boss. Is there anything I can ask about without you pleading the Fifth?"

"Try me."

"Korin?"

"No."

"Brodsky?"

"No."

"Last night?"

"Well," Hannah's brown skin lost some of its color, "what exactly about last night?"

"Were you on or off the clock?"

"On, I'm always on," she confided. "Why do you ask?"

"I've never been with a whore before and I just wanted to make certain last night counted."

"I didn't realize you were keeping score, but men are always keeping score, aren't they?" She sounded let down. "That's why you shoved the gun into my mouth, because you felt emasculated."

"You do seem to enjoy things of mine in your mouth, Dr. Freud. But there's truth in what you say. Men keep score, one way or another. Do you enjoy having to fuck men because your bosses think it's a good idea?"

"Men and women," she corrected. "Sometimes, yes, I do. Have you loved every job you've ever had or loved every aspect of any job you've ever had? No, I think not," she answered for me and correctly.

"I've never had to be with anyone I didn't want to be with."

"That fact and a dollar will get you on the subway. Maybe they'll print that on your tombstone. Have you ever slept with a woman you didn't enjoy? Do you suppose any of the women you've been with have turned to the convent because they'd never meet anyone of your sexual prowess again?"

"Maybe one or two," I laughed even though it killed me to do it. "I see your point."

"Sometimes I have to fuck people I wouldn't even speak to on the street, but I know that going in. There are no false expectations and no crushing disappointments, only the occassional pleasant surprise," she sighed. "Like—"

"Like me?"

"Yes, like you."

"I bet you say that to all the schmucks stupid enough to listen. Nice try, but could you cool it with the thick lips and the lies. Manipulation makes me nauseous and I already have a head start in that direction."

"Fine."

Hannah hopped off the desk and went next door to let the boys know she hadn't harvested any results during our private little session or maybe she went to see if the phone call was finished. If there actually had been one, at all.

"Dylan," her face was white and twisted when she reappeared, "they're dead! Come."

"For heaven's sake, can't we just do this without the dramatics?" I stood up in sections, trying not to rock the boat. "Ask me your questions and I'll answer. I wanna go home and sleep for a month."

"Get down," she led by example and sprawled herself, stomach down, against the floor. "Here!" Hannah weakly tossed MacClough's tape-handled .38 in my general direction. "Get down!"

"Whatever you say. Maybe I can catch some winks while I'm stretched out."

On my stomach now, I popped out the .38's cylinder, expecting to find six empty slots where bullets used to be. As was the pattern of late, I didn't get what I expected. The six slots were full of bullets. I removed one of the six, thinking that they must be blanks. I thought wrong. I put the perfectly formed piece of ammunition back into its chamber and clicked the cylinder in place. Giving me a loaded gun knocked a few inches off my skeptical pedestal, but I still had my doubts. Maybe they'd removed the firing pin. I wouldn't know if they had. What did a firing pin look like, anyway?

"Don't you think you're overdoing this a bit?" I asked Hannah, slithering up behind her an elbow at a time.

"This is no game, Dylan," she waved me on with a flash of black metal, an automatic pistol of some kind. It was carried in her left hand which had been hidden from me by the office door. "Me first."

I crawled behind her, my face a few inches from the soles of her aerobic shoes. She made the turn into David Ben Avraam's office and came to a dead stop. I said my farewell to her sneakers and slinked up along side her. This was no game.

I thought I recognized the work. The first whispers of dawn filtered into the still office through three small holes in the smoky glass. Three small holes that hadn't been there fifteen minutes before. My eyes followed one of the faint beams of light to the office's side wall. Nothing now stood between light and wall, but something once had. Juri's body slumped against the wall like a carelessly assembled sack of hand-me-downs tossed out of a moving car. One of his eyes was missing, replaced by space and a trickle of blood.

David Ben Avraam still had both of his dead eyes and his passing from this life had been more orderly. He wasn't smiling for the second time since we'd met, but he wasn't exactly frowning either. He looked astonished as if he died thinking it wasn't supposed to happen this way. It took two shots to kill him, so maybe he had a moment to ponder. Just below his right collarbone, a wet, red flower had painted itself through his once-white polo shirt. That didn't kill him. The neck shot had done that. Two shots! The man with the quiet rifle was losing his touch.

"Let's get the fuck outta here," I suggested less than politely. "Where's my car?"

"Brooklyn Heights. I followed Juri here in the BMW."

"I finally got a spot in Brooklyn Heights," I said almost to myself.

"What?"

"Nevermind."

We crawled back into the windowless office and stood up. Hannah looked shaken, but controlled. I didn't care to know how I looked.

"I have to make a call," she explained, putting the black metal down on the desk.

"The cops?"

"Certainly not," she picked up the phone and started pushing buttons.

"Couldn't you do that once we get out of here? I know some payphones close by where no one's been assassinated recently."

Hannah ignored me, turning her back. She gave a few short bursts of Hebrew into the mouthpiece. I guess somebody'd picked up on the other end of the line. I picked her automatic off the desk and tucked it inside my belt. I kept MacClough's .38 in my hand at my side. The woman screamed her parts of the conversation now, mostly waving and pointing at the temporary morgue next door. She put the phone back into its cradle.

"Come, Dylan, the cleaning crew will be here soon," she turned back to where I was standing.

"Where are we going?" I asked.

"To an assigned safe house."

"No, we're not. We're going to my house and on the way you and I are gonna have a long talk," I raised the pistol.

Her eyes flashed to the barren desktop.

"Looking for this?" I pointed to the black machined handle that hung above my belt. "I have a good idea who did in your boss and the zealous boy. I just wouldn't feel very secure in your safe house. You see, there's a message he wants me to deliver and only one person he wants me to deliver it to. Until that's done, I'm safer on the street than with your friends."

"What message? To whom?"

"Nice grammar," I nodded, a slight dizzyness reminding me that I shouldn't have. "We'll talk about it in your car. What's the fastest path to the car with the fewest windows?"

"I thought you weren't worried about being shot." Her voice was rich in sarcasm.

"It's not me I'm worried about."

"Oh," she understood. "We turn left out the door, down the hallway to a back staircase. It leads to the warehouse. David's . . . the BMW is parked there."

She wasn't lying. The maroon 2002 and the Kiev car were parked in parallel loading bays. We moved toward the BMW.

"You drive," I instructed, "but don't get in just yet. Where's the bay door controls?"

"I can open the warehouse doors from inside the car," she educated me.

"Okay, let's get in together, slowly."

Patiently waiting keys dangled out of the ignition. She tested the stick for neutral and started the engine. I held the .38 in my right hand, close to the passenger door, pointed across my body. Hannah's right hand made a move in that direction.

"Stop!"

"Dylan, the remote door control is in the glove compartment. I can't will the damned thing opened. Maybe you'd like to try."

"Go ahead and do what you have to do."

She pulled what looked like a calculator out of the glove box, punched in a few numbers, and the corrugated steel door began to raise itself onto rails hung just below the ceiling.

"Great," I complimented her work, "now give me the remote control and we'll be leaving."

"What for?"

"Here," I snatched it out of her palm, "I'll show you." I carefully rolled down my window and tossed out the little device. "You know the way to Sound Hill. Let's go."

She found first, stood on the gas, hung a fast right and an easy left.

We were out on Rockaway Boulevard in the morning air; no bullets, no broken glass. Out-of-state truckers stretched their legs on side streets and yawned at their watches, waiting for the world to catch up to them.

"Slow down," I told her. "We're outta there. I'm not up to making awkward explanations to a grumpy cop."

"Why did you do that?" Hannah asked.

"The remote control? I thought it might be bugged or something. Your friends'll find us soon enough. I don't need them crawling up my behind."

She laughed, a nervous laugh, like a skipping record.

"Kinda stupid, huh? I was brought up on too many Matt Helm movies."

"No, Dylan, on the contrary. It was bugged. And stop pointing that gun at me. I'm not about to jump out of a moving car. In any case, you're my assignment. I can't afford to lose track of you."

"You'll forgive me for not doing as you ask."

"I suppose I'll have to."

"Take the Cross Island Expressway up to Northern Boulevard," I directed.

"That's not—"

"—the way to Sound Hill," I finished. "Well, it's the long way. Just do it."

The sun was showing itself now, no longer whispering about its arrival. The flow of cars in the opposite direction thickened by the minute. Some forgetful cars kept their headlights on. Some shut them off as they passed. I wanted coffee more than anything.

"Pull over and park."

"Here?"

"Anywhere along here is fine," I said with vague interest, not wanting to reveal my intentions just yet. "I'm gonna give your credibility a little test now." I put the white-handled pistol in my pocket. "Right here is good."

She brought the car to a lazy stop, yanked on the handbrake, quieted the motor, and let out the clutch. She did some make-believe stretching to cover her assessment of our surroundings. Nothing clicked. I could see the puzzlement in her eyes.

"Let's stretch our legs," I suggested. "Leave the keys where they are."

Hannah got out first. I removed her automatic from my belt and popped it into the glove box. I followed her out, locking my door, then circled the car to meet her. I locked her door as well.

"You've locked the keys in the car."

"Your gun too."

We crossed to the north side of the avenue and walked with our backs to the sun for a block.

"Here we are," I opened the door to the Hertz Car Rental Office. "After you."

She stepped by me in silence, the puzzled look gone from her copper eyes. Hannah found a chair and thumbed through some ragged magazines. She worked hard at acting detached, disaffected, and disinterested. I moved to the counter.

"Good morning, sir," the reservation girl fought back a yawn and flashed me a 'why-aren't-you-home-sleeping' kind of smile. "How may we help you today?"

"I'd like to rent a Taurus or a Sable," I flipped my American Express card in her direction. "I have no corporate discounts. I don't want any added liability or collision coverage and I'll need the car for three days or so."

"Fine, Mr . . . Klein," she read off my charge card and tapped on a computer keyboard simultaneously. "Is there anything else?"

"Yes, I wonder if you've got a map of Westchester County, and do you have a public restroom?"

"Well," she kept typing, "the bathroom's not public, but I don't see why you can't use it. Go through that door," she nodded her head to the right, "turn left and it's the first door on the right. I'll search for that map in the meantime."

"Thanks."

The cold water felt like cool comforting kisses on my forehead. I folded about ten sheets of toilet paper and drowned the white stack in more running water. Pressing the wet tissues against the soreness at the back of my neck, I let it rest there while I ran out some liquid of my own. I checked my watch and decided to give Hannah another minute or two. I wanted to make certain she'd have enough time to borrow the phone to call her boss. She'd tell him we were at a Hertz office on Northern Boulevard in Great Neck and that we were destined for somewhere in Westchester. She'd also try to convince the reservations clerk to keep the phone call their little secret.

"Thanks again," I stepped back up to the counter. "I feel like a new man."

"You're welcome, Mr. Klein. Here are the keys to the silver Taurus in spot number seven. Please sign here and here." She handed me a pen and a thick white form with two circled 'Xs'. "I'm sorry, but we don't seem to have a map of Westchester."

"That's alright," I handed back the pen and signed form.

"Here," the reservation clerk gave me a copy of the form and my charge card. "Enjoy your car, Mr. Klein. It's been a pleasure serving you."

"Honey," I said over my shoulder to Hannah, "did you make that phone call?"

"No, what phone call was that?" she answered as calmly as a summer breeze, but the sudden shock in the counter girl's eyes told me the truth.

I flipped the keys to the calm liar: "You drive, okay dear?"

Once planted inside the car, I molded my fingers around the grip of Johnny's spare revolver. I was almost feeling comfortable with it—almost.

"I take it we're not going to Westchester at all," Hannah half-asked, turning left onto the boulevard.

"You take it correctly. Keep heading east."

"Your instincts for this sort of work are very good, Dylan."

"I wish I'd never gotten the opportunity to find that out."

"In this life you never get what you wish for, but somehow manage to arrange for what you'd never wish."

"Spy, whore, and philosopher too," I shook my head, "a real Rennaissance woman, aren't you?" I didn't let her answer, "Turn off at the end of the Roslyn overpass and follow the bend."

The desk clerk at the beige clapboard motel looked at the two of us suspiciously through his lingering sleep. I told him we'd be a day or two and that the airline had lost my damned luggage and that my damned flight had been delayed on the ground in Denver for three very long hours. His suspicion dissolved, but his sleepiness persisted. The names on the registration card were those of my Aunt Lindy and Uncle Saul. I was too tired and the day too young for me to get creative. I asked the clerk for coffee and aspirins. He gave me a knowing smile and said that's what he usually had for breakfast himself. He promised to bring two cups and a few tablets around to our room as soon as he reached full consciousness, but that might be a while.

Our room was dark and noisy. Cars buzzed above our heads, speeding along the overpass. The room's solitary window framed a perfect view of the litter at the base of the overpass and its green metal supports. Roslyn was probably one of the five wealthiest villages in Nassau County, but from here it looked and sounded an awful lot like Brighton Beach. Hannah spread herself across the brown and orange comforter covering the queen-sized mattress. Part of me was busy admitting that I wanted to be there next to her. Another part was smirking at the tasteless motel decor, which seemed to have been done by the designer who'd assembled the late Juri's wardrobe.

I found the bathroom. It was pink and black and almost as large as the rest of our lodgings. I took the white tape and metal out of my pocket and removed the bullets. I buried the six pellets back in my pants and flushed the toilet to cover my tracks. I stepped out of the water closet holding the pistol and tossed it into the drawer of a night stand next to the bed. There were three short knocks at the door.

"Your coffee and aspirin, Mr. Rose," the desk clerk, most of the sleep gone from his eyes, handed me a frayed rattan tray. "I'll put the coffee on your bill."

"Here," I slipped him twenty bucks.

"What's this for?" he wondered.

"For the aspirin and giving us enough time to let it work. We," I pointed my head at the woman spread out quietly across the covers, "have some catching up to do."

"Yeah, acetylsalicylic acid's a tricky drug. Effects different people differently. About how long does it usually take to work on you?" he asked, perfectly poker faced.

"Six hours or so, if I'm left completely undisturbed."

"How do you define 'undisturbed?'"

"As if I weren't here at all." I explained.

"Sorry, friend. Twenty bucks don't buy you six hours in limbo around here. Roslyn's got a high cost of living."

"I can see that," I said handing him another twenty.

He didn't thank me or wish me good day. No, he just closed the door as if he were leaving an empty room. I turned to the bed. The Renaissance woman's eyes were sealed by sleep. I swallowed the aspirins with a hot flood of coffee and pulled a chair up to the bed. I listened to the flying cars above the roof and watched Hannah sleeping until I fell in, unwillingly, behind her.

Captain Queeg's Marbles

The road was paved in that old beige sort of concrete. You know, the type with incongruous bits of black and white stone mixed in for filler. Sunshine fell everywhere—from all the right and wrong, possible and impossible angles—through the blue windshield onto my pink shades. Normally, I hated sunglasses, but I wasn't hating them now. The sun's bouncing glare stitched little red acid trails wherever it touched glass or sand or blue salt water. There was an ocean of blue salt water on the left side of the world, somewhere; I could swear it.

Neat rows of evenly spaced broccoli trees threw mushroom-shaped shadows across the beige pavement at one another. Closer to the sky, above my head, their branches touched to form a comfortable tunnel for passing traffic. I liked it that way. All was quiet, except for the telltale lapping of the world's blue ocean. Suddenly a shrill siren broke the silence, warning me.

Hannah sat upright against a pillow sandwiched between her back and the headboard. She held MacClough's impotent .38 carelessly in her left palm. It's nozzle was pointed in my general direction.

"What time is it?"

"High noon, Dylan. Didn't you hear the siren?" she asked incredulously.

"I thought I dreamed it, the alarm, I mean," I yawned, rubbing the newest bump on my body. "It was a nice dream up to that point. How long 'til your friends arrive?"

"I haven't called them yet."

"Just like you didn't call from the Hertz office. Come on!"

"I wanted to listen to your story without them around," she almost sounded sincere. "You're right, you know. I am a whore. Too often I'm used like a worm on a hook. My superiors reel in the fish and mount them on their study walls. I just get pulled out of the fish's mouth and get put on another hook. I'm getting to be a curious little worm and your maneuvering has brought me enough time to quench my thirst."

"I'm not sure I'm getting you."

"Earlier, for example, in David's office, if things had gone according to form, I would have been dismissed like a schoolgirl as soon as my perceived ability to manipulate you had worn thin."

"That's why you were making such an obvious target of yourself."

"Was I that obvious? Well . . . yes. It's sometimes an effective dynamic in interrogation, but its value is short lived. I am frequently around to hear the questions asked. Seldom am I present to listen to the final answers."

"You're breakin' my heart," I sneered. "If you haven't notified your pals as to our whereabouts, what's the gun for?"

"Added incentive."

"Lady, I got all the incentive I need. I got enough incentive to export to the Third World. I want three things from you and I'll make you a happy little worm. Two outta three won't cut it. I won't argue and I won't negotiate," I slapped the top of the night table with my right palm. "It's yes or no."

"One . . ."

"One, you put the pistol back where you found it sleeping. Two, you tell me the truth about Korin. Three, you arrange for Mr. Brodsky to meet me tonight at a time and place of my—"

"But—"

"But nothing. Brodsky meets me tonight or you get put back on the hook like before and get tossed in the pond without hearing those answers you're so thirsty for."

"I cannot guarantee Brodsky's answer," she said, putting the revolver back into the nightstand drawer, "but maybe what you tell me will help convince him. That is all I can promise."

"On the Sunday my mom was buried," I began without pause, "I drop kicked my mourning stool and went to Nathan's."

"Rather unconventional of you."

"I hate the religious mumbo jumbo and the ritualized goodbyes. So after lunch, I take a long slow drive through Brighton Beach. I'm looking for something. I'm not exactly sure what it is, but I found it in Alexander Korin's house. My car stalled . . ."

I served the rest of the story to her in bite-sized pieces, like a toddler's meal. I fed her enough details to choke a starving pig. Hannah even got to hear about the stand girl's ice green eyes and gingham apron. The only missing ingredient was MacClough's involvement. I didn't see the need to get him in any deeper than he already was. She swallowed it all silently, her face bearing the stamp of rapt neutrality.

On only three occasions during the tale did the false daughter alter her expression: First, when I described the blood red dot put through Alexander Korin's forehead. Again, as I detailed the discovery of the little Russian's headless torso and, finally, when I mentioned the demise of a certain Joseph Piccolo, Jr. The meager changes in the listener's facial display were not indicative of disgust or remorse or even of loathing. No, Hannah's full lips, twisted brow, and flashing eyes communicated only surprise.

". . . car parked directly under the Blue Sabre sign. I sat out front trying to convince myself that this was all one great coincidence. I remained unconvinced. That's when I phoned you and got your 'damsel-in-distress' routine. Let me guess," I threw my hands up, "I was getting closer to the truth faster than you'd anticipated and the broken lock and frightened girl bit was meant to keep me off balance by making me question my own conclusions about your involvement. Right?"

She answered with continuing silence.

"I'll go on then," I informed her. "You had the stage set well, but after my call, or maybe before, you got another. It was from Juri or Ben Avraam telling you that I'd been spotted, spotting them. Maybe the cargo agent had whispered in their ears. You got told that no matter how realistic the set design and how convincing an actress you were, the initial plan was off and that you should keep me occupied until Juri could keep his appointment with the back of my neck."

"So, Korin is dead. Are you positive?" Hannah ignored my speculations and questioned me as if she couldn't, or didn't, want to accept the facts.

"Well, the last time I checked he was quite dead; low on blood, stiff of muscle, and short above the shoulders. Weren't you listening to me?"

"Yes, Mr. Klein," a bright voice boomed, not from the woman's lips or even from the direction of the bed, but rather from the dark doorway of the small room. "Hannah," the man's voice took on a paternal tone, "will you excuse us now? Mr. Klein and I need some time alone."

She made no remark as she rose up off the ugly comforter to plant her feet on the dirty peach carpeting. The calm liar shook out her black hair and palm-pressed some wrinkles out of her blouse. Her eyes did not acknowledge my presence. She walked to the door and through it as if she were leaving an empty room.

When the bolt clicked shut, the brightly voiced gentlemen stepped out of the shadows and into the lighted heart of the boxy room. His hairline receded into uncontrolled waves of gray. Once, when he was younger and there was more of it, his hair had been dark and curly. Hints of days past survived in his ample eyebrows. The lines smiled around the corners of his eyes, but the eyes themselves were blue vacuums, incapable of matching the gestures of his crinkled skin. They were the eyes of a witness, scarred by what they'd seen. His nose changed direction twice as it plunged from a thin bridge to a bubbled tip. That nose had intimate knowledge of the human knuckle. The neat white teeth peeking out from behind his crooked lips didn't figure to be original equipment. His hairless chin was strong and square, but age and gravity had fudged the border between it and his neck.

Even if I hadn't already deduced his identity, I might've recognized him from a grainy old photo I'd held in my hand in a lawyer's office in Brighton Beach about a thousand years ago.

"Second row from the bottom, third from the left," I stated with a degree of self satisfaction.

"Yes, the photo your friend Mr. Korin showed you."

"How are the acoustics in the next room?" I asked, standing up to take his measure.

"They're quite irrelevant, Mr. Klein. Let it suffice to say that I was privileged to hear your tale of woe from start to finish." He held his age-speckled right hand out to me, "Mikhail Brodsky."

"Thanks for making it official," I squeezed his hand, "but where's your badge? Or don't the Israelis feel the need to carry I.D.?"

"You've had your little joke, Mr. Klein, now sit down!" There was an implied threat in his tone.

I sat down.

"That was quite a cock and bull story your friend Mr. Korin told you, but he is—"

"Was," I corrected.

"Was," he repeated, tilting his head in mock deference. "Your friend was a most convincing liar."

"Yeah, almost as convincing as Hannah."

Brodsky slapped me across the mouth with the back of his hand hard enough to rock the chair. "Don't ever compare one of my people to that scum. Is that clear?"

"As clear as the sound in the next room," I answered, trying to work open the night stand drawer that held the gun. "Let me straighten you out on something. Alexander Korin wasn't my friend. I liked the guy well enough, but at the time of his death he was my employer."

"No, Mr. Klein, it is you who requires some straightening out. Alexander Korin was neither your friend nor your employer," Brodsky explained in his awkward jumble of accents. "Alexander Korin, the kindly neighborhood lawyer serving his community of fellow expatriates, never existed."

"You've gotta stop watchin' those *Twilight Zone* reruns, Mr. Brodsky. They're affecting your reasoning."

"My patience may be waning, but I assure you my powers of reason are fully intact."

I went for the pistol and had it turned to his abdomen before he could react.

"Are you going to disembowel me with invisible bullets, Mr. Klein," he wondered, a broad smile spreading across his face, "or are your hands so fast that you've gotten the cartridges out of your pocket and into the gun without me noticing? Hannah is a thorough worker."

Reflexively, I felt for the bullets in my pocket. He swatted the powerless pistol out of my hand.

"Stop this foolishness!" he demanded, his vacant eyes searching the rug for MacClough's weapon.

"Okay, if that wasn't Korin's topless carcass making raspberry jam on the desk that night, whose was it? No John the Baptist jokes, please."

"His name is Sergei Krylov," Brodsky answered unenthusiastically.

"His name isn't anything. The only proper phrase using the word 'is' in connection with the man you call Krylov is, 'is dead,' or 'is very dead.'"

"I have only your words to prove it and that is completely unsatisfactory," he said matter of factly.

"That's too fuckin' bad because the only other proof is in the trunk of a black Lincoln Town Car."

"Not necessarily. I'd be very interested to have my laboratory go over that stained piece of note paper you mentioned to Hannah. By the way, Mr. Klein, would you care to tell me where that paper is? You neglected to include that detail in your story," the smile ran away from his face.

"I'm almost as dumb as I look, but not quite. No, I wouldn't care to tell you where that crimson paper is. Why don't you try searching my house? It's as good a place to start looking as any."

"Thank you for your permission. The men I have assigned that task should be arriving in Sound Hill . . . ," he checked his watch, "within the half hour. Now they won't have to suffer the guilt of entering someone's house uninvited."

"Not for nothin', but can we back up a few steps here?"

"Yes, yes, what is it?" he asked impatiently, moving to collect the tape-handled revolver.

"Who was Krylov to you? Why the alias? Why—"

"You'll excuse me now," Brodsky cut me off, checking his timepiece again. "Hannah will be in shortly to keep you company. You may ask her your petty questions."

"Asking is only half the fun."

"She'll have my permission to answer truthfully, if she is so inclined," he slipped the gun carelessly into his pocket and moved to the door.

"I don't like you too well, Mr. Brodsky," I spoke to his back.

The words almost embarrassed me as they left my lips. I wanted to disown them, although I'd never spoken any that I'd meant more. It was shocking to think how often, as an adult, I'd felt dislike for someone without ever expressing it. And in the same breath, I realized the converse was true. But that's part of being an adult, isn't it? Dancing around your feelings. It's strange what you think about.

"I don't imagine you do," he turned to show me the shadow of his profile. "I'm certain you enjoyed your Mr. Korin's company much more."

"That's true enough."

"But it shouldn't be so. And when Hannah answers your question, you'll comprehend my meaning. Understanding it won't sway your feelings, though," he turned back to me fully, now. His tone was the paternal one with which he had previously addressed the false daughter. "We humans are funny. We convince ourselves that like and dislike are learned things, but that is sophistry, Mr. Klein, pure and simple. We do not choose whom to like and dislike. We just do or don't, and fill in the justifications after the fact. We are animals, Mr. Klein, though we spend our lives trying to deny it."

I sat slack jawed and silent as he turned back to the door.

"As you told Hannah," the lifeless voice had returned, "the assassin wanted you to deliver the message of Kry . . . Korin's death to me. Consider it done. Now sit patiently while we try to confirm that and figure out just what to do with you."

I retrieved the six bullets from my pocket and rolled them around in my palm. They clicked like Captain Queeg's marbles and that made me think of strawberries and insanity. I was hungry for one and getting closer to the other. I gave a moment's thought to attempting an unauthorized exit through the little room's solitary window, but Brodsky would have that contigency covered. I didn't really want escape, anyway, and Brodsky knew as much. The need to know consumed me.

"How are you feeling, Dylan?" Hannah inquired, taking a seat on the bed's edge.

"Curious, sore, hungry, and curious," I rubbed my neck.

"Food is coming," she assured me. "Would you like some ice for your head?"

"No, let's ignore it and maybe the pain will go away. Did you speak with your boss?" I changed subjects.

"I am to answer your questions as completely as my knowledge of the subjects will allow," she answered in bored monotone. "However, to facilitate the process I must check your familiarity with certain historical events."

"History! You've found a subject I'm not totally inept at."

"How are you with the Second World War?"

"Far from inept, very far," I boasted. "Remember, I told you about the discussion of the subject I had with your dearly departed, make-believe father."

"Yes, I remember. Do you know what the Cheka and GPU were?"

"Forerunners of the KGB in the Soviet Union," I winked in self satisfaction.

"That is basically accurate," Hannah was unimpressed. "Ask your first question."

"Not just yet. Nod yes or no if I'm right. The man I knew as Korin worked for the aforementioned organizations."

She nodded in the affirmative: "He was connected with the latter two during his lifetime. Dylan, you know the names Barbi and Von Braun?"

"Of course."

"Then you understand what they have in common other than their obvious ties to Nazi Germany."

"If you mean they should've been tried as war criminals, but were protected by the Allies, then I understand. But—"

"That is precisely what I meant. Why do you suppose they were insulated?"

"The Allies saw them as valuable assets to garner in the building Cold War," I responded impatiently. "Come on, you can't be comparing Alexander Korin or Sergei Krylov, or whatever the fuck his name was, to those two."

"Yes, that is exactly what I'm doing. Life, after all, is a matter of degree." Her copper eyes were deadly serious.

"Can we stop dancing now? My feet are getting tired. I've been jerked around long enough by everyone I've dealt with for the last week. Just tell me what you're prepared to tell me about Krylov without makin' me play twenty questions. Any historical facts I'm unsure of, I'll ask about."

"I agree, things will be easier that way," Hannah inhaled deeply. "Every generation educated in the West since the end of World War II has been told that Hitler's Germany was the most murderous nation-state that has ever existed in the history of our world. They have been told wrong. Stalin—"

"—is reputed to have killed anywhere from ten to forty million of his own people during the great purges," I interrupted, "blah, blah, blah."

"Some estimates are as high as seventy million, but we'll use the range you have provided. Stalin did not just snap his fingers and make people vanish. No, he needed a secret army to mutilate his imagined enemies. Sergei Alexander Krylov was a loyal soldier in that secret army. So, when Germany crossed into Russia on that June day in 1941, Sergei Krylov was already a very skilled destroyer of human life. He was certainly as competent a killer as any man in the invading waves. It was a talent that would serve him well in the hard years to come.

"Krylov was not a typical party bully, however. No, he was bright, affable and ultimately flexible. He recognized that to survive an occupation one must possess more than the knack for destruction. After all, the invaders would get better at that with practice. Sergei must've felt quite pleased that he'd studied German as a second language. He'd also studied English on his own, though the government had prohibited it from time to time since the Revolution. Sergei Krylov had a gift for anticipation. As others retreated from the advancing Germans, Krylov moved west to meet them in the Ukraine.

"Although it is unclear exactly how he managed it, Krylov attached himself to one of the spearhead Nazi divisions slicing through Russia. I imagine he told them that he'd always hated Communism, that he was about to be executed for disloyalty when the invasion began. Maybe he licked their boots and named them as his saviors. Whatever he said, I'm sure it was said in perfect German. Apparently, the division commander was an intelligent enough soldier to divine Krylov's value as an interpreter and also as someone who knew the territory. Sergei must also have appealed to the Nazi sense of humor."

"Wait!" I threw my palms up, still unable to fully accept what my ears were hearing. "Let me take it from here. Now Krylov, who's just finished murdering his countrymen in the name of Stalin, lands a new gig assisting in the destruction of his countrymen in the name of Adolf Hitler. As Krylov and his adopted army race through the Ukraine they happen upon a village in which a man named Mikhail Brodsky lives. How'm I doin'?"

"I'll stop you when you stray too far off course," she yawned. "Continue."

"The story Kor . . . Krylov told me in his office was basically true, then. Only he wasn't one of the villagers. He was the interpreter. He picked out the one survivor alright, but not by puking on him.

No, Krylov saw the look of recognition in Brodsky's eyes. Maybe Brodsky had been a fellow thug and—"

"You've just strayed," Hannah chopped off my sentence abruptly. "Brodsky did recognize Krylov, but not as an accomplice. He recognized Krylov as one of the men who'd arrested his father in the middle of the night some three years earlier. Needless to say, the father was never seen or heard from again."

"So Krylov sees this look in Brodsky's eyes," I picked up. "He's not certain why the look is there, but realizes that he's got to deal with it. Krylov can convince the Nazis to kill the man with the unrelenting stare. That would be easy enough, but what if the villager was given a chance to speak and renounced the interpreter as a former member of Stalin's death squads. Krylov couldn't take the chance, no matter how slim it might be.

"By now Krylov knows the Nazi routine. They'll kill some villagers as an example. From the group chosen to be executed, one or two will be spared to show that the Master Race can be charitable as well as strict, Krylov whispers in the commander's ear. He's asked nothing in return for his services until now. Can he, Krylov, please pick the exception. He tells the colonel that it would be good fun for the troops, a good laugh, a boost for morale. The colonel, bored with the task himself, agrees.

"Brodsky, grateful and confused, says nothing as his fellow villagers are stripped, raped, hanged and shot. It's too late for him to speak up now. No one will listen. No one will care. The threat to Krylov is ended, temporarily. Krylov and the conquerers move on to the next village, leaving Brodsky to fester in his own guilt. The worst kind of guilt. The guilt of the survivor. That's what this is all about, isn't it?"

"Partially, yes, it is," Hannah replied without hesitation, "but not totally, not at all."

"You'll have to pardon my ignorance, but I don't get the connection between Klaus Barbi, Wernher Von Braun, Sergei Krylov and myself," I confessed with false disappointment.

"Dylan, you surprise me. You did such a keen job of filling in the events of almost fifty years past that I should've thought the rest would be a cake walk," she laughed that nervous, skipping-record laugh of hers. "Actually, it gets fairly complicated from here on in, so I'll try to keep it as simple as possible."

"I'd appreciate that. When's the food getting here?"

"If it doesn't come shortly, I'll go check or would you prefer I do that now?"

"No, go on."

"As Krylov smelled a change in the fortunes of war, he once again flip-flopped his allegiance. He had to reach the Allied lines and there were only two groups headed that way; the retreating Germans or the advancing Red Army. Sergei realized that a retreating army has very little need of interpreters, especially ones that had witnessed what he had witnessed. The Nazis would have cast him off like a lead suitcase from a sinking ship.

"As he had been of great help to the German Army, so was he to the army of his rediscovered motherland. Krylov seemed to his Red Army commander to be a man of unusual talent in anticipating the tactics of the opposition. In fact, it wasn't anticipation at all. It's a great irony that Sergei Krylov was probably amongst the first Red Army troops to enter Berlin."

"And once there?"

"Here again the details are sketchy," she screwed up her face as if to apologize, "but we can make some pretty good guesses. He had to get to the Allied lines and again there were only two groups headed that way; the Germans hoping to surrender to the Americans and the Red Army hurrying to envelope as much of Germany as possible before surrender.

"His choice was the obvious one. He wanted to be captured by the Americans, too. Krylov foresaw that the victory party between the Soviets and the Allies would be a short one and that the Americans would be less suspicious of and more impressed with him in the guise of a captured German officer than as a AWOL Red corporal. He was quite correct in his assumptions.

"On February 24, 1945, Major Hans Zimmer walked into an outpost headquarters of the American Third Army and surrendered. Only God knows where the real Hans Zimmer was buried. Zimmer, in properly respectful tones, informed captors that he'd be willing to discuss any military matters they wished, but only with an Army Intelligence officer or a member of the OSS. If they would not supply him with such an officer, it would be name, rank, and serial number only. He got his wish, and more.

"For some time, already, the Allies had been rummaging through the ranks of captured Nazis, like old ladies picking through rags at a garage sale, to find which ones were 'keepers' and which ones were war criminals. Can you imagine the look on his interrogator's face when Hans Zimmer revealed his true identity? Any idiot could see Krylov's potential value. Here was a man who knew the intricacies of the Soviet Intelligence network, had firsthand knowledge of the Red Army's advance, had current knowledge of German defenses. The list went on and on. Even if none of those benefits were exploited, Krylov could always be used as trade bait with the Soviets or as fodder for the inevitable war crimes trials."

"Someone clearly must've recognized his value," I interjected the obvious.

"No, Dylan, not someone," she corrected. "Everyone."

"What?"

"You see, whereas men like Barbi exaggerated their potential utility, Krylov did not have to. The Americans spent months trying to corroborate the details of Krylov's story. When they were satisfied that he was telling the truth, he was debriefed and shipped to British Intelligence for retraining and instruction. The Americans were still amateurs at the espionage game at that time and didn't want to mishandle their prize.

"Krylov was a good student and taught his teachers a few tricks. As he went through his training, he was busy amassing as much information about the people he was now working for as possible. You see, the British and the Americans both assumed that Krylov was no security risk to them. After all, he couldn't cross back to the other side. He'd committed war crimes against his own people and everybody knew how bad the Russians were about forgiving and forgetting. It was a bad assumption. A very bad assumption.

"For the first few years, Krylov was kept on the western side of the fence, interviewing defectors, checking the validity of field intelligence, etc. But," Hannah closed her left hand, leaving only the index finger at attention, "when the fence became a curtain, Krylov underwent a little plastic surgery—thickening the nose bridge, cropping the ears, bowing his legs—and was sent into East Germany during the Berlin airlift. Do you know where his first stop was after he settled into his cover?" she asked, almost laughing.

"The Soviet Embassy?"

"Well, no, but close enough," she smiled approvingly. "The Bulgarian Embassy. The Soviet Embassy would've been too much of a risk. What if he were recognized by some low-level official unconcerned with his value to the State. Krylov might be shot on sight. And, in any case, once in the Soviet Embassy there was no out. The Bulgarian Embassy lowered the risk of recognition and gave him a possible escape in case negotiations went poorly. They did not, however, go poorly."

"Look, this is all thoroughly interesting stuff, but you're talking forty years ago here," I stated with emphatic impatience. "What's all this got to do with me?"

"Please, Dylan. You wanted answers and you're getting them. There was no guarantee of you liking them," the calm liar admonished me. "Shall I—

"Yeah, yeah. Go on."

"The Americans weren't the only ones willing to foresake morality for advantage. The Russians jumped at Krylov's offer to 'turn' for them. After all, he'd been killing his own people before the war. America's nuclear monopoly made looking the other way that much easier for the Russians."

"And the Cold War was job security for Krylov."

"Yes, the best kind. For forty years he's been doing very nasty jobs for both sides to everyone's satisfaction."

"Not everyone's, apparently," I corrected.

"Until recently, then."

I gave her that. "You, your boss, Blue Sabre, the Kiev Car Service?"

"I am not fully at liberty to discuss those matters," she answered in the rehearsed tones of a press secretary. "Let us say that we work for a certain foreign government with the unwritten approval of your own. As long as we don't gather and/or make available intelligence damaging to the vital interests of the United States, we are tolerated. When we stumble across such information, through no efforts of our own, of course, we are only too glad to share that strategic information with your government."

"Who are you trying to convince? I couldn't care less about your unwritten approval. The connection between all the players, mainly myself, is still escaping me. Do you guys sell programs to help keep score?"

"One of our functions, not a top priority," she spoke overly loud, reaching her left arm under her blouse and behind her back, "but one of our jobs is to keep a watch out for war criminals. Usually, we take no precipitous actions on our own," Hannah pulled her hand forward from behind her back. MacClough's pistol was in it. She held her right index finger across her lips, motioning me not to speak. "No," she continued, "we usually inform some do-good community group and public pressure takes care of the rest. To be perfectly frank, Dylan, the younger ones among us don't see the point in it any longer. We have our own battles to fight. It makes us look bad. All the world sees are foolish old men being persecuted in the last days of their lives for crimes committed half a century ago. It makes us look bad," she repeated, "and at the moment we don't need to look any worse than we are."

I lightened the load of her left hand. "It must get sticky when you happen upon a war criminal who is in the employ of your host country," I sympathized, placing Captain Queeg's marbles back in their slots as quietly as possible.

"Yes, extremely," Hannah agreed, but shook her head in contradiction to her words.

She feigned coughing to cover her search for a pad and pencil. When she finally located them, Hannah rotated her hands violently as if to stimulate my speech.

"Are you alright?" was the only thing that occured to me.

She stopped scribbling long enough to give me a look which indicated her disappointment in my part of the performance.

"It doesn't make any sense," I started up again. "Why would Krylov hire me, a total amateur at this stuff, to find the man most dangerous to him?"

"Because," she continued writing, not looking up to meet my eyes, "you are an amateur. I'm certain Krylov never expected you to get so far as to find Brodsky. You were a joker thrown into the deck to shake up everybody's hand, a wrench thrown into the machinery. If he were alive, he'd be most proud of himself."

"What for?"

"For picking you. Look how far you've gotten. You've flushed out several agents, blown the cover of two of our business fronts and got Brodsky out into the open. It's quite amazing, really."

"But that's no answer," I was genuinely agitated.

"You, Dylan. Why you?" She put the folded note in my palm and curled my fingers shut around it. "Is that what's bothering you?"

"That," I pocketed the note, "and a few other things like why was Joey Piccolo killed?"

"You might as well ask how Krylov managed to survive as long as he did with so many potential enemies. He had a gift for knowing people's talents and weaknesses," she pantomimed my planned escape as she spoke.

I nodded my comprehension: "Fuck you and your boss and the horse shit you rode in on. I've never heard such a load of crap in my life."

"It's all quite true. I promise you."

"Yeah, as I recall you promised me some food awhile ago. Where's that? Your credibility wasn't at a high water mark with me to begin with. Now you're digging into the negative numbers," I chided, opening up the room's one window as slowly and silently as it would allow.

"The burden of belief is yours, Mr. Klein," she answered smugly. "I'll go check on your food. A man should be in with it shortly. Good afternoon."

This once, her word was gold. Through the door I could hear the food tray rattle in the hands of its inexperienced carrier. He was probably better with guns. The door swung open, stopping its arch an inch from the tips of my shoes.

"Mr. Klein," a rough, careless voice beckoned, "your food."

Now he stepped into the room and tried my name again. He screamed a few harsh syllables to himself, probably a choice Hebrew curseword. My waiter had seen the open window. A steady stream of anxious Hebrew flew from his lips, directed at the ad hoc eavesdropping system Brodsky and his mates had set up during my nap. Two unsynchronized sets of shoes galloped down the hallway sounding like a racehorse not fully recovered from a recent stroke. The hoofs came to rest at the door's threshold.

"Outside! Outside!" he barked in English at the ailing thoroughbred.

The gallop started up again in the direction of the motel's lobby. I thought about pulling Johnny's pistol on my waiter and doing a sort of hostage duet. Instead, I rubbed the back of my neck for reference and clocked Brodsky's man as he moved past. I guess there's a technique to sapping someone cleanly. It took me two passes to bring him down, but down he went, tray and all. In the excitement, he'd neglected to rest the food somewhere to free up his hands. I checked the unconscious bundle of humanity for signs of life. I found some. I also found his wallet, pistol and car keys. Car keys! My left hand told me I still had mine.

I removed the clip from his automatic and tossed the cartridge out of the open window through which Brodsky's people had assumed I'd exited. I threw the gun—a twin to Hannah's—under the bed. I buried his wallet and keys in my pants and scanned the food tray's wreckage for a little added insurance. I found it in the form of a steak knife, a foot or two from a rug-tainted veal chop. I wondered which one of the overpriced restaurants along Old Northern Boulevard they'd ordered out from. As I said, it's funny what you think about.

I palmed MacClough's .38 against my left leg to hide it from the desk clerk. Looping my rented car's key ring around my right pinky, I took a quartet of bills from the sleeping waiter's wallet. The wood handled insurance, tucked between my belt and buttocks, scraped layers of skin off my ass with each step.

"I don't know where they're headed," the front man volunteered without my asking.

"Who's 'they'?" I asked, slowing down my pace.

"Your wife and one of the guys who checked into Room 6 a few hours after you."

"Oh, that. Don't worry about it. Here," I chucked the folded twenties at the counter and missed. The bills fell apart and floated to the floor like four green butterflies. "That should cover the room. Use the leftovers as a hedge against the high cost of living."

"Thanks," he said, stepping around the partition to scoop up the fallen Jacksons. "What about your luggage?"

"Luggage?" I whispered the question and then recalled the story I'd told him earlier. "When it gets here, keep it."

"But Mr.—"

"Which car in the lot is yours?" I cut off his protestations.

"What?"

"Which car—"

"The brown Hyundai," he responded haltingly. "Why?"

"I wouldn't want you to have to spend today's profits on new tires. Bye."

"Yeah, whatever," the desk clerk spoke to my back.

I was outside. There was no sign of Hannah, or of anyone particularly ominous looking. I moved quickly down the wooden treads to the street and followed the contours of the clapboarded building until I reached the dirt parking lot. There was no panic in my movements. I was counting on the false daughter of the false lawyer to protect me. I also figured Brodsky's people couldn't stand the publicity of an execution in broad daylight.

There were two cars in the lot, excluding Hertz's silver Taurus and the desk clerk's brown Hyundai. One was a metallic green Mercedes 300 E sedan—a match for the sleeping waiter's keys—and the other, a black BMW 735i. I laughed at the Israeli fascination for German cars and withdrew the chaffing steak knife from its niche against my bleeding skin. The buzzing of cars on the overpass masked the hissing escape of air from the slashed sidewalls.

In the Ford's rearview, I could see two of the three remaining cars listing noticeably to one side. I was away from there, but I had to ditch the rent-a-car in a hurry. The longer I drove it, the more like an albatross it would become.

"MacClough's Rusty Scupper," Johnny answered.

"It's me!"

"Klein?"

"Yeah."

"Where've ya been?"

"No time for that now. Long story. I need you to pick me up," I was sounding out of breath, but I hadn't really run anywhere.

"What's the matter?"

"Not now, Johnny, please."

"Alright. Where are you?"

"Port Washington train station, but I can't stay here. I got a cab waiting. Pick a spot that only you know about and I'll meet you there."

"Hey, will you guys shut up!" MacClough yelled at his customers, "I'm tryin' to think." That was followed by a few seconds of silence. "Do what I tell ya."

"Go ahead."

"Give the driver an address in Old Brookville along 107, 12 Cow Path Rd, anything. When you get on 107 offer the guy as much money as it takes to get him to drop you at the rest stop on the L.I.E. between exits—"

"I know it, but that's an awfully public place."

"That's the idea, genius. Make sure he doesn't call in the second leg of the journey. I'll be there soon enough."

"Thanks, MacClough."

He was still cursing when I hung up the phone.

I gave the driver the address Johnny had used as an example. It must've been convincing enough. We pulled off the curb without any questions. I laid out across the back seat, back against a door, and began to read Hannah's note in the orange light of a sinking sun.

Playin' Poker With Mr. Sandman

I got to the rest stop first and was poorer for my timing. Cab drivers tend to be the victims of robbery. Not mine. No. Mine robbed me. His silence was expensive. It cost me the last of the sleeping waiter's pocket cash plus almost every penny of mine. He left me with a dollar's worth of phone calls. A real prince, that cabbie. He tried to justify his larceny by exclaiming that this type of thing could cost him his job. What type of thing, I wondered? Was it against company policy to take bribes or just taking such large ones? I neglected to ask.

This rest stop was true to its name. It really was just a rest stop, only a rest stop. No HoJos here, nor any Dennys, McDonalds or Burger Kings. No food here at all. No gas either: just parking spots and payphones and a stupid old railway car for window dressing. During business hours it served as toilet space and a tourist info booth. Now it was just window dressing. Stuffed horses would've been more fun or maybe a decommissioned B-29. The road signs would read, "Park your car/Hit the hay/Catch forty winks/By the Enola Gay." But no, there was only this ancient piece of red junk caught in a time warp. Visitors to the westbound rest stop were not so fortunate as I. There was no railway car over there. They could only stare enviously across the six lanes of traffic. I palmed my last four quarters, put a shoulder up against the trackless coach, and waited to be rescued by John Francis MacClough.

Trouble preceded his arrival in the form of a bland Chevy

sedan. It was chromeless and colored in a vague metallic blue. The kind of blue that looks sun faded even before the factory paint is dry. I didn't notice it pull in off the expressway, but its lack of personality and creeping pace made it as conspicuous as a pea to a sleepless princess. At first, I dismissed any possible connection between its presence and mine. Maybe the driver'd come to catch a closer look at the railway car. But as the Chevy pulled nearer to my position, I decided to reconsider my premature dismissal.

The dying light and glare made it impossible to catch a glimpse of the driver. I wanted it to be a state trooper or a county cop out hunting for DWI meat. I soon enough realized that that prospect might not be in my best interests. If a cop got curious about me, I'd be hard pressed to explain the two wallets (both free of the burden of cash) in my pockets and the .38 strapped tightly—too tightly—to my ankle. The need to explain never arose.

The blue box on wheels stopped for a five count and then picked up its pace. It came to rest again quietly at my feet. An electric motor whined as the passenger side window dropped to reveal a green-sunglassed man in his mid-twenties wearing a white, short-sleeved shirt and last year's power tie. His hair was blond and cropped. His skin was ruddy and freckled. His arms were well muscled and lightly downed. His manner was threateningly cordial.

"Mr. Klein," he let a black vinyl card case fall open in his left palm.

I guess he was trying to impress me with his credentials, but in that light he might as well have been showing me Pete Rose's rookie card.

"Mr. Klein," he repeated no less patiently, "please step into the back seat and come with us." He phrased it like a request, but his tone suggested a command.

I thought about running, but didn't. I wasn't up to challenging six lanes of Long Island Expressway traffic at dusk. Not yet, anyway.

"'Us,' who?" I asked evenly.

The flaxen headed man turned his credentials toward his sunglasses and laughed, "I guess that would be difficult to see from where you're standing."

"Thanks for understanding, but that's not the answer I was

searching for." I decided to try and kill some time until MacClough showed.

"This is official business, Mr. Klein. I'll be happy to explain when you get in the car." His words were insistent, but were spoken without anger.

"I've got a detective shield in my wallet. That doesn't make me the Man from Uncle."

"Who?" the blond man asked with genuine surprise.

"Nevermind. It was before your time," I consoled him with a phrase I'd never imagined myself uttering. "In any case, you're gonna have to be a little less tight lipped or I'm not gettin' any closer to your car than I am now."

Another electric motor whined as a second window, the rear passenger's, slid into the door.

"Yes, Mr. Klein. I've seen that shield before," a familiar voice testified, "but it will be of little use to you today."

The voice belonged to a relaxed, fleshy-faced man. The last and only time I'd seen that rotund face or heard that voice was on the night of Krylov's beheading. On that night it was me sitting in the car.

"It's a long way and a lotta exits from the 61st precinct, Officer Rizzo, or whatever your name is today." I winked and smiled with knowing sarcasm. "Is Newkirk with you or is he back in Brooklyn pretending to be stupid?"

"Look who's driving, Mr. Klein," Rizzo instructed.

I bent down and looked past the sunglassed farm boy in the front seat. Behind the wheel a light-skinned black man gracefully removed his own gold rimmed aviators to give me an unobstructed look.

"Wave hello to the nice man, Newkirk," the back seat driver instructed.

Newkirk sneered, rolling his eyes, bowing his head defiantly rather than waving. I felt confident the anger in his gesturing wasn't intended for me.

"That'll do, *I guess*," the fat-faced man stated disapprovingly, having caught the brunt of the driver's anger. "Now that we've gotten reacquainted, it's time—"

"Time for what?" I butted in. "Anyway, I haven't been properly introduced to your third. Is he Curly, Shemp, or Little Joe?"

Four door locks popped up in one quadraphonic click as the trio stirred in their seats.

"Please get in, Mr. Klein," the unnamed member of the three patiently requested. Rizzo kicked open the rear passenger door.

"Get in!" Rizzo commanded, abandoning his phony jovial tone.

I started to reach down my leg for Johnny's spare piece. It was a dumb move done mostly out of exhaustion and despair, I guess.

"Don't!" the farm boy warned, showing me the body of a black matted automatic. "Stand up straight, sir," the threatening cordiality returned, "and step slowly into the rear of the car."

I stood up straight, hands behind my head, and did a short, slow march to the rear door. MacClough's '66 Thunderbird pulled in off the expressway. I raised my arms up above my head in the ultimate gesture of surrender in an attempt to get Johnny's attention. The boys in the dull Chevy found it all pretty funny.

"Put your flaps down, Klein," Rizzo chortled, "and get in already. The Virgin Mary could have twins in the time you're takin'."

When I stepped around the open car door, the blond man shot out of the car, positioning himself behind me. He frisked me, relieved my ankle of its additional weight and guided me into the car using his left hand to shield my head. I wanted to turn around to check on MacClough, but didn't. I couldn't afford to tip my hand, if I had a hand at all, and that depended on whether Johnny'd noticed me.

"Good man," Rizzo smiled and then wiped his face expressionless. "Move."

Newkirk put the Chevy into drive, taking his time to do so. He cast his sunglassed eyes to the rearview mirror to see if his tardiness had annoyed his fat-faced boss. A red flush exploded onto Rizzo's puffy hide and the right corner of his mouth twitched excitedly. When Newkirk was certain that he'd helped to bring a little misery into Rizzo's life, he smiled, turned his shaded eyes from the mirror and let the car roll toward the expressway. I noticed that the car's interior was as dull as the face it showed the outside world.

"You've got some very interesting friends, Mr. Klein," Rizzo looked to me, his face still pink, but with the corner of his mouth at rest.

"Ain't that the truth," the farm boy added his two cents.

"Yeah," Newkirk chimed in disinterestedly.

"It's nice of you to say. You wouldn't mind being a little more specific, would you? I wouldn't want the wrong people to get the wrong ideas." My tone was as sincere as a rabbi's at an interfaith marriage.

"Sure," my back seat partner commiserated, "we know how it is. You have so many friends; it could get confusing. How, for conversation's sake, is your buddy Alexander?"

"Alexander Applebaum? He's fine, owns a carpet outlet on Staten Island. You know, I haven't spoken to him—"

Rizzo cut me off by placing the barrel of his black automatic in the soft alcove under my left earlobe where the neck and jawbone meet. "Alexander Korin, Mr. Klein, how is he?"

"Dead. Very dead and doing his best imitation of Marie Antoinette," I choked out with a smile, knowing that the gun was more for show than threat.

The man attached to the hand holding the gun seemed unmoved and unconvinced by my reply. "Where is he, Klein?"

"The last I heard of him, he was stiffening nicely in the trunk of the Lincoln I was driving the night you and I and Newkirk first met."

Rizzo pulled the pistol away and quietly considered my answer. I took the opportunity to rub my neck and roll my head around as if to loosen any tension having a gun placed under my ear might cause. I caught a glimpse of MacClough two cars behind in the far right lane driving in the Chevy's blind spot. He was good.

"Look, Mr. Klein," the blond man in the front seat threw his left arm over the seat and turned to face me. He removed his green shades to show me his long lashes and hard hazel eyes in an obvious attempt to humanize his words. "You've got to understand."

"I'd love to."

"We're in a pretty tight spot," the farm boy went on.

"As far as tight spots go," I interrupted, "I'd have to say the one I'm in looks a whole lot less roomier than yours, Mr. . . ." I trailed off.

"My name is unimportant. You may call me whatever makes you feel comfortable," he paused as if waiting to be christened. I did not oblige and he continued looking somewhat disappointed, "I realize that it's odd to say that three men with automatic weapons holding you against your will are in a tougher position than yourself, but it's true just the same."

"Come on, already with the bullshit. Can you be any more vague or what? Maybe, if you start talkin' to me like a human being with more than just a brain stem in his skull, I'll try and be as straight with you as I can. But until then, you can all stick your guns up your butts and play intestinal roulette," I told my carmates in an aggravated growl just testy enough to be believed.

Newkirk snickered and then squelched it before he was told to. Rizzo's reddening complexion let me know he was more annoyed by the black man's laugh than by my bravado. Newkirk, if that was his name, knew just what buttons to push.

"Will you two stop acting like a married couple," the front seat passenger scolded. "I'm sorry for this, Mr. Klein. We've treated you pretty shabbily, haven't we? Pressure'll make you do that. And there's enough pressure on me and my men to force us into worse mistakes than we've made with you so far." I was being given a back-handed warning.

"Yeah, and so . . ."

"We're connected with the NSA, Mr. Klein. The National—"

"—Security Agency," I finished.

"Your friend, Mr. Korin,—"

"Wasn't my friend," I corrected. "Was an acquaintance. Was someone trying to hire me. Wasn't my friend."

"As you wish, Mr. Klein. As you wish," the farm boy's patience was beginning to wear a little thin. "Mr. Korin is also connected with our organization, but in a slightly different capacity. On the evening you claim to have seen Mr. Korin dead, he was to make a rather sensitive delivery to us. Needless to say, we're still waiting for the package and the courier."

"Why tell me any of this?" I asked as innocently as Bambi.

"Because you been such a pal," Rizzo responded, grabbing and twisting at my innocent collar.

"Easy . . . easy," the hazel-eyed inquisitor purred, "there's no need for that . . . ," his voice trailing off without finishing the thought or his sentence.

There was no need to break bones, yet. Even without completing the line, the implications were clear enough. The man in the front seat knew that.

"I'm telling you what I can, Mr. Klein, so that you might see the advantages in cooperating voluntarily. The fact is," he nodded reassuringly, "that we're fairly uncomfortable with hard stuff."

The fat-faced man squirmed at those words, pushing his experienced knuckles into my Adam's apple.

"Some of us," the farm boy corrected, "are less uncomfortable with it than others."

Rizzo released me with a shove and a grunt.

"Well," I massaged my neck and reflexively straightened my shirt collar, "so far you've told me a lot of nothin' and my friend here," I leaned towards Rizzo, "doesn't show any signs of discomfort." I rolled my head back again to check on MacClough's position. His car was gone. He'd lost me. And if that was so, I was really lost. That possibility rattled around my insides like a grasshopper in a garbage can.

"You're suddenly not looking very well, Mr. Klein."

"I'm suddenly not feeling very well," I spoke the truth.

"Enough stalling, Mr. Klein," the farm boy interrogator put his green glasses back on. He'd had enough humanity for one day. "From that night in Brighton Beach until the second before we approached you today, I want you to describe, in detail, everything that's happened to you. Everything! I want to know who you've spoken to and what about. Who you've seen. When and where. And try not to skip the part about our Israeli friends. That'll really piss Mr. Rizzo off. Am I clear?

"Then," he continued without my answer, "we'll backtrack some more. You might go over your relationship with Mr. Korin. And when you've talked yourself out, maybe, we'll feel better."

Newkirk cursed in machine gun staccato and whipped us into the far right lane. That's one of the last things I remember before the night got suddenly, totally black. The very last thing I recall featured a swerving cesspool drainage tanker with a gilded facsimile of Long Island showing on its flank, the left front fender of the dull blue Chevy, a guardrail, an exit sign, my right cheek and breaking glass.

"You can sleep it off next year," words from another world and a firm hand shook me. My head flopped from shoulder to shoulder like a rag doll's: no muscle tone, no resistance. "Get up!"

I steadied my head and, with my eyes still sewn shut, I brought my right palm up to my face to survey any potential damage. The potential was realized. A moist stiffness in my beard and the tacky goo on my skin indicated that I'd done some bleeding. That, or else someone'd poured maple syrup over my head while I was out. The latter seemed unlikely. I opened my eyes.

The world wasn't totally black at all. Johnny MacClough sat sour-faced and stiff-backed behind the big wheel of his Thunderbird. We were off the expressway somewhere and a soft blue darkness worked hard at making the light from the old Ford's headlamps more than just a moot expenditure of energy. You could actually trace the overlapping funnels of light against the passive screen of deepening night. This, of course, is a revelation only to the city-raised. Urban streetlight blots out more than just the stars.

"So, you're alive, after all," MacClough spit out the side of his worried mouth.

"No thanks to you," I shot back haltingly. The right side of my jaw, where my face had hit the blue Chevy's window, wasn't functioning up to specs. "It was you, wasn't it? You cut that fucking cesspool truck off."

"I did and saved your flat Jewish be-hind in the process," he confessed, showing hints of a smile, but holding it back like an untimely sneeze. "I saw the fat boy put the rod to your throat. Things looked kinda serious for you and my options were a little limited, me being in another car."

I bowed to him. A burst of fire ignited in my chin, shot up through my skull, and into my ear. The car started spinning like a potter's wheel and the contents of my stomach shot up my throat.

"Whoa!" MacClough's quick right hand pushed my head between my knees. "Take it easy. You just turned greener than Fifth Avenue on St. Patrick's Day. Nobody gets sick in this car, not even friends."

"Alright, let me up," I coughed when enough of my stomach had resettled and my inner ear had brought the potter's wheel to a standstill. He relaxed his grip. "Where are we?"

MacClough acted deaf to the question and came up with one of his choosing: "Feeling human yet?"

"I haven't felt human for thirty-odd years. Why should I ruin a good thing now? Where are we?" I persisted loudly enough to be heard in the next time zone.

"Can't say."

"What kinda shit is—"

He quieted me with a vertical index finger across very horizontal lips, a gesture most popular with a certain false daughter. It looked substantially better on her, but Johnny's version was no less effective. When I'd been sufficiently silenced, he reformed his fingers into a hitch-hiker's salute—fist closed, thumb erect—and shook that hand over his right shoulder directing my gaze at the floor of the rear seat. An itchy, old army blanket, faded light green with time, covered something twisted and bumpy and almost humanform.

"Company?" I smiled knowingly and quickly rubbed my jaw with regret.

"Company," he confirmed.

"Which one?"

"Just full of questions, aren't we? Your fat friend from the backseat," MacClough relented without further prodding.

"Why him?"

"I'd like to say it's because I didn't appreciate his sticking a gun to your neck or that I recognized him as one of the circle jerkers who came to Sound Hill to milk me about you, but I can't."

"Well, if those aren't the reasons . . ." I drifted.

"Proximity, Einstein, proximity," Johnny shook his head with mock pity. "Minnesota Fats was the closest one to you when I got back to where you were. It was hard enough pulling your bleeding ass out before a big crowd gathered. I had to flash my shield to get him into my car without questions being asked."

"How long till we get to wherever it is we're headed?"

MacClough moved his mouth to answer, but was interrupted by some nasal moans muffled by the weathered blanket.

"Sleeping Beauty awakes!" I announced.

"Nah," the ex-detective contradicted, "he'll be out for a little while yet."

"What makes you so sure? Was he hurt worse than me in the accident?"

"No, not in the accident, after the accident. I gave him some gun butt. Makes even the most hard-to-manage people amazingly cooperative. I was in the mood to give him an overdose, but we'll need him."

"Great, but what's all the hush hush crap for if he's playin' poker with Mr. Sandman?" I sounded annoyed.

"I don't trust his type, especially when they're sleepin'."

Big Print and Little Words

I'd stopped noticing headlights against the night and the pain in my jaw by the time Johnny'd clicked the Thunderbird into park. We rested on a deeply grooved patch of blacktop that passed as a driveway, more or less. A rainforest of dormant forsythia and weeds gone wild had swallowed up a chainlink fence just outside the front door.

The house was a lime-green, salt box affair covered in cracked asbestos shingles. Two chipped and weathered slabs of concrete, slapped down on one another without the benefit of a level or a T-square, were the current excuse for front steps and a porch. This little work of art was lighted by one too-bright bulb surrounded by an austere glass fixture that kind of looked like a jam jar with the label steamed off. You know, the sorta' jar kids catch bees in or where dads keep screws they'll never use.

"Cozy little dump," I let Johnny know I was less than impressed, as I worked my way out of his car.

"Yeah, honey, a real fixer-upper-handyman's special, "Mac-Clough shot back cooly without missing a beat. "It'll grow on ya and it's perfect for us, anyway."

"How so?"

"Lonely. Quiet. Especially quiet."

"I don't know. Maybe we oughta consider a new real estate agent." I tried smiling and got reminded that my healing processes, along with the rest of me, had been heavily overtaxed lately.

"Maybe you should think about shutting up," the ex-detective suggested in a flat tone of voice I'd never heard from him before, "and maybe helpin' me carry your fat-piece-a-shit friend here across the threshold."

I didn't feel like discussing his tone of voice, so I bent down and grabbed some hands and blanket and started pulling.

"Christ!" I growled through clenched teeth, "can we stop playin' tug-a-war for a minute. My jaw's fuckin' killin' me."

"Drop him," MacClough commanded. When I hesitated, he repeated the command in that odd cool tone.

I let go, slamming the old Ford's door behind me.

"Get up there on the steps," he ordered.

I obeyed.

"Here!" MacClough flipped me some keys looped through a garbage bag twisty. "Open up and wait just inside."

As I attempted to match key to lock, the cheap ring slipped out of my palm and landed on a worn rubber mat that might once have read, "Welcome." As I knelt to scoop the keys, I heard a very human groan followed by the sickening clap of metal on meat. I could testify as an expert witness in any court about just how sickening a sound that clap could be. Somehow, I managed to open the palace gates in spite of my very wet and now shaking hands.

I stepped inside. John carried the ill-covered collection of toneless muscle right in behind me, laying it down on the floor with paradoxical gentility. Having delivered the package, he brushed past my position and clicked on a light switch. MacClough had been here before. I could sense that much—for what it was worth.

Muted yellow light from two wall sconces—not quite as Spartan in design as the outside fixture, but almost—revealed a sparsely furnished rectangular room with a low ceiling, age-darkened wood floors, and a twisted lump of arms and legs deposited center stage. I couldn't take my eyes off Johnny MacClough's face, though. I was pinned to its chilly intensity, its frozen straight lips and empty eyes. His brusque tone matched his face. I didn't know this guy, only who he used to be. No, this was who he used to be. I knew Johnny "Let the Good Times Roll" MacClough, proprietor and most faithful patron of Sound Hill's Rusty Scupper. Standing there now, a few steps from me, was John Francis MacClough, Detective (second grade), New York City Police Department. He was a man on the job, at work, a man I'd never really met. I forced my gaze away from his hard face to look at the ceiling cracks and the bargain store wall hangings of dogs playing poker, but my eyes found him again, while his eyes were fixed to the faded green army blanket.

"Go soak your head in the sink or get some ice for it. The kitchen and toilet are that way," John tilted his skull to the left. "There should be a few six packs in the box and a bottle of vodka above the stove. We'll," MacClough thrust his square chin toward the unconscious Rizzo, "be in the bedroom. Bring us some beers and the vodka."

"Vodka? You don't drink—"

"Matches," he cut me off.

"Matches?"

"Do you have a pack a matches on you?"

I didn't, but John was too impatient for me to tell him so.

"If you don't, hunt some down in the kitchen and bring 'em with you."

"You don't," I started up again.

"Yeah, yeah. Smoke or drink vodka," he finished for me without changing expression. "But maybe fatboy does."

I found the bathroom . A naked bulb hung down from the ceiling, shedding just enough light on the subject so a man could find the bowl without resorting to trial and error. The pedestal sink, walls and stall shower were done up in early mildew. My reflection looked like shit in the bevel-edged wall mirror. I considered blaming the scratched and faded foil backing to the mirror, but even I had trouble with lies that big.

I ran some cold water and splashed as much of the dried blood out of my beard and off my skin as I could. The water was probably rusty, but the light wasn't strong enough for me to see. Thank God! I did an about-face and found fresh towels on the door. Fresh towels? They must've been provided by the beer and vodka man. I also found knee grooves worn into the door just above toilet level which I chose not to think about.

MacClough was standing in the kitchen, drinking down a Budweiser and looking almost as I'd known him before tonight. I walked by him, opened the top refrigerator door, and grabbed some ice.

"Save some of that for fatso," Johnny stopped sipping for a second to warn me. "He'll need it a lot more than you do. Sit down and have one. We've gotta talk and he'll be out for a while."

"I thought you were gonna meet me in there, remember? Remember about the beer and the vodka and the matches?"

"Yeah, Klein. I remember. I also remembered you weren't a cop. That's why we gotta talk."

I found something shaped like a chair and used it for sitting.

"This," MacClough waved his beer around like a conductor's baton, "is an old NYPD safehouse. It just so happens I forgot to turn the front door keys in upon retirement. After you called, I made a few calls of my own."

"Hence the beer, vodka, and candle burning in the window," I spoke.

"What?"

"The porch light. The porch light!"

"Will you just sit there and shut up, please," he handed me a beer. "Drink it!"

"I don't—"

"Drink it, You'll need it."

I wasn't in the mood to argue.

"They're gonna indict you for Piccolo," Johnny laid it out matter of factly between a sip and two gulps.

"What?" I made like Old Faithful and sprayed some beer into the holes in the linoleum. "I thought you told me that they knew it wasn't me who offed Piccolo."

"It smells. The whole thing smells like last week's anchovies. It smells like pressure, like someone wants to squeeze you."

"Malone and Fazzano tried to squeeze me already and I wouldn't play. What makes them think I'll play now?"

"It's a new game with new players. The D.A.'s office is handlin' it now. That's politics," MacClough choked on the last word as if he'd swallowed battery acid instead of Budweiser. "I spoke to Fazzano direct. He and the Jolly Dumb Giant got yanked off the case. No way they were goin' after you. It's not like they bought your story or anything, but that don't equal murder. They figured it for a sour drug deal."

"Fazzano told you all this?" I raised my eyebrows up as high as they'd go without surgery. "I thought detectives hated other detectives nosin' in where they didn't belong."

"They do, but they hate politics worse. Fuckin' politicians." He grabbed another beer.

"So."

"So even without that side a beef in the bedroom, I was gonna stash you here awhile until we figured out what to do."

"I need to ask him some questions," I pointed my beer in the general direction of the bedroom.

"His name's Lawrence Dante or so says his N.S.A. paperwork," MacClough pulled something black and rectangular out of his back pocket and tossed it at my feet. "The N.S.A. carries a big punch."

"Big enough to get somebody indicted on a trumped-up murder charge?" I asked, studying the credentials.

"Big enough to get him convicted."

"They don't want me convicted," I threw the black folder back to Johnny with an air of careless confidence. "I know what they want, it's just that I can't give it to 'em."

"First off, I wouldn't be so certain about what they don't want. I've seen these intelligence fuckers ruin people's lives 'cause it was a slow day at the office. Second, would you care to let me in on what makes you such a hot property?"

"The little dead Russian." I took a cold swallow.

"Yeah, and so what's the little red stiff got to do with the price of tomatoes in Moscow?"

I told him. I told him about parking spots in Brooklyn Heights and about bullet holes at Blue Sabre. I told him about rented cars from Great Neck and about beige motels in Roslyn. I told him about Micki and Hannah and David and Juri and about Stalin and Hitler and Brodsky and Korin. I told him about Korin and Krylov. It was a lot of telling, but I told him.

"Get outta here!" was all MacClough could manage at first. Then: "Why you? I mean, I've seen a shitload of coincidences in my life that no one would ever believe, but come on. You're tellin' me all this baggage got dumped on your lap, because you happened to be in the wrong place at the wrong time."

"No, Johnny, the deeper I'm in this the less I believe in chance and coincidence. There's a line around the block of invisible hands takin' turns at yankin' my chain. Only the longer this stuff drags on, the more visible the hands are getting."

"And the more bumps you get on your brain."

Another one of those very human groans reached us in the kitchen.

"Speaking of bumps on the brain . . ." I smiled.

Not MacClough. His comfortable features went blank and were replaced by his cool game face before I could breathe again.

"You want answers," he pointed down at me. "I'm gonna help you get 'em. It's gonna get ugly; no good cop/bad cop tonight. You just ask the questions and listen. I'll know when it's the truth and when it's horseshit. Don't worry about that. Ready!" MacClough asked, tensing his own muscles in response.

"Sorta,"

"No sorta, Klein," he lifted me out of my chair via my neck and twisted collar. "I may have to kill that scumbag in there. Understand? So there can't be any maybes or almosts, none!" The detective shook me and pulled my face nose to nose with his. "Do you want those answers?"

I wanted them and said so.

"Take the vodka, a bag of ice, and some Buds."

"Matches?" I reminded him.

"Found a pack when you got lost in the toilet. Don't—" he was interrupted by another, louder expression of pain and awakening. "Don't take too long."

MacClough left me alone to scavenge up the goods. The beers traveled in my pockets, the zip-lock bag of cubed water in my right fist, and the fresh bottle of 100 proof Stolichnaya under my left arm. I was all set according to the guidelines of one John Francis MacClough.

Although it was a short trip to the bedroom, I did a lot of thinking on the way. The mind's amazing like that. I thought about how the people closest to me sometimes turned out to be, for the most part, strangers. I wondered about just how many men had fallen prey to nighttime interrogations at the hand of John Mac-Clough *et al.* I wondered about the knot in my stomach. It wasn't a nervous knot or a guilty knot. Numbness had become too big a part of my emotional life for that. The knot was about answers and how much I was willing to spend and let others spend to get them. The knot was about Johnny and about how close a friend he was no matter what he really turned out to be.

The fat man lay on a makeshift rack, albeit a more comfortable one than those in vogue during the Spanish Inquisition. Dante's arms were stretched above his head and handcuffed separately to legs on the bedframe. His own legs received similar treatment, only clothesline was used as the restraining medium. The top third of a red rubber ball protruded between his lips. The whale-bellied agent's white shirttails hung out over his wrinkled, blue suit pants.

Carrying my supplies to MacClough, I stumbled over a compost heap of manufactured goods, including the green blanket, Dante's belt, shoes, socks, suit jacket, and holster. The N.S.A. agent swung his bruised and swollen head from side to side, as if trying to simultaneously pop out the rubber ball and shake off his pain. He didn't seem to be having much success with either.

"Ice!" Johnny snapped. "Gimme the ice."

My right fist surrendered it. MacClough grabbed the clear bag with one mit and steadied Dante's swinging chin with the other. Without hestitation, he slammed the icebag down on the fat man's puffy, blue face. The man I'd known as Rizzo struggled vainly against the cuffs, ropes and a firm left hand.

Using a free foot, MacClough pulled a plastic milk crate underneath him and eased his body down. Pressing his lips to the restrained man's left ear, MacClough whispered forcefully: "Listen scumbag, you've done a few things that really piss me off. First, you impersonate a cop; then you come into my bar and try to jerk me around. Those two things are enough to make me wanna hurt you, but you gotta make it worse. You and your friends are tryin' to crucify Klein for somethin' we both know he didn't do. Right?" MacClough released Dante's head, but the fat man held it still. "Right?" the question was repeated and so was the lack of response.

Johnny removed the icebag and slapped whale belly across the most swollen part of his face. Dante's body went rigid with pain as blood began to flow out of a neat rip in his cheek.

"Listen, prick," MacClough began again, "I don't have time for the usual Cha-Cha. Answer the questions the first time and don't bother lying. I've got reason enough to cut your balls off already. If you wanna add a little extra motivation, that's fine. I'll just make it hurt that much more and make it last that much longer.

"My buddy's gonna ask you some questions. Give him the same respect you'd give me. If we like your answers, I'll drop you off somewhere still breathing. Then you can call off the indictment bullshit and you can live happily ever after. But if your answers suck like your taste in clothing, then I'm gonna kill you. Understand?"

This time Dante shook his head indicating that he'd gotten the message.

"Good," MacClough patted Dante's face almost affectionately and put the icebag over the open wound. "I'm gonna take the ball outta your mouth in a minute. Scream, don't scream. I don't care. No one's around to hear except the three of us." Johnny removed the ball.

Dante tried unsuccessfully to spit in Johnny's face. Apparently, rubber balls tend to dry out one's mouth. I thought I caught a hint of a smile on MacClough's cool face. I flinched in anticipation of MacClough's response, but brutality failed to follow.

"Okay, asshole," the ex-detective stood up, "that was your one shot for the night, your last shot. And you fuckin' blew it. "Klein," he turned to me, "ask away."

Suddenly, I was as dry for questions as the fat man was for saliva. I could feel sweat running down my backside as chills began to shake me inside out. My right hand found the neck of the vodka bottle and the rest of me found that oddly comforting. All the frustration I'd ever felt welled up through my legs, past my guts, and into my right arm. Dante saw it coming in my face.

"Don't!" his twisted face begged.

But I did. I slammed the body of the bottle into where his ribs should've been. That much fat could distort DaVinci's map of human anatomy. I hit something painful, alright. The wind went out of his sails faster than if I'd opened his lungs from the inside. There was no air left when I hit him again. Something grabbed my arm on the third pass and the bottle was gone.

I recognized the look of surprise on John MacClough's face. It was the same look I'd worn earlier. The look that says, "I know you, but I don't." My frustration ran away.

"Okay, Klein. That was your one shot for the night," Johnny rubbed the back of my neck, but maintained that stern look. "Just ask questions."

"Sergei Krylov," I blurted out.

Dante's partially-swollen-shut eyes parted like the Red Sea for Moses.

"Alexander Korin was Sergei Krylov," I continued. "What was his connection to the N.S.A.?"

The fat man made like he'd gone deaf. MacClough gave him a

few second and repeated my question. That got a like response.

"Just what we need, Klein, a hero," Johnny mocked. "I thought we had an understanding, scumbag," he addressed the handcuffed agent.

"You thought wrong," Dante rasped out through a distorted smile. "What you gonna do now," he coughed and swallowed some air, "mister tough cop? Ya gonna empty out your gun and play make believe Russian Roulette with me, huh? That may go over big with spic street dealers," he gulped air again, "but it don't scare me?"

"Fair enough," the ex-detective surprised me again. "Klein, open a beer for the man. Don't spit it out at me."

MacClough poured the beer down our prisoner's throat slowly at first, but accelerated the pace beyond the recipient's ability to swallow the liquid. Dante choked and heaved. Johnny latched one hand around Dante's throat and clapped the other one over the heavy man's mouth.

"I warned you, deadman. I warned you. No, I'm not gonna play with an empty .38. I'm gonna burn you to death one part at a time," MacClough loosened his throat grip to let the beer go down.

Dante tried head swinging again to no avail. Now I knew what the matches were for.

"Klein," Johnny turned to me. "Flip me that rubber ball."

I picked it clean off the floor and tossed it into a waiting left hand. All MacClough needed to do was to make the pivot and a straight throw to first for a double play. Instead, he crammed it back into the panicky man's mouth.

"Watch him for a second, a good barbeque always makes me wanna piss."

MacClough left and I took his seat. "He means it, Dante. He's going to burn you and I'm not going to stop him. I'm no fuckin' spy and you know it. I'm no traitor. Krylov is dead. I just need to know a few things to help me stay alive. Is not helpin' me worth becomin' a french fry?"

I finished my speech making and began pacing.

"Stop that, Klein," John came back in, "he's the one that's got reason to be nervous."

"Let's give him another—"

"Chance. No. No good cop/bad cop. He knew what was comin'.

He fucked up. Not us. This guy and his friends are ready to send you to Attica for life. Fuck him."

With that, MacClough ripped open Dante's shirt sending cheap plastic buttons flying throughout the room. One ricocheted off the wall and hit me in the chin. I was surprised that I retained enough presence of mind to feel it.

The fat man's belly was even more prodigious than expected. Maybe it was his sickly white skin and withered gray tree of chest hair that enhanced the size. Whatever, the bulge of white fat looked natural on him, as if he'd been born with it.

MacClough undid the vodka bottle's metal cap and took a mouthful. That changed his expression for a second. Christ, it changed mine. Instead of replacing the bottle cap, Johnny placed a thumb over the bottle's opening and proceeded to squirt a neat stripe of the clear liquid nipple to nipple on the government man's chest. Those famous matches appeared in the ex-detective's left palm. His skilled fingers wiggled one match free and bent it against the striking board.

"This won't hurt that much, asshole. Your burning hair may stink up the place, but remember this was your choice." And with that hint of rationalization, the match was lighted.

Dante's whole body tensed, even the well-camouflaged muscle beneath his massive belly stood at attention. He began to pound the back of his head into the matress. The neat rip in his purple cheek widened with each impact, mixing blood with bruise, sweat with tears. The room began to stink, but not from any burning hairs. MacClough smiled with macabre satisfaction and blew out the match, but not before it scorched his fingers.

Johnny, fingers in mouth, turned to me: "He'll talk to you, now. Come get me when you're done. Yeah," the smiling inquisitor stuck his head back in the room, "give the prick a beer."

I did and then we talked.

I found my Sound Hill friend half asleep, feet up on the kitchen table.

"Have a nice chat?" he wondered aloud, removing his feet from the formica before I could slap them down.

"Lovely stuff."

"And so . . ."

"His story checks out with Hannah's. I mean, some of the details from the false daughter's story are missin'—the way he tells it. But some of fat boy's facts were missin' this afternoon." I looked at the glow-in-the-dark wallclock. "Yesterday afternoon," I amended.

"Great," Johnny yawned, "so the little Russian was James Bond, Benedict Arnold, and Philby all rolled up into one bundle. Still doesn't explain why everybody's got such a hard-on for you."

"They think I helped him escape."

"Who?" MacClough raised his eyebrows.

"Who what? Who thinks I helped him escape or who do they think I helped to escape?" I answered his question with a two part one of my own.

"Both."

"The N.S.A. thinks I helped Kor . . . Krylov escape."

"Escape! Escape from what? Funeral expenses. The guy's probably dog food by now," Johnny choked on a gulp of new beer. "Didn't you bother tellin' your buddy Dante that this guy Krylov's a little short in the forehead department?"

"Christ, I told them in the car before you rerouted the cesspool tanker."

"And they didn't believe you, a nice Jewish boy from Brighton Beach," he shook his head in mock disgust.

"No, they didn't believe me. In fact, if you hadn't done that bit of creative driving, I'd be tied down on a bed in some safehouse with vodka on my chest." I took a sip of Johnny's beer.

"I don't get it."

"Get what?"

"Well, if this stiff Krylov is all that he's cracked up to be, then the N.S.A. should throw a party for the murderer. Look," MacClough put down the beer he'd just repossessed from me. "One," his right index finger went up, "Krylov's workin' both sides of the fence. He's a total security risk. Two," the middle finger, "he's a major potential embarrassment to the government. Just what America needs, a scandal about protecting ex-Nazi double agents. Three—"

"He wasn't really a Nazi."

"Whatever. Three," the thumb now, "things are warmin' up a little between us and the Reds. A scandal could hurt them as bad or worse than us. And if I read the newspaper correctly, the current renter at the White House wouldn't be keen on that. Ya see? It doesn't hold water. I'm surprised the N.S.A. didn't kill the little bastard themselves. Certainly woulda done a neater job of it."

"You read newspapers?"

"Uh huh, but only ones with big print and little words."

"Two things," it was my turn to make a list. "One, like I said, they don't think he's dead. Two, Krylov promised big carrots to prevent getting hit by an N.S.A. stick."

"You're losin' me, Klein," the newspaper reader threw his hands up and shirked his shoulders.

"You were right about the N.S.A. wanting to make Krylov into a bad memory. According to fat boy, they were planning a bon voyage party for the Russian. But apparently Krylov reads the papers, too, and maybe an occasional tea leaf. The Israelis told me in the motel that what separated Krylov from the pack was his ability to anticipate. It's what kept him alive under Stalin and through the war. He knew just when to switch sides, when his services were at a premium, and when they were about to drop in value.

"So before the goodbye party could be mapped out and approved, Krylov approached the N.S.A. He confessed to all his sins; Soviet and otherwise. He—"

"Why did't they introduce him to Casper the friendly ghost the minute they got done debriefing him?" the ex-cop asked incredulously.

"Because Krylov had big red carrots for the red, white and blue rabbit. He promised to provide the N.S.A., the C.I.A., the N.B.A., anyone who was interested, with a list of Soviet moles in our State Department and some rather highly placed ones at the Pentagon." I massaged my almost forgotten jaw. "To show he was acting in good faith, Krylov threw 'em a few bones as a sample."

"Fat man went for it."

"Actually, fat man's bosses. Unfortuantely for Dante, the job got dumped in his lap."

"Big lap for a big job."

"You're so witty, MacClough . . . Anyway, they cut a deal with the Russian. He'll turn over almost all the detailed info he had, under certain conditions."

"What's this 'almost all' shit?" MacClough made quotation marks in space.

"Well, if he turned it all over, there wouldn't be much need for the N.S.A. to guarantee his health. Now, would there?" I didn't wait for an an answer to continue. "Krylov agreed to do this if he were allowed a few months to get some personal things in order and if he were permitted to arrange his own fake demise. That way—"

"That way the KGB would think it was the C.I.A. or some other American intelligence branch cutting its loses upon discovering Krylov was a switch hitter." MacClough patted himself on the back.

"Right. And the Soviets are happy because their secrets will be safe with a dead man. And the N.S.A. agreed to let Krylov arrange his own departure so the KGB wouldn't get suspicious. See, everybody's happy. There's even a bonus. Upon Krylov's natural death, the information withheld from the Americans—Krylov's life insurance—was to be delivered to the N.S.A."

"And you just happened to show up the night of the big performance."

"No, John, nothing just happened. Krylov wanted me there. Somehow, I was part of the plan," I looked in the refrigerator for anything but beer. "Why do you think Dante and Newkirk—I forgot to ask if Newkirk was his real name—let me slide so easy that night."

"And here I was thinkin' my courtesy shield carried a lot a weight."

"Sorry."

"I'll get over it."

"Something went wrong with Krylov's little passion play. Dante thinks the Russians got wind of it and made like a bad TV show by putting real bullets in the prop gun, but he would think that," I sipped some jarred water. It *was* rusty.

"The guy may be fat, but his thinkin' is sound. Didn't you say the shooter's voice had a Russian ring to it with a bit of a shabby English accent thrown in for effect?"

"Yeah, that's basically what I said," I answered, scratching my beard, only to find some left-over dried blood. "But that's too easy. Too simple."

"Pardon me, Mister Master Spy. Snap out of it, Klein," Johnny clicked his fingers together. "It's time for you to go back to checkin' up on grandmas and their crutches. Christ, you're not even very good at that. So stop tryin' to out-guess the professionals."

"So—"

"Wait a second. If Dante figures the Soviets did Krylov in, what the fuck is the N.S.A. squeezing your nuts for?" MacClough wondered as if he'd just discovered logic.

"They're not convinced he's dead, remember? They only have my word on that. So maybe if I'm pushed far enough, maybe I'll panic and lead 'em to Krylov."

"Makes sense," the ex-cop concurred.

"Great minds think alike," I chided.

"Fuck you."

"Anyway, even if Krylov is dead, there's a chance I'm connected enough to know where the little Russian buried his bones and carrots. Meanwhile, all I got is a thousand-dollar check I'll probably never be able to cash, and a stained piece of yellow paper."

"You don't even have that much," MacClough smiled like a leprechaun who'd just found the pot of gold. "I do."

"Keep it! You know there's another reason for the rough stuff and the trumped indictment. I'm—"

MacClough interrupted for the umpteenth time tonight: "You're the only lead they got, the only card they've got to play. So, they're playing' it."

"Right again," I applauded like a bored spectator at a golf match. "Krylov was Dante, Newkirk, and the farm boy's responsibility. Word from on high is they better produce Krylov in one form or another or find some of those big carrots."

"If they don't?"

"If they don't, they'll be out of a job or probably worse."

"Hey," Johnny's ears pricked up, "you and fat boy got along so well tonight, maybe you and him could become partners when the N.S.A. cuts his cord."

I ignored that. "You wouldn't have killed him." It was worded like a statement of fact, but spoken like a question.

"You're never gonna know the answer to that, so don't rephrase it and don't ask it again." The bar owner pressed hard against his tired face with nervous fingers. "I've gotta go clean your future partner up and drop him off. Have a beer and get some sleep. The couch folds out. I'll be back before the sun."

"Bring me a big coffee and the paper. I've lost touch with the Mets for a few days."

"I'm sure all twenty-four of them are real concerned about that," MacClough clapped my shoulder. "Which paper you want?"

"Any one with big print and little words."

Fred Astaire

The couch folded out, but MacClough failed to say just how far. It would've slept a small dog comfortably. Maybe not, since the mattress had less stuffing than a small Christmas turkey. One good thing about exhaustion, though, it helps you overlook minor inconveniences, like bonsai convertible couches with underfed sleeping cushions. I thought about moving into the bedroom, now that Johnny'd taken Dante out for delivery, but I didn't have the energy for sheet changing or even keeping my eyes open.

I slept eyes facing east. I knew that because a low beam of sunlight, sneaking into the green shack through a rip in the ancient canvas window shade, forced my left eye shut as soon as it opened. Cupping my hands to block the uninvited sun, I pulled my left eyelid up again and then my right. The place was still pretty dark except for those spots where too many years had cut ragged paths for the sun.

I gave Johnny a shout and got the same response as those nuts who try to contact Houdini every Halloween: None. I rubbed my hand across a new-found pain in my back before attempting to get up. Maybe we just should've let the fat N.S.A. man sleep a night on the couch. He probably would've talked with less effort from us, but no less suffering for him. MacClough wasn't resting in the bedroom. I'd had bigger surprises in my life. It'd taken quite some time to get Dante cleaned up and knocked out again. The '66 Thunderbird didn't pull away from the gate until around four in the a.m. And knowing Johnny, he'd be making a few well-placed phone calls before returning.

A bath would've been great, if there had been a bath. A shower would've sufficed, but mildew and rusty water. . . I took a shower anyway. Fungus and dirty water have never felt better. Never! There was even some glycerin soap, and a generic shampoo with ingredients that would've made as good a breakfast cereal as hair cleanser.

Squinting from the sting of residual soap, I reached for a towel. One got handed to me and that saved me from groping the back of the bathroom door.

"Thanks, MacClough." My voice was muffled by the towel over my face. "Just put the paper and the coffee down on the table. I'll be right out."

But when I unmasked myself, there was no paper and no coffee and no Johnny MacClough. There were, however, two square-headed men with thick, black brows, marine haircuts and ill-fitting gray suits. Their ties were too thin and their lapels too wide. Oh, but their guns were just right.

The one closest to me followed my gaze to his gun and promptly put it away. His partner followed in kind. I must've had a pretty powerful stare.

"Yes, Mr. Klein. You are please getting dressed and accompanying us," he couldn't have hid that Russian accent behind a barn. "Your friend, Mr. MacClough," he pronounced MacCluff, "is being—"

"MacClough, like cow." I corrected.

"Yes, your friend is being entertained very comfortably by our comrades this good morning. Please, just come along and I assure you that nothing vill happen negatively to either yourself or your friend."

"And if I don't?" I asked, already knowing the answer.

"I, sir, am only a messenger, an—how do you say in English. . . ," he turned to the silent partner and muttered something in Russian, or what I assumed to be Russian.

"Errand boy," the quiet one spoke.

"I am an errand boy and in no position to make decisions about you or your friend, but I think ve both could make guesses," he smiled as innocently as an angel with brass knuckles.

"Can I get dressed first or are we going to a nudist colony?"

"Get dressed." The angel no longer smiled. "I have already asked you to do so before."

I was thinking that this guy's syntax had to be a put on, but I didn't challenge him on it. If they had Johnny, I wouldn't want to ruffle anyone's feathers. I dried myself off and threw on my less-than-fresh clothes. Fricsky and Fracsky wandered carelessly around the tiny house, opening the refrigerator doors, cabinet doors, and the bedroom door. Frankly, they paid so little attention to me that I was certain their buddies were entertaining MacClough.

"Well, are we off to see the wizard?"

The twin Russian bears looked at each other for help, but, evidently, neither one knew about ruby slippers or the tin man.

"Ve are going now," the more vocal of the two spoke up. "There is no need to bind your hands, but there must be a. . . ," he struggled again for the word, putting his right hand over his eyes.

"A blindfold," I offered, like a guess in a game of charades.

"A blindfold. Yes, a blindfold." He put one on me.

I tried to do all those things there in the backseat—I'm pretty sure it was the backseat—that I'd seen people do in the movies or on TV. I listened for bumps and potholes. I kept account of stops and starts. I tried to judge our speed by increases in interior noise. I also attempted to guess at the time our journey took. I was a failure at bumps, potholes, stops, starts, and noise. Time? I was better with time. Our jaunt took no more than twenty minutes and no less than fifteen. Big deal! For all I know the distance covered may have been three blocks. Don't laugh. I've met some New York cabbies that've turned trips around the corner into a search for the headwaters of the Nile.

My lids and pupils did all those funky things they do when exposed to the shock of a bright sun. But before they could stop doing them and focus on something, I got rushed up some steps and into a huge vestibule or hall. The only details I could make out about the building's exterior was that it was immense and old. There were days when I'd been less observant, but none came immediately to mind.

By the time I'd stopped rubbing my abused and baggy eyes, the two gray-suited square heads had gone. Their replacement was a considerably more elegant figure of a man. He was a taller, thinner man than myself, with a high-crowned balding head, a sharp-sloping nose, a long round chin and bright, smiling blue eyes. He wore a well-tailored, light blue, double-breasted suit with a pink-hued shirt and a yellow and blue silk tie. The only discordant note to his clothing was a red star pinned to his left lapel. We shook hands.

"Let me guess," I let go of his calm, firm hand, "the Soviet compound in Glen Cove."

"Were this a game show, Mr. Klein, you'd have won the grand prize." His voice mirrored his calm, firm manner. His underlying accent was surely Russian, but there was nothing dime store-ish about the English overtones. "As this is not a game show, would you settle for some freshly brewed coffee and pastries?"

"Coffee suits me, besides I couldn't afford the taxes on the grand prize. You know my name. How about your's?"

"No, Mr. Klein, I think not. I realize that's awfully rude of me, but things are better this way. Please follow me."

We wound up in a large, over-stuffed Victorian room that was sort of a combination library/office. Flouncy red velvet curtains partially obscured the view of carpet-green gardens just outside a full set of French doors. A silver tray of the promised pastries and a silver coffee pot rested on the top of a dark wood desk supported by thick, curvy legs which ended with carved wooden animal paws. The elegant man sat down behind the desk and motioned me into a red leather wing chair opposite him. He poured coffee into two delicate white china cups.

"Cream and sugar?" he asked like a practiced butler.

"Just the former."

"Cream then." He poured again, stirred and handed me the fragile cup on a matching plate.

"Before we get to be breakfast buddies," I rested the cup and saucer on my crossed legs, "there are a few things we need to straighten out."

"They are. . ."

"The two men who brought me here told me you're detaining a friend of mine. Let's understand this. I'm not saying a word to you until I'm certain my friend's safe."

A long index finger immediately began twirling the dial of a brass and ceramic phone. Speaking Russian into the mouth piece, he then handed me to the phone.

"MacClough?"

"Yeah."

"You OK?"

"Fine. Don't worry. They didn't use any rough stuff with me. They got nice guns," he almost laughed.

"Yup, I saw a few myself. Now listen," I spoke up enough for the elegant man to hear, "you'll be leaving in a few minutes," I looked at the man behind the desk for a change of expression, but none came. "When you get back to the bar, give me a call and tell me what kinda newspaper I wanted. Until then, I'm not talking. See you later. Put one of your friends back on the phone."

I handed the phone back. Some more Russian was spoken and then, "Very well, Mr. Klein. I understand your sentiments, but I assure you Mr. MacClough would've been released unharmed without your brave gesture. We wanted him only to prevent you from resisting initially. His abduction simply helped to guarantee there would be no need for violence between us. My man estimates it will take at least one half hour until your friend calls. So enjoy your coffee and relax. You may stretch your legs, if you wish, but please contain yourself on this floor of the building. I will take leave of you now." He rose with the grace of Fred Astaire.

"Just one thing," I sipped at my coffee, "if you don't mind?"

"And that would be?" the tall-man showed the first signs of strain in his voice and on his brow.

"If you weren't worried about me knowing where I was being taken, what was the blindfold routine for?"

The signs of strain went away: "Oh that! Actually, it was to make you feel at ease, more secure. It was rather over-dramatic, but we couldn't have you thinking harm might come your way just because you could lead the local militia back to where you were held. As our gesture with Mr. MacClough should indicate, our motives are purely peaceful. I only wish to talk."

"We'll see when he calls."

"As you say. Will you answer one question for me, Mr. Klein?"

"Depends."

"How many left and right turns did the driver make coming here?" the elegant man asked with the look of a curious child.

"What?"

"I assume you spent your time while blindfolded listening for changes in road noise, counting stops and potholes and calculating the number of right and left turns."

"Sorry," I shook my head in disgust. "I didn't count the turns, about the only thing I didn't think to do."

Fred Astaire pouted and hurried wordlessly out of the room. It almost seemed like he was genuinely disappointed. For all of his public school grammar and butlerish manner, I got the feeling that I'd rather not be on the other side of this smooth Russian's anger.

I was generous with the silver-potted coffee. The pastries were just alright, but hunger twisted my arm into having a few. I strolled over the hand-made oriental rugs, thumbing some leatherbound books that lined the built-in, walnut-stained shelves. Most of the books were English classics, a few French, no Russian. All of the books were basically untouched and unread, but they made for nice wallcovering.

A man in brown overalls and a Mets cap was riding a tractor mower over the backyard carpet. For some stupid reason, like his headgear, I waved at him madly. I waved at him as if I were Robinson Crusoe and he'd come to rescue me. The man in the brown overalls ignored Robinson Crusoe, Mets cap notwithstanding. I turned away from the French doors and caught Fred Astaire coming my way. His face appeared as I'd first seen it: with no signs of stress, nor strain, nor disappointment.

"There is a call for you, Mr. Klein. Use the phone on the desk," he nodded gracefully, pointing the way.

"MacClough?" my voice cracked unexpectedly.

"You O.K.?" It was Johnny.

"Yeah, so far. I think that condition should persist."

"Where are you?"

"Nah, Johnny," I looked into the elegant man's eyes, "I think my host would feel me a rude person if I told ya now."

Fred Astaire smiled approvingly.

"What kinda paper did I want, MacClough?" I went on.

"Big print and little words. Now what do I win?"

"A kick in the ass. Are you in the bar?"

"Yeah."

"Hold on." I palmed the mouthpiece.

I turned to the smooth Russian. "What's the time?"

Making the letter 'C' with his fingers, he pushed back the sleeves on his right wrist: "Nine twenty-one, Mr. Klein."

"If you're in the bar and it's after nine, Stan Long must be there having a little before-hours amber breakfast. Put him on."

I looked at the other man in the room with me to see if this impromptu request was getting under his skin. If it was, I couldn't say from his reaction.

"Yeah, Klein," a rough, disturbed man shouted in my ear, "your car stuck out in God-knows-where again?"

"No Stan, just wanted to interrupt your breakfast."

"Fuck you!" he hung up.

"Are you satisfied, Mr. Klein?" Astaire asked, crossing back behind the desk.

"Well, unless you kidnapped all of Sound Hill, I guess Mac-Clough's fine."

The elegant man must've pressed a buzzer on the desk somewhere, for no sooner had he seated himself than another person entered the room. The steps were short and quick and muffled by the weave of the rugs. The height of my chair's backrest prevented me from seeing him until he passed my position.

"Hello, again, Mr. Klein," a light-skinned black man, sporting a white gauze and adhesive tape bandage across his right cheek, reached out to shake my hand. "No need to get up."

I shook it. "Is your name really Newkirk?"

"It suits me, don't you think?" He smiled, but not without pain.

"How'd'ya get that?" I pointed at the gauze patch.

"Compliments of your friend, I believe. No hard feelings, though. I'll pay more attention to old Thunderbirds that try to drive in my blind spot from now on. Take care, Mr. Klein."

Newkirk left, but not before depositing a file on Mr. Astaire's desk.

"You're takin' some awful big chances with me, aren't you Fred?" I let my private name for him leak out?

"Fred?" he rubbed his long chin contemplatively. "Very well. No, Mr. Klein, I'm not taking big chances. I am not by nature a gambling fellow. I simply understand the rules of the game I play well enough to know that it won't be in anyone's best interest to discuss where you've been today, whom you've met and what, if anything, you've discussed."

"Care to teach me the rules? Can't play the sport, if I don't know the rules," I'd gotten his veiled threat, but didn't want to show it.

"Come now, Mr. Klein, you and Mr. MacClough have done extraordinarily well for players without a rulebook, but let me backtrack. So now you see that the man you know as Newkirk works for us and the N.S.A. Of what value is that to anyone? Do you imagine calling the local FBI office will change anything? They'll laugh at you. In fact, it wouldn't be a major revelation to me if your government already knows about Newkirk.

"It's madness, I know. But that's the game. Both your government and mine have people working in each other's intelligence networks. Some we know about, some not. The ones we know about are not shot at dawn. No, quite the opposite. They are valuable to the maintenance of stability between our two nations. In love, familiarity may breed contempt. In our business, though, it breeds stability.

"The more we know about each other, the less likely we are to act precipitously. We know about your spy satellites. You know about ours. We know what you photograph and . . . Need I continue? By telling anyone about Newkirk or about being here, you'll only be rocking a boat that needs as little rocking as possible. You see that, don't you?"

"Nice speech, Fred," I bowed. "I even agree with some of it. But you didn't bring me here for a reunion with Newkirk and then warn me against tattling. You wanna talk about someone sorta like Newkirk, but more of a major leaguer. I'm not much of a gambler myself, but I'd bet that file's chock full of goodies about him."

"Sergei Krylov." The old dancer appeared relieved and leaned back.

"Fat file."

"This!" he picked it up with a smirk of incredulity. "This is nothing, a blurb, a synopsis, a precis. No, Mr. Klein, the whole file would leave no space in this rather expansive room for the two of us."

"I didn't—"

"You needn't proclaim your innocence to me, Mr. Klein. Give me some credit for being skilled at my job. I am aware that you had no premeditated part in helping Krylov escape."

"What is it with you guys?" I raised my voice and my behind out of the red leather chair. "Krylov is dead. I'm not Madame Defarge, but I can tell when someone's had his head chopped off. Death usually follows shortly thereafter."

"Sit down!" Fred commanded. "As you must have determined for yourself by now, we were well aware of the deal that Krylov had made with the Americans. In the name of superpower stability, we'd intended to intercept Mr. Krylov on the evening in question and prevent him from making a foolish mistake. Unfortunately, something went very wrong."

"You're sitting there with a straight face tellin' me you guys weren't the ones who ventilated his skull and then removed it for good measure. I don't buy it. His death made your life easier."

"On the contrary, Mr. Klein, it's made not only your life, but mine as well exponentially more difficult." The elegant man frowned with the dexterity of a circus clown sans greasepaint. "We realize the Americans believe we either seized or quieted Krylov. It's simply not so. This is not to say that under different circumstances we would not have liked to see him dead.

"Did you know that just prior to his deal with the Americans, he'd approached us with promises of a similar nature? Certainly, after we debriefed Krylov and determined if he'd set up any booby traps to be triggered by his untimely death and/or disappearance, we would have disposed of him. But to do it so impetuously and violently makes no sense for us. We are, after all, many things, but we're not druglords, decapitating operatives just to make a point."

"Hey, do me a favor. Don't plead non-violence with me. From what I've seen of your business, you could teach Attila the Hun a few tricks and then some." I gestured for more coffee and Fred poured me a cup. "But let's say I swallow the line you're feedin' me. Who am I? Like you said, if I tried to rat you out, the FBI'd just laugh at me. So why's it so important to convince me?"

"Valid question, Mr. Klein."

"Hurrah for me. And so . . ."

"It's important that you be convinced in order to facilitate your efforts on our behalf."

"Now wait—" I tried to interject.

Fred went on: "Don't you agree that someone who is committed to and believes in their job is a more effective worker? Yes, I'm certain you see that. You also must understand that even with Mr. Newkirk placed where he is, it would be impossible for us to explain to your government that whatever misfortune that has befallen Mr. Krylov is certainly not of our doing.

"Krylov involved you in this mess for some purpose. Dead or alive, we need to know what he intended. We also need to know where he was hiding the documents he promised the Americans. It would be very embarrassing to my employers if those documents should ever fall into the wrong hands. And I want to know why the Israelis are so interested in all of this. You hold the key Mr. Klein, even if you're not conscious of what or where it is. For your own well-being and that of your friends, I'd strongly suggest you work hard to find the answers I need."

"I was wondering when you'd take the gloves off," I spilled coffee on the rug, accidentally on purpose. "Oh, silly me, look what I've done now."

"Yes, Mr. Klein, silly you." Mr. Astaire was annoyed. "I should've thought you'd realize that cooperating would be to your benefit. I'm quite sure Mr. Newkirk could be of great assistance in the quashing of certain pending criminal indictments."

"I see your point," I said and I did. "I imagine there won't be any need for me to contact you."

"Not necessary."

"I can answer one of your questions right now, free of charge. And I won't be uncovering any secrets."

"Yes," the elegant man's syllable was spoken with practiced nonchalance.

"The chief Israeli agent is an unhappy fellow named Brodsky. He doesn't believe Kryov's dead either. You guys aren't a very trusting bunch, are you? Anyway, about fifty years ago Stalin took a disliking to Brodsky's family and arranged for a little purging. Nothing serious; what's a parent or two, after all? It seems the purger in this case was an eager young lad named Krylov. During the war, apparently, Brodsky and Krylov had a chance encounter. Only this time Krylov was purging for the visiting team. It's a touching story, really. Suffice it to say, that the Israeli involvement in this is easily explained. It's just personal."

"No, Mr. Klein. In this business, it's never just personal."

"I—"

"You'll be leaving now, Mr. Klein," the old hoofer declared, looking down at the file on his desk. "One of the men who brought you here will escort you to the Long Island Railroad station in town and give you a ticket for out east."

"I wouldn't want you to go to all that expense."

"You and I will never meet or speak to one another again. Try to remember that you have great incentive for acting on our behalf.

At the same time, remind yourself that any heroics would result in unpleasantness for not only yourself, but those closest to you. Good day to you, Mr. Klein."

I didn't hear square-head one come in, but I surely felt his meaty fingers on my shoulder. I raised up before he could motivate me. I moved to the door and he followed. Apparently, he and I were no longer on friendly talking terms. At the door I peered over my right shoulder to catch a parting glance at Fred Astaire and his high crowned forehead.

"How's Ginger these days?" I shouted past the gray suit.

Fred was serious about never speaking to me again. He kept reading as if he hadn't heard the stupid question. Square-head shoved me out the door, through the huge hallway, out the front doors, down the steps, and into a sad brown Chevy Impala with its motor running. Earlier they'd treated me like royalty. Well, no. As I recall my history, the Soviets treated their royalty rather badly. In any case, they'd handled me with kid gloves. Now I was getting the bum's rush like Typhoid Mary from a soup kitchen.

The ride into town was brief, pretty, and quiet. Like I said, square-head and I were no longer chums. We passed rich men's castles that were now conference centers with personal computers in each room and bowling alleys in the basements. We passed the YMCA where I'd played basketball once or twice and not exceptionally well. But mostly we passed unique houses with haphazard trees, houses built on hilltops, houses built before communities were planned and plots allotted like squares on a gameboard. Sound Hill is still like that. There aren't any developments where the land's been flattened like the deck of an aircraft carrier and the native vegetation is chipped in favor of shrubs that highlight exterior paint schemes. But sadly, that, too, shall pass.

We rode across the tracks before stopping opposite a Burger King. Square-head smiled at me and produced a cardboard ticket out of a suit pocket. I took it and got out of the sad Chevy before he could help me.

"Klein!" my chauffer shouted at me through an open window.

"Yeah," I don't know why I answered.

"This isn't Kansas anymore." The heavy-browed Russian choked from laughing like he'd swallowed a chicken bone but loved the flavor.

He drove on. So he'd understood my earlier allusion to "Oz." So what? Was everyone's purpose on earth to keep me off-balance? No, not even I was that paranoid. It was just everyone I knew. I grabbed a train schedule from the ticket office and sat on a bench staring at numbers and humming, out of tune, of course, "They Can't Take That Away From Me."

The Employees and the Dead

Who was I to hate the Long Island Railroad? I'd been Brooklyn born and raised so it was my birthright to hate things about the city, like the subways, for instance. It was one of the privileges accorded a borough dweller. Other privileges on the list included paying enormous taxes for invisible services and standing on mile-long lines for three hours in the snow in December to pay too much money to see a movie in too small a theater that only had seating in the first three rows and no two seats together. The supreme privilege, of course, for any New York City resident was to live in a tiny, squalid apartment with a bathtub in the living room and to pay rent that would cross the eyes of the Sultan of Brunei. So, like I said, who was I to hate the Long Island Railroad?

During my brief years in Sound Hill, I'd pretty much ignored the railroad, and it, me. My ancient Volkswagen and I had managed; sometimes not so well, but we managed. All native Islanders hated the LIRR. It was one of their birthrights and privileges. The only ones who bore the system no malice were the employees and the dead. No. I take that back. From what I could gather, the employees hated it too. As for the dead, I could afford to wait awhile to ask.

I was hating the railroad today. Not only did I have forty-three minutes to kill, if the rusty, sooty diesel was on schedule, but I had to go west to go east. Don't ask! I just had to. The system's set up that way.

I had a pocket full of four quarters. I gave a thought to calling John MacClough, but figured that could wait until I got back home, if I ever got back home. I thought about a burger, but four bits wouldn't buy me the bun. I considered buying the paper, any paper, but the vending machines were as empty as the two wallets in my pockets. I just sat under the near-noon sun on a bench by the tracks. I daydreamed about a fresh change of clothes, reconsidered my dispassion for the subway and passed my railroad ticket from palm to palm.

I never used the ticket.

A persistent foreign car horn cut through my contemplation like a screaming baby at the next table ruining lunch in a restaurant. I didn't know whom the cries were meant for and didn't care to know. I wasn't interested enough in seeing a stolen parking spot or near collision. With my luck of late, I'd wind up in the middle of a fight and get bopped on the head. No, I moved to the opposite end of the platform, figuring the sun would follow and the horn blowing would stop eventually. I batted .500. The sun followed.

I looked. And the second I did, the noise rested like God on the seventh day. Its memory, however, still haunted my ears. There, where square-head had dropped me, sat a maroon BMW 2002. I looked away. I turned back. Glare prevented me from getting a good view of the driver, but I could make an educated guess. Maybe she'd buy me a burger or, better still, take me home. We might even go east without driving west first.

I dragged my feet to the car, not bothering to see if the sun would follow.

One Stringed Guitar

The only thing I could think to do was kiss her. I guess even Satan could look like a lover in hell, if hell were bad enough. Lately, hell had been bad enough.

She tasted like fresh lemons with faint reminders of stale tea. Somehow, that tasted like salvation. I don't know how I tasted, but her probably practiced response said she didn't care. Given the sighs and push and power in her kisses, I might've convinced myself there was something on my breath besides coffee. I doubted whether that something was salvation.

We stopped kissing. We stopped with short, soft kisses; our lips barely touching. They were delicate kisses, like butterflies landing in the snow. We stopped with the kinds of kisses that meant we'd kiss again, soon. It was good that we let up. Kissing through an open car window is rough on the lower back, especially when you've spent the previous night on a foldout couch for fleas.

"Buy me lunch?" I could be such a romantic.

"Yes, Dylan," Hannah screwed up her rich lips, "but not here." She threw a thumb at Burger King.

"Have it your way."

She didn't get the joke. Either that or she did a great pan face. Hannah leaned over and pushed the BMW's passenger door open. The seat's warm leather soothed me as did her fingers running through my beard.

"Your cheek is swollen," the false daughter half asked and stated.

"Got hit by a cesspool truck. It's a long story like the rest of my recent life," I sighed with no resulting relief. "What's on the menu?"

She didn't answer, but let out the clutch. We drove south along Glen Cove Road in silence. I guess we'd done enough talking and kissing for now, even though my back was feeling better. After one tight turn and three minutes, we were driving through Sea Cliff.

Sea Cliff was a town very much like Sound Hill. The irregular streets were lined with gingerbread houses, century-old bungalows, and tall, contorted trees, some of which had probably shaded Indian campsites. Nothing was moving in Sea Cliff, not even the leaves. Empty stores with moot "We're Open" signs in their windows quietly guarded either side of the main street. I didn't see a working restaurant among them. Eventually, we got to the still, brown waters of Hempstead Harbor which lead out into the Sound.

"Nice tour," I broke the no talking rule, "but that's not what this is for, is it?"

She wouldn't break the rules with me, but kept on driving along the shore. There was a left turn, another, and then the car rested. It was a lonely street of scattered, tired bungalows. The one we stopped in front of was a lime-green, salt box affair covered in cracked asbestos shingles. It had two concrete slabs for a porch and sat surrounded by overgrown weeds and an obscured chainlink fence. It looked worse under the high noon sun than by the light of a jam jar fixture.

"You know about last night," I tried striking up a conversation again.

"Yes, Dylan, and about your visit to the compound this morning," she said casually as if we were discussing yesterday's box scores.

"You know a whole lotta things."

"It is my business to know. That is how one manages to continue breathing for any length of time doing what I do."

"Funny," I snickered cruelly, "I bet you Krylov would've given me the same response."

Hannah didn't like that comparison, not that she said so. She just squirmed in her seat as if she was sitting on a cup full of worms. She changed the subject: "How did your meeting with Tankloff go?"

"Tankloff?"

"State security office. A tall, svelt gentleman, balding . . ."

"Oh, Fred Astaire," I said. "He makes a good pot of coffee, but his pastries suck. He also doesn't believe Krylov's dead. So what's new? Nobody believes the little man's dead."

"I believe."

We were moving again, following the harbor's contour south. By mutual consent, the no-talking rule was back in effect. I busied my eyes watching some schmuck in an electric blue wet suit trying to windsurf across the brown water to Port Washington. I guess he had trouble figuring out that wind really was a major ingredient in the sport. Like I said, not even the leaves were moving in Sea Cliff today.

Hannah was busy driving and saying nothing. Her lips and face twitched and moved just ever so slightly as if she were hashing something out or replaying both sides of a conversation in her head. Whatever it was, she wasn't prepared to share it with the class. She must've been in the mood for a trip down memory lane though, because she made a point of passing a certain beige clapboard motel snuggled underneath the Roslyn Overpass.

"Why do you believe me?" I started up again.

"Just be satisfied that I do, won't you, please?" Her tone sounded genuine enough, but then, so had Krylov's.

"None of any of this satisfies me, but I'll accept that you believe me for now," I relented, as we got on the LIE heading east. "The Soviets are very curious about you and your little gang of revenging angels. I'm working for them now, you know?"

"I did not think your meeting this morning was to discuss the virtues of pre-revolutionary Russian literature. Work with him, Dylan. Do what he says. He is known to be a very hard man."

"I sensed that already. Why are you so anxious to have me help him?" The short hairs on the back of my neck stood at attention.

"Because you do not know enough to hurt anyone and I have no desire to see any harm come to you." She stopped looking at the road and slid her right palm along the inside of my left thigh.

"I'm glad you feel that way. I told him this grudge between Brodsky and Krylov was a personal thing."

"And what did Tankloff say to that?" She wondered.

"Didn't buy it for a second. Said nothin' in his business—"

"Was personal," Hannah cut me off and finished. "And he's quite correct in that. It is less personal than I led you to believe yesterday."

"That's big of you. Everybody lies to me, but at least you admit it when it suits you."

"Listen, Dylan," she withdrew her hand from my thigh, "if you think back to yesterday, everything we said was being listened to and recorded. I could not very well have given you the whole picture. They never would have allowed me to let you escape. If you knew the truth, you never would have seen the light of day again. Those men in the motel yesterday are not the Keystone Cops.

"I convinced Brodsky that the only way we would ever discover the truth about Krylov was to let you escape. If you knew where he was, maybe you'd be shaken enough to lead us to him. If you were a co-conspirator with Krylov, maybe he'd lose faith in you and come out of hiding to quiet you. After all, he could scarcely afford any loose cannons rolling along the deck. If he came out of hiding, we might catch him making a false step. Even if you were as innocent as a lamb, we wanted that yellow piece of paper to check for blood and DNA. If none of the above happened, then we were no worse off than when we started. How could Brodsky argue with that logic?" Hannah asked rhetorically.

"And you convinced him to let you follow me. So I get to be the bait on the hook this time and you get to be the fisherman for once. Glad I could be of service," I chided. "Would you care to tell me what the deal is with Brodsky and Krylov if it isn't personal?"

"Do you remember the reasons the Americans wanted Krylov so badly after the war?" She wanted an answer this time.

"Yeah, and so."

"He had value on many levels then and that is truer now."

"Care to elaborate or is this gonna be a game of twenty questions?"

"The Israelis are nervous, Dylan. They—"

I stopped her: "What's this 'They' stuff. The last time I checked my scorecard you were playin' for them."

"They," the fisherman plowed on, "sense a shift in American policy coming, a shift toward negotiating with the PLO. If the new Soviet government can last long enough to carry out some of the changes they've promised, the Cold War may fade away. And if that happens, it will reduce Israel's importance in the Middle East as an ally of the United States. Israel couldn't stand to lose the billions of American dollars that literally prop up its economy. The politicians are also worried about being forced into a position where they'll either have to choose between getting into bed with Arafat or losing the money.

"At the same time, the Soviets have shown interest in re-establishing diplomatic ties with Israel. To this point, the overtures have been quiet ones, passed on through third parties. This is attractive to Israel. On a superficial level, Israel might gain the release of most of the Soviet Jews. Come election time, that would be quite a trophy to show the voters. But with the possible change in American policy, Israel could sorely use another suitor and potential source of money. Other countries have successfully manipulated U.S. policy by playing one superpower against the other. Israel's never had to do that before, but recognizes the impending need. Even if the Cold War thaws, there'll still be severe competition between the superpowers."

"Slow down." I raised my arms, palms out, like a traffic cop.

Hannah eased off the gas pedal and started to downshift.

"Not the car," I admonished her like a cranky husband teaching his wife to drive. "Slow down with the superpower politics rag. I'm sure you've got your facts straight. After all, it's your business to know, but the last time I checked there were Soviet troops in Afganistan, Contras in Nicaragua, Cubans in Angola . . . Let's not even bring up the twenty thousand nuclear warheads each side has or the guy in the White House who wants to throw a space net over the continent. I can say with a fair amount of confidence, the Cold War's not ending next week. But even if it were, what's this got to do with a dead spy from Brighton Beach?"

"Desparation," my chauffeur answered without hesitation. "The Israelis are taking a stab in the dark."

"You're losin' me again."

"It's so obvious, Dylan," it was her turn to be cranky. "Brodsky's not here to kill Krylov. He is here to bring him back to Israel. Can't you see why no one believes you about Krylov being dead?" Hannah didn't wait for me my answer. "None of them—the N.S.A., the Soviet's, the Israelis—can afford to believe you. They have too much invested in him.

"Israel was hoping that Krylov would possess some information so embarrassing to the Americans that they'd rethink their shift to the PLO. If he is dead, they'd like to get hold of the documentation he squirreled away and maybe find the blackmail they need there.

There was even some thought that Krylov's mere existence, considering his past record, would be enough to shame the Americans.

"If that line of blackmail wouldn't work, the Israelis planned to make a gift of Krylov to the Soviets as a gesture of good faith when diplomatic ties were reformed."

"Like a dowry," I added.

"Yes, very much like a dowry. And if the Soviets refused the dowry, the Israelis would've conveniently brought him to justice as a war criminial the next time the government needed to divert attention away from a real issue."

"You're right. It sounds pretty desperate to me," I almost laughed.

"Yes, almost as desperate as flying into a hostile foreign country, capturing an airport, and freeing a planeload of hostages," she offered with sarcastic pride. "Israelis are used to taking desperate chances."

"Different ballpark. Different game. Bigger stakes."

"Agreed."

"So, if you work for the Israelis and you're supposed to be tracing my steps, why are you telling me this? Aren't you afraid that giving me all this info is gonna change my plan of attack?"

"Dylan," she spoke the syllables as if something unexpected had just occurred to her, "did you read my note?"

"Yeah, some note: 'Don't cash the check!' What are you, my banker all of a sudden? Besides, it doesn't answer my other questions."

"You're not thinking, Dylan," she lectured me like a third-grade teacher. "It answers everything. I couldn't have you cash it until I explained."

I dropped it for now, feeling suddenly tired. "Where are we going, anyway?"

"To your bed, Dylan Klein. To your bed, if you'll please shut up and think."

I'd wanted her since she was a voice on the phone. And having had a taste of her, I wanted her more. I wanted her even though I could feel she was playing me like a one-stringed guitar. I wanted her enough to keep still when we passed the red railroad car at the reststop just past exit 51.

She was already wet when I pressed my left hand to her panties.

It's Either Raining

No brass bands played. No sparkly red majorettes twirled. No tartan kilted men with pipes and snares and furry black busbies marched. No milky white high school girls with lettered sweaters, saddle shoes, and blue berets chanted. No shops closed. No auburn-haired toddlers climbed on their daddies shoulders to see. No one did anything to mark my return to Sound Hill. And even if they had, I was too worked up to notice. For the better part of the last hour, Hannah and I had done everything possible to tease and excite one another while keeping most of our clothes on and trying to avoid the center median. Humans are never more in touch with their animal pasts than when they're one lick or kiss or stroke away from orgasm.

Her soaked cotton panties were on the floor at my feet near my fallen pants and less than dry briefs. I was inside of her, finally, her bare brown legs forming a sweet circle around the very bottom of my back. My left hand cupped the smooth—flexed curves of her buttocks, drops of her rolling onto my fingers. I braced my right forearm against the inside of the front door cushioning her back from the pounding my intensifying thrusts created.

Hannah ran her short nails along the back of my neck, skillfully using my own sweat as lubrication to prevent deep scratching. As I pushed harder, her arms swallowed my head and neck, burying my face in the wet valley of her dress. I bit blindly at her solid nipples through the drenched dress. When my teeth found their mark, she shuddered, her legs scissoring so tightly I could barely breathe.

When the circle loosened, she forced her tongue into my right ear, her faint sighing begging me to let go.

Which I did. I let go, pounding harder, harder . . . My force against her mass nearly snapping my right arm in two, but I wasn't complaining. God, nothing ever does feel quite that good. I fell to the floor with her as one, still inside her, the door still on its hinges, the cool wood flooring sending a chill along my wet spine.

Hannah released me, sliding down my chest, matching her lips with mine, but not kissing them. She ran her tongue across my lips and mustache, licking up the small pool of saliva. Drops of her sweat splashed onto my cheeks, burning my already foggy eyes. Hannah traveled further down, mouthing and biting at my neck, her thicket of ebony hair mingling with the curl of my beard. I just lay there. Her head vanished, reappearing somewhere below my waist and above my knees, high above my knees.

She was licking at me, almost cat-like, washing her scent from my skin and hair. I was beyond physical stimulation for the moment. Christ, I didn't even know where my legs were, exactly. My orgasms are so intense, but so short-lived that it's the floating relaxation and the bittersweet scent of the aftermath that give the experience a life worth remembering.

But Hannah was doing what she was doing for herself. As her licking passed from feline to human, and then some, she tensed for orgasm by surrounding my left leg and rubbing her thighs against my shin. Her pleasure was smashing through any barriers that remained between me and arousal, but before the walls tumbled, her inevitable sighs and shudders filled the room. The air smelled lovely and she was gone, really.

I felt more human now. The slippery, cold flooring and the pain in the bottom of my back told me so. I could hear the shower running. A shower sounded great. Unfortunately, I wasn't up to standing, so I rolled over onto my belly and reacquainted myself with the living room. I should've remained supine.

Brodsky's men. I'd forgotten about their visit when I was in Roslyn in an ugly bed playing with Captain Queeg's marbles. I was glad for the forgetting. Recall might've dampened the sex. But then again, no. Not that it would have ever won any design awards to begin with, but my house'd never looked like an old wino's throw-up either. Bits and shreds of fabric and furniture were strewn about as if the room's contents had been thrown into a giant food processor on pulse mode. Apparently, Brodsky's chaps did their job with all the skill and caring of an old Brooklyn dentist. They worked cheap and fast and rarely found what they were searching for.

I tried to care, but couldn't. Maybe I'd care later. Sex is amazing like that. I stood, finally, dragging my feet like Frankenstein's monster toward the running water.

The bathroom steam was kind to me. I couldn't see my reflection in the mirror. So now I was Dracula or maybe just Claude Raines. Man, my brain gets weak, sometimes. I had my saturated shirt over my head when it him me. Bang!

"You worked for him," I screamed through the shirt and the steam and the plastic curtain. "You worked for Krylov." I pulled the shirt back on.

"Yes, Dylan," was her careless response. "It's taken you an awfully long time to figure that out. Now please come in here. There are places I need you to reach."

"No!" I said like a petulant brat refusing spinach. "Reach them yourself."

"Dylan," her shining back mop stuck out of the shower, "don't be that way. There's much to talk about and explain, later."

I pulled my shirt off and swallowed the spinach.

She was no less beautiful now, nude and speckled with clear drops of hot water. The shower I'd been looking forward to seemed suddenly unimportant. I separated my lips to speak, but she pressed her index finger across them, as she'd done in the diner in Brooklyn. I let the gesture stop me. I didn't know what to say, anyhow.

I pulled her to me, hard, by her hair. I pressed my dry lips to hers so forcefully that I could feel her square, white teeth cutting into the pink skin of her mouth, so forcefully that I could taste the iron of my own blood. I spun her around, grabbing cruelly at her breasts with my left hand and ramming my right hand inside her. She was moist enough, but I knew I was hurting her. I wanted to hurt her. When I realized that, I stopped.

I turned her to face me, gently. Streams of tears ran down her brown cheeks, winding through drops left by the shower.

"I deserved that," she choked out.

"No one deserves that," I kissed at her tears. "I'm sorry."
Hannah smiled shyly; "You don't understand."
"I don't. I don't understand any of it. Make me understand," I pleaded.
"I will, Dylan," she ran her hand across my own tears. "I will."

We lay, my front conforming to the sloping curves of her back, on wet sheets in the false darkness of the bedroom. It was late afternoon and the sun was already west of Manhattan, but not far enough west to darken the house like a good pair of window shades. She spoke first.

"Krylov recruited me a few years ago. You know," Hannah now rolled over to face me, "he had a great talent for reading people. You, for example. In one brief encounter, he knew more about your own resourcefulness than you could ever imagine. It was no different with me. Krylov played upon my dissatisfaction with the right wing and their treatment of the Palestinians. He was also uniquely familiar with how woman are used and tossed away in this business."

"Bait on the hook," I couldn't help interrupting.

"Exactly so, bait on the hook. In some ways I was like a mistress to a man who always swears to leave his wife, but never does. Somehow, I never got off the hook. He'd say my time was coming, my time was coming," the mistress laughed too loudly. "In other ways, Dylan, I *was* like a daughter. The old man passing his skills onto the next generation. And considerable skills they were. So, our initial introductions weren't completely false."

"I know," I said, "that I promised to let you finish, but you're being a little vague."

"Yes, well . . . once I threw in with him, Krylov knew there was no turning back. I couldn't go to the Israelis and tell them I'd been working for this man. At the least, I'd never again be trusted. At worst . . . You can imagine. So he believed he could use me for bait forever, as long as it suited him. Though he did teach me things I couldn't have learned elsewhere and, for the most part, he treated me better than my own government."

"You said, 'he believed he could use'," I quoted. "Was he wrong?"

"Do you recall me saying before that I was the first?" she answered my question with another.

"Yeah. The first what?"

"Maybe it was his age," she stared at the ceiling wistfully, "or his health. Maybe it was my age, maybe my sex. I was never certain."

"The first what?" I repeated, louder this time.

"The first person Sergei Krylov ever underestimated." Hannah's voice was both proud and unbelieving.

"You never did stop working for the Israelis, even now," I pushed her away.

"Yes and no, Dylan. I understand your anger, but this is not a black and white shoot 'em up. The good guys and bad guys exchange hats and shirts and their goodness and badness. Don't you—"

"Answer the question." I demanded.

"The answer will always be yes and no." The words were sincere enough. "Krylov was right, I hate a lot of my government's policies and the way my life on this earth has been used. And please don't lecture me about choices or I'll be sick. Under orders, I stayed close to Krylov, waiting for the opportune time for him to be reeled in by his teeth through me and the hook. But if you play in the visiting team's stadium long enough, it begins to feel like home. I was too long in the water, Dylan."

"Listen," I managed, banging my head lightly against the headboard. "Can you tell me what I've got to do with any of this?"

"Yes. I'm sorry. I was getting there.

"Krylov could feel the walls closing in from all sides. It's almost funny," her voice smiled, "all the promises were going to come true for me. The Israelis suddenly remembered I was alive and closer to the man they wanted more than anyone else on the planet. I'd be out of the water soon, back to the homefield advantage.

"As for Sergei," her tone was almost affectionate, "he had amassed a small fortune over the years; hard currency, gold, bonds, everything. And he had a storehouse of marketable information that could quadruple his net worth in a New York minute. I could've shared it all with him, and when he died, it would be mine. I was more deserving of that inheritance than any real daughter could ever have been."

"But."

"The 'but', Dylan, is where you come in. To spend this fortune, to get to it, I had to help him escape. A very difficult task considering the other interested parties. Death, or a reasonable facsimile thereof, was the only type of escape that had any chance of success."

"Even death isn't working out too well; take it from me," I shook my head for emphasis, though Hannah couldn't see me.

"You underestimate yourself, Dylan. You've done better than I expected. In any case, we had to fake Krylov's death in such a manner as to throw suspicion on the three competing powers. And once all three were convinced of his death, we needed them to feel secure in the knowledge that whatever pertinent intelligence he'd hoarded was now inaccessible or had died with him."

"Tough job."

"You were the key," she came off the bed to sit on the floor opposite me. "We needed a clean man, an innocent man, but one with certain qualities. Not just anyone would do. We needed someone loyal enough to believe in his own word. It wouldn't have served us well if the man we picked stuck his tail between his legs and ran at the first sign of trouble, regardless of payment or promise. We needed someone who was curious by nature and possessed some rudimentary investigatory skills. We needed an advocate, admittedly an unwitting one. Someone to plead our case to the interested parties, to convince them that Krylov was dead. If you believed, they'd believe, eventually.

"To help them believe our advocate, we had to choose a man who, even under the most strenuous testing and careful scrutiny, would be found to have no reason to lie, no possible self-interest at all. At the very least, our chosen had to be a man whose association with Alexander Korin was both brief and a matter of chance. Dylan," she waved her hands in frustration, "do you have any clue how hard it is to manufacture chance? We were running out of time and candidates. The resourceful ones were too crooked and the innocent ones were too innocent and lacking.

"Sergei couldn't have kept the flies off of himself much longer. We would have to have taken a shot with one of the weak candidates, because sooner or later one of the interested parties would have had Krylov killed and taken the loss like a bad investment at tax time. It was that very possibility that gave the plan life in the first place.

"What I am trying to say, Dylan, is that you stumbled into it," Hannah's eyes turned down sadly. "You were the perfect candidate. To Sergei, you were manna from heaven. If your mother had passed on one day sooner or later, had she been buried on any other day of the week, had your car stalled on any other street, had you not set off the Lincoln's alarm . . . There are infinite ifs. And if any single one had happened, we wouldn't be here together, now. I'm sorry, Dylan."

"Why are you telling me this?" I couldn't look at her.

"Because you asked."

"Too simple," I barked. "By telling me, you're shooting big holes in your own plan. Your advocate is no longer unwitting. He no longer believes. If he no longer believes, then the interested parties will catch on. I may have even persuaded them a little, but they're far from convinced. Come on." I goaded, "I've had quite an education recently. It doesn't hang together."

"I'm afraid it does," she contradicted.

"Bullshit! The Russians don't have him. The N.S.A. doesn't have him and, as of yesterday, Brodsky and the Hebrew Mafia didn't have him. Now I only got a B in Symbolic Logic, but given that none of the three parties has him, I feel I can draw some very reasonable conclusions."

"Don't be so confident," Hannah warned.

"One," I went on anyway, "Korin or Krylov is alive somewhere having a good laugh. Two, he didn't underestimate you at all. Once he recruited you for him team, you signed a lifetime contract. Three, having told me enough about you and your real boss's little plan to ruin that plan, you've handed me a death sentence. Like I said before, I'm not unwitting and I don't believe. For the plan to continue working, you can't afford to have me around."

"It's either raining or it isn't. . . ." she trailed off.

"Stop talking in circles. Is it or isn't it. What is going on? Are you fucking sick? Do you always fuck your potential victims and then test their basic understanding of logic before you kill them?"

"Dylan," she slapped me, hard, "stop being so dramatic. No one's going to kill you. I just wanted to show you that logic can be impeccable and wrong. Krylov's not laughing anymore nor am I working for anyone but myself. As for death sentences, they've already been carried out."

"You know I have a friend that warned me about people who talk in circles."

"You're no threat to a plan that was smothered at birth." Hannah assured me.

"The circle's getting bigger," I rolled my eyes with displeasure.

"Sergei Krylov is dead!" she blurted out.
"How do you know?"
"I killed him."
I was lying down, so my jaw didn't have that far to travel before hitting the floor. The earth got awfully quiet, awfully fast. What was left of my head was racing. I didn't know to where.
"Prove it!" I threw down the gauntlet with the aplomb of a fighting ten year old.
"Stand up," she ordered, leading by example.
I stood, gravity reminding me that I was totally nude. Hannah, just as bare yet more resistant to the laws of physics, moved quietly behind me.
"The bullet passed your cheek here," she scratched my left cheek in the correct spot. "You should've felt its heat. Here," Hannah drove the heel of her palm into the back of my skull.
I winced. The spot was still sore from mending and memory. Before I could speak, she drew her body tightly against mine and tilted my head back to her mouth.
"Don't mention my note or the check, please. Not in here," the executioner whispered. Then loudly: "Kyrlov fell onto the desk, crushing the berries you brought him. You tensed in anticipation and I struck you."
I turned to face her. The light brown woman imposed herself upon me, my helpless arms encircling her. She pressed and I pulled so tightly that I could feel her breasts flattening against my abdomen. Her copperish eyes met my gaze.
"It wasn't the plan," she barely spoke.
"That much I got."
"I don't know. I hated him suddenly. He deserved to die. Not for what he'd done to me, but for the countless, senseless murders. I couldn't bring myself to help him escape nor could I risk turning him over to my government and have him go unpunished for his crimes. I believe what I told you previously. Even if he were put on trial, and that would only have been a last resort, a matter of political convenience, it would have looked horrible to the rest of the world. I would not chance it. So, instead of the blank I was scheduled to fire, I loaded the clip with live rounds."
"Why the—"
"Why the mutilation, you were about to ask? Actually, it was part of the plan. Only we didn't use the freshly dead body-double

already hidden in the house. We used the real product instead," she giggled.

"Double?" I wondered, though I was getting the picture.

"Yes, well, he wasn't a double, exactly. He wasn't cosmetically altered in any manner! That sort of high tech nonsense would have only drawn attention to the plan, attention no one wanted. Unfortuantely for the poor man, he had a very similar build to Krylov's and remarkably similar hands. You had to be convinced that the headless body you found was the man you knew as Alexander Korin.

"Actually," she let go of me, "fooling you would have been the easiest part of the plot. You'd only met Korin once, before that evening. And on that occasion you were distracted by your mother's death, the memories of your old doctor's house and the trouble with your car. Perfect. You were absolutely perfect. You see a man you barely know get shot. You wake up groggy, wracked with pain in a dark room. You find a headless torso wearing the same clothes and jewelry as the man whose execution you witnessed. With its head intact, the body would be the right height. And given the loss of blood and passage of time, what would anyone have assumed?"

"They would've assumed the body was Korin's." I gave the obvious answer. I was getting good at obvious answers.

"And if you had any doubt, the shots through the window would erase them or at least distract you," Hannah walked to the damp bed, picked up a cover and tossed it around her shoulders.

"Who was the voice on the phone?" I asked about the dime-store Englishman.

"A hired hand. I'd use him before. He'd never met Krylov."

"He did the hacking and the shooting, then," I yawned, feeling chilly myself.

"I did the shooting." she corrected proudly. "I'm quite a good shot."

"My car window?" I asked about the night in the diner parking lot.

"The hired hand. If you recall, I was quite busy that evening."

"I recall," the corner of my mouth smiled reflexively. "Ben Avraam and Juri?"

Her ripe lips went taut as all the emotion in her face seemed to drain down through her legs and onto the floor; "I don't know, probably the Americans sending a message." Hannah seemed unconvinced.

"When did you send the hired hand to the happy hunting ground?"

"That night, after the diner," she answered in a bit of a stutter, still thinking about the dead men at Blue Sabre. "It was part of the plan to give you carrot and stick motivation, to push you in the right directions."

"You're a lovely carrot."

The avenging angel ignored that. "You were doing better than expected, thanks to your friend MacClough. The stick no longer seemed necessary. Don't mourn the hired hand. He's the fool that murdered Piccolo. Idiot! I picked my help poorly for the job. Piccolo's death was unnecessary, but you brought him into it."

"Hey, lady, fuck you! I'm sorry I didn't run the maze like a good little rat. I was busy trying to save my life."

"You're right, of course," the executioner handed me a blanket. "Forgive me."

I thought about throwing the cover down, but the only place I threw it was over my cold skin. "Alright," I could feel myself surrendering, letting go, "Krylov deserved to die. He deserved to die and you killed him. Joe Piccolo was a scumbag, maybe not enough of a scumbag to deserve his fate, but I did drag him into it. And I was the innocent man."

"You still are," she corrected.

"No. The minute Joey Piccolo stopped breathing, I stopped being innocent forever."

There was no dispute or correction from the other human being in the room.

"So you killed Krylov," I rewound the tape to just before my *mea culpa*. "Why carry out the rest of the gag when you'd already made a moot point out of the punchline?"

"I was playing for time, stalling," she confessed, glad to get it off her chest.

"At my expense."

"At your expense. Up to the point of loading my weapon, I hadn't decided what I was going to do. Then, when I put the bullet into his brain and you were lying there unconscious, I had to choose quickly, I don't want to die, Dylan," Hannah drew close to me, staring at me so intensely I couldn't turn away. "I am no soldier of god or radical lunatic who gives no second thought after my target or enemy is dealt with. If I were, I would've strapped a bag of *plastique* on my back, given Krylov a great big hug, and blown us both to the boardwalk.

"There was quite a crowd waiting down the steps from old Dr. Potamkin's house that night. You know first hand that the N.S.A. was there. Tankloff and his posse were probably ready to head the Americans off at the pass. And I had positioned Brodsky's men myself. Remember the car that followed you as you pulled the Lincoln away from Korin's driveway?" The question required no answer. "For all I know, representatives from every nation on earth might've been there. So, until I could decide what to do . . ."

"You went on with the plan as if nothing had changed," I completed the thought. "I don't like it, but it's what I would've done. You bided time with Brodsky by tellin' him I was the fly in the ointment, that somehow Krylov had gotten to me or that I was the little Russian's plant to begin with."

"Basically, yes."

"So the Americans go to pick up Krylov, thinking he'll be sitting behind his desk smiling, drinkin' cheap Scotch, and smokin' a cigar. They must've had a good laugh, walkin' up Dr. Potamkin's steps, picturing the Russians and the Israelis chasing all over Long Island after me and the body of some poor putz who was probably a retired pattern cutter from the garment district. Probably laughed until they found the cold, nude body of the pattern cutter stiffening nicely in the closet. No wonder everyone is so fond of me."

"Dylan, I suppose it really doesn't matter, but the other man had quite a substantial criminal record."

"You suppose correctly," I gave her a mocking bow. "It wouldn't matter if he had a yellow sheet from here to Minsk. And while we're on the subject of yellow paper. . ."

"A red herring of sort," Hannah saved me the effort of formulating a question.

"Nice pun; yellow note paper covered in blood and raspberry juice, red herring. Cute."

"It was just a little improvisation of mine to keep you confused and off guard. And when the interested parties found out about it, the stained paper became a straw for them to grab at. If they grabbed hard enough, it would prove that you had convinced them of Krylov's death and that they were desperate to confirm it. Even with the flimsiest of evidence."

"But the paper wouldn't really prove anything," I scoffed. "Given the proper planning, you could've supplied them with a few quarts of blood."

"Exactly, Dylan. That is why the race for the paper is such a good measure of your performance and their desperation."

"But how—"

"No more questions, Dylan," the brown-skinned woman yawned, rubbing her eyes with the backs of her hands. "I could use a drink."

"I have beer in—"

"Not here, please." Hannah's tone was gentle and reasonable enough, but she shook her head violently from side to side, mouthing the words, "No. No. No."

"Okay, I guess I could use some fresh air, too," I winked and she smiled back. "But there is just one more question."

"Yes," no sign of her smile remained.

"Your clothes are still soaked. What are you gonna wear?"

We both laughed too long and too loudly. She vowed to manage and excused herself. Nature was calling and another shower, a solo shower, seemed like a good idea. Nature was on the line for me as well, but there wasn't any empty coffee cups around that I could remember.

I moved to hunt for clothing among the ruins. The room was truly dark now, darker than any window shade could make it. Actually, it'd been dark for a time. I just hadn't wanted to notice.

Gift Horse Laughing

Having grown up in Brighton Beach and a million miles away from the nearest chapter of the 4H Club, there were always a few farm-related cliches which were lost on me. Well, they weren't exactly lost on me, but I had to guess at the terminology. I never quite got why you weren't supposed to look a gift horse in the mouth. I'm still not clear on what a gift horse is meant to signify. I know that's dumb, but I'm from Brooklyn. There are a bunch of horse farms around Sound Hill; I wonder if any raise gift horses.

I was free now, basically, Hannah had seen to that like old Abe Lincoln had seen to the slaves. Only problem is that I comprehend Lincoln's reasoning a whole lot better. My bedroom had been bugged, my entire house, probably. She knew that coming in. But instead of blasting adolescent white boy music on the box or running every faucet in the county to cover our conversation, she pretty much spoke directly into the microphones, making certain our listening audience could jot down every word.

Sure, I'd gotten my answers, most of them anyway. I knew who'd killed whom and why, with one or two exceptions. Hannah had given me an alibi, but at the same time sealed her fate. Once I could lay it out for the interested parties—if any had missed our broadcast—I'd be out of it. I was released, off the hook and as satisfied as a handless priest shipwrecked on a lifeless island.

There, in the vacuum of the dark, I was looking so far down my gift horse's throat that it could've used my shoelace tips for toothpicks. That is, if I were wearing shoes. And as I kept asking myself why she'd done it, I could feel the horse's mouth closing over the soles of my feet. The phone rang before I got digested completely.

I found a lamp. It hurt my eyes more than the ringing phone annoyed me. The light was a waste as Brodsky's men had managed to bury Bell's invention like pirate treasure. I was no bat, but even I could follow that stubborn ringing to its source.

"Klein?"

"Who'd you expect to answer?" I went question for question.

"Geeze, Klein," MacClough scoffed, "maybe one of your friends from the Russian Embassy. You've been keepin' some strange company lately."

"If I remember right, they were keeping you company."

"Yeah. Nice bunch of guys, if you don't like smilin' or talkin' much. You'll have to explain that routine to me when we've got a spare week. Listen," was Johnny's idea of how to switch subjects, "listen, looks like you're not gonna need a cheap lawyer after all. The D.A.'s office all of a sudden got chilly on the subject of you and Piccolo. Too chilly, too sudden if you ask me. But luck changes."

"The last guy who told me about luck changing got his head shaved off," I warned. "When did you find out about the D.A.'s fickleness?"

"This morning, just after me, you and Stan had our little talk. Funny thing is, someone whispered the info in my ear without me askin'. It smells like you got friends in high places."

"They're in high places," I agreed, "but you'd have to stretch the definition from here to Sheepshead Bay Road and back to call 'em friends. Anyway, I'll be over in a few minutes, with company."

"Should I break out the good vodka?" the barman prodded.

"Cute, Johnny. Wrong company," I complimented, then corrected.

"The girl?"

"The girl."

Click. MacClough was gone, but she was there, wrapped in a towel in the doorway. Why had she announced her guilt to the world? I walked up to her wearing that question on my face. She'd seen it coming from across the semi-destroyed bedroom and stopped me from the asking.

"Dylan," Hannah kissed me like a cousin, on the cheek, "go shower while I hunt for some clothes."

I showered, but all the soap and shampoo on earth couldn't wash off the gift horse smell.

I had nice legs, but she looked better in my diaper pinned cut-off sweats than I ever could. The pulled-in waist served to accentuate her already positive curves. And somehow she redesigned one of my faded gray T-shirts into a manageable halter.

In the rubble of my rooms I found a blue pair of ripped chinos for the basis of my evening wear. Underneath my dresser—used to be my grandfather's—I dug up a pair of maroon tassled loafers that were no longer maroon and had long since lost their tassles. The heels were worn to the nails, but the soles still had a few miles of leather left. My white Oxford button-down was so covered with fabric pills that if I shaved them off, the shirt would've disintegrated.

We nodded feigned approval to one another, but didn't speak. Me, for fear of exploding. As for my emancipator, I could only guess she'd said enough. At the door I bowed like a foppish cavalier, gesturing for the lady to leave first.

The night was lighter than my room with wisps of pink just disappearing in the west. The air was cool for summer in the city, but just right for the town of Sound Hill. No fire hydrants poured water into the black gutter. No fat mothers sat in polyester housedresses in bargain store beach chairs on brick stoops, yelling at their kids to shut up and come in. No old fathers came home late, dragging their feet through screen doors to scream at their wives to get off their beach chairs and make supper. God, I really missed Brooklyn, sometimes. Hannah snaked her arm inside mine as we walked to the Rusty Scupper.

We made a natural detour and stood at the railing of the marina. It was mostly quiet, except for the gentle slapping water and shrill drunken laughter coming from one of the bigger yatchs berthed about fifty yards away. We gazed out at the bay and the night, not at each other.

"How many of the interested parties were listening to us in there?" I asked, finally, pointing back toward my house.

"All of them, maybe. Brodsky, definitely. Don't fret, Dylan. The word will spread fast enough to make your head spin," she plunked her chin onto the rail like a tired puppy, with her hands and forearms spread out to either side. "You are bursting to know why I admitted killing him when I knew people were listening."

"Yeah," I whistled, letting some of the built-up steam escape. "That and about the check. You said inside that you went on with the plan until you could decide what to do. I guess this means you've decided."

"I've decided," the puppy raised her weary head to look at me. "I like you. I can even imagine myself loving you. I don't know if I have that capacity any longer. I'm not certain I ever did, but I'm not answering your questions, am I? No," she waved at me not to speak, "I'm not.

"Krylov let me get close to him and, yes, he underestimated me, but he trusted no one completely and very few people, even partially. His mistrust served him well. He never let on as to where I could collect his files in case something went wrong. Sergei would joke that my not knowing was like an added insurance policy. My being kept in the dark, he'd joke, served two purposes. It made me into his best possible bodyguard and prevented me from shooting him in the back myself."

"You were right about his underestimating you," I congratulated her. "At least you didn't shoot him in the back."

"But I didn't know where the files were," Hannah slapped her forehead.

"So you do now." I half asked and suggested.

"No," the mistress-daughter shot me down, "but I think I have figured out how to put my hands on them."

"The check?" I tilted my head skeptically.

"The check. That stupid check you tried to buy off Piccolo's help with."

I counted the seconds, the seconds until she inquired as to the current whereabouts of that check. I could've been counting forever.

"Krylov was so very good," she grabbed my shirt. "Giving you that check was yet another insurance policy. Don't you see? If the escape fell through and he wound up as a guest of the Soviets, the Americans, or the Israelis, he'd have an out, a bargaining chip for his life. The check was like a hidden locker key or the overtired letter in the lawyer's office. If he were captured, they could neither torture it nor cajole it out of him, because he didn't have it on him.

He was an evil bastard, but a brilliant evil bastard."

"And if everything went according to schedule," I carried on, "he'd have sent someone round early the next morning to collect it from me. Nice fairy tale, but I've eaten some ripe Swiss cheese with smaller holes than this story," I turned in disgust toward the Scupper. "You're forgetting one rather large detail. Your hired hand had his mits on the check the night you wasted Krylov. He lifted it off Piccolo and served it back to me on a silver platter."

"Wait!" Hannah commanded. "I didn't know about the check's significance then. Can't you understand? I was improvising, but trying to stay as close to the plan as possible. As far as I could tell, you were supposed to keep the money you were paid. At the time, I thought it was meant to pacify and encourage you to keep your commitment to your employer, whether he was dead or alive. How did I know you were meant to have it for safe keeping? Think, Dylan. I had the check in my possession, if I knew its value then, why would I have given it back? We practically had to order you to take it."

"That's the most convoluted logic I've ever heard," It was. "But it's got a twisted sort of symmetry to it." It did. "So, I guess I'll have to believe you." I didn't. Most of me wanted to, but the knot in my stomach wouldn't let me swallow. I just couldn't stop looking at that gift horse's mouth.

"I know it seems strange," she concurred with my assessment.

"I surrender!" I folded my hands atop my head. "I'm convinced." I lied. "Anyway, you still haven't given me a clue about your decision."

"Have you ever wanted to be rich, Dylan?" she floated to me.

"No. I enjoy following poor, half-dead men with broken hips who buy rotting fruit and dented cans without labels. I love sitting in my car for hours in the winter, watching my breath and pissing in coffee cups. Why do you ask?"

"We can be rich, Dylan," Hannah hugged me, pressing her left cheek against my chest. "Not very rich, but comfortable enough. We'd never have to work again, never. Have you ever walked into a clothing store when your only worries were fit and quality of material?"

"If you can't tell, I seldom walk into clothing stores, with or without worries. But I'm not so blind I can't see your point." I wasn't. "We're back to the check . . ."

"Yes. I'm not asking you to betray your country," she pushed off my chest to talk to my eyes. "I know you wouldn't. You could never enjoy the profit and I couldn't enjoy you that way. We'll use Krylov's nest egg and destroy the files. Whatever your answer, I'm out of this."

"But you signed your own death warrant before when you destroyed mine. They can't let you walk. You confessed to killing Krylov, and even if everyone agrees the old guy deserved it, they're gonna make you pay."

"Give me credit, Dylan," she untangled herself. "I like you very much and you're a beautiful lover, but there's a limit to my generosity. I'm no sacrificial lamb trading my hide for your's."

"I'm either dumb or ignorant," I turned my palms to the night and jerked my shoulders to show I didn't understand. "Take your pick."

"Krylov's insurance policy is transferable to us. The interested parties will never know we destroyed the files. As long as they believe we have access to them, they won't touch us. They wouldn't dare, at least not for the time being. By the time one of them gets impatient enough to try something, we would have bought protection. And after a few years, when there's been some turnover amongst the interested parties and the anger has dissipated over Krylov's unscheduled departure, we can pass the word that the files have been destroyed as a gesture of goodwill."

"Some people have long memories and they're usually not the forgiving types." I cautioned.

"You're forgetting, Dylan," Hannah poo-pooed my warning. "In this business it's never personal."

"I'm not sure I'm up to that kinda good life. Besides, looking over my shoulder just gives me a stiff neck."

"Just think about it," she stepped around behind me and massaged my shoulders, "you owe me that much."

I did, but wouldn't commit verbally. "Let's get that drink," was all I said.

As we turned our backs on the bay, a wind came up. Careless loose sails flapped their goodbyes and old pipes, turned into the wind, whistled. I couldn't help thinking how much the moving air reminded me of a gift horse laughing.

Three Guys Named Biff

The Scupper was boomingly busy, relatively. A thin kid with pimples, wiry, shoulder-length brown hair, a sleeveless denim jacket, square-toed black boots, and a Confederate flag bandanna hanging out of his right rear pocket, celebrated his coming of age by playing eight ball with a similarly dressed, round-faced, doofy kind of guy in his late thirties. When doofy stretched to make a shot, his belly rolled out onto the green felt like pizza dough.

Stan Long sat in his reserved seat at the bar, directly opposite the Guiness Stout beer pull, working on some Scotch with his tongue and the black-caked sludge beneath his finger nails with a toothpick. In spite of Johnny's best efforts, and those of the owner before him, the wood floor below Stan's seat took on a gray, waxy, opaque sheen. Neither the floor nor those nails would ever come clean.

Three summertime sailors with c-note deck shoes and pastel dockers and dollars coming out of their nostrils, played a passive game of darts between sips of Remy and water. One of them enjoyed tossing back his sun-streaked hair and swishing the cognac around in the snifter. He did both so frequently, one could believe he was an actor preparing for the part. Maybe he was. The other two talked too loudly of seasons at the "Vineyard" and smiled so much it made my mouth ache to look at them.

A few locals huddled around the Budweiser tap scanning the scene with heads on swivels like radar antennae. The sour pose of their faces had nothing to do with the Bud being flat or the dying pink of the sky. It had everything to do with what their radar picked up; westerners and bikers and three guys named Biff. The enemy had landed. The invasion was on. They were powerless to stop it. Rejecting foreign beers was their major form of protest.

MacClough ignored us for a measured amount of time, not wanting to seem too involved or over-anxious. He couldn't know his calculations were for naught.

"John Francis MacClough," he extended his right hand, "what's your pleasure this evening?"

"Hannah," she took his palm with her right and squeezed it hard enough to cause a small crack in Johnny's smile and glad-handing Irishman routine, "Campari and soda with a twist."

"You've got good taste in drinks, lady," MacClough winked, "but as for company . . ." he shook his head, smiling at me.

"Black and tan," I gave my order to the back of his head.

"Klein," the ex-cop spoke to the Campari bottle, "I know what your order is better than my badge number. Did my friend here say I used to be a detective?" MacClough questioned, putting her sparkling pink cocktail on the bar.

"He didn't have to tell me," she fenced back. "Would you like a sip, Dylan?" she crossed her legs and turned to me.

"Nah," I waved her off with one hand while pulling the beer and stout foam to my lips with the other. "I'm not in the mood for cough syrup tonight."

"You're exactly right," she smiled. "For years I have been trying to place the flavor of Campari. It does rather taste like Vick's Formula 44."

I was only half listening, watching a bit of the pool game, listening about the summers I'd missed at Martha's Vineyard and wondering where the barman had hidden the check. Johnny and Hannah engaged each other in some nonsense conversation that was more a battle of wits and nerve than discussion. They'd taken to one another like a hungry mongoose to a cobra on steroids.

My eyes wandered over to MacClough's academy graduation picture. He didn't look much older now, except for his eyes. They'd seen too much to deny the years. Maybe he was mellowing with age, because there was a new addition to the right of the beat-up photo and frame. Another cheap frame displayed a collection of weathered currency; a one dollar bill, a five, a ten, a twenty, and a dreary-looking check. The first currency of each denomination he'd taken in as proprietor of the Rusty Scupper. I was surprised he didn't have his first charge receipt up there. Hey, the whole thing surprised me. The money on the wall bit was totally pizzeria in nature. And John had never struck me as the pizzeria type. Christ, it was hard enough to get him to hang his liquor license and graduation photo. Why the display? Why now, so long after opening?

The check up there amongst the dirty reserve notes was made out to "Cash" for one thousand U.S. dollars. The signature was a scrawl. It was Korin's check, the hidden locker key, the insurance policy and, if I could believe Hannah, my meal ticket. MacClough knew what he was doing. I rationalized furiously: No one ever looks at those stupid displays. I'd be cool, nonchalant, detached. I choked on my black and tan, coughing some onto my pill-ly white shirt.

"Dylan!

"Klein!"

Hannah was slapping me between the shoulder blades by the time Johnny'd gotten around the bar. At least no one tried the Heimlich maneuver.

"I'm fine," I moved away from the bar, brushing drops of beer and stout off my shirt. "Wrong pipe. That's all. Can't a man choke in peace around here?"

"Walk me to my car, won't you?" Hannah asked me, finishing her cough medicine and placing the empty high ball glass on the rutted bar. "Nice to have met you John Francis," she lied, raising herself up from the bar stool like royalty.

"Safe home, lady," John Francis offered, as if cursing in a foreign tongue.

"Be back in a minute, John Francis," I scrunched up my lips for a sarcastic kiss.

"I'll try not to breathe while you're gone."

She was out ahead of me, already walking back to her car and my house. The wind that had come up on our way into the Scupper had stayed up and intensified. Even from the rear, I could see her vainly pulling at her hair to keep it out of her eyes. That slowed her progress enough to let me catch her. I grabbed her shoulders.

"You're going to cash the check, but you're not going to come away with me, Dylan. Are you?" She looked worried, even more so than when she'd discovered the bodies at Blue Sabre. "I can't blame you," she was crying now, but hadn't noticed yet. "You're free, out of this dirty business. It wasn't your fight or game to start with. We used you, manipulated you."

"Listen," I shook her.

She wouldn't. "What I said before about loving you, I meant it. None of what happened between you and I as lovers was manipulation. You have to believe me."

I was almost willing to, but there was that skeptical knot in my guts again.

"Okay," I fed her some of my own ambiguity. "Okay. Just calm down."

"I'm fine," Hannah's muscles stiffened against the tears she realized were there. "I'm fine. Just let me go. I've got much to do, and precious little time in which to do it. Let me go," she pulled away in earnest. "You don't owe me anything now."

"What will happen to you?" I asked after her.

"I'll have a small grace period," she and the tears had stopped, but the panicked look remained. "Eventually though, they'll discover that I don't hold the key to those files. And then . . ." she moved again.

"They'll kill you."

"They'll have to," Hannah spoke over her shoulder, quickening the pace.

"Will you be safe tonight?" I asked, grabbing her to a standstill.

"Why?"

"Will you?" I repeated more forcefully.

"I should be," the panic wore down some "unless they find out immediately that you have the key and don't intend to form an alliance with me. Even then, the wheels don't usually turn so fast."

"You know I can't give you the check. I might hate a lot, maybe most, of what this country does with my tax money. I might even believe it sucks that we protected war criminals for so long, but I couldn't risk Krylov's files falling into unfriendly hands."

"I've known that all along, Dylan. I never asked for the check for myself. "We could be happy, though."

"Where will you go tonight?" I asked, ignoring the allusion to her earlier proposal.

"Back to Brooklyn Heights."

"You'll be safe there?"

"Dylan," her fuse was getting shorter, "I've already explained about the grace period."

"I never said I wouldn't go with you," was my futile attempt to buy a minute's worth of thinking.

"That's very gallant of you, but give me a measure of credit for my ability to read people." Hannah pressed her ripe lips to my cheek.

"Give me tonight to think, just tonight."

"What good will one night do?" she shook her head at my naivete.

"It won't hurt, will it?"

"One night, no. I suppose not," she wore the pleasant, bored smile of a condemned man. "But I can't see any new options for you to pull from the hat."

"Then let me sleep on the hat and see what happens. I'll come pick up my car in the morning and we'll talk then."

"Yes, Dylan," fatalism was setting in like rigor mortis, "we'll talk then."

"Promise me you won't do anything until the morning," I demanded from an exceedingly weak position.

"Scout's honor," the brown-skinned woman laughed sadly, bringing some rigid fingers to her brow.

She turned in the direction of my house and took off. I hesitated at first, but started after her.

"No, Dylan," Hannah stopped for the last time, pratically whispering. "I'd rather go on alone."

"What about your clothes?" It was a pretty unimportant question, but it's what came to mind.

"Bring them in the morning. Good night."

I stood my ground, watching her disappear into the darkness that was Sound Hill. I listened to the BMW's throaty engine, the wind carrying its sound and some of the exhaust to me. When even that was gone, I walked to the spot at the marina railing where we'd talked before the Scupper. The big yatch was gone from its berth, probably turning loose circles in the middle of the Sound. I wanted another drink.

The Rusty Scupper had lost some of its patrons in my absence. The bikers were on the road somewhere; on the road to another bar, another beer and another game of eight ball. There was an empty glass, a dirty toothpick and a pile of nail grit at the bar, but no Stan Long. The lynch mob by the Budweiser tap had abandoned their gathering place and gone home to consider what brand of Mexican beer not to drink tomorrow. So it was me and MacClough and three guys named Biff.

"Thank God you're back. I can breathe again," the barman joked. Then: "Watch out for her, Klein. She'll eat you alive."

"Strange thing is, John, I'm not the one who has to worry," I spoke carelessly, staring right at the new money display.

He followed my gaze. "Like it?"

"As long as it works."

"It'll work," the smart ex-cop assured me. "Don't you worry."

"I told you, MacClough, I'm not the one who's got that problem."

"Then why do—"

"Night. Bye. Good night." The trio of Biffs cut Johnny off mid-question and threw a ten dollar bill on the bar as if they were donating to charity.

MacClough did the business-like thing and thanked them anyway. He was savy enough to wait until they'd left to call them assholes.

"Don't put it in the register," I reached over the bar and grabbed his arm. "There'll be a spot for it up there," I pointed at the new currency display with my free hand, "by tomorrow."

"That's it!" MacClough wrenched his arm loose of my grasp, putting the ten in his pocket, "If you got nothin' to worry about, why you got that puss that looks like your pet tarantula got run over by a bus? And what are you gonna do with the check?"

"I'm gonna save someone's life with the check," I answered the latter question first. "And I got a sour look on because I'm not sure how to do it. That's why you gotta help me."

"I'm about as lost as the tribes of Israel following Moses through the desert."

"It's worse than that, MacClough," I put on a crooked smile. "Those are my footprints you're following around in the sand and Moses is nowhere in sight."

"You're scaring me," the bartender looked around for customers he knew weren't there and poured himself a guilty glass of beer. "Ya talkin' in circles like ya were born to it. Can we get outta the desert now, before the sand starts burnin' my toes?"

I took him out of the desert and put him back in Alexander Korin's office the night the little Russian was killed, back before I knew Sergei Krylov ever existed. I walked him through the steps of murder as Hannah had led me through the dance only hours before.

I took him out of the desert and into a study with unread, leather-bound books, flouncy curtains, French doors, and an elegant man who served fine coffee. I walked MacClough through Fred Astaire's sweet promises and harsh threats. I reintroduced Mr. Newkirk, explaining that the thin black man was thin and black and shrewd for both the red, white and blue and just the red.

I took him out of the desert, out of Kansas, out of Oz. I took him to the railroad station. I took him back to Sea Cliff, back to the safehouse, back to Sound Hill.

I took him out of the desert and into Hannah. I sang the executioner's song as she had sung it for me. Note for note, as she had sung it for the listeners. I introduced him to the gift horse smell and the knotful of doubts in my gut that wouldn't go away. I stood him at the rail of the marina and explained about how the check was like a hidden locker key and an insurance policy. I stood across from him at the bar trying to justify my freedom for her life.

"Its got a twisted kinda logic," MacClough held his chin in one hand and a beer in the other."

"I know it. I thought the same thing," I used both hands on my chin. "I wanna believe her, Johnny, but this whole thing's got me so fucked up . . . Anyway, I'm out of it if I wanna be and she's the one who supplied me with the out. I can't chance her story being true and me just sitting back and letting her get offed."

"Yes you can," the ex-detective offered unenthusiastically.

"No, John. I might be able to rationalize Piccolo's death. I didn't know exactly what I was getting him into. And even that doesn't sit well with me. No, John. I couldn't live with this one."

"The files, Klein. You can't risk her gettin' those either."

"Not until we have a look at 'em, anyway." I tried muffling my words with my hands but MacClough heard them in spite of that.

"You *are* nuts. You know that? How would we know what to look for? What if the shit's coded? What if—"

"What if, my ass," I cut him off angrily for fear he might convince me. "Maybe it is in code and maybe it isn't. But unless you got another option, I'm havin' a look."

"Hey genius," Johnny slapped my face with affection, "what good is canned food to a starvin' man without an opener?"

"Now who's talkin' in circles?"

"Think, Klein. You're like the starvin' man only you got the opener and no clue where the can is. You know this check," MacClough grabbed the cheap frame and pointed, "is the key to a lock, but no one's told you where the lock is. Krylov didn't tell ya. Did you ask the girl? Of course you didn't. You couldn't afford to let on that you might do this."

"Look, John. I'm taking the check back to the bank in Brighton Beach it's written against. I don't know, maybe they'll give me a grand for it. Somehow, I don't think so. Krylov was too calculating to risk anyone cashing the check before he could have it back. If I get the money for it, we know Hannah guessed wrong about the check and there's nothing I could do to save her skin. By the way," I coughed, "how'd you like to drive me to Brooklyn Heights tomorrow?"

"I wouldn't," he lied, "but I will."

"You're in this too deep already, MacClough. So all you have to do is drop me by car and go."

"I'm not a fuckin' cabbie, Klein. If I'm drivin' you in, I'm in. Besides, you already lost one of my guns and I'm not givin' you another. Someone's gotta watch your ass and I just elected myself."

"Thanks, John," I shook his hand.

"We'll be there when the bank doors open," he smiled, shaking back.

"One thing, MacClough. I told her I'd be at her house in the morning."

"Call her."

"Phone's too risky."

"Then she'll just have to wait."

"But—"

"Trust me Klein, she'll wait. If it was your neck in the noose, you'd wait."

"Okay, I'm leaving. You want me to help you close up, MacClough?"

"Nah, go get some rest. I'm gonna stay open another hour, anyway. I'll come collect your ass around 7:00."

"Bring coffee," I requested and walked to the door. "John," I called back as he started to sweep around the pool table.

"What now?"

"What were you and Hannah bickering about before at the bar? I wasn't really listening."

"We were arguing about the size of your dick. I told her issues that small weren't worth discussing. She disagreed. I guess she's got an eye for details."

"Come on, MacClough," I urged.

"Go home and rest up. We'll be busy tomorrow."

"John."

"Christ, Klein," he ceased collecting dirt and turned. "If ya must know she was curious as to why you and myself wound up out here. 'Why had we escaped?' as she put it."

"And her asking made you mad?" I wondered.

"No," he scratched at the shadow of his beard. "It was my answers that bothered me."

I thought about pursuing the matter, but didn't. The word escape would have bothered me too, probably because it was true. I had lots of stock answers about living in Sound Hill. I even believed some of them.

"Goodnight, John." I closed the door.

Unless the moon was out raising up werewolves, Sound Hill was black and empty by this time of night. And tonight, the werewolves were sleeping. But black, silent streets are no threat here, anyway. The best-lit places in the world are the most dangerous. I'd like to think that. So I walked back to what was left of my house with the dark, the quiet, and the knot in my belly for company.

Counting Cars

I was outside at 7:00, waiting and watching my breath. The chill was unexpected, but, as last night's pink sky had promised, the air today was blue and cloudless. Five or six cars passed me heading to the marina. I kept a loose count. In Sound Hill that many cars constitutes either serious traffic or a parade. In Brooklyn, five or six cars isn't even a long line at the car wash or a good start for a funeral procession.

As a kid I used to think the number of cars trailing a hearse was a measure of how much the dead were loved in life. Whenever my dad took us out driving, I'd spy any passing motorcade and count the cars behind the hearse. Ten or more cars, at two or three persons a car, meant the deceased had been well loved and would be missed. Five to nine cars were iffy, a gray area. Four or less made me look away. I couldn't help wondering how many cars would follow me. Kids are like that.

The seventh car I counted was MacClough's. I sank into the Thunderbird's bucket and groped for the coffee in Johnny's right mitt. I felt only a little better than the last time I'd sat in this seat. At least my cheek was less swollen and my beard was free of blood. But sleep hadn't come easily last night. My unremembered dreams had worn me down so much, I might've been better staying awake. I was both wired and tired.

The ride was long on traffic and short on conversation. No one sang "A Hundred Bottles of Beer . . ." or "Heart and Soul." Johnny's expression remained constant and cool, but not as inhuman as that night at the green bungalow. I just sipped my coffee, and counted the cars behind any passing hearse. I wondered how many might follow Hannah, if I screwed up today. I wondered if any would have the chance.

The immense art deco bank fit the rest of Brighton Beach like a woman's size seven shoe would fit King Kong. Next to the Chrysler building, it would've done nicely. On the corners of Brighton Beach Avenue and Coney Island Avenue, bordered in the rear by a beach club, across from Mrs. Stahl's Knishes and at the bend of the elevated subway tracks, it didn't go. I even thought that when I had my first passbook account there, before I knew what art deco was.

MacClough parked at an expired meter, throwing his police parking permit on the top of the dashboard.

"I thought you were supposed to turn those in," I said, stepping out of the low-to-the-ground Ford.

"I was also supposed to give back my shield," he answered, flashing the blue and gold badge, of which I had a small copy, in my face.

We walked out of the checkerboard track shadows and into the sun. The chill of eastern Long Island had no business here. Hoards of kids were already streaming down the subway steps carrying Frisbees and huge radios and coolers full of beer they were too young to drink.

The bank's heavy brass doors were pulled back to expose the real entrance; revolving glass panels. Its insides were cool and dark with marble floors, hanging globed fixtures, and cartoon-like murals of construction workers with shiny metal caps at labor, steam shovels belching white smoke and propeller planes flying. MacClough handed me the check and I asked a security guard, old enough to have helped build the bank, where I might cash it. He pointed to some metal poles with green velvet ropes and a few people impatiently waiting behind them. I waited too.

"Good morning, sir," the gaunt fellow hadn't said it enough yet today not to mean it. "What can we do for you?"

"Cash this!" I slid the worse for wear check across the granite counter. I looked back at Johnny who was busy with the old bank guard, probably an ex-cop.

The teller studied the little rectangular piece of paper like an anthropologist with a parcel of the Dead Sea Scrolls.

"Something wrong?" I asked, knowing that just the opposite was true. The longer he took, the more hemming and hawing he did, meant the closer I was getting to those files.

"No, sir," his reply was unconvincing. And when he picked up the phone to his left, I knew just how little conviction there was in his denial. "Yes Mr. Allen. Griggs here. Griggs, teller number six," was all I could discern before the teller turned his back to me and began whispering. Eventually, Mr. Allen and Mr. Griggs finished telling secrets. The teller put down the phone and faced me, wearing the sheepish look of a man bearing someone else's bad news.

"I thought there was nothing wrong," I sounded appropriately impatient.

"That's correct, sir. Nothing major, anyway," Griggs reformulated his position.

"Do I get my money or don't I?"

"If you'll just take this," he slid the check back to me, "to the gentleman at the third desk on your right."

"Mr. Allen?"

"Yes," Griggs looked relieved. "The man in the beige suit."

As I moved to that third desk and beige suit, I heard Griggs cry out: "Next!" and "Good morning." His greeting had already become disingenuous, thanks to me.

I winked at MacClough and he smiled back. The bank guard was eagerly chewing off Johnny's ear with cop chatter. My chauffeur and body guard tried hard to seem interested, which probably wasn't easy.

"Good day, Mr. . . , eh, sir," a round black man of forty stood and shook my hand nervously. Small beads of sweat collected on his forehead and over his prim mustache. "How can I be of assistance."

His uneasy manner seemed to pass through his hand and into me. The knot in my belly reappeared and its presence must've showed on my face. I could see its reflection on MacClough. He took his ear back from the talky, old bank guard and moved to me slowly. I faked a cough and shook my head "no" at him and mouthed the words: "Set up." Hell, even an amateur like me could spot this one. Mr. Allen might've been a bang up bank manager, but his acting career was doomed. I went on with it, anyway.

"My name's Klein. Seems your tellers are reluctant to cash a perfectly good check," I passed it to his twitching left hand.

"Yes, well. . . ," Mr. Allen over inspected the check. "Oh, you need to endorse it, sir," was the best he could do.

"Couldn't the teller have saved me the trip over here by instructing me to do that?" I was going along with the set-up, but I didn't have to make it easy.

"He's new, Mr. Klein, and didn't want to make a thousand-dollar mistake. I'm certain you understand." Allen was comfortable enough with that lie. He probably tells it a couple of times a day. In banking, that's sort of like saying, "the check's in the mail" or "the truck broke down on the bridge."

"Pen?" I asked, patting mootly at my pockets.

"Here you are," Mr. Allen handed me a black and gold Montblanc.

I endorsed the check and returned the fancy pen. I yawned, turning to find MacClough. He was gone. The bank guard, too. The intestinal knot dropped into my crotch. I got light-headed. I stared at the wall cartoons, remembering my mother's hand holding mine as we waited on line here. I remember holding the brown passbook in my other hand. We'd always go to the bank, then to the deli, then to Dr. Potamkin.

"Mr. Klein. Mr. Klein," the jittery manager snapped me out of my trance. "This envelope was left here for the person who attempted to cash the check you brought in at this branch. Here."

I took the white envelope, hesitated a minute, and opened it. I could see Mr. Allen anxiously licking the perspiration off his top lip. I still couldn't find Johnny. There was a key; I'd figured there'd be one. There was also a copy of a bank signature card bearing my forged autograph. It was an excellent likeness of my ugly hieroglyphics. The card authorized me access to a safety deposit box. I slid the key and the card along Mr. Allen's desk.

"This way, Mr. Klein," Allen picked up the key and the card.

He shot out of his seat, launched by tension, and headed to the rear of the bank. I followed, but lagged a bit as I continued to search for the ex-detective. I caught up to the manic manager without catching a glimpse of MacClough. Mr. Allen and I stood just outside a sealed and shiny steel gate guarded by an unsmiling security man with a thick neck, no hair, cold eyes, and a large, holstered sidearm.

"Buzz us in, will you," Mr. Allen half asked, half ordered.

"Certainly, sir," the guard agreed too easily and pressed a button on the wall at his back.

A lock clicked and the steel door popped open an inch or two. The eager, but still unsmiling, sentry pulled the door back fully and ushered us through it like a well-versed butler. Once past the threshold, the bars clicked shut behind us. I turned back out of habit and saw the security guard now smiling through the spaces between the bars. Where was MacClough?

My escort and I walked ahead a few more feet to the base of a green metal door. Mr. Allen defeated its lock with some handy keys and we were in. What we were in was more of a hallway than a room, per se. It was rectangular, with like shaped florescent fixtures recessed into a soundproof dropped-tile ceiling. The floors were covered in olive green carpeting and the walls were ivory white. Three evenly spaced opaque glass and wood doors lined the walls. The glass on each door displayed a single black numeral. The door to my left was door 1. To my right, door 6. At the far end of the hall stood the identical twin door to the one at my back. I couldn't say for sure, but I was willing to bet the twin door led to the vault room and that the numbered doors were entrances to observation rooms.

"Please wait for me in room 3, Mr. Klein," Allen's voice was shaking now. "I'll deliver your box to you in one moment. He was through the far green door before I could think of objecting.

His voice wasn't the only thing shaking in the bank. This was the end of the line for whatever was coming my way. MacClough was gone and I'd be alone beyond anyone's reach or anyone's help. My quaking hands tried vainly to open every door but 3. Both green doors were locked. I checked them, too. I would've procrastinated longer, if I thought there might be some advantage in waiting, but I just didn't see any. And believe me, I looked hard, real hard.

I tensed my face up, twisted the door handle to my assigned room and shoved the door in so vigorously that I landed on my bony knees. The door slammed quickly behind me. Someone fat and familiar to me laughed. The lights came up.

Newkirk stood over me, shaking his head with disapproval. At the back wall, the farm boy held MacClough, his face bloodied and already bruised, by the arms. When Johnny smiled in defiance to greet me, red poured down his chin. Dante, his hand balled up into a meaty fist, was positioned directly in front of the ex-cop.

"It's a pity you didn't keep us waiting a little longer, Klein," the fat man's sarcasm made his belly jiggle. "Would've given me some more time to repay your friend here." He slapped MacClough with the back of his hand.

I threw my arm up to Newkirk, gesturing for him to help me stand. He obliged me. Just as I was tensing to take a run at Dante, the switch hitting agent stuck a gun in my ribs. I rethought that run.

"How'd'ya know about the check and the box?" I made it a toss-up question.

"Tipped off," MacClough gurgled through the blood.

"Hey!" Dante threw an elbow into Johnny's ribs. "No one asked you." Then he turned to me: "Sorry your friend had to ruin the surprise, but yeah, we were put onto it."

I thought of asking about the snitch, but decided against it. The inquiry could have only one answer. I already knew that answer. Hannah was the sole living candidate for snitch honors and I didn't need any confirmation. Besides, Johnny would've replied whether or not he knew the correct answer, just to piss fat boy off. And fat boy was itching to be pissed off.

"If you knew—" a rapping at the cloudy glass cut me off.

"Come in," the farm boy, replete with sunglasses, called out to the knocker.

Mr. Allen pushed the door open like a faint breeze. He stepped in, head down, with even less force. His agitated hands were laden with a yard long, gray metal box.

Here," he placed the deposit box on a green marble ledge built into the wall, his eyes still watching the carpet. "When you're finished, just ring this bell," Allen pointed with a shaky finger to a black buzzer mounted above the ledge, "and someone will come collect the box." He looked up and saw MacClough's black and blue and crimson kisser: "Oh, save me, Jesus!" He left us with that sentiment and his hand covering his mouth to hold back the vomit.

"Just one thing before I open it," I tried to head off their natural impatience.

"One thing, just one," Newkirk allowed, for the same reason as MacClough before. He enjoyed aggravating Dante.

"If you knew how to get at what you were lookin' for, why'd you wait around for us to show up? I know Dante wanted to do a little payback for the other night," I continued before Newkirk could stop me, "but shouldn't that have been put on the back burner until you got your hands on the files? You could get to us anytime. Maybe," I shrugged my shoulder, "I'm just missing something."

"You're not missing a thing, Klein," Newkirk eased the .9 millimeter away from my ribs. "For one thing, we only found out about this little unveiling party of yours a few hours ago. It would've taken court orders and strings pulled from on high to get us in here before business hours. We couldn't chance telling half the free world about it. Even a good cover story would've raised too many eyebrows and made too many people suspicious, maybe the wrong people, and just think about the chance of this tip being a false lead. We already look bad enough without compounding the bad image. No, sir, we just waited for the party to begin. We enjoy crashing parties," he cleared his throat. "Okay, Klein, you got your answer, now open up."

The lid was hinged about three quarters of the way along the top of the box. I flipped it up and pulled it back. Money, lots of it, filled every visible inch of the metal receptacle. There were neatly rubberbanded stacks of used twenties, hundreds, and even a pile or two of thousand dollar bills. I couldn't resist picking up a stack and rustling it by my ear. John was the only one who appreciated my B-movie gesture.

"Screw the cash, Klein," Dante shouted at me. "Pull it outta there now or I'll crush your buddy's jaw. Now!" he slapped MacClough for emphasis.

I piled the green stacks on the matching marble ledge until all the bills were out of the deposit box. There, under the welded part of the lid, sat some plain white envelopes just like the one Mr. Allen had given me out front. I took them out, too.

"Open them, sir," the well-mannered farm boy commanded.

"Now!" whale belly chimed in.

"Eat me, you fat piece a shit," I taunted Dante.

He came at me, forgetting about MacClough for the moment. Sometimes people get sloppy when they're angry. Dante was angry. Dante got sloppy. I stuck my tongue out at him like a red flag. He saw that alright. His eyes widened. It was my left leg he didn't see, but he felt it sure enough. Boom! My foot got him square in the nuts and the air went out of him like helium from the Hindenburgh. He turned colors and slammed to the floor holding his balls and coughing. I was sort of hoping he'd swallow his tongue, but it didn't seem likely.

The farm boy let go of MacClough and began a charge at me. Johnny fell to the floor. Newkirk shifted his gun from my direction toward the charging man with the sunglasses.

"Hold your ground," Newkirk ordered. The gun made raising his voice unnecessary. "The prick deserved it," the black man referred to Dante. "I'll see about the files. Why don't you see if you can raise our colleague up from the near dead."

The farm boy took Newkirk's advice to heart and knelt over the downed agent.

"Back to business, Mr. Klein," the gun-bearing man smiled at me knowingly. "The envelopes."

I was out of cards to play, so I opened an envelope. No secret files here, just a note.

"Read it, loud and slow," the pistol holder instructed.

"Dear Mr. Klein, If you are reading this letter, I have been dead for a day, maybe a week. That really depends upon the speed with which you acted to cash my check. As you can see, the check was only an initial payment for your services. The money contained in this box is for you. I will not have any need of it here in hell.

"If you are the man I thought you were, by now you must know that I was not the man you thought me to be. My name was Sergei Krylov and I was guilty of all the crimes I have been accused of. I am certain to have wasted at least some of your time with the wild goose chase I sent you on. I will not waste any more of it by trying to justify my life.

"You will be contacted by several people in an attempt to gain access to some secret files. They do not exist. They never did. My training and experience taught me to never leave a paper trail, but that the threat of one could be an amazing weapon. This threat has kept me alive the last several months.

"I like you, Mr. Klein. I have not liked many people in my life. I am sorry to have brought you into this so shortly after the death of your mother, but I had few options remaining. Please try and understand. I am certain that you are not the reason my escape failed. You are a good man, better than even you are aware.

"The only compensation I can offer you is the money in this box and the documents contained in the accompanying envelope. As you are a man of some principles, I wish to assure you that none of these funds were accumulated through illegal means. They are the results of wise investments. Buy your mother a lovely headstone, please. I know I shall never meet her like, here. Take care, Mr. Klein." I took a breath, finally. "It's signed by Alexander Korin."

"Touching," Newkirk commented sarcastically. "The other envelope, open it."

This one was chubbier, its contents straining the glued seams of white paper. That made it difficult to open for fear of ripping something inside.

"Here!" a friendly, if somewhat groggy, voice called out.

Everyone's head, even the now breathing Dante's, turned to look at MacClough, propped up by the back wall, holding a .38 in one hand and a key chain nail clipper in the other.

"Catch!: he tossed the little clipper to me. "Use the nail file. You," he raised his voice and pointed the police special at Newkirk, "pop the shell outta the chamber, drop the clip on the floor, then the hardware. When that's done, kick the piece as close to me as you can. Understand?"

Newkirk nodded his head to indicate his comprehension.

"Do it," the ex-cop watched the bullet fall out of the chamber. "And you," Johnny shifted his attention to the kneeling agent and his charge, "do just the same with your weapon and fat boy's."

MacClough's wishes became farm boy's commands.

"That was sloppy of you," the bleeding man scolded, "to leave my .38 on me. No. It's just that you guys are all a bunch of arrogant cocksuckers. Okay, Klein, let 'er rip."

I cut a neat slit along the envelope's top edge. The triple folded papers within practically popped out of their own accord. I helped to birth them a little. Krylov hadn't lied in the note. There were no national security secrets here; Soviet or American, coded or otherwise. There were two Power of Attorney forms, one made out in Korin's name and the other in Krylov's. Both gave me the power. There was a will, naming me as sole heir, and a confession of sins dating back half a century.

MacClough opened up his mouth to issue instructions, but, oddly enough, Dante beat him to it.

"Get the fuck outta here," he choked. "Take the money and get the fuck out."

"How about the confession?" I asked in a suddenly conciliatory tone.

"What confession is that?" the farm boy wondered, taking over for the struggling fat man.

"Krylov's," I replied as innocently as William Blake's lamb.

"Never heard of him," it was Newkirk's turn. "Have you, Dante?"

"Heard of who?" he forced out.

"Who's that?" farm boy crooked his head with wonder.

"If you never heard of this guy, what are we all doin' in here together?" I banged my head against their stonewalling once more.

"That's what we'd like to know?" the three stooges practically spoke in unison.

"Let's stop bothering the nice men and go," MacClough suggested, pulling up his trouser cuff to holster the .38.

Newkirk, anticipating my lack of storage space, handed me his sport coat. I needed every inch of every pocket in my pants, Johnny's pants, and the loaner jacket. I pushed the black buzzer to call Mr. Allen and we stepped outside into the ivory hallway without looking back.

"Two down, one to go," Johnny was sounding like a sportscaster.

"Care to translate?"

"The N.S.A. won't be thrilled, but they'll be satisfied. Now that they know there was no loose ends to tie, the little dead Russian's become a non-person, a fiction. To them, Korin or Krylov never existed. That's why they didn't want to acknowledge the confession. Taking it would've been an indirect admission of Krylov's reality and their involvement with that reality," the sportcaster slapped the back of my head softly. "Get it?"

"I got it halfway through your brilliant analysis." I chided. "How you feeling?"

"Worse than I look, but better than the fat prick in there," he thumbed over his left shoulder, laughing. "No. I don't have to go to the hospital, if that's what you're thinkin'," he lied, trying to hold his ribs together with his arms.

"When we get back to Sound Hill?"

"Maybe," his ribs answered.

When Allen finally worked up the courage to come through the green metal door, he praised Jesus and nearly fainted at the sight of MacClough.

"The box is back in room 3, Mr. Allen. You can collect it after you escort us out of the bank," I simply ordered.

Johnny waved his shield in the bank man's face as an added

incentive against the wrong decisions. The smiling guard planted outside the steel bars had pulled up his roots and gone, but MacClough spotted the chatty old security man picking his nose by an empty counter near the front window.

"Hey, Klein, give me that jacket," the ex-cop demanded Newkirk's newly relined sport coat.

I complied and he limped quickly ahead, asking me to grab him on the way out. I hung back with the delicate Mr. Allen. I saw MacClough bend, then hug his prey around the shoulders, mouthing something into the fossil's ear. They stood face to face for a few seconds and they separated, the older man's face turning whiter than a cloud. Johnny rejoined me at the spinning doors and we wished Mr. Allen, good day, forever.

Once outside, we hesitated under the entrance overhang. The skies had opened without our knowledge or consent. Drops bounced off the blacktop like rubber bullets, punishing the legs of betrayed summer vacationers now desperately seeking escape from Brighton Beach. A few, unlike Sergei Krylov, were successful.

Two shirtless teenage boys in long shorts and rubber sandals raced against the rain, showing off. One slid on the concrete, peeling back the skin on his right shin and knee. Up almost immediatley, he hopped and winced to defy the pain. His competitor noticed a crowd of bikini-topped girls watching from across Coney Island Avenue. He slapped his bleeding friend on the bicep and pointed at the crowd. He was suddenly cured and walked to the bus stop like DeGaulle marching into Paris. We walked to the car like ourselves.

"What did you say to the breathing antique back in the bank?" I wanted to know.

"I stuck my gun in his ribs and told him to take a good close look at how fucked up my face was," MacClough smiled, cracking some blood that had dried on his lips. "I informed him that the next time he faked chest pains to set me up, his face would look far worse than mine even after the mortician prettied him up."

"Let's go." I urged.

"To her—" a grumbling M train, squealing on the wet tracks, drowned him out. "To her house?

I waited until the M train was a memory. "Please."

The first half of the ride along Ocean Parkway was mostly a silent affair. Johnny kept his eyes straight as the boulevard itself, pursing his puffy, scabbing lips as if to whistle, but his lungs balking at the requisite production of rushing air. I watched him. I watched steam rise off the hot, rain-polished pavement. I ran my fingers across the long chrome buttons of the old Ford's radio, as if sliding them along the keys of some grand piano.

"Try turning the radio on first. I find it helps," MacClough's sarcastic advice broke our silence.

"I just wanted to play with the buttons, John . . ."

"Yeah."

"There's a question I've always wanted to ask you, but it never seemed appropriate," I stated almost shyly.

"So, it's appropriate now?" he wanted to know.

"No, not really, but I'll ask it anyway. Why do you spell your last name like a Scotsman?"

"That's the earth-shattering question?"

"I never said it was earth-shattering, but it is the question?"

"Well, me boy," Johnny, shaking his head, fell into a brogue as thick as a bomb shelter's walls, "me grandda weren't much iv a drinkin' man, mind ya, but when the vessel carryin' himself and his family to America passed the great lady of the harbor, he could not help but partake in a wee sip of the Irish. The wee sips added up, don't ya know. So me poor grandda, through no fault of his own, is drunker than a field mouse drownin' in a still. When the immigration man asks for his family name, grandda says, 'MacClough; M-a-c-C-l-o-u-g-h.' Me grandma's taken aback. 'What av ya done, man, to your good family's name?' she wants to know. 'Well, lady,' he says, 'the Irish have a bad enough score against 'em in dis country widout 'em tinkin' dat I'm anodder shanty mick. Now dey're tinkin' I'm anodder fallin' down, tightwad Scot. It serves dem Protestant devils right.'"

"Never dropped the 'a'?"

"Never." he confirmed, easing off the gas pedal.

MacClough straddled his T-bird parallel to my tired blue Volkswagen. It hadn't moved or changed much in the few days I'd left it, but I could see that several brown-shirted Department of Traffic agents had taken this opportunity to adorn its windshield with some beige pieces of cardboard. But what's a c-note and a half's worth of parking tickets when you've got ten times that much between your ass and the vinyl it's sitting on? It still hurts, only not as much.

"What about the Soviets?" I asked myself out loud.

"What?"

"Okay, the N.S.A.'ll be satisfied, but what—"

"They'll feel the same way the N.S.A. does," Johnny cut me off, "once Newkirk relays what happened at the bank to your buddy at the Russian compound."

"Two down," I repeated his earlier sports report.

"Exactly. Now there's only her," MacClough nodded his head toward her building, "to deal with."

"What do ya think Brodsky's gonna do with her when he finds out the insurance policy was a fraud?" I questioned, talking into the car door and looking up to her high window.

"I'll stay here and wait, but take this," the ex-detective ignored my query and handed me his gun. "Don't lose this one."

I wanted to tell him to leave, to go get his ribs taped up, to go back to Sound Hill and start spending the money. Instead, I took the gun and tucked it under my shirt.

"Shit!" I slapped my thigh.

"What now?" he wondered impatiently.

"I left her clothes back at my house."

"That's the last thing on earth she'd be worryin' about today. Go!"

"Yeah," I closed the heavy car door behind me.

The skies had peppered the planet enough for now. My car was hardly wet, but a plastic gleam covered the streets. It's a false coating that fools the eyes into believing that things are sweet and clean and fresh again. In Brooklyn, it's an especially big lie. I opened up the VW's door and emptied my green-lined pockets onto the forgotten silk shirts in the backseat. I threw my coagulated parking tickets in for good measure.

It might have been deja vu, but for the time of day. I couldn't reconcile that. As before, the doors in my path and the steps beneath my feet fell away at my touch and melted at the pressure of my soles. I was at her landing, the sweat soaking through the back of my shirt just as it had the last time I'd visited. I pulled out MacClough's .38 and tiptoed through her passive door. I found her in the living room, again. She was still dressed in the makeshift ensemble I'd scraped together for her.

Guns are ugly things. Guns are uglier things in a dead woman's mouth. There wasn't much blood on her face. Most of it had run out onto the floor through a hole in the back of her head. Some of it had even leaked onto the slacks of the man bending over her.

"Get out of here, Mr. Klein," the kneeling, white-haired man directed, without deigning to face me.

"Up on your feet, Brodsky," I ordered in return, my thumb pulling back the hammer on Johnny's pistol until we both heard it click into place. "Hands straight up, then the rest of you, slowly. How'd you know it was me coming through the door?"

"Where else would you go upon leaving the bank?" the old Israeli asked, following my instructions to the letter. "After her," he looked down at Hannah's body in disgust and nudged it with his right shoe tip, "little recital yesterday, did you imagine you would not be followed? Are you that foolish a man? Yes," Brodsky smiled, answering his own question, "you are a very foolish man."

"You got lotsa questions and some pretty funny opinions for a man with a gun pointed at his nuts and a dead girl at his feet. At the same pace as before, put your hand into your coat. Pull out your weapon. Drop it on the floor and kick it over to me. Or is that your gun in her mouth?" I wondered.

"This," he nudged the stiffening flesh again, "is not my handy work. Here," from his suit jacket he produced the twin to the gun in Hannah's dormant mouth. "She killed herself, Mr.Klein. I guess she grew too impatient for her white knight," he laughed at me. "Her white knight indeed!"

"Is there a note?" I asked, debating whether to pull the trigger or agree with Brodsky's disdain for me.

"A note!" he took a step toward me before remembering the barrel and bullet aimed at his balls. "Why should she write a note? She knew her situation was hopeless. What could you have done for her? Nothing. And she understood that. Would you have liked her to sum that up for you in a few concise paragraphs? Idiot!"

"No note," I tried, unsuccessfully, to keep my voice from shaking. "No note," I repeated, "that's bad for you, Mr. Brodsky, very bad."

His face was practiced wax. It told me nothing I could say or do would faze him, but his eyes belied traces of fear. The angry quaking in my voice forced him to stare at MacClough's .38.

"If I had done this," Brodsky nodded at the body, neglecting to nudge it with his wingtips this time, "you would never have found me here."

"Tell it to the judge." I chided, my voice no longer shaking.

"And what would you tell the judge, Mr. Klein?" His eyes were back to their cold-faded blue and his mouth was back to asking questions.

"You held her here, I'd say, waiting until your man on the inside called you about the files. When you got the word that the files were a myth as big as penis envy, you punished her for killing off your government's bargaining chip. With the little Russian dead, those files were your last hope and her *only* hope. As long as she might gain access to Krylov's records, you couldn't risk hurting her. But when you got the bad news, you blew her brain out the back of her head. Too bad you got caught tryin' to cover your tracks."

The ancient sour man didn't say a word. He confidently shook his head, no. And I was beginning to believe.

"Okay," I tried to convince myself. "You never intended to use Krylov as a bargaining chip at all. You meant to execute him to relieve yourself of the survivor's guilt that's been haunting you for forty years. When she killed him, she frustrated your last chance at freedom from the guilt."

"I might very well have killed him, Mr. Klein," Brodsky admitted. "I shall never have the pleasure to know, but I did not kill Hannah for that or any other reason. I came here to find out what that performance was all about in your bedroom yesterday."

"I can't figure that one out myself," I acknowledged.

"No, of course not," disdain returned to his voice. "You are too busy being relieved. She knew I'd be curious to find out what cards she had to play."

"You'll never know." I reminded him with cruel satisfaction.

"No, Mr. Klein, I never will. She's robbed me twice, but at such a cost," Brodsky sounded like a rabbi at a stranger's funeral. "I hope it was worth it. May I put my arms down now?"

"Would you have killed her?" I asked, ignoring his request.

"Eventually, yes. I would have to and she understood that," his head tilted down, and he shook it in disappointment. "But nothing this dramatic. And despite my frustrations, I would never have done it myself. Maybe. Krylov, maybe. But not her. May I?" he waved his tired arms.

"Put 'em down. I'll call the cops," I undid the .38's anxious hammer and placed it back under my shirt as a lone fly buzzed my right ear.

"That will be unnecessary, Mr. Klein. . . ," he paused. "Please," was the only heartfelt thing I would ever hear him say.

"Here!" I tossed him the only pack of money I'd neglected to empty from my pockets.

He fumbled trying to catch it, dropping the crisp bills into the tacky crimson pool around Hannah's uncaring head.

"What for?" Brodsky was curious about the money.

"I want at least ten cars behind the hearse. That should pay for 'em and a few tanks of gas."

"There will be no hearse nor cars to follow," the words were practically inaudible for his laughing. "You are truly a foolish man. I hope you get more comfortable with your guilt, Mr. Klein. I do. It seems you have been robbed as well."

"Of what?"

"Of many, many good nights of sleep. Goodbye now, Mr. Klein."

I started for the door without protest. I never found arguing with the truth a very fruitful activity. I did turn to catch one last glimpse of Hannah, but focused instead on a lone fly gorging himself in the sticky liquid which had once filled Hannah's lips.

Johnny sat patiently in his Thunderbird, pretending to read Krylov's confession. Maybe he really was reading. I don't know. I hesitated on the front steps and noticed that the sun had chased away the earth's false gleam. I didn't look back.

I leaned down on MacClough's door, waiting for the window to drop completely.

"Three down," I gave him the score.

"What's wrong, then?" he asked, seeing it in my face.

"She's dead."

"Murdered?"

"Suicide. Gun barrel in mouth. Goodbye!"

"Women don't—"

"Commit violent suicide," I finished. "She would. She did."

"Did you call the cops?"

"Not necessary. Brodsky's handling it."

"Brodsky? He—"

"No, John. He didn't. Even if he did, he'd never hear a cell door slam behind him."

"What makes you so sure he didn't do the deed?"

"He just didn't, John. Trust me."

"I don't like it."

"Not less than me, MacClough. Not less than me."

"So, let's say I believe Brodsky. I still don't like not calling the cops."

"You wouldn't. Just go home, John. Please, just go home. I'll call you later."

"Will you be okay?"

"No, but I'll get home fine."

"I know it, but—"

"Here," I returned his .38. "Bye, MacClough."

He put his car in drive. I could feel the little jump.

"John."

"What?"

"Thanks," I shook his hand. "I owe you—"

"Nothin', Well . . . maybe a new sign for the Scupper."

"Yeah, maybe."

He was gone, probably cursing at himself for not getting the law. No, not probably.

I left my parking spot in Brooklyn Heights. Someone had, after all, died in the neighborhood. It wouldn't be vacant for more than a few minutes, nor would Hannah's apartment. New York is like that.

Sunday Breezes Revisited

On this Sunday the sun's light was too brilliant for life to go sleeping. That much hadn't changed in the year. Some things had.

The Rusty Scupper had a new, green neon sign. Unfortunately, MacClough was forced to keep it inside his storeroom. Seems the zoning commission or the buildings commission or the Society for the Preservation of Eastern Suffolk County didn't care much for hanging green neon on what had once been a meeting hall for whalers. They did give him a heavy metal plaque to hang by the front door declaring the Scupper a site of some historic significance. That plaque meant more money as the bar now appeared on tourist maps. It also meant more headaches as he couldn't even put in new bathroom fixtures without petitioning the governor and his grandson's pet monkey. Ain't bureaucracy a grand thing? I suppose I should've bought him a big screen TV instead.

I moved out of the little rented house by the marina and into an old barn a mile past the edge of town. It was more of a shed than a barn, but I liked to think of it as a barn. I bought the structure and a few acres from an old potato farmer. He thought I was crazy, but I could afford to be crazy. I had never wanted to be so alone for so long before. I learned how to sleep again, though never quite as well as I had. I also learned that crickets at night in the summer are louder than any elevated subway train could ever be.

I'd given up long nights in the Volkswagen and pissing into empty coffee cups. My office was closed and the phone disconnected. No one cried about it, not even my landlord. He was going to convert the space into an illegal summer rental. The locals were right. The invasion was on. The enemy was here. And now, some of the troops were exchanging uniforms.

My brothers and I were speaking again. The fact that I had contributed to my nieces' and nephews' college funds sort of supplied the peace talks with some momentum. I guess they would've talked to me anyway. I'd like to think that. My Dad was holding up. He kept saying how much he hated Florida, but he'd managed to spend a lot of time down there. I saw that it was good for him to hate it. We all did. He wasn't hating it today. He was here today, under our bright sun.

No one wailed or fainted and there were no limo drivers to wear black or to keep me posted on the Mets game. The unveiling of my mother's tombstone had gone smoothly. No one jumped on the casket last year, so no one jumped on the grave today. My brothers even brought their kids. The rabbi droned on in two languages and we sang along. In his thankfully brief eulogy, he repeated some of last year's memorized lies concerning the wonder that was my mother's life. I imagine that was a service he provides for all his flock or anyone who could pay the price.

After the official ceremony, we broke up into little cliques of kissing and hugging humanity. My Dad and Uncle Saul stopped off by Dead Uncle Larry to reminisce. Aunt Lindy gave catering instructions to my sisters-in-law and I held court with the kids. My brothers stood shoulder to shoulder at the foot of mom's grave, quietly missing her. I was jealous of that feeling. The rabbi was the first to take off, hoping to earn a little pocket change by trolling for families in need of a blessing. Saul and Lindy were next, taking most of the kids. Then my sisters-in-law hit the road with the remainder of the brood. Eventually, it was just the four of us, Jeffrey, Joshie, my Dad and myself. We didn't speak. Dad started for his car and Joshie followed.

"Come on, Dylan," Jeffrey tugged at my arm. "I'll ride with you."

"I don't need a chaperone, Jeff," I removed my arm from his grip. "Go with them. I'll catch up."

"Oh, no, not this time, buddy." Jeffrey always called me buddy when he was angry with me. "You're not gonna upset Dad like you did the day of the funeral."

"That's right, I'm not," I seconded the motion. "But it won't be because you're ordering me around. Shit, Jeffrey," I always called him Jeffrey when I was mad at him, "you don't even like Daddy that much."

"You're wrong about that. You always have misread that in me. Besides that's not the point. I'm the one who has to deal with Dad when you fuck up," he drove a finger into my shoulder.

"I won't fuck up, Jeffrey. Now get outta here. I wanna spend some time with Mom, alone."

"See you soon." It was more of an order than a goodbye. He chased after Dad and Joshie, shaking his head in distrust.

When the only thing I could see of their car was the settling haze of dust it had kicked up, I stepped to the foot of my Mother's grave. I tried hard to miss her like they did, but when you have to try to feel . . . The effort was doomed, so my eyes wandered.

This part of the cemetery was pretty old and as full as a Tokyo subway car at rush hour. I looked up, spotting a jet moving slowly from the east. Its painted fuselage was the only white visible against the severely blue sky. I watched it for a little while in its glide toward JFK, making bets with myself as to its country of registry. But I turned impatiently away, wondering where MacClough could be. Christ, he'd already missed the ceremony. I resolved not to wait and started for my car.

"It is a lovely headstone," a ghost called behind me.

"And speaking of heads," I turned back around, "I notice you still have yours."

"Yes, Dylan Klein," the little Russian slapped his sunken cheeks for effect, "it is still very much in place. You do not appear very surprised by my return from hell," he smiled to cover disappointment and pain. The disappointment might've been feigned, but the distress was visceral and quite real.

"Nothing about you could surprise me."

But before little Lazarus could respond, he started to swoon. I ran to catch him. He was light as a scarecrow and bone thin under his clinging black suit jacket. Someone *had* worn black after all. His once meaty face had imploded, collapsing into hollow cheeks and hanging gray skin. Not even theatrical makeup could turn a man that gray. The bulb behind his copper eyes was dim and the smell of him was making me sick. I propped up the stick figure.

"Thank you for catching me," he smiled.

"Don't flatter yourself. It was reflex."

The smile ran away from his face as he coughed blood and yellow mucous into a crusty hanky. His legs went rubbery again like a pug headed for queer street, but he righted himself this time.

"I'm alright," Krylov waved his stained handkerchief at me.

"Yeah, and I'm the king of Siam. How long've you known you were dying?" It was my turn to ask morbid questions.

"For quite some time, since—" he stopped to hack some more of himself into his spotted bandanna, "since before we met."

"That's why you were so curious about my Mother that day. Well," I forced a chilly laugh, "part of you is human, after all."

"Condemnation doesn't suit you, Mr. Klein," he shook his head just as Brodsky had when standing over Hannah's body. "No, it does not fit you at all. My eyes are not so blind that I cannot see you still like me in spite of all you know."

"That's pity you see," I refuted uncomfortably.

"No, Dylan. I would not recognize pity if it was closer to me than my own frail shadow. Believe me. I would not recognize it."

"If you knew you were dying, why—" I took up a new line of questioning and he guessed the direction.

"Why did I sacrifice so many others just to give myself an extra year or two? Is that what you were going to ask? I think so, yes," he coughed up the last syllable. "It is precisely because I saw the end so near that I did what I did. I wanted one year of peace, one year to live without looking over my shoulder, one year to drink only cheap Scotch and smoke long cigars, one year for myself. I had earned that much."

"But the trail of bodies . . ." now I shook my head.

"Do not expect regrets from me, Dylan Klein. I cannot begin regretting now. I have had my year and guilt will not sprout wings on me now."

"You're right," I acquiesced, to build him up. "I can't help liking you. Your friend, Mr. Brodsky, forewarned me about just that. But you're a liar," I chopped him down. "You regret what you've done to me. That's why you're here. Don't even deny it. You can't help liking me either. After all the death you've been responsible for, you want absolution from *me*. You even hedged your bets by lining my pockets."

"Absolution!" the scarecrow stood rigid. "Now, Dylan Klein, it is you who flatters himself."

"Maybe so. Maybe so. Do you know what all your money did

besides buy this grand headstone?" I yelled while pointing at the granite block.

His silence was answer enough.

"It gave me time to think, to figure things out. You shouldn't've faked the suicide," I scolded. "It made things too neat, too tidy like a gift-wrapped package from an expensive store. Everything else concerning your disappearance had been messy, chancy, too difficult to decipher. Christ, you had the intelligence communities of three countries tripping over their own dicks trying to make heads and tails of the situation. Hannah might have run. I could've bought that. I might even have accepted a scenario where she got handled with extreme prejudice by one of the three interested parties that had grown angry or impatient. It would've been stupid and sloppy, but it would've fit."

"But you believed at first . . ." he trailed off.

"At that point, I would've believed the world was flat."

That bothered him. I could see it in his life-drained eyes. Even this close to death, he was compelled to find the flaws in his technique.

"Explain yourself. What exact—"

"First," I cut him off, "you clear a few things up for me, okay?"

The ghost didn't answer, but I got the feeling we had a deal.

"There wasn't any hired help, like Hannah said, was there?"

"No, none. The less players on my team the better." Then, to demonstrate, he covered his gray mouth with the soiled hanky: "Good morning, Mr. Klein. Sorry about the bruises," he repeated, in a remotely British accent, the words I'd heard over the phone the night of his staged beheading.

"You were the guy with the silent rifle."

"Yes and no. I did the talking. Hannah did the shooting. She was a better shot than me. I took good care of the two Israelis, though," he spoke proudly, "if you intended to ask."

"I intended to, yes. Don't tell me it was Hannah that did Piccolo," I took a threatening step forward.

"She was quite capable of it," he ignored the threat, "but no, that was my doing. To look at me now, you could not believe it. Yes, well, your involving him necessitated his demise. I could not get back the check and leave him in any condition to describe me. I, after all, was supposed to be a dead headless corpse."

"Hannah's confession to a live radio audience was part of the plan?" I asked too angrily.

"Naturally, along with everything else she did. Everything! Her only surprise came in the form of the bullet I fed her for breakfast," he said too proudly.

"Goodbye!" I ordered, pushing little Lazarus away, but not hard enough to force him to the earth. "Goodbye!"

"You—" he came at me, not to fight, but to regain lost ground. He halted his advance at the pebble and dust announcement of a stopping car.

I turned to see John Francis MacClough pulling a circular green wreath out of his backseat. He approach me in a hurry, juggling the wreath, straightening his suit and finger-combing his hair.

"Here," the landmark owner handed me the ring of dyed-green carnations. "Sorry I'm late."

"MacClough, fifteen minutes is late. Now you're gonna have to wait for the next relative," I shook his hand. "Thanks for coming, anyway. Go on over and lay it by the tombstone," I played hot potato with flowers, giving them back to Johnny.

"What's his problem?" the ex-cop wondered, pointing a finger at the once and future ghost disappearing behind a forest of tree-shaped tombstones.

"He was just looking for a funeral party."

"Think he'll find it?"

"Not to worry, Johnny. It'll find him soon enough."

"Yeah, Klein," MacClough squeezed the back of my neck. "whatever you say."